BOOK FIVE OF THE LIFE & DEATH CYCLE

CHILDREN

OF

CYPRESS

E.S. BARRISON

Dedicated to Grandma Rhoda & Grandpa David

Teachers exist in all forms.

I hope I brought your lessons to the page.

To Kainan
Knoll
Hutch's Creek
To Heims Norte
Newbir
Arm
The Capitol
Maedee's Outlook
Ab Aeterno
Grover's Marsh
Opal's Canyon
Stilette
To Rosada
To Volfium
To Heims Sur
To Prove

rt
Graycott
To Spinoza
To Evylain
To Delilah
Errat
To Yilk

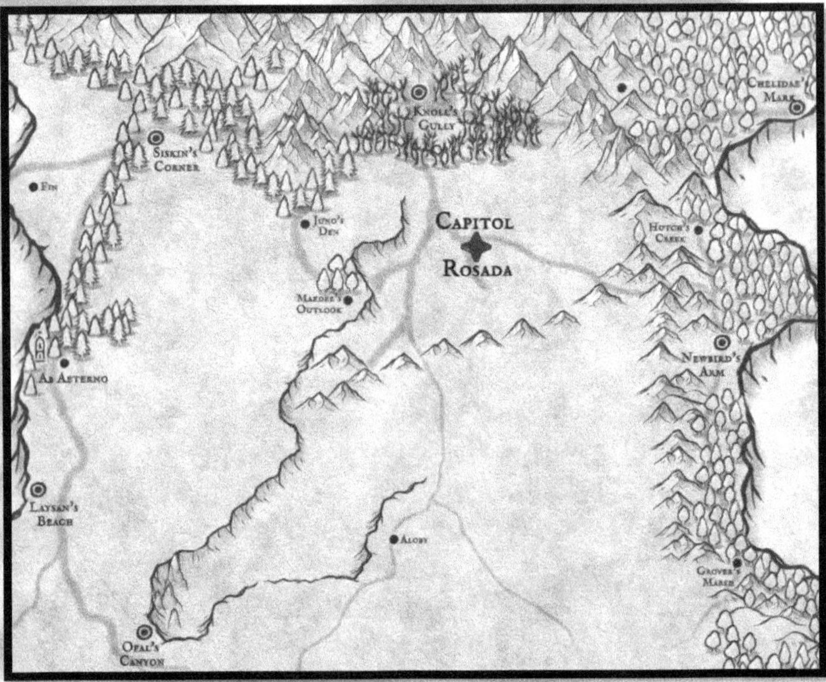

CHELIDAE
MARK
KNOLL'S
GULLY
SISKIN'S
CORNER
FIN
JUNO'S
DEN
CAPITOL
ROSADA
HUTCH'S
CREEK
MARDEE'S
OUTLOOK
NEWBIRD'S
ARM
AB AETERNO
LAYSAN'S
BEACH
ALOBY
GROVER'S
MARSH
OPAL'S
CANYON

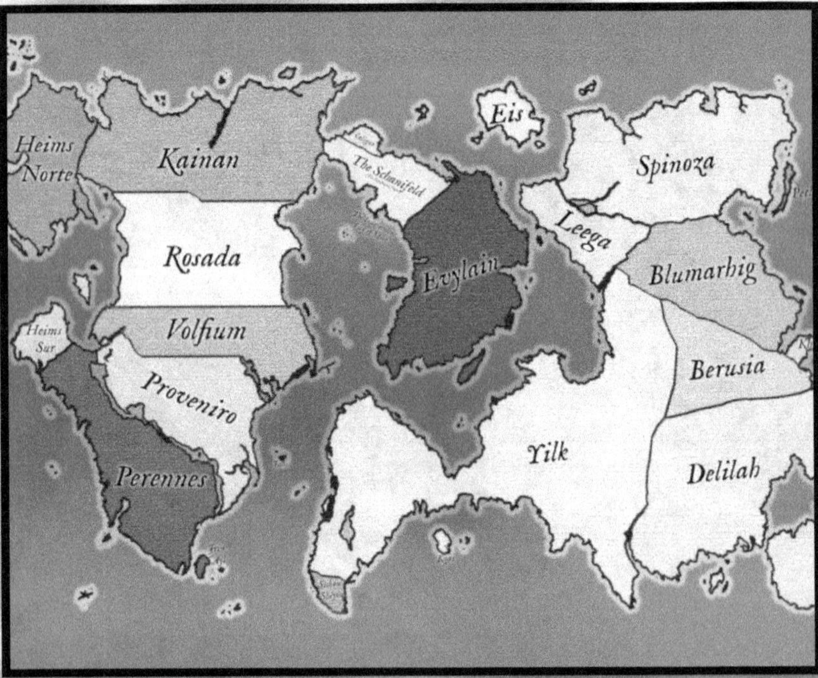

Eis
Heims
Norte
Kainan
The Schanifeld
Spinoza
Rosada
Evylain
Leega
Blumarhig
Volfium
Heims
Sur
Proveniro
Berusia
Perennes
Yilk
Delilah

The Council of Mist Keepers

NINGURSU
The God of Death

AELIA
The Healer

TOMAS
The Peacemaker

JULIETTA
The Painter

JIANG
Null

MALAIKA
The Cartographer

ALOJZY
The Architect

CAROLINE
The Illusionist

BRENT
The Story Collector

AN INADEQUATE CAFÉ

The boy's eyes bled. They hadn't stopped bleeding, not as the leaves fell from the trees, not as the Guard's occupation grew in numbers, nor as the first snow powdered the broken city. Each morning, as Todd removed the bandage from the boy's eyes, he prayed that the bleeding might stop.

"Stay still, Garrett," he muttered as he reapplied the bandage. "We'll get some food once you're good."

The boy didn't respond. He never did, his attention blank, his lips pursed into a permanent frown. Todd pleaded for the child to speak, but no matter what he asked, no matter what he did, the child had nothing to say. His head instead lulled into Todd's shoulder, and all fell silent.

Todd adjusted Garrett in his arms, then, with a grunt, crawled from his makeshift structure. Compiled with old canvas tarps and rotting wood, it looked no different from the collection of structures occupying the alleyway. It was one of the few places left in the Capital, undiscovered by the Guard. Yet Todd knew that this home would be short-lived. Soon, the Guard would come, and he'd be forced to run and find another hideaway.

This had been his life over the last couple of months. After escaping the clutches of the Order of the Effluvium and abandoning the Guard for the second time in his life, Todd had finally been reunited with his son. But the worst had already occurred. Some young guard had brought the child to Todd, coated in blood, with both eyes torn from their sockets. Without thanking the Guard, Todd fled with a few of his old squadron, and they spent a week hiding in the sewers before going their separate ways. Where did they go? Todd didn't know. But when he came to the border of the Capital, he discovered all the gates were closed, and the Guard was multiplying on every road.

Now, Todd was left wandering the city alone, taking residency in different alleyways, hostels, and boarding houses each night. He couldn't leave the Capital. The entire city had been placed on lockdown ever since the Senate had been found slaughtered in their chamber. The blame fell onto a terrorist known solely as Rhodana the Forest Queen. Until she was captured, no one would be allowed in or out of the city walls.

Although Todd had a feeling, if this was who he thought, that she was already gone.

He had met this so-called Rhodana back in the City of Mert over a year earlier. With her arrival, his world was turned upside-down. Now, he was far away from that small little general store he ran, with his small tattoo parlor and his wife's ridiculous fortune-telling business. Now it was gone. Even if he returned to Mert, he had nothing. No home. A dead wife. And a blinded son.

Now, Todd carried Garrett on his hip, that constant reminder of his last shred of self. He had to defend Garrett with everything. So, as they stepped outside, he pulled the hood of Garrett's jacket over the child's head. While Todd, for the most part, was uninteresting, a child with missing eyes could garner way more attention than needed. Garrett never fussed over the hood. In fact, he hardly responded to anything, as if lost in a permanent trance.

"If you behave, I'll get ya some pancakes, a'ight? With chocolate. Ya hear?"

Garrett grunted a response.

I don't got the moxie for this. Lex woulda known what to say. Any time his late wife entered his thoughts, Todd's heart sank. After leaving Mert, Todd rejoined the Guard to protect her and Garrett. Yet, it was all for nothing. His dear Elexis still ended up in the crossfires of rebellion, and only in her last breaths did they reunite. He promised her that he would find Garrett.

But he didn't keep him safe.

He snatched a newspaper from the front porch of a café as he entered. While cafes like this always bustled in Mert, here in the Capital of Rosada, they sat empty and silent. No one looked up as he entered, nor did they say a word as he sat at one of the tables. They served him a cup of tea without a word, leaving him with a menu.
He grumbled a thank you to the server, then opened his newspaper. In the seat across from him, Garrett played with his fingers.

"Here, Garrett. Play with this." Todd removed a wooden toy soldier from his coat pocket. He placed it on the table across from Garrett, then guided his hand to the toy.

The child's trance broke for a moment. He grimaced, then picked the soldier up, lifting it in the air and mumbling an incomprehensible phrase.

Garrett used to have words. He was never the most talkative child, but he did speak. Now, he never said anything.

It was hard not to think nonstop about Garrett, but Todd forced himself to redirect his attention to the newspaper.

Most of the articles did little to hold his interest. He couldn't care less about the countless laws being implemented across Rosada. Curfews dominated the streets, while even a simple rumor could send people to the Pit for storytelling. While Knoll's Gully had fallen months earlier, and their towers had long abandoned their domain, their aggressive dominance had infiltrated the rest of the country. To be sent to the Pit might as well have been the end; with no fresh food or water, the constant watch of the Guard, and the torturous cleansing rituals delivered by the Order, entering the nation's Pits was worse than death.

Between the different articles, adverts for the nation's most-wanted criminals decorated the page. For the most part, Todd did not recognize most of the names. A few repeated. Dr. Hue Lieu appeared in almost every paper, wanted for her involvement in Knoll's Fall. A rebellious doctor appealed to Todd—she might be able to help him with Garrett. Yet, there were no pictures of her in the paper, and even if Todd wanted to find her, he had no clue where to look.

Other than Dr. Lieu and a few other unfamiliar names, Todd often paused over the large adverts for the

Forest Queen. It made his stomach turn. It wasn't hatred but a sort of distaste that left him nauseous. She had upended his life with a flick of her finger.

Rhodana the Forest Queen.

Her name had been whispered amongst the guards like a curse. They called her Rhodana, but her true name was Briannabella Smidt. Wherever she went, chaos followed. While the adverts for her arrest said she was responsible for the Senate's collapse, Todd didn't quite believe she was responsible. She never did have a violent tendency.

But no matter who slaughtered Senator Cordova and the others, it led to martial law dictating the streets and an invisible hand making all the decisions. Many assumed it was an elder within the Order of the Effluvium; others claimed it to be a radical captain of the Guard. Whoever it was, it was as though someone had taken a syringe and yanked color from the streets, leaving every tree dying and smoke rising between the cobblestones.

While whispers of magic, Todd ignored such claims. It was the same story, again and again, of a leader with too much power. What did it matter who played puppet master? The story would continue as it always had.

His only vow now belonged to his son. No one else.

Todd peered around in search of the café server and continued to search through the paper. He tore a few odd jobs from the classified section before turning to the opinion pieces in the back. Pages upon pages of people writing about the terrors of storytelling, the recent crop harvest, or their support for the Order filled the columns. Only the large, bold titles broke the text.

As he reached the end of the paper, he stopped at a different title.

Why aren't we talking about the missing eyeballs?

Todd glanced at his son, still playing with the toy soldier, then returned to the paper.

We like to say ignorance is bliss. That's why everyone has been ignoring the people on the street with their blood-riddled eyes.

I know you've seen them. We all have just been ignoring them.

I saw the first victim three months ago when I was at my local café. They were only sitting there, minding their own business, and their eyes began to bleed. Before I had a chance to help them, their friend dragged them from the café, and they vanished down the street.

I have witnessed five others with these symptoms. Some have no eyes remaining; others permanently bleed. In my research, over two hundred people across the country have exhibited this obscure illness.

But the Order of the Effluvium doesn't want you to know about this. Because if you knew the truth, then their power would suffer.

This is their fault and their fault alone.

Todd read the article over twice and bit his lip. There was no author attached to the article. A smart move, no doubt. But this meant, if the author was honest, that others had exhibited the same pain as Garrett.

If they had, was there a cure? Was this merely just a disease ripping through Rosada?

But the author said it was the Order of the Effluvium's responsibility. Had they harnessed magic just to torture random citizens...like Garrett?

But Garrett's eyes were not just bleeding but had also been removed from their head. It was different from what the author mentioned.

Surely, it was a coincidence.

He pushed the paper away and leaned back, watching as his son continued to fiddle with the soldier. The server had yet to take his order. From behind Garrett, he caught a glimpse of the kitchen, where the chef worked without looking up from the stove.

Todd leaned back, crossing his arms. The server still didn't appear; the constant clacking of the stove was the only solace as he waited. *What's taking so long?* The sooner he ate, the sooner he and Garrett could get moving. He hated to stay still for too long. What if the Guard came and saw Garrett? Or what if they recognized him?

Even worse, what if someone noticed the black stamp entwined in the dragon tattoo along his arm?

At one point, the chef tore their attention away from the stove. They locked eyes with Todd and then returned to their work, not speaking a word.

"'Scuse me!" Todd called. "Y'know where that damn server is?"

The chef didn't respond.

"Oi!" Todd rose from his seat and marched over to the counter.

"He'll get to you when he gets to you," the chef grunted.

"I been waiting here for a good fifteen minutes!"

"Ain't that long."

Todd gripped the counter and leaned forward. "Listen, I got a boy here who's hungry. Why don't you go get your damn server out here...or better yet, you can take my order!"

The chef continued on the griddle without looking up at Todd. "It ain't my job."

"Fine, then we're leaving! Hope this place gets shut down. What kind of damn establishment are you running here?"

The chef continued with his cooking. Todd huffed and returned to Garrett. The boy fidgeted for a moment as Todd lifted him out of the chair, then relaxed against his shoulder.

"We're gonna find a better place, a'ight? You don't want to eat none of these meals."

The boy pressed his forehead into Todd's shoulder.

Todd marched from the café, his anger twisting in his throat. *You would think some small café like that would want any business they can get. Not like there's anyone out on these streets anymore. Damn terrible place if you ask me.*

He marched a few paces forward, pausing only when Garrett tugged on his shirt.

"Toy..." the child mumbled.

"What?"

"Toy."

"Toy?" He groaned. "You left your toy in the café, didn't you?"

Garrett nodded.

Todd resisted the urge to curse, pivoting back to the café. He marched through the door, straight to the toy soldier lying on the table.

As he picked it up, the door to the kitchen opened.

Good, I'll give that damn server a piece of my mind.

With the door opening, rather than greeting the sole server, over a dozen people exited from the kitchen. Unassumingly dressed, they could be any one person on the street, but not someone who belonged in the back of a kitchen.

"What the hell is going on?" He spat as the last person exited the restaurant without acknowledging him.

The server finally stood in the doorway with their arms crossed over their broad chest. "So you were the one pitching a fit up here, huh?"

"Well, I was waiting for you to take my damn order!"

"Ever heard of patience?"

"It was fifteen minutes!"

"Well, I'm the only server here, and I had something else to do."

"You work here!" Todd scoffed. "What, does this café not serve food no more?"

"It does, to the right customers."

"Right customer?"

The server kept that smug smile on his face as he spoke. "Tell me a three-sentence story, and I'll tell you."

"Stories are illegal," Todd grumbled.

"Don't think that matters to you."

Todd shifted Garrett in his arms and glanced over his shoulder. The road remained clear. No guard stood watch.

Tell him a story, Toddle. It's not like you care about any of this nonsense. Lex's voice played in his mind. She would have told a story without hindrance or delay, as she used to with their son.

If only he had listened when she used to tell them.

"A'ight, fine," Todd muttered, finding some ridiculous tale on the tip of his tongue. "There once was a boy in a field. He transformed into a dragon out of fear. There he took flight way into the night...never to return here."

The server smirked. "Very good. How'd it feel?"

"I ain't playing these games. Tell me what is going on cause I don't like nothing like this."

"Fine, follow me," the server motioned Todd into the kitchen.

Todd paused, shifting Garrett again in his arms. Would it make sense to follow this man? He didn't even know his name—he was just some server who was acting a tad strange.

But, if Todd knew anything from his time in the Guard, strange meant something was afoot. In this case, he hoped the strange nature would help him and Garrett.

The server led him through a tight kitchen, past the otherwise nonchalant chef, and towards a cellar. After fiddling with the three complicated locks, the door swung open. Rather than a collection of jars, a stairwell greeted them, breathing in the cold winter air. A single light hung from the ceiling.

"Follow down there. You'll arrive at a witch tunnel. Follow it. You'll get to safety," the server said.

Every one of his defenses shot up as he stared down the stairway, deep into the dark tunnels. Lex would follow, that much he was certain. His heart told him to trust Lex's intuition, but his head begged him to leave. "Seriously? You want me to go into your *basement*?"

"It's not a basement. It'll take you to one of our safe houses."

"Yeah, that seems like a load of bull."

"Why would I lie?"

"Plenty of reasons. Don't have to name them."

"I thought maybe you'd want to help your son...but if you'd rather stay on the streets, fine."

"My son ain't none of your business."

"I never said he was. I am just...concerned for him."
"Well, don't be. He's fine. We're fine, and I ain't signing up for some damn prison or nothing." Todd stepped back from the doorway.

The server closed the door with a shrug. "Suit yourself. You know where to find us."

Todd didn't humor the server with a response, turning away from him and leaving the café like a storm marching across the sky.

DOMAIN

Brent lay on the floor, eyeing the pineapple perched at the end of the hall. Large fangs filled its mouth while its dark eyes bled with smoke. His rationale told him it was a story, but as much as he tried to ignore it, the story continued its ongoing mockery.

He rolled onto his back and closed his eyes. *It's just a story. Pineapples don't have mouths.* The story popped up while he wandered the desolate halls of the Library of Mist Keepers.

Well, what remained of it.

Ever since he escaped with the spirits of past Mist Keepers, the Library sat abandoned, its shelves toppled, and its ceilings bowing under pressure.

At least until Bria returned to it and created a palace with its remnants.

The palace served as her new domain, giving Brent access to the Library where hundreds of years of stories loitered in the Mist. While he pieced together the pasts of the other eight Mist Keepers from these tales, with them, nightmares lingered, composed of his thoughts, and projected like any other illusion.

It was hard to shake the stories that loitered in each of the halls. Brent had spent weeks locked in the Library, the Mist as his only companion. The head of the Council of Mist Keepers, the cunning skull known as Ningursu, trapped him. Only when Brent finally broke the spell, casting Ningursu's grasp aside, did he manage to escape. But with the escape came nightmares. He had grown weak after being attacked by Ningursu's magic. Every movement creaked through his body, and if he closed his eyes, he woke with pernicious tales assaulting his brain.

And now, after resting his eyes for only five minutes, he sat face-to-face with a vicious pineapple.

Go away. I'm not here to deal with you. He counted backward under his breath from ten before repeating his quiet mantra. His name. His history. And his constant. *Bria.*

Just the thought of her quelled him. The past couple of months had been strange. After sight was erased, in a desperate attempt by Ningursu to eliminate communication between Life and Death, Brent resorted to communicating with Bria through tap-code and notes. It wasn't the same; they occupied two different planes. Brent now loitered, not quite dead and not quite alive, in the Mist. He tried to push through the Mist, just as he helped Bria see the world of the dead almost two years earlier, but the barrier remained.

Brent sighed and sat up from the floor, rubbing his eyes. The pineapple finally vanished, leaving Brent with nothing more than the swampy hallways of the abandoned Library.

His knees trembled as he walked, and he gripped the wall until finding his cane resting by a bookshelf. His body ached as he walked along the path, and his head pounded with every existing story. They'd grown stronger. The Mist harbored the story of everyone, living and dead. He did use the stories of the dead to release their souls into the afterlife; it didn't stop their stories from lingering.

Here in the Library, it was the story of the Council of Mist Keepers that gathered his attention.

Brent had scribbled countless stories on the available walls, empty tables, and destroyed picture frames. He did not waste time when the stories came to him and frantically wrote in the first space available. His old teacher, Caroline, had the clearest story, which he etched on the blank canvases in an old storage closet. She had been a precocious young woman, a fisherwoman with a vendetta against a mythical fish, who openly welcomed the idea of the Mist. Her quest to find herself had been light, easy to track.

While other stories still eluded.

He had gathered parts of Alojzy's tale, the Architect of the Library. None of that story surprised him; Alojzy had been a temperamental man even before joining the Council. He lost trust in his family and misplaced his paranoia. But Brent could not be certain how many more walls the man had constructed.

Brent had yet to write Malaika's story on the walls. He scribbled it across a notebook after reconnecting with her in the City of Mert. She composed a map of the world out of Mist, and in her quest to explore, she'd distanced herself from the Council. She had countless resources, from her friendship with her unindoctrinated Mist Keeper, Szyman, to her missing airship, the *Mystical Cheer*.

The stories grew muddy beyond Malaika, though. While Brent saw some parts of Jiang's past, marred by war, lost love, and failure, the others left little for him to uncover. Julietta's past had been rewritten so many times that finding the truth was like unwinding a tangled ball of yarn. Tomás's story lingered, but years marred the story with uncertainty. Brent had not found Aelia's story, and any time he dared look at Ningursu's tale, it sent his head spinning.

His mind had limits. If he dared to look too far into any story, it may lead him astray.

And he had no desire to get lost in the stories...again.

Since he escaped Ningursu's clutches a few months earlier, the stories taunted him. A year earlier, the immortal alchemist Tehuti Thema Tarek Kamilah Kafele Kek created a concoction that medicated his mind, clearing Brent's mind of the stories brought to him by the nightmarish Diabolo. While the Diabolo continued to interfere with his thoughts, it gave him a chance to breathe.

But, as a prisoner, he lost that medication. The Diabolo slowly clawed away at his mind.

Then, like a gasp, it withered, nothing more than a faint shadow.

He wished it could have been with celebration. Instead, now, a new disease riddled his body. Ningursu infected him with rot, ordering it to eat away at the Diabolo and, in turn, Brent's mind.

The stories grew stronger. Stranger, even.

And if he dared blink wrong, they returned without warning.

Yet, he still returned to the Library. When Bria disappeared in her own conquests, he wandered the shelves, seeking out tales, compiling them for his notes. His goal was simple, for now: if he wanted to change the Mist Keepers, he needed to understand them.

With this newfound understanding, Brent had decided to build a school. He only had two students, Yaz and Chander, but he imagined countless other confused individuals with inclinations to the Mist. A misunderstanding of the Mist could lead to further harm, further uncertainty, and further failure.

That much he had seen.

Back when he was a prisoner, he met countless failed Mist Keepers loitering in the crypts. The spirits, as they'd been dubbed, had deteriorated into a childlike state, lost in their own imaginations and dreams. What could Brent do to stop others from being turned into distant dreams?

This new school was his solution.

But every time he thought of the school, his stomach crawled. He hadn't even started his first lesson. The notebook he kept in his pocket, with countless ideas for this school, weighed heavily. What gave him the authority to run it? He had been a Mist Keeper for all of two years; even with a collection of stories, a gathering of history in his hands, it did not mean he was the authority on the Mist.

What if he was wrong?

What if he made a mistake?

It was with these thoughts that he limped up the stairs, away from the Library shelves, and towards the sunlight. It trickled in from the atrium above, decorated with the vermillion roots of cypress trees. Brent followed along the stairs. Here, at least, stories did not bother him the same way anymore. Instead, a breath of fresh air and a wash of color welcomed him to the palace above the Library.

Composed of branches, roots, and leaves, the palace represented every aspect of the Forest Queen. Here, unscathed by the Order of the Effluvium, magic could thrive. Stories could be whispered.

And life could be pretty.

Brent always smiled upon entering the palace. While the actual furnishings were few and far between, the atrium itself served as a welcome to all. With countless rooms and winding stairs, the palace wove together with vines. A piece of art telling a story that the stone structures of tyrants never dreamt of enacting.

There, standing at the steps of the palace, staring out into the swamp, waited Bria.

Brent walked over to her. Her gaze remained fixated ahead, where a collection of houses composed of equally lush and vibrant trees gathered. A handful of Magii and storytellers, marked with the black stamp on their wrists, loitered between the homes.

With his cane, Brent tapped the ground beside Bria.

-... .-....- *Bria.*

She tilted her head to the side, then removed a notebook from her pocket. A vine rose from the floor, reconstructing itself into a table, where she rested the notebook.

Brent removed a pen from his pocket and flipped open the notebook to the first clean page.

When did you get back? He wrote.

"About an hour ago," Bria whispered, arms crossed over her chest. Her voice lacked ease, tugged downward by the constant weight of decisions.

How many did you bring this time?

"Seventeen, from Laysan's Beach."

Brent glanced back out at the gathering of houses. In a short time, this swamp became Bria's kingdom.

Although she was but a reluctant queen.

CHAPTER THREE

CONSTRUCTING PARADISE

Bria glowered at the toilet.

Well, what should have been a toilet.

While she willed the trees to do her bidding, the stone still mocked her whenever she harnessed its elements. She'd only started understanding the true prowess of her magic, all thanks to her...mother. The mere thought made her throat tighten with tears. She'd only been reunited with her mother, Angelana Gonzo, a few months earlier by a fluke chance. Their relationship had been tenuous at the start, but she helped Bria finally understand the unlimited power deep within her core.

She placed her hand on the stone again. *Come on. Just shape correctly.*

The stone shifted beneath her fingers. She recognized the elements in plants without a problem and could feel them shifting beneath her fingers. But it was harder to identify the elements in the stone. Was that quartz or diamond? Silica or alumina? Or something else? If she had the book that her mother gave her, *The Rules of the Apothecary*, then she might be able to differentiate them.

As she released her fingers, the stone retracted. It curved inwards, and a spark of hope ignited in Bria's chest.

But it didn't stop arching, forming a hole in the center of the stone.

She cursed under her breath and sank against the wall again.

Beside her, the familiar rhythmic tapping tugged at her attention.

−... .−....−

Brent stayed with her since she arrived back from Laysan's Beach. Silent, invisible — it was easy to forget she wasn't alone. But then again, in some ways, she *was* alone. Sure, she and Brent occupied the same space, but it was more like exchanging letters. He was there, but he wasn't. Just like the wind.

Even as he wrote in the notebook on the ground, it wasn't like he was there with her.

That's not a toilet.

"You don't think I know that?" She spat, pressing her head against the wall. "I can see it in my mind, but it's not coming together. It seems so simple."

Then take a break. You need rest.

"I can't! I want this place to be comfortable for everyone. It's the least I can do."

You've done more than enough.

"But it's still not...home."

Bria hadn't returned home since she fled the Senate Chambers a couple months prior. With her escape, she left the Capitol destroyed, and behind her, rumors flew that she had massacred everyone in the Senate. She hadn't pulled the trigger, but part of her felt responsible. Hadn't she sparked all of this? Back in Newbird's Arm, she told the vagrant population to rise. In Knoll, she destroyed the towers. Now, the Order of the Effluvium had doubled down, gathering Magii, storytellers, and any other opponent in their Pits. The least Bria could do was help them escape the country through her tunnels and palace, deep into the swamps of Volfium.

But that was all it was: a swamp. She constructed houses, but there was no electricity and no plumbing. Food was scarce. The closest town was still a tedious hike through the sludge. Unless, of course, Bria used the Tunnels.

You need to rest. Brent wrote. *You do not have to do this alone.*

"I can't..." Bria whispered.

It's just a toilet. We have other places to go.

"That's easy for you to say."

Bria. The punctuated sentence gave her chills. She could almost hear Brent saying it.

Her branched arm, composed from the roots of the little branch behind her ear, shifted. At that moment, a second appendage formed into the shape of a hand resting on her shoulder. It told her that Brent touched her, and for a brief second, at least, she could feel him.

The newly formed hand squeezed her shoulder.

She shook her head. "I can't rest. If I want this to work, I need to finish."

You've been working at this for weeks. There's no shame in asking for help.

Bria frowned, still glaring at the failed latrine.

Come with me.

She almost objected but instead lifted the book from the ground. Carrying it close, she rose to her feet. The hand-like appendage on her shoulder tugged her away from the bathroom and out into the hallway. There, it withered, and in its place, a soft tapping guided her. Every few steps, another couple of taps echoed against the floor. There, Brent would touch her arm again, allowing her to turn in the right direction. It had taken time for them to get used to this communication method, but it worked in its own way.

She ran her fingers over the walls as she walked. Every part of this palace came from her. Bria had to remind herself of that. This was her sculpture. After returning to the Library of the Council, she'd climbed out of its dark embrace into the humid air, where a swamp of vermillion trees waited for her. There, she constructed a palace out of trees, with limbs bowing into permanent fixtures: balconies, stairways, an entrance hall, and later, a small collection of houses at its base.

Brent led Bria to the end of one of those balconies overlooking the swampy interior of the Library and tapped on the handrail to get her attention.
Bria opened the notebook again. Brent's writing came at once. *I know this is your creation...but you can ask for help.*

Bria glanced at the different balconies overlooking the Library. Each one had come together, woven like a tapestry. While the structure of the palace came together with a single breath, it took her time to form these stable structures with the beauty of any skilled architect.

You've made all the furniture. You built this palace. But please, rest. Others can help with the remaining pieces.

"You act like it would be easy for me to find someone."

There are people waiting for you who would love to help.

"I can't return to the Capital." Even if Bria had wanted to return to that little speakeasy on the outskirts of the Capital, she knew it was too risky. It'd been three months. Her mother's body would have been burned by now; Death's Mourn had already passed. What would everyone think? She had abandoned Marisol in the middle of the plaza, right outside of the Capitol building. The others she had led no doubt sought her out. But instead, she did what she had always done: she ran away from the destruction carved by her own hand.

They're waiting for you.

"They're fine without me."

Our dog isn't.

Bria huffed, leaning her head back to stare at the ceiling. She swallowed the tears in her throat. She had left their dog, Nix, back at the speakeasy. Marisol surely watched her, but that box-headed dog had been their ongoing companion over the last year.

It was another thing she added to her regrets.

So many regrets.

They weighed on her like a storm. She couldn't shake them.

"Why can't you get her?" Bria asked, glancing back at the notebook.

I would if I could. But didn't we agree that Ningursu was most likely in Rosada? He would know of my arrival immediately. A pause followed his writing before resuming at a slow scrawl. *You don't have to go if you don't want to, but remember there are people who will help you. You're not alone.*

Bria traced the edge of the notebook. "I'll think about it."

And I'm here to help however I can.

"But you're not *here*. You're *there*, and you have your own work to do."

I know.

"I have to do what I can. I'm not some...leader or queen who will end this war. I can protect people, but I can't save them. So if that means I have to go to every Pit in Rosada and free every last wrongly prosecuted person...I will. Maybe from them, someone will come along who won't run away from their problems."

I know. But you're more than that.

"Brent..."

But do what you need to do. Just promise me that you will rest.

"I'll try," Bria whispered. But even that statement felt vacant on her lips.

She stayed there with Brent until the sun fell, basking in the comfortable silence as he scribbled a ridiculous story on the page. His stories comforted her. They brewed with nonsense, speaking of talking pieces of bread and spiral-tailed cockatoos that jumped to the moon, but they tugged at her heart enough to incite a smile. The Order of the Effluvium sought to ban such tales. While Brent told silly stories in the notebook, other tales spoke of rebellion and freedom.

Back home, in Newbird's Arm, Brent used to tell the legend of *Rhodana the Forest Queen*. This was long before he knew of Bria's own powers. Rather than telling the tale that the Order governed, the quiet song that everyone hummed, Brent would weave adventures out of nothing.

Now, he collected stories like breathing.

But his stories ultimately grew quiet, and Brent left to return to Mert, to resume his only quest. He had told her all about it, written with excitement about how he was building a school for those with inclinations to the Mist. For children, he said, like that girl, Yaz, who they had rescued back in Knoll.

Finally, after everything, Brent Harley had found his purpose. He had always loved children, and now he could help them before they succumbed to the overwhelming nature of their magic.

It left Bria alone with her castle. She turned her attention to a nearby window, where the refugees loitered in the swamp. Amongst them, she caught a glimpse of the eclectically dressed Horton, a performer who had traveled with Brent under the name of Ms. Honey. A few weeks earlier, Bria had returned to Knoll, where she ran into Horton and their sister Hortense. Upon talking with the siblings and a handful of other leaders in Knoll's Pit, Horton agreed to come to the swamp with her. They happily took over the role of patron, welcoming each group of refugees and helping them find their place. It allowed Bria the chance to continue her quests.

Despite the refugees' presence, they did little to quell Bria's loneliness. Overall, she offered them protection. They could leave if they wanted, venture home if they saw fit, but overall, she had no clue what to do with them. Was she raising an army? Not at all. Building a civilization? Probably not.

She had merely collected these refugees, trying to replace the guilt in her gut with fulfillment.

When she did choose to leave her palace, a small crowd always gathered. So far, she rescued less than fifty refugees, but when they gathered, it suffocated her. She just wanted to fall back into the trees and avoid everyone and everything.

But then, she would be forced to reckon with her own thoughts.

So instead of stepping outside or falling backward into the swamp, or even working on the latrine upstairs, Bria ventured down into the Library. She navigated past the droves of books, wading through the small swamp she'd created along its floors. The doors hung open permanently on their hinges, allowing the Tunnels to greet her.

At the junction of the Tunnels, she removed a gas mask hanging from the wall. It was as routine as breathing at this point. Without even thinking, she strapped the gas mask to her face and adjusted the filter. With a single inhale to test the flow of oxygen, she turned down one of the Tunnels, letting the twists and turns guide her. A yellow smoke tainted Rosada and other parts of the globe, creating a film over any connection she had with her magic. While it hadn't interfered with her swamp or even lingered in the Tunnels, the moment she dared exit, it threatened everything that defined her.

Bria followed the Tunnels, unalarmed by the changing of climates. The magic was familiar. Created by the Mist Keepers, Bria had mastered their pathways, using them to travel the world. Why they still worked for her while the Mist hid Brent and the world of the dead, she didn't quite know. Perhaps she had laid her mark across them. The Tunnels, in a way, had become hers. After all, she had traveled so many of these paths in her youth. Now, it was like she'd been transported back in time, a child exploring the Tunnels, discovering new places and new aspects of her magic. The excitement used to carry her forward, with the constant question of where she would go next.

As she traveled the Tunnels, the roots grew more sporadic, and in their place, an arid, iridescent interior dotted the path. Bria adjusted the gas mask on her face as she walked, letting the branch behind her ear weave over the edges of the mask.

At the end of the Tunnels, she placed her hand against the iridescent stone, where Bria found herself standing in a high-walled canyon. The stones glimmered in the moonlight while a twisting creek babbled between the collection of rocks. In the distance, the dim light of the fire waved to her.

She kept her focus, listening to the stones, the minimal foliage, and the sky as she moved. It'd been a long time since she visited the Pit of Opal's Canyon. She would typically avoid the actual shanty town, instead exploring the gorgeous walls and desert flowers. But this time, she strode towards the makeshift town, her heart pounding in her ears.

This was it.

This was what she had to do.

This was who she had become.

With each step, she recited her plan to herself. She'd completed this plan half a dozen times already, but each time, it sent fear rippling through her stomach. What if someone turned her over to the Guard? What if they attacked her for the prize?

The questions gathered in her thoughts. They embellished her nausea.

But it was all she could do now.

As she neared the crackling fire, a distant song blessed the air. Her little branch tightened over her face as its words became clear.

Rhodana,
The Forest Queen,
We hear your deep melody,
Will you speak when you're ready
Rhodana

Bria froze. They were calling for her. She couldn't deny it. Her story had left its mark across the nation, into the deepest depths of the pits and the hearts of the people. She closed her eyes, pushing the tears back. The song always changed, as if it knew her own fate.

But that had to be a coincidence.

Stories evolved as they passed from person to person.

It had nothing to do with *her*.

Why did Rhodana's song always change? What did it mean?

She broke her own trance and approached the fire. Even the flames called her name.

A few of the vagrants around the fire turned as she approached. One removed a rusted pistol from their belt, extending it with trembling hands.

"I'm not here to hurt you," Bria said, raising her hands.

"Who are you?" Another vagrant asked.

She glanced at them. "A friend."

"And what does that mean?"

Bria inhaled, then held out her branched hand. In its palm, a camellia bloomed. "Because I'm Rhodana...the Forest Queen. And I'm here—"

Before she finished her sentence, someone grabbed hold of her from behind and unbuckled her mask. The yellow smoke bombarded her.

It suffocated her.

Before dragging her down into darkness.

CHAPTER FOUR

WHERE THE MIST LEARNS

Chander still couldn't believe that he wandered the streets of Neorama. While at first glance, all the buildings and people looked *alive*, seeming to change in appearance like the clouds did in the sky. Once he looked beyond the Mist, even the peculiarity of the town became obvious. The buildings did not match, taken from different parts of the world. One structure reminded him of a Rosadian farmhouse, while the next bore colors closer to the structures in the City of Mert. Even the people came from different places and eras. One ghost wore furs from the north, while another wore the thin draping of the south. Here, in this ghost town, your past didn't matter; here, you belonged.

Yet it still struck Chander with the deepest awe. Only a few months earlier, he learned of his inclination to the Mist. His magic, which allowed him to see through the eyes of others, came from the Mist, and if he chose, he could be a Mist Keeper like Brent.

He wasn't the only one who could see this ghost town. Beside him, his friend Yaz marveled at the same structures. With her wide-framed glasses and excited exclamations, she gave Chander permission to be himself. Despite everything she had gone through, from dealing with her magic that could summon monsters as well as facing the Council of Mist Keepers, she kept her childlike enthusiasm.

Chander was glad to call her his adopted sister. Though he would never say that outright to her.

Especially while tensions with his real sister, Anandi, ran high.

Anandi, unlike Chander and Yaz, could not see the ghost town. While she used to be able to see certain things, like the dragon that took them away from Rosada, all of that had vanished. Instead, Anandi had surrounded herself with a reality unscathed by the Mist, hiding away in the Pinstripe Tavern, following around the pinstripe Mitzi like a lost puppy.

Now, she hardly spoke to Chander. What would Chander even say to his sister? It was almost impossible to describe the ghost town or the Mist Keepers to someone unfamiliar with them. He'd seen Timothée, one of the men who helped Chander and his sisters escape Rosada, try to explain it to his partner, Micca. Yet the conversation resulted in arguments that shook the entire tavern.

It was a different world. A different place.

Where life and death intertwined.

And things seemed okay.

Yaz bumped into his shoulder as they walked along the paths. He winced once, blinking three times to refocus his vision. As his vision stabilized, he nearly walked into one of the multiple ghosts wandering the paths. They didn't give him any mind, going about their days like any other citizen in a town. They paid no mind to the "good" Mist Keepers that visited. To them, the Mist Keepers were not some crazed gods, as Yaz had described them. They were just...people.

Chander didn't want to be a god, anyway. That seemed like too much work.

He followed Yaz as she marched through town. Her attention turned as Zephyr, the dragon, took flight with the Mist Keeper Malaika on her back. Yaz waved frantically, and the Mist Keeper waved back. Malaika had become a presence in Neorama. Upbeat, with wild curly hair and a large smile, she cast a different shadow compared to the others.

Another Mist Keeper, Tomás, stood at the end of the road, where a stone mansion waited, with iron gates and dark windows. They spoke with their heads down to the architect of the town, a hairy man who spoke like his mouth was always full.

"Hi Tomás! Hi Szyman!" Yaz piped up from beside Chander as they approached the cohort of Mist Keepers. "Is Brent around?"

Tomás glanced over at them. A scar ran down his face, cutting away at his left eye and leaving an empty socket. He spoke softly as though trying to keep the world around them calm. "He should be back soon."

Yaz's face fell. Ever since Chander had met Yaz, she had been enamored by both Brent Harley, the Mist Keeper, and Bria Smidt, the Forest Queen. She said something about her owing them her life, but Chander never quite believed her. A petty crush seemed more likely.

The town architect turned to Yaz. "We're getting close to being ready for school, just so y'know. He'll be around more once that is ready to go."

Yaz kicked the dirt. "Alright."

Brent had told Chander and Yaz about the plans for the school. Once they had everything together, they would begin school, where anyone of any age could learn how to harness the Mist. The ghost town, he promised, would be safe. No one would find them - not the Order of the Effluvium, not any of the "bad" Mist Keepers, and not the Rosadian Guard.

"Can we go to the schoolhouse, Szyman?" Yaz asked the town's architect.

"You know where it is. If Brent shows up, we'll let him know you're looking for him."

"Oh, thank you!" Yaz continued to beam. Then, before they said anything else, she tugged Chander's sleeve toward the stone mansion. He winced harder at this touch, shaking his head once to refocus on the structure. With its cracked columns and sloping roof, it blended in with the pulsing smoke. The first time Chander saw the building, he had disregarded it. What could be so special about a dilapidated structure?

But inside told a different story.

Yaz pushed open the door. It opened without resistance to a small entranceway framed by a set of winding stairs. A single archway climbed beneath the stairwell, leading into a classroom lined with desks. On the far wall, a chalkboard stared over the desk. Rows of books towered along the walls. Other hallways extended from the entranceway, leading to an old kitchen and dining hall, with other empty rooms locked behind closed doors.

"It hasn't really changed, Yaz," Chander said.

"Then why hasn't class started?"

"Brent's probably still preparing lessons. There's more to the school than a classroom."

Yaz huffed.

"C'mon, we can go upstairs if you want."

With less pep in her step, Yaz returned to the stairwell. Chander followed her upstairs, where rows of rooms decorated the hallway. Upon opening the door to the first room, they found two beds and a window overlooking the city.

"You think this is for us to live in?" Yaz asked.

"Something like that. There's going to be a handful of us learning from the Mist Keepers, remember?"

"Oh, yeah," Yaz entered the room, glancing at the bare walls. "Who else will be here, do you think?"

"Not sure. Don't know how many of us there are."

"I hope it's not the monsters we saw in the Sanitorium..." Yaz hugged herself.

Chander remembered. They had followed Brent to the Sanitorium, only to discover that a collection of monsters, with misshapen faces and distant stares, waited for them. Brent reassured them that they were just other types of Mist Keepers.

Would they have to share a classroom with them? Chander wasn't sure how he felt about that as a whole.

Chander rubbed his hands together and closed his eyes. For a moment, he saw through Yaz's eyes, staring straight back at him. He shook his head to push the vision away. Brent had helped him tame his magic. A year ago, if he touched anyone, their perspective would haunt his every move, paralyzing him in place. Brent instead helped him.

Focus on the present. Focus on your senses. Chander inhaled once and pushed Yaz's vision from his mind. He had seen things that he never wanted to see; intimate moments that belonged in the privacy of bedrooms, bloody moments that belonged to the battlefields, and somber minutes that belonged to the dying. By the time he was ten years old, he needed a tonic to sleep.

But after the Order took him, Anandi, and his grandfather away, he was left reeling in nightmares.

His sister was jealous of his sight, but for Chander, it had always been a burden. He would trade anything to get rid of it.

But, rather, it kept getting stronger.

Now, thirteen years old, if someone bumped his shoulder, he claimed their eyes.

He had to remember the mantra.

His constants in life, his happiness.

The present.

"Chander? Did you hear what I said?" Yaz interjected his thoughts.

"What?" Chander shook his head and glanced at Yaz. She stood on her tiptoes by the window.

"Brent's here! Look!"

He joined her side. Brent spoke outside of the schoolhouse with Tomás and Szyman. He shifted in place, balancing a few books in one arm and gripping a cane with his free hand. His right leg trembled, and even from a distance, the exhaustion was clear on his face. Every time Chander saw Brent, illness riddled him. Did he sleep at all? Eat? He would vanish for days at a time, returning with books to fill his schoolhouse. But every time he returned, more color disappeared from his already pale face, and his eyes glossed over as he stared into a world beyond Chander's own understanding.

After finishing his conversation with the other Mist Keepers, Brent turned to the schoolhouse. Yaz immediately jumped from the window and bolted downstairs. Chander kept his gaze on Tomás and Szyman for a moment longer. The two men exchanged a few more words, not glancing in Chander's direction.

Without anyway to stall, Chander left the window behind and joined Yaz downstairs.

Yaz had already cornered Brent by the time Chander joined them. Jumping between her feet, she spoke to Brent with excitement.

"Is the school gonna open soon?" Yaz asked.

"Yes, I...I mean, we'll be starting in the next week or so." Brent lifted his attention to Chander and nodded once. "I look forward to working with both of you. We're going to learn about what being a Mist Keeper means together, a'ight?"

Chander crossed his arms. "If you don't know what it means, why bother teaching us?"

"I like to think that...that teaching is a part of learning."

"What do you mean?" Yaz asked.

Brent motioned for them to follow him into the classroom. He leaned his cane against the wall, then slowly began to unload the books onto the shelves. With each book, he paused, blinked once, and then placed it in a specific spot on the shelves. After placing his second book, he said, "I think I told you both that I haven't been a Mist Keeper long. I'm not like Caroline, Tomás, or Malaika, who have been Mist Keepers for centuries. But, because of the stories...I mean, because I collect stories and I understand their meaning...it means I've gathered a lot of knowledge about the Mist Keepers." Brent turned back to Chander and Yaz. "I need to sort through this information...and we're gonna do it together and learn from it."

"But how's that gonna help us?" Chander kept his questions pointed.

"Part of being a Mist Keeper is understanding where we came from and how we can grow from the Mistakes of others."

"Mistakes like the Diabolo..." Yaz mumbled.

Brent grimaced and nodded once before turning back to the bookcase. He ran his finger along the shelving, closing his eyes once as he traced the book's spines. His bottom lip trembled as he recited a few words under his breath.

He's not doing too well, Chander realized. But before he could pry, Brent returned to them with a smile.

"Did you choose your bedroom upstairs?" he asked.

"You mean the rooms up there are for us?" Yaz wrung her hands together, eyes widening behind her glasses.

"Yeah. It'll be where all the students will stay if they want."

"There're a lot of rooms, though!"

"I know. There will be more students over time."

"Like who?"

"I'm not sure yet. But if we found both of you, then there's gotta be others, right?"

Yaz grinned.

"Go on, both of you. Choose whatever room you like, a'ight? Upstairs though. Downstairs rooms are for adults. Got it?"

"Okay! Can I go now?"

"Go for it."

"Thank you, Brent!" Yaz spun at once, hurrying from the room with untampered excitement.

Chander didn't follow Yaz, eyeing Brent closely. As soon as Yaz disappeared from the room, Brent sank onto one of the nearby desks. He stared at his trembling hand. His eyes dimmed. In a certain light, it was as though Brent was a mirage composed of only Mist.

"Is everything a'ight, Chander?" Brent asked him.

"What's wrong with you?"

"Huh?"

"Are you sick or something? You don't look good," Chander replied.

Brent sighed and clenched his fists closed. He turned his head toward the ceiling and exhaled. "I am sick. But you don't need to worry about it."

"Shouldn't you see a doctor then or something?"

"Tomás is working on some potential solutions."

"What will he do? He's not a doctor. You should go to the Sanitorium."

"I will. Don't worry, though. It's not anything you need to fret yourself over, a'ight?"

"Why? Cause I'm a *kid*?"

"No, no," Brent groaned as he shifted on the desk. "It's not something anyone can really fix, a'ight? I mean...I'll be okay. You gotta focus on you right now."

"Yeah, well, just cause I'm a kid doesn't mean I can't help. I've seen a lot more than most kids my age."

"I know. I'll let you know if you can help, a'ight?"

"Fine," Chander grunted. For a moment, he closed his eyes. There, he watched as Yaz selected her bedroom overlooking the main road toward the school. If only his sight carried her excitement, but it was merely a glimpse into what she saw.

Then he blinked, and he stood again in the classroom.

In the present.

Where he yearned to remain.

CHAPTER FIVE

CRAWL SPACE

The wall had eyes.

And the desk had a tongue.

Brent clenched his jaw, pressing between his knuckles. *Go away. You're not real.*

The desk's shadow shifted in the morning light, moving against the wall.

And the eyes blinked.

You're not real. Brent lowered his head to his knees and counted backward from ten. Walls did not have eyes. Desks did not have tongues.

It was all in his head.

Brent had spent hours working in the classroom, organizing books and straightening out the desks. He tried to quell his nerves by writing on the chalkboard, but the sound of the chalk on the slate burned his ears. After two minutes of writing, he tossed the chalk to the floor and sank to his knees.

Where he stayed arguing with the wall until the purple tinge of evening arrived.

The wall continued to watch him. Its eyes switched from yellow to red, never blinking.

Beneath the eyes, the desk smiled, opening its mouth wide as if to feast.

"Stay back!" Brent jumped to his feet. He clenched his hands, summoning the surrounding Mist. What could fight a monster like this? It lived in the walls—lurking.

A dragon could, right? It could demolish the building with a single gasp.

He opened his hands, summoning forth another story. He imagined a dragon flying through the sky, igniting fear in all who stood in its way.

But when the Mist wrapped around his story, rather than creating a dragon, in its place flew a giant dragonfly, buzzing and flittering around Brent's head.

"Agh! Away, you fiend!" Brent waved his hands to force the giant insect away.

Except now he wasn't Brent, but a knight fighting a giant beast.

He grabbed his cane from the floor and flung it across the room. It hit the far wall with a clang. He winced.

"Horrid beast…" He hissed and sank back into one of the desks. The room had returned to normal.

And once again, he was Brent Harley.

His head fell against the desk. Sweat matted his hair, and his head spun as he tried to recenter himself. *My name is Brent Harley. I'm in my schoolhouse. I built this to help.*

And Bria Smidt is my constant.

"Bria…" he whispered. He ran his fingers over the betrothal mark on his hand. Back when they were in Knoll, they had an unofficial marriage ceremony, sealing their relationship with a mark on each of their hands. With magic woven into the ink, it connected them, constantly changing to depict safety or fear. Right now, the root-shaped fixtures on his hand rested.

As he hoped Bria did as well.

He kept his head on the desk, clenching his eyes shut even as the door to the classroom opened.

"Brent? Are you doing alright there?"

"Hmph," he grunted and opened one eye. Timothée, the burly circus performer, stood in the entranceway. On his back, he carried a small ghost child whose eyes had turned into holes in his head. He stared aimlessly into nothing.

"You don't look too good. Do you need anything?" Timothée asked.

"Nah, I'm a'ight. I just...the stories get to me, and it can be kinda overwhelming. But I'm a'ight." Brent straightened in his seat. "What're you doing here?"

"I wanted to see how this school's coming along."

"You thinking of attending?"

"Nah, this Mist Keeper bull isn't anything for me. I kind of like the idea of existing and doing what I want, like Szyman is doing out there." Timothée smiled beneath his curled mustache. It had grown thicker, hiding his upper lip. "Rather use my magic to make people happy."

"Given the choice, I'd be the same way."

To Brent, Szyman and Timothée proved that being a Mist Keeper was not a role set in stone as the Council had led him to believe. Back when he first learned of his apprenticeship, the Council said that he would die to become a Mist Keeper. It was only a means of control, to illicit fear and keep the true nature of the Mist at bay.

Mist Keepers were just a subset of Magii, really. They could choose to be the keepers of the afterlife, or they could continue, like so many people did, to live their lives.

But how many had struggled with their overwhelming magic? How many wondered if there was more?

"Well, you're always welcome to sit in on any lessons…learn a little. No one is forced to be a Mist Keeper here," Brent replied.

"I'll see. Got this little one to care for," Timothée motioned to the ghost boy. "Poor Preston's not doing too great. Think all the arguing I'm doing with Micca is making it worse."

"Sounds about right." Brent had known Micca since he was a boy. While Micca was smart, he had no magical inclination, so when sight was erased, in a mere blink, Micca no longer saw countless people. It had led to frustration and confusion.

"Well, I'm gonna go see Kek. Get their thoughts on this little man here," Timothée said.

"Have they been of any help?"

"Hard when they can't see him, unfortunately. Just taking notes on observations. Kek thinks Preston might hold the key to fixing all this, but not really sure. You can come if you want. Might be good for you to see Kek about all of…this." Timothée motioned to Brent.

"Not sure what they can do."

"Up your meds?"

"Maybe," Brent grunted as he climbed from his seat. "I'll come, though. Probably a good idea to get away from all of this for a bit."

He glanced over at the back wall. "You don't scare me."

But the wall chuckled back at him with a malicious grin.

The walk to the Sanitorium in the City of Mert took time. Brent had to stop every few minutes to catch his breath. It grew worse as they entered the city, with the cobblestones threatening to trip him with every few steps. It felt like the walk would take forever until finally, they reached the sterile white building near the city centre.

Kek had set up a side entranceway at the Sanitorium that allowed their trusted colleagues to come and go as they saw fit. A single tapped password granted access to the entrance: -.... ...-

Timothée tapped it without thinking against that door, and it swung open, allowing them to ascend the narrow stairwell to the top floor of the Sanitorium, where Kek's private suite waited above the wards. They'd created this Sanitorium from nothing, serving as a place to help those ill from both magical and non-magical ailments alike.

Brent caught his breath at the top of the stairs, gripping the wall as Timothée knocked on the second door. "Dr. Kafele?"

With a few clicks of the lock, the door swung open. Kek stood there in a long robe, their hair slicked back behind their ears.

"Ah, hello, Timothée."

"Is this a bad time?" Timothée peaked inside.

"Oh, not at all. Just catching up on my sleep. Come in," Kek paused, glancing at the wall. "Brent, are you here too?"

"He is—how did you know?"

"The shadow," Kek motioned to the wall.

Brent glanced at his fuzzy shadow against the wall. He waved once, and a half-form hand did the same.

"Yes, hello, Brent. Come in, all of you."

Kek led them into the suite. Brent paused at the threshold. Last time he had been here, he'd been recovering from the Diabolo for the first time, reunited with Bria, and recounting the taste of raccoon.

Had he really eaten a raccoon, then? Or was it a story?

He didn't ponder it as he entered the suite. Kek already had a tray of cheeses laid out on the table. Varden, the red-headed giant with empty, bloodshot eyes, sat there, not acknowledging their presence.

"How has Preston been?" Kek asked as they munched on a piece of cheese.

"The same, to be honest," Timothée paused, shifting the small ghost child into his arms. "But I have noticed something odd."

"And that is?"

"He doesn't seem to notice anyone who is living...unless they're Mist Keeper type people. He can sense the other ghosts, but he can't sense if Micca is there or anyone else," Timothée said.

Brent leaned forward on his cane, furrowing his brow. He hadn't taken notice of the other ghosts; they seemed to fade in and out as usual. But he had been preoccupied.

"Peculiar. Quite peculiar," Kek laced their hands together, staring at the pieces of cheese. "Varden, did you hear that?"

Varden turned his head slightly.

"Go talk more with Varden about this. He understands this whole sight thing more than I do. I want to speak with Mr. Harley here."

Timothée obliged, joining Varden at the table. Before Brent heard what they said, Kek slammed a notebook on a table and opened it.

"Well," Kek pointed at the notebook. "Tell me. What is occurring in that convoluted head of yours?"

Brent picked up the pen. *I'm*—he stopped. It would be easy to lie. But what good would that do? *I'm losing myself again.*

"Elaborate," Kek said, weaving their hands beneath their chin.

So Brent continued. *Every morning, I'm battling who I was in my dreams with who I actually am. Some days, it's within moments, but other days, I sit there for minutes to redis-cover myself. I've resorted to locking my door and hiding my shoes, hoping that I don't wander in a false state of existence. Shite, today I thought the wall had become a monster.*

Kek asked, "Is it your Diabolo resurfacing? Or the stories themselves?"

I don't know the last time I heard my Diabolo. He's been quiet.

Kek closed their eyes, "And what of the scar left behind by Ningursu? What is its current state?"

Not much different. It's expanded down my leg slightly. Makes it difficult to walk. Brent tapped the pen on the paper, leaving behind a few inconsequential marks.

"Has it lightened in color at all?"

No.

"Is it vascular?"

What?

Kek crossed their arms. "Does it look like if you pinched it hard enough, it would bleed?"

Brent lifted his shirt up slightly, glancing at the twisted black marks on his stomach. *I suppose so. They look like veins.*

Kek's attention fell on the back wall, licked their lip once, exhaled, then spoke, voice level and calm, "I was worried this might happen."

Brent's hand shook as he wrote. *What?*

"I've been speaking with Tomás and Varden. As I believe they mentioned to you a couple months ago, whatever Ningursu did to you, it is focusing on the Diabolo you harbor inside your body."

Right. Brent tried to push from his mind the time he'd spent trapped in the Library. With a pineapple as his best friend, he wandered the shelves until Ningursu ultimately captured him again. There, Brent made friends with the spirits, a collection of unsuccessful Mist Keepers used as experiments by the Council, and helped Kek escape Ningursu's clutches. All of this came with a cost. Ningursu wrapped him in a black smoke, and it laced to his skin, threatening to take over his body.

The plan had been for Ningursu to occupy his body, using it as a vessel for his mind. Brent fought back, but the black smoke remained.

Kek continued, "Well, I had my own worries based on my knowledge of your...disease, as I call it."

Brent didn't write a response, waiting.

"The medication I gave you over a year ago was designed to help clear your mind and give you focus. It was not designed to destroy the Diabolo. But...now the

Diabolo is dying at Ningursu's hand, freeing your mind from its clutches."

Isn't that good?

"It would be…if your magic didn't manifest in this way. I would have to run tests, of course, but I believe that the Diabolo served as a buffer for your magic. It prevented it from overwhelming you in one go and allowed you to harness it more than anyone else." Kek bit their bottom lip, then said, "With your Diabolo disappearing, your magic is growing…and fast."

His magic was growing? He'd already seen new talents weave through his magic; the ability to use the stories to impact Brent scribbled frantically, his print lacing together in near illegible chicken scratch. *You're saying that the Diabolo helped me?*

Kek nodded.

So it's either keep the Diabolo at the cost of my mind or let my magic grow uncontrollably?

Another nod.

Either way, I lose control.

"You were managing the Diabolo. In some ways, it was part of you," Kek replied.

With medication.

"Some diseases are chronic."

Brent tensed as the gong in his head vibrated, a headache etching its way into his mind. His next sentence came in rushed print. *What is going to happen to me?*

"If we fix the rot on your body, your Diabolo may come back and provide that buffer for you, with the proper controls, of course. But if we don't, if we can't figure it out, then the stories you see, in my opinion, will overwhelm you. You will alternate between yourself and someone else, imagination and reality. But it won't be like last time. Where last time, you used the stories to cope with the Diabolo, hiding your mind beneath layers of stories, this time...you will lose all sense of reality. You will be nothing but a shell."

So Ningursu can crawl into it.

"Exactly."

Brent stared at his hands. His fingers did not stop trembling while his throat tightened.

"I'll investigate potential remedies, but it will be hard without having an eye on you. For now, I'd recommend not taking your dosage. Give the Diabolo a chance to breathe, to act as a buffer for your mind."

Brent shook his head, his sight blurring. Carefully, he wrote the next words. *How long do I have left?*

"I cannot be certain, Brent, I am sorry."

CHAPTER SIX

A MUSICAL SPIRIT

Brent sat in silence for a time, not budging even when Timothée left with Varden, instead spending the time to ponder what Kek told him. He had two options: welcome his Diabolo once again to inch its way into his mind, or keep it buried and open his mind to all the stories. Neither option appealed to him. He had truly gotten stronger with his magic, and he reveled in its ability over the last few months. The stories breathed around him, and with his thoughts under control, they did not elicit fear.

Now, in Mert, he was back where he began.

Assaulted by the Mist.

With fear of becoming an empty shell.

He didn't tell Kek when he left, sneaking out through the door and down into the ward beneath the suite. The infamous Ward Nine harbored countless victims of magical duress. As he moved forward, the stories of his own time here haunted him: the bloodthirsty Edith carving "Reaper" into his arm, the dizzying spell alternating between reality and fiction, and then Bria, with a dramatic flair, freeing him from the sterile white room.

He paused outside of one room with the curtains pulled open. Inside, a woman played the violin. As she played, the Mist danced, producing an array of colors at her feet. Brent placed his hand against the window and watched. Like so many others, she had been abandoned by the Mist, left struggling in the confusion brought on by her magic. Did the Mist speak to her through song? Was her violin the only way to reply?

"She is an untrained Mist Keeper, as I am sure you noticed," a voice came behind Brent.

He turned. Tomás stood there, his arms crossed, gaze fixated at the window.

"So she's a spirit?"

"Not quite. She is still alive and could still enter the Mist if she dared choose," Tomás replied. "Music has been a fascinating source of comfort for many of our spirits. One of my peers, long ago, used music as well, playing the flute to produce comfort. It wasn't strong enough for them, though."

"How many spirits have there been? We only rescued a handful from the crypts…right?"

"Thousands. Many faded away by now…" Tomás sighed. "Fading may be the best option for many of them. Sometimes, it is not worth trying to save them."

"But we have to try."

"Yes, many have thought that. After all, you're not the first one to create a school."

"What do you mean?"

Tomás motioned for Brent to follow him down the hallway. As they walked, he continued. "Aelia gathered about twenty of us as children and attempted to raise us into the role of Mist Keeper. Teodozia, Imelda, Estefano…just to name a few. Some are the spirits you see now; some worse…"

"Diabolo?"

"Diabolo." Tomás slowed as they reached another door at the end of the ward with a set of three locks. He removed a key and began his slow unlock. "What Aelia did is quite similar to what you are doing now…and that is where my hesitancy lies. The training was cumbersome, to say the least."

As Tomás paused, Brent glanced over him once. The story circled around him: an orphan boy taken by a strange woman, forced to work with the Mist, divulge himself in it, and surround himself in its torturous grasp.

He was a boy who lost friends, lost childhood, and lost freedom.

"I am sure you are collecting the tale now, aren't you?" Tomás asked.

"I see parts of it."

"So you can see my own hesitancy, can't you? It is something we must ask ourselves: is it worth torturing more souls to create a collection of new Mist Keepers? Is it worth putting them through these trials?" Tomás dropped the first key to the ground, then removed the next one. "Ningursu and Aelia realized, after their failure with this school, that focusing on one apprentice was easier. It provided fewer errors...or so they thought. We still lost many, still produced a multitude of mistakes...but I like to think we have less now than we would have if Ningursu and Aelia continued their first path."

"But how many untrained Mist Keepers suffered a worse fate?" Brent asked, glancing back down the ward. "The ones here are struggling, lost and confused. The spirits have been experimented on for centuries. And now we have children like Chander and Yaz, begging for...for an explanation or help or...or something."

"How many have avoided Ningursu, though? Perhaps there are more like Timothée out there, surviving and living, rather than forced into a single role." Tomás asked as he turned the last key.

"I'm not trying to create an army of Mist Keepers. No one will be forced to learn if they don't want to...I mean...I want to help all these people understand their magic and have a choice. Shouldn't we all have a choice in how our magic manifests...or if we want to become Mist Keepers in the first place? I mean, I never had a choice in any of this shite...did you?"

Tomás gripped the knob. "I...did not."

"Because Aelia decided your fate."

"I suppose so."

"This time will be different, a'ight? There's more of us. We'll take our time. I've been...I mean...I've been working on the plan. Please Tomás...I mean...you are the oldest of all of us here. I need...I want your help in all of this. Please.

Tomás sighed. "Very well. But I hope you have considered the spirits in all of this."

"I have."

"Then let us speak with them now...as I am sure you have considered."

Brent didn't say a word as Tomás opened the door. Plumes of yellow seeped around them as they entered. Tomás closed it as soon as they both entered, then turned the dial on the nearby gas lamp. The dim light highlighted the set of rooms lining the wall, like the ones in the ward outside. Through the smudged windows, figures moved about, indistinguishable. It might have been better than the crypt, but not by much. *From one prison to the next.*

"We've been keeping it dim in here, turning the lights up slowly to adjust their eyes. Most of them haven't been in daylight in centuries." Tomás said as he approached one of the windowed doors.

Brent joined his side, reaching for the doorknob. Tomás stopped him.

"Brent, I know you are struggling with your stories again. So, I do not advise you to open this door. Not yet, at least. While I cannot sense their stories, their minds are even too much for me. It leaves me spinning…I cannot imagine the impact on you."

"How can we help them then? They…they can't stay in here forever. This is just like the crypt."

"I've been working with one of them regularly since they arrived. Here, I'll introduce you. His mind is clearer than most."

Brent followed Tomás down the dark hallway, wincing as waves of yellow smoke passed over his nose. Stories danced on the plumes, but he pushed them away with a flick of his hand. *My name is Brent Harley. I am not a spirit. I am a Mist Keeper. A true Mist Keeper.*

And I am here to help.

At the end of the hall sat another room with a glass-paned door. This time, Tomás reached for the knob and turned it.

Rather than the dim glow of the hall, a calming light greeted them, welcoming Brent and Tomás into a small bedroom with a collection of books. A piano sat against the wall, where a thin man with a long neck and punched-in chin played a calm tune. As he played, the music filled the room, catching the Mist in its song and forming images with each beat.

Like the woman and her violin upstairs.

"Milo? Are you there?" Tomás asked.

The man perked and turned to face them. With thinning strands of gray hair on his head and wide silver eyes, he looked more human than most of the other spirits. Part of his chin had collapsed, and his skin still steamed with yellow smoke. With shaking skeletal fingers, he affixed a pair of glasses onto his face, then grinned.

"Milo?" Brent asked, "You mean Julietta's Milo?"

The spirit turned back to the piano and tapped on the keys: -.--. ... .-.-.- / - .....- -.----. ... / --. .-.-.-

Yes. That's me.

"And he knows tap-code!?"

Tomás nodded. "He lost his ability to speak after years in the crypt. After evaluating him and realizing he still had some awareness, I started to teach him. He picked it

74

up rather quickly, especially once I got him a piano. Sure, I can read his mind, but it's not as effective when his thoughts are jumbled."

"But he's the Milo that Julietta was always talking about! Did she know?"

Milo tapped on his keyboard again. *Yes.*

Tomás added, "I think that is why he has survived. Julietta visited him regularly, whether aware it was him or not. Once free of the nightmares in the crypt, he started to return to his old self."

"And you believe he can help the other spirits?"

"Yes. He isn't affected by their stories or minds like you or me. Milo, would you like to show Brent here what you've done?"

Milo climbed to his feet, then, with a hurried strut, motioned for Brent to follow.

Every step Milo took came with an uneven sway. With one leg longer than the other, he struggled to stay balanced, having to grab hold of the wall for stability. He marveled at the simple structures of doorknobs and the pristine paint on the walls. How long had he been a prisoner? Where had he lived before the Library? Had he once been a Mist Keeper, able to release souls at a whim?

What was his story?

Brent would collect it someday.

Milo approached a door. Its window pulsed with yellow smoke. Within it, Brent caught a glimpse of one of the spirits pacing in its room.

Tomás held his arm out to prevent Brent from approaching while Milo slipped into the room where he opened the blinds. Milo nodded toward Brent and Tomás, then approached the spirit sitting on the bed.

"That's Yūki. One of Jiang's failures, if I recall." Tomás said.

"What happened with her?" Brent asked.

"Her magic. It was similar to yours, in a way. She created illusions of monsters and beasts. But one day, she created a beast all too powerful, and...it overwhelmed her. She essentially thought herself a sea serpent and crawled into the sea. Jiang rescued her...only to discover that she had become engorged like a sponge. She continued to slither across the ground like the serpent...until recently."

And that's what I want to prevent going forward. Brent placed his hand against the glass. Milo's shadow approached Yūki, and then he removed a small object from his pocket. With nervous hands, he brought the object to his lips.

A gnawing sound exited the object, bouncing around the room. With its harmonic tune, images filled the room, pulling back at the yellow smoke. A storyteller in his own right, Milo told a tale to Yūki about safety, about friendship, and about her own magic. Yūki watched in awe, her dark eyes glimmering with a touch of hope.

"He's telling them stories," Brent whispered.

"His music is helping them find themselves again, yes," Tomás replied. "In the past couple weeks, the yellow smoke isn't so harrowing, and they have started to display a sense of self in their actions. Their thoughts are still jumbled, but there are brief moments of clarity."

Brent grinned, unable to pull his attention away from Milo and Yūki. The way Milo continued to play his harmonica, it captured everything Brent believed the Council could become: helpful, kind, and fantastic.

With Milo's help, the school would thrive.

Brent would make sure of it. Even if it cost him his mind.

CHAPTER SEVEN

THE WORLD BENEATH

Todd adjusted his makeshift blanket on the ground, peering out from the alleyway by the coffee shop. The collection of strangers who had filed from the kitchen had yet to return. He knew well enough by now that something was amiss. This was not the normal coming and going of patrons to the café. There was something more unusual. His years of training with the Guard told him to look for odd behavior: people ducking into shadows, notes passed on strips of newspaper, and whispers spoken with heads touching. A cohort of individuals fleeing a café? That set his alarm bells ringing.

But he wasn't in the Guard anymore, and Garrett still sat there within him, his bandaged head turned ahead, unspeaking. He couldn't go investigating or running to authorities; any wrong move and his own son would be discovered.

The alley allowed him to watch, though. He kept Garrett on his lap, letting the little boy play with the wooden toys they had collected over the last couple months. The form of play was anything but cohesive. Garrett whacked the two toys together. Frankly, Todd could barely tell what the toys were supposed to be; at first, he thought one was a dog, but another time, it looked like a dragon. The second toy was more human in its features, but even then, Todd couldn't tell if it was monster or man.

Nor did it matter.

He adjusted Garrett's sleeves, hiding the nipping bites on his wrists from the cold air, then placed the hole-riddled blanket across his lap. The winter air nipped at his face, tugging at his eyelids, keeping him attentive. He couldn't recall the last time he had slept a full night. But now, with his curiosity locked on that strange café, it was all for the best.

If the past year had taught him anything, it was to be alert. One wrong look, one incorrect nod, and life as he knew it would be flipped. Pretending this café didn't exist wasn't an option.

And part of him wondered if it could provide him with safety. What if, behind that door, he found Garrett a new home away from harm?

But what would that look like?

The City of Mert had infiltrated his life, stole his livelihood, and led him back to Rosada.

Meanwhile, Rosada was a land without exceptions.

In the north waited Kainan, but they were even worse than Rosada. In the south, Volfium might be open to his presence...but he did not speak the language or carry the necessary skills to immigrate there.

What good could a café do?

"Sorry I ain't that knowledgeable about nothing, Garrett," Todd adjusted the boy on his lap again.

The classified adverts lay open in the newspaper beside him. Their ongoing lists of credentials and papers mocked him. Even if he had the skills, he had no records. A twice deserter of the Guard—even if he had documentation, it would be marked with the black stamp.

Just like the hidden emblem on his wrist.

Even if I could find a job, it's not like I got no skills. It ain't like a tattooist is gonna be respected around these parts. He'd learned how to tattoo when in the Pit, but outside those walls, the idea of a tattoo was as taboo as a story. Tattoos told tales, embossed on the skin, a permanent mark of defiance. The only marks allowed, so decreed by the Order and, in turn, the government, were the betrothal marks...as well as the black stamps.

Survive. That was all he could do now. Survive.

As night coated the city with a blanket, Todd settled farther back into the alley. Guards marched through the streets, checking each crevasse and corner for storytellers and Magii. One glanced Todd's way, only to shrug him off, disregarding the scene. Todd had gotten used to the guards ignoring him. While years ago, any vagrant sleeping in the streets would find themselves in the Pit, with so many new detainees, someone resting on the streets proved minimally invasive.

Todd could live like this, but how long could Garrett?

His mind raced as a half-sleep washed over him. He envisioned dropping Garrett off at an orphanage, where at least the boy could be fed and given a warm bed. But every time he grew close to making such a decision, he pictured Lex, with her soft, pale features, clinging to Garrett and promising she would never leave his side.

He couldn't leave Garrett now. Not when the world had turned dark.

As sleep finally started to cradle him, footsteps pulled Todd back to life.

The cohort of individuals he saw in the café tiptoed through the darkness with about ten new faces on their heels. Checking each corner, they approached the café again, opening the door a crack and ushering each person inside.

The new cohort each bore a familiar exhaustion, one that Todd had been carrying for weeks. They wore tattered clothes, empty stares, and trembling limbs. He was no different from them.

And if they followed, what stopped him?

Perhaps this café held all the answers that he needed.

His gut told him not to stand, not to gather his son into his arms, and not to approach the café. He had already got himself out of the situation. Why bother getting involved in such detrimental activities? But…looking at Garrett, playing with the indistinguishable toys, his gaze empty, his voice unheard, Todd knew that he could not continue down the same path. The past three months brought no success. How long could he keep Garrett in the streets?

If something went wrong, he could blame himself as a fool.

But at least this offered one thing: a chance.

You gotta take a risk at some point. Besides, Lex would trust these people in the café, right? She had always been naïve, trusting people, believing them to be the best versions of themselves. Everything she did was for Garrett. Would she have let Garrett stay on the streets for so long? Or would she have put her faith in this café owner?

Todd swallowed and finally climbed to his feet, holding Garrett tight. The last of the cohort entered the shop.

Just before they closed the door, he raced forward, ignoring the dizziness crawling through his head.

He stumbled to the door as it shut and banged his hand against the glass pane. The last person in the group turned, raised their brow, then called into another room. After a moment, the same server from the previous day appeared.

They cracked open the door with a smile.

"Ah, so you came crawling back now?"

"Don't get all cocky with me. Yeah, I came back cause my kid's gotta sleep with a roof over his head at some point, a'ight? So you gonna let me in or what?"

"Hmm...not sure if I should now. Maybe you have a guard or someone coming," the server crossed his arms over his broad chest.

"I've been sitting in that alley all day. I don't got time to find a guard or nothing."

"You had time to sit in an alley."

"I was with my son!" Todd shouted.

Garrett did not flinch.

The server glanced at Garrett, then back at Todd, "A'ight, fine, c'mon in. It's not like you could get us in much trouble anyway...at least not yet."

"What d'ya mean?"

"You'll see. C'mon," the server motioned for Todd to follow back into the kitchen.

Todd glanced one last time at the street, then followed the server into the back, where the others waited. No one glanced in his direction, each keeping their attention on the floor. One individual worked on the pantry door locks, while another spoke to each of the vagrants in a low voice.

"As I told you, there's safety down here. Probably a good place for you and your boy here." The server said. "I think we'll be able to help."

"Fine. Let's go then," Todd said.

"Tell me a story if you wanna go," the server said as the cellar door opened.

Todd glowered and instead took a step forward.

The server stopped him. "Story or leave."

"I told you one already!"

"Gotta tell me another one."

Todd glanced at Garrett in his arms. *This better be worth breaking the law.* He huffed once, then whispered a small tale he heard Lex tell Garett in another life. "Once, there was a little boy who dreamed a dream so quiet no one heard. A simple dream, for a night without nightmares and a day without tears. He sat beneath his window, wishing for that dream. Until one day, a star came tumbling down and granted him that very thing."

"Cute," the server smiled. Then, with a dramatic bow, he stepped to the side, allowing Todd to follow the cohort down into the cellar.

The wooden steps creaked as Todd stepped onto them. He repositioned Garrett so the boy's head rested on his chest and took each step one at a time, gripping the railing with his free hand. The server closed the door behind him, allowing only a trickle of light to travel along the stairway from the lantern at the bottom of the stairs.

Much to Todd's displeasure, the stairway did lead into a cellar. With everyone crammed together, he could hardly move his elbows without bumping into one of the other vagrants.

"You gonna suffocate us down here?" he spat at the server.

"Just hang on there," the server stood on his tiptoes and called out, "Jayme! Third panel over, second code, four times, a'ight!?"

Todd couldn't see this so-called Jayme, but he heard the familiar tap-code against the wooden paneling on the far wall. He didn't understand the code. While he had been trained on some of it back in the Guard, he never committed it to memory, thinking it a relic of a hundred years prior.

But, as the last bit of code echoed throughout the cellar, the wall paneling fell away, opening to a long tunnel whistling with wind and dripping water.

"Is that a witch tunnel?" Todd grunted. "The Guard knows all about those, I'm sure."

"They don't know every passage, though," the server said.

"You could be leading us straight into a trap."

"We're not. Don't worry."

"And I should trust you?"

The server chuckled and strolled past Todd, saying, "Listen, you're welcome to stay in the cellar...but you showed up on your own, so stop being so skeptical. We're only here to help."

Todd froze, watching as the group slowly moved down the tunnels. Once again, the temptation to turn tugged at him. But he could hear Lex telling him to go, feel her guiding him forward. What good would staying here do? Garrett needed someplace safer.

With a grunt, he followed behind the group, making sure to stay a few paces back from the end of the line. If things went wrong, then at least he could run.

Other than the tunnel growing darker and the occasional whiff of sewage running through the air, everything continued uneventfully. The tunnel narrowed, then widened, while little conversations passed between any of the individuals. Even Garrett remained quiet, head on Todd's chest, his attention turned ahead. Occasionally, the server glanced back at Todd, but otherwise, no conversation was exchanged.

Until they reached a dead end.

"Nils!" Someone called from the front of the group, "What's the code here?"

The server perked up, "It's the fifth panel, code number twelve, repeat thrice."

After a pause, the tap-code echoed around the tunnel, the same pattern three times. Todd joined the server's side.

"So your name is Nils then?" Todd whispered.

"Does it matter?" The server replied.

Todd shrugged. *At least it is some information.*

He wouldn't give his name up so easily.

As the last of the tap-code echoed, the wall creaked, opening up into the tunnel. One at a time, each person entered the new room on the other side.

Todd glanced one last time down the tunnel, waiting for Nils to step into the room. When the server finally entered, he turned around and motioned Todd to follow.

Grunting once, Todd stepped through the doorway.

Then froze.

He had heard rumors about these places in the Guard but never saw one in person. There, in front of him, waited a small tavern—a speakeasy, really—where nearly thirty people gathered. Despite the dark, candlelit room, people laughed, and children darted between the tables.

"Thought these things were fake..." Todd mumbled.

"Nah, there's a group of 'em," Nils replied. "This is a tiny one under one of the apothecaries here."

"So we're still in the city?"

"We only bring a handful of ya out of the Capital at a time. Reduces risk. Don't worry, you're all safe here, though," Nils said.

"But—"

"Trust me. They ain't found this place in thirty years. Unless someone goes running to the Guard now, I think we're still safe."

Todd opened his mouth to reply, but Nils cut him off.

"Don't worry, my friend. Get a drink, relax. You're safe."

Before Todd could find any other response, the bartender called Nils over to them. With a wave, Nils left Todd standing there, surrounded by strangers, in a dimly lit speakeasy.

If anything, it meant he had a roof over his head for the night.

Even if it meant being surrounded by whispers of stories and a hint of repulsive magic.

CHAPTER EIGHT

THE QUEEN'S RETURN

Bria jolted awake, gasping. The air weighed heavily, pulling at her lungs. She could hardly see through the yellow haze, and in a panic, she felt along the side of the cot until her fingers found the elongated structure of her gas mask. Fumbling, she pulled it on and adjusted the filter, hyperventilating until her head finally stopped spinning.

She found herself in a canvas tent, brought to life by the dim daylight battering on the outside of the structure. A thin cot rested beneath her.

What happened? She slowly climbed to her feet. Dust matted her hair. Her branched arm hung at her side, unwoven, like a set of discombobulated vines. All the while, chilled morning air danced around her as she peeked her head out of the tent.

Glistening stones greeted her, the sunlight dancing on their surface with each beat. Yet, nothing else shimmered with the same determination. Everything else remained in the drab, colorless reality of the Pit.

Right. I came to Opal's Canyon. She wrung her hands together. What had happened? She arrived, promising to help them leave. But then, her mask fell off, and the disease-riddled yellow smoke debilitated her. Or had someone removed it? The whole night had been a blur.

"Well, well, well, look who finally woke from her beauty rest."

Bria recognized that voice. She slowly turned to where Edith stood, waiting beside the tent with her arms crossed. The metallurgist had long haunted Bria. They had met in Mert, where Edith was quick to seek blood from the Mist Keepers—and, more specifically, Brent. Since then, she always managed to follow Bria, coming to Knoll's Gully and killing the Seer, Madame Owiti, to forcing Bria into a series of trainings that left her both exhausted and overstimulated.

"What are you doing here?" Bria asked.

"Waiting for you, of course."

"But...how did you know I'd be here?"

"I didn't. I've been using the Pools to check all the large Pits each day. Figured I'd cross paths with you at some point."

"There's a pool near here?" Bria skimmed the horizon. The Pools, once constructed long ago by Kek's own hand, tainted the earth. Powerful and magical, the Pools could be used as transportation, communication, and as the base for countless potions and concoctions. As valuable as it was, Bria knew it was too dangerous to leave scattered across the world. It gave power to all the wrong people.

And Bria had not forgotten her promise to destroy the Pools.

But Edith knew this plan all too well, "Don't go thinking I'll let you destroy it now. That's Kek's property."

Bria flared her nostrils but did not reply.

"Besides, Hue is waiting for you back in the Capital. Promised her if I found you, I'd bring you straight there. I might have broken that promise a little, though."

"What do you mean?" Bria clenched her fist. Her head still spun from the yellow smoke. Even her other arm had yet to reform.

"You're still here, aren't you? Figured if you saw me, you might attack. So, debilitated you a little. Unfortunately, I couldn't carry you back to the Capital discreetly...so here we still are."

Bria reached for her mask. "So you removed my mask?"

"Now you get it," Edith chuckled.

Bria glowered back and hissed, "If my head wasn't spinning, I'd send you into the trees."

"Too bad, so sad."

"How is this not impacting your magic?"

"Oh, it is. Just my magic isn't tied to my life force...and I got other skills besides turning stone into metal." Edith tapped the long knife hooked into her belt. "So, I suggest you come with me."

Bria stepped away, "No. I said I would get everyone to safety."

"Oh, come now, what's one more day in the Pit going to do?"

"I made a promise."

"And you already broke it. Come now, Hue is waiting. Don't want to upset the new leader now, do you? Especially after you caused your mommy's death?"

Bria willed her branched arm to reform. Before the hand even fully returned, she sent it forward, reaching for Edith.

Edith acted faster, removing her knife with one swift motion and slicing Bria's branched arm in two.

Wincing, Bria stumbled back, letting the remaining branches withdraw to her shoulder. She bit her tongue to stop the tears.

"Not so strong now, hm?" Edith returned her blade. "This Diabolic smoke is getting stronger, huh? That's what I call this stuff that Ningursu spat all over the world. Good name, right?"

Bria didn't reply.

"You're no fun. Is that what being a queen does? Make you boring?"

"Just take me to Hue if that's what you're here to do, Edith. I don't have time for your antics."

Edith stooped into a dramatic bow. "Very well, Your Majesty...but on one condition."

"And what's that?"

She removed a long piece of cloth from her coat. "Cover your eyes."

"Pardon?"

"I don't need you knowing where this Pool is."

"It's not like I have the strength to destroy it right now."

"Yes, but you will later," Edith held out the strip of cloth. "Either wear it, or I suppose I can knock you out again. If I were you, I'd take the first option."

Bria snatched the cloth from Edith. It wasn't worth the argument. After all, the sooner she saw Hue, the sooner she could refocus on her own mission.

"This better not be a trick," she said, then covered the eye sockets of her gas mask with the strip of red fabric.

Bria let Edith lead her away from Opal's Pit. Even with the strip of fabric covering her mask, she managed to listen to the elements as she walked. The same silicon and iron followed her from the ground, no differentiation in her surroundings. A slight glare from the sun entered her vision from the right, shifting away from her as Edith led her closer to the Pool.

So we headed northwest, through the canyon, to get here, Bria recounted as the liquid touched her ankles. But would it be enough for her to find her way back if she could remember?

As soon as it wrapped around her feet, Edith tugged her forward, and she toppled into Pool.

Within seconds, she reemerged for air inside a porcelain tub. The blindfold drooped from her face, falling around her neck. Bria carefully removed her gas mask, peering around the lavatory where Edith stood wiping the liquid from her body.

Bria recognized the location at once: one of the bathrooms in the storytelling tavern on the outskirts of the Capital, where she had stayed before the Senate fell. It was in this very bathroom that Christof grabbed hold of her and knocked her unconscious.

And within an hour of that misstep, Bria watched her mother die, and a new target fell on her back.

She had tried not to think about that day. After her mother took her last breath, she let her emotions take control. Her anger carried her to the Capitol Building. Why? Had she planned to kill Christof? What had been the plan?

She still didn't know.

But it led to a moment when she stood face-to-face with Jemma Reds, the pious young woman from back home.

Yet, it wasn't Jemma, but rather someone else controlled by Ningursu and seeking a path of control and domination.

And under Jemma's hand, Senator Cordova fell.

"You gonna sit in that tub all day? C'mon. Hue's probably downstairs," Edith tugged Bria from the tub.

Stumbling over the edge of the fixture, Bria straightened her body and followed Edith from the room. There was a comfort in these hallways. Years ago, she came to this tavern to just listen to stories. It was one of the first places she'd taken Brent when he discovered the Tunnels.

And here, she had let her walls collapse and finally let Brent truly see her in full.

She paused at the stairs, glancing back down the hallway. If Brent stood beside her, he could recall the story in a heartbeat.

But her recollection was short-lived as Edith continued to lead her down the stairwell. As they entered the kitchen, Edith chanted, "Look who I found!"

Bria froze in the entranceway. Her throat tightened.

Marisol, with her long black hair wrapped into a bun, rose from the table. Tears filled her dark eyes, and a wide smile spread across her face.

"Bria!?"

"Marisol, I—"

Before Bria could finish her sentence, Marisol pulled her into a hug. Tears bubbled in Bria's eyes, and she broke down sobbing in her friend's arms. The warmth of her arms, the mere touch, it was like being wrapped in a warm blanket. When was the last time she felt real touch? With Brent, it was all an illusion. She could only imagine his touch...but was it even there?

"I'm so sorry..." Bria choked.

"Hey! No apologizing! You did what you had to do."

"I was being dumb..."

"No, no, you were doing what you had to–don't call yourself that. Besides, you've done such amazing things since! We've been following what has been going on with the Pits. We knew it was you—really! Do not apologize! You're a hero!" Marisol squeezed Bria's hands before shifting her attention slightly to the ground. "Oh, look! Nix is here to cheer you up!"

"Nix?" Bria glanced at the ground. Her heart sank.

Her misty dog, Nix, did not wait at her feet.

Nothing waited there but the kitchen floor.

"Where?" Bria asked.

"Right here!" Marisol motioned to the ground. "Don't you see her?"

Bria shook her head.

Marisol furrowed her brow, "Other people have been saying that, too. Maybe there's something wrong with me..."

"No...I don't think there is," Bria murmured, her throat tightening. "Nix is part of the Mist."

Another bout of tears suffocated her.

Just like with Brent, she couldn't even see her dog.

CHAPTER NINE

AN ARMY IN WAITING

"Where were you, Bria?" Marisol asked as she placed a glass of scotch on the table.

Bria eyed the drink, the final tears leaving her ducts dry. She had accepted not seeing Brent or the world of the dead...but she hadn't considered that her own misty dog would succumb to the same fate. She had fully expected to be greeted by Nix's wagging tail and lopsided tongue...once she returned.

But even that had been taken from her.

She picked up the glass, glancing across at Marisol. They sat in the speakeasy beneath the tavern, where the old barkeep, Lester, prepared drinks and whispered stories. His aunt Doris greeted Bria with a smile from the barstool as she arrived. While the speakeasy held its secrets, the bustle of countless Magii and other members of the so-called rebellion loitered. Bria recognized some of them, but rather than saying hello, she kept her eyes downcast.

In the far corner, she caught a glimpse of Edith, who had taken a seat with a gathering of Kek's Magii - Tristan, a master of fire; Mayim, a master of water; and Fritjof, a master of air. They had trained her back in Knoll in their own way, helping her come to terms with the depths of her magic. She knew they waited for her to lead them to glory against the Council of Mist Keepers.

Just like everyone else looked towards her for guidance against the Order of the Effluvium.

But she wasn't *Lana*. Sure, she had magic, but Lana had worked for years in the Pit to gain everyone's trust. Bria had no right taking her place.

"Bria?" Marisol pried again.

"Sorry..." She placed the glass down, "What were you saying?"

"I was asking what happened to you. We thought that you were captured, but then there were the rumors about vagrants escaping the Pit. We thought it might be you...but you didn't return. We didn't know what happened."

Bria sighed and stared at her hands. Her branched fingers curled in on themselves. "I was finding a place where we could be safe."

"Alone?"

"Not...exactly." Bria could feel Marisol's magic tugging at her tongue, but she resisted spilling everything. She explained to Marisol that she had traveled far from Rosada to a hideaway where the Order could not touch her. She explained her communication with Brent through private tap-code and scribbled letters, how he helped her create the new fortress before she ventured out into the Pits driven by her own shame and promise to make things right.

"You could have sent us a message," Marisol said as Bria finished.

"I know. I just...wasn't ready."

Marisol didn't ask any further questions, finishing off her glass of scotch and glancing around the room before saying, "Well, Hue will be glad you're here. She got here soon after you went missing with the others from Knoll and took over for Lana. She and her brother are constantly sending tap-code messages to reinforcements around the country. Newbird's Arm has become our biggest ally—thanks to you, of course."

"Newbird's Arm is okay then?" Bria straightened her back slightly. She had last left Newbird's Arm with a slew of guards imprisoned and destruction in her wake. Despite her intentions to stay, her grandmama encouraged her to leave. To defend. To fight.

And to lead.

"From what we have heard, yes. After their senator died, I think it spawned a new sense of rebellion. But...we've been missing something in all of this."

Bria shrank. "You don't need me."

Someone interjected, "Yes. We do."

Bria glanced over her shoulder. Hue, the doctor from Knoll's Gully, strode towards the table. She had pulled her gray-streaked hair back into a ponytail, her thin-rimmed glasses resting on the tip of her nose.

She joined Marisol and Bria at the table, then waved to the bartender. "Les! Can you get another round over here, please?"

The bartender grunted but obliged with another bottle of scotch. "That's the last free bottle."

"Oh, stop. What would Mami say?"

"Mami's not here." The bartender smirked, then returned to his post.

Hue filled up her own glass, chuckling. "Just because he stuck around in this tavern doesn't mean he makes all the rules."

Marisol answered Bria's question before she even asked, "Hue and Lester are siblings."

"Oh, I see." Bria glanced back at Lester. There was certainly a family resemblance—similar hair and face shape—but otherwise, she never would have guessed that they were related.

"Lester kept the tavern; I went to school. I never did think I'd end up back here using this tavern just like my Auntie did. But we're not here to reminisce about my past." Hue took a swig of her drink. "I am glad you are back, Bria. We need you."

Bria looked away from Hue. "You don't need me."

"We do not have anyone with your type of magic. You can–"

"What? Cause destruction? Hurt people?" Bria shook her head.

"You have done more good than harm. Think of all the Pits you have liberated over the last couple months."

"It's only what I have to do...to make up for what I did."

"Make up for what?" Marisol asked. "If you mean what you did in the plaza a couple months ago, it was brilliant! It has completely derailed the Order. It gave people time to flee while they reconstructed themselves."

"Not just that. I've harmed people. I'm being called a terrorist."

Hue replied, "Only by those who are scared. The Order is using you as a scapegoat, but everyone is singing your song."

"They shouldn't be singing it!" Bria clamored to her feet, gripping the table tight. The wood gathered at her fingertips, lacing around her nails. She released it, swallowing her tears. "That song has followed me since childhood. It has basically dictated everything I have done...and I wish people would stop singing it. No good comes out of it."

"It gives people hope. Isn't that enough?" Hue asked.

Bria's bottom lip quivered.

"And now that you're back, we may have a chance to thrive."

Bria stared at her fingers.

"It's what Lana would want."

"I know," Bria whispered. "It doesn't mean I have to like it, though."

Bria sat with Marisol and Hue, listening as they detailed the events that had occurred in Rosada over the last couple of months. Rosada had grown bleak. The Capital had closed its walls, vetting each person who dared to enter or leave. Guards never left their posts. Hundreds of people slept in the streets, waiting to be sent to the Pits or brought in for magical experimentation. Each night, at the first sign of sundown, the Capital fell into a restless sleep. No nightlife, no celebrations. Everything that once had been alive in the Capital, with its bolstering streets and freedom to speak, had dimmed.

The only glimmer came from the group of speakeasies throughout the Capital, which Hue dubbed the Witch Network. Through hidden fronts throughout the Capital, they gathered those without homes, those exhibiting magic, and those yearning to tell stories.

And all of them waited for the Forest Queen to return.

With the weight of her song on her back, Bria left the speakeasy and walked back up the stairs of the tavern and back to her old room. Old Lady Doris sat in her usual rocking chair, smiling as Bria passed her.

It was like entering a foreign land. Of course Bria knew the tavern, but it didn't hold the same excitement anymore. All the rush she received from the secret stories and the wallops of magic vanished with the dimming colors. She moved through the rooms, trying to imagine a different life. Hue said she was raised here with her brother Lester. What sort of life was that? Did they play games, laugh, and sneak in lovers? What about their parents? Did they dance in the kitchen while listening to storytellers in their speakeasy?

What would it be like to have a life like that?

She tried to imagine her and Brent in a home that belonged to them. He would tell stories at the kitchen table while she bundled flowers into a bouquet. Would they dance to silent music? Sit in their respective chairs, reading stories and sharing tidbits? It was hard to imagine.

That future didn't exist.

It never would.

It never could.

Bria climbed up the stairs to the rows of empty rooms. She paused outside the lavatory, her skin crawling. Christof had snagged her as she walked past; she should have been on alert. Sure, the Guard hadn't invaded the tavern in decades, but it didn't mean foes didn't lurk in the shadows. Now, every flicker of light sent Bria's stomach churning, and she had to count each one as she walked to ensure a second shadow did not appear.

There are seven lights in the hall. Seven shadows. No more. No less.

Then, an eighth shadow appeared with the opening of a nearby door.

Bria froze, reaching for the wood along the wall. It curled under her fingers.

Her stomach dropped as the shadow fell from the person leaving a nearby room. With mismatched eyes and sleek black hair, Gisela Kai exited the room. A chill ran through the air as her attention caught Bria.

"So, you decided to return then?" She asked.

Bria didn't respond. She last encountered Gisela and her partner Yeshua down in the speakeasy. There, she imprisoned Gisela and Yeshua until they told her of an incomprehensible prophecy that predicted the Council's success if the puzzle pieces fell into place.

Now, it was all coming true.

"Doesn't surprise me. Yeshua said you would be back." Gisela shrugged and strode past Bria.

"Wait! What are you doing free?"

"It's not like I can leave with Yeshua in his current state."

"Current state..." Bria eyed the door. *Right. The Erasure. It's impacting the Seers, too.* She glanced back at Gisela. "Is he okay?"

"Why do you care?"

"I'm just wondering."

Gisela scoffed, "Whatever. Go talk to him if you want...as long as you promise not to use his eye sockets as planters."

"I wouldn't do that."

"Of course you wouldn't. I must be thinking of a different nymph."

Bria gawked after Gisela, unsure how to reply. A nymph? Surely, the woman was just trying to get under her skin. *I'm not a nymph. I'm human.*

Right?

She rubbed her branched arm and turned to the door.

She pushed the door open and peeked into the room.

Her throat tightened at the sight.

Inside sat not only Yeshua but four other individuals. With their heads bowed, it reminded Bria of a prayer circle.

But with a step forward, they turned toward her.

All stared at her with their eyes painted entirely with red, dried blood staining their cheeks. Yeshua sat against the far wall. Beside him sat another familiar face.

"Tilda?" Bria whispered.

She turned her head towards Bria's voice. The woman's usual slicked-back hair rested in unkempt strands against her face, her bloodied eyes as vacant, clothes stained. If Bria hardly recognized the woman, who once held a professional air and poise, serving as a detective in Mert and as one of Kek's loyal followers.

"Hello, Bria," she said.

Bria took a moment to find her words. "When did you get here?"

"Right after Lana died. As I intended," Tilda replied.

"As you intended?"

"I told Lana that if certain events occurred, it would lead to an inevitable death. Who the victim would be was unclear...but I knew it would be someone of Rhodana's blood." Tilda laced her hands together. "The last vision I had was of her death, just as I arrived here in the Capital."

"Why didn't you tell me?" Bria asked.

"Because if I did...you would be the one to die."

"And you didn't think I should have that choice?" Bria glanced at the two unfamiliar Seers sitting on the beds. Black stamps sat on their wrists, the mark of vagrancy as much of a plague as their missing eyes. "My death might have saved all of you from this fate."

"Your life will protect everyone else for years to come."

"And the life of a few hundred Seers is not worth the lives of millions," Yeshua finally added from his spot, his gaze not lifting from the floor.

"A few hundred Seers..." Bria glanced again at the unfamiliar Seers. Brent had told her how it impacted the Seers in Mert. She hadn't seen it in person, but now, staring at these individual Seers, their eyes gone, blood staining their cheeks, she realized the true extent of her loss of sight. People had lost more than just the Second World, but their livelihoods.

And it wasn't just Kek's Seers; countless people across the world had lost their sight, not even aware of an ongoing war. People had been just living their lives; now, Ningursu had ripped it from them. How many Seers sat in pits across Rosada, blind and targeted by more than just their stamps?

"This is not your fault, Bria," Tilda said, "Remember that."

Bria shook her head, swallowing once. How could they say it wasn't her fault? The choices she made led to all of this; she chose a path of destruction. No matter the intention, the damage remained.

She had to fix this.

Somehow, she had to make things right.

She exchanged another glance around the room. The Seers all sat, defeated and lost. Their world was taken from them. Not just their vision but their understanding of the world as a whole.

"What can I do to help?" Bria finally asked, her voice tight.

Tilda smiled as she responded, "Right now, you could fetch us some hot cocoa. I think we all need something sweet and warm."

PLAYING WITH SMOKE

Chander sat on a boulder outside of Neorama, watching as Yaz and Malaika fed the dragon, Zephyr. The long strips of red meat dripped like blood, sputtering about as they flew straight into Zephyr's mouth. Yaz laughed as the dragon caught the strips of meat while Malaika placed her hands on her hips, smiling widely as the dragon spun in the air.

Yet, Chander could not bring himself to join in the festivities, with his mind constantly wandering back to Anandi in Mert. What was she doing right now? He had hardly spoken with his sister over the last couple of weeks. She preferred to humor herself with recipes while clinging to the words of her new favorite person, Mitzi.

He closed his eyes. It'd been so long since he hugged Anandi that he couldn't even see her actions.

"Chander! Don't go falling asleep over there. I don't want to be the one to carry you," Malaika called over to him.

He blinked once. The dragon had landed before Yaz and Malaika, its head resting on the ground. Yaz ran her hands over the dragon's narrow snout.

"I'm not sleeping," he grunted.

"Well, then stop being a buzzkill and come join us," Malaika motioned for him to join.

Chander grunted, then hopped off the boulder. As he approached, the dragon huffed, sending a plume of smoke around them.

As the smoke settled, Malaika twirled her hand once in the air. The remaining Mist wove before her, forming a complicated globe. She spun it once with her fingers, letting each of the continents fill out, their details etched into the globe, from the tallest peaks to the deepest valleys. Yaz removed her glasses, cleaned them, and put them back, eyes wide with awe.

"Have I ever shown you one of my maps?" Malaika asked them.

"I don't think so," Yaz replied.

Chander took a step forward to get a better look at the map.

With a swift motion, Malaika adjusted the globe, refocusing on a northern section of the map. She pinched the image, and as if looking through a spyglass, the section enlarged, where the City of Mert waited. From the globe, the city seemed more like a stone carving instead of the collection of colorful homes and towering complexes that bordered the Chessboard Plains.

"Wait! Is that us?" Yaz asked, pointing to three small dots out on the plains.

"That they are," Malaika said. She pinched the map again. The image enhanced, and there they stood, on the very map, miniature versions of themselves.

"Wowee!" Yaz exclaimed.

"That's interesting," Chander added.

"It's no flying whales, or whatever it is that Brent can do...but I suppose it's still quite a feat, isn't it?" Malaika spun the globe around again, running her finger along the surface.

"No! I think it's swell!" Yaz said. "Can you see anyone with that?"

"Not exactly. I have to know who to look for. But even then, it's not an exact science." She sighed and waved her hand through the smoke. The globe disappeared. "There are some people I can't find."

"Like who?"

"Ningursu, for one."

"Ningursu..." Chander mumbled. He'd heard the name tossed around; the leader of the Council, a pernicious God in his own right, he manipulated the Mist Keepers.

Chander hoped he would never have to meet it.

Malaika continued, not responding to Chander. "I also have a friend...Teodozia. She has been missing for a while. I'm hoping I can find her on the map...but she never appears."

"Do you know where she could be?" Yaz asked.

"Not a clue..." Malaika ran her hand through her curls and turned her attention to the sky. "I used to have this airship, the Mystical Cheer. I searched the skies and the earth for Teodozia, but she never appeared. Now I don't even have the airship, though."

"What happened to it?"

"One of my crew. When we landed here, I asked her to dock the ship...but she ran off with it and most of my crew. If I ever find her again, I'll wring her neck. Though...not sure how I'd wring the neck of a dead pirate." Malaika paused, seeming to ponder her options. "Perhaps Dee will have some ideas. I'll need to ask her later. Have you two met Dee—sorry, Dobroslawa? She was one of my crewmates and a great friend. You'd probably learn a lot from her. Let me tell you—"

As Malaika entered her long-winded ramble, Chander's mind wandered back to the dragon. Zephyr watched him intently, her silver eyes focused, locking onto his gaze. He couldn't pull his attention away; it was almost as though the dragon could see through him and understand his every move.

What do you want? Chander approached the beast. Carefully, he placed his fingers on its snout.

And with a sudden jolt, the world around him blurred.

Through a field of color beyond his imagination, he saw *himself* standing before the dragon. Waves of smoke riddled the air. Yet, unlike the smoke Chander usually saw, this glowed, extending off people, buildings, and even trees. In the distance, the very shadow of Mert shone with this aura as well.

Chander blinked again, and the vision dissipated, allowing him to stare at Zephyr once again.

"Chander, you alright there?" Malaika asked.

"Yeah...yeah..." Chander shook his head. "Just...yeah, I'm fine."

"You sure there?"

"Yeah, just was petting Zephyr is all."

He stepped back from the dragon. His whole life, he only saw through the eyes of other humans. While Zephyr was different from the average creature just months earlier, touching her did not impact his own vision.

Why now? What changed?

"Well, let me know if you need anything," Malaika said, letting the Mist fall from her fingers. "We should probably head back, though. It's getting late."

Together, they bid Zephyr farewell and made their way back across the black-and-white flowered field toward Neorama. Yaz followed in step with Malaika, leaving Chander dwindling a few steps behind them.

"Do you think you'll ever find your friend, Teodozia?" Yaz asked Malaika.

Malaika shrugged. "I've got a plan to find her, but just gotta find the right time to leave. I might take Zephyr with me. That dragon deserves to fly."

"Have you ever ridden on a dragon?"

"Oh, yes. My papa used to have this pretty old beast named Pam. She and I were quite close...and we had our fair share of adventures."

"Wowee!" Yaz exclaimed. "So you know what you're doing with Zephyr?"

"Sort of, yes. Although, every dragon is a bit different." Malaika smiled to herself. "I miss dear Pam. She was a loyal girl—a constant companion, really. But she had to go home. I think that every dragon needs to go home eventually—that is just where their spirit is pulled."

"Where's their home?"

"Spinoza, in the..." Malaika oriented herself, turning her attention away from the setting sun. "East. Spinoza is east of here...I think."

"Oh! I think Ningursu took me there. I remember seeing dragons and smoke..." Yaz's voice trailed. She didn't speak much of her time with Ningursu and the Council. Chander never pressured her, either. It sounded horrific, at least from the small tidbits Yaz had shared. From what Yaz told him, they used her to control monsters, casting her in a blanket of nightmares. Yaz always held her head high, keeping her nightmares in her pocket.

Really, Chander couldn't help admiring her for such a feat.

He could hardly keep his head straight after brushing hands with a stranger.

They didn't speak much as they walked back to Neorama. The ghost town sat like a mirage, pulsing in and out of their vision. With each flicker, it altered from solid to gas, opaque to transparent. Its single road acted like a wind tunnel, and with its collection of odd buildings, it belonged both everywhere and nowhere at the same time.

As they entered the town, Chander could easily see down the road, straight to the other end, where a gathering of individuals walked towards the school. Most recognizable, Brent stood the tallest, his curly hair blowing in the wind while he hunched over his cane.

"Brent's back!" Yaz exclaimed, her eyes lighting up at the Mist Keeper's arrival.

"Saw him on the map before…was wondering if he was on his way back or not," Malaika added.

Yaz wiggled her hand out of Malaika's hand, then darted forward toward the group by the school. Brent turned in her direction and waved,

"She's obsessed with him," Malaika chuckled.

"It's kinda weird," Chander grumbled.

"Eh, he saved her life, and she's, what, eight years old? Let her have a hero. There's certainly worse people to fawn over."

"I guess—" A scream cut his sentence short.

Yaz stumbled back from the group. Brent waved to the others behind him to go inside, kneeling beside Yaz. Chander squinted, trying to get a better look at the group, but they soon vanished inside the schoolhouse.

He hurried forward with Malaika. Yaz held her face in her hands, shaking her head back and forth.

"What's going on?" Malaika asked as they approached.

Yaz didn't reply, still holding her head in her hands.

"Yaz?" Chander joined her side, "You alright?"

"No…the monster…it's here…" Yaz sobbed.

Chander glanced at Brent and crossed his arms. "What does she mean?"

Brent sucked in his lips, fidgeting with the top of his cane. He quickly exchanged a look with Malaika before saying, "One of the spirits is here for a lesson. We're, I mean, we're gonna have our first lesson today—or at least try to, if you all want to join."

"Spirits..." Chander wracked his brain. "You mean one of the creatures we saw in the Sanitorium?"

"That's right. His name is Milo...and he won't hurt you," Brent turned back to Yaz.

She glanced at him, eyes red and tearful.

"Milo won't hurt you, Yaz. He wants to learn about the Mist Keepers just like you, a'ight?"

"But what if he turns evil like the others?"

"He won't."

"But what if he does?"

"Well, we'll make sure to put him someplace safe. A'ight?"

"Promise?"

"Promise."

Yaz sniffled and wiped her nose with the back of her sleeve. When Brent offered her a hand, she took it, hoisting herself off the ground.

Brent grinned at her. "Atta girl. You up for your first lesson then? I know it's late, but better late than never, right?"

"So we're really gonna have a school?"

"Yeah, I think so. If you wanna be part of it."

"Yeah!"

"What about you, Chander? Are you up for it?"

Chander shrugged. What did he have to lose? They'd been talking about this school for months. While he expected a more traditional introduction to class, there was nothing traditional about being a Mist Keeper in the first place.

"Might as well," Chander finally replied.

"A'ight, then let's get this started. But remember, Milo will be inside the schoolhouse—so just be brave, a'ight?"

Yaz gulped and nodded once.

"You want me to stay, Brent?" Malaika asked from behind Chander.

"If you got the time," Brent said as he turned.

"Eh, might as well. I think this'll be its own sort of adventure."

As Brent led them into the schoolhouse, Chander joined Yaz's side. After inhaling once, he offered a hand to Yaz. There was no reason to be scared, but his insides spun nonetheless. It wasn't over that so-called spirit, Milo, or being a room full of Mist Keepers. Chander couldn't quite put his finger on what caused his stomach to churn.

But as Yaz accepted his hand, he knew one thing: the moment he stepped into that classroom, he might finally be able to see the truth through his own eyes.

Not those of a dragon.

CHAPTER ELEVEN

LESSON ONE

Brent fidgeted with the chalk, glancing over the classroom. It was time. After all these months, he stood there, ready to lead a lecture. Sure, he only had three students—Chander, Yaz, and Milo—and sure, Malaika and Tomás stood in the back of the room, ready to judge him, but it was still a class.

He'd mulled for weeks over how to start. Wasn't it all just like a story? It wasn't an adventure written in heroics and journeys but one of anecdotes and knowledge. With the right structure, he could tell the tale—and with the tale, his pupils could learn.

He glanced over the room one last time. Yaz had taken a seat at the front, the farthest she could away from Milo, who had crouched in the back of the room, rubbing his hands together. The spirit eyed the room with care, flinching at even the slightest breeze. Every now and again, Milo and Chander locked eyes. Chander would stare at the spirit before refocusing on Brent.

They're waiting. For a moment, Brent swore he heard his Diabolo. But the thought belonged to him and only him. Slowly, he lifted the chalk and turned to the blackboard. As he pressed the chalk to the surface, the noise rippled through his ears like a train screeching down the tracks.

Was there a train coming for him now? Chugging along, entering the building?

No. That's a story. Just write.

He lifted the chalk and, with his fingers shaking, scratched onto the blackboard.

Lesson One: What is a Mist Keeper?

He stared at the words for a minute. This was the first lesson, the one he had been planning for all these weeks. The introduction. The truth.

Brent turned back to the classroom. "So I wanted to start off with this basic question: What is a Mist Keeper? Does anyone know?"

Yaz raised her hand abruptly.

"Go on."

Yaz inhaled once, then said, "The Mist Keepers are protectors of the dead."

Brent scribbled 'protectors' on the wall. "Very good. Anyone else? Just call it out."

At first, silence.

Then, a tap.

Milo tapped on his desk, forming a single word:--. --- -.. ...

Brent wrote the very word on the wall, "Gods."

Silence followed again. Brent could imagine a full classroom. How many more words might be shouted?

Tomás must have read his thoughts, adding to the list from his spot in the back of the room. "We're Death."

Brent nodded, adding the word to the chalkboard.

"And we're also dead," Malaika added with a sly smile.

And Brent added another word to the board.

Then the silence fell. Chander squirmed in his seat, staring at his hands.

"Chander, c'mon," Yaz hissed back at him.

He fidgeted, then whispered, "Lost. The Mist Keepers are lost."

Brent wrote the word on the chalkboard, then paused to add his own word. "People."

With the final letter written, he dropped the chalk and wiped the dust from his hands to turn back to the class-room. He inhaled once, then said, "Everyone sees the Mist Keepers differently, and each Mist Keeper has carried the title with a different belief. But at their core, the

Mist Keepers are what cultures across the globe have described as deities, describing them as malicious to peaceful in their own tales. None of our descriptors are wrong...but I think what we forget is that Mist Keepers are people like you and me. They are not as powerful as the stars. They are people. Nothing more, nothing less."

He paused, expecting Tomás or Malaika to interject.

But all remained silent.

He continued. "It's not to say that Mist Keepers aren't, well...powerful. We have an innate ability inside each of us—the ability to release the souls of the dead from their bodies. We will teach you how to do that if you so choose, but that is not the point of this lesson.

"Today, I am here to just tell you what a Mist Keeper really is and why each of you is a Mist Keeper as well. We are not going to make any decisions about our past or our future...today, we will just learn. Because I think that, really, you all should know everything about yourselves, your magic, and the Mist Keepers before you commit to any sort of future. You're young. You have a chance to live. A'ight?"

"Yes!" Yaz exclaimed. Milo nodded from his spot, while Chander didn't say a word.

Brent inhaled. *Teach them what you wish Caroline had taught you.* He eyed Tomás and Malaika. Part of him wished his old teacher had joined them, but she had stayed in Mert. She'd been aloof over the past few weeks, avoiding most conversations. Some days, she disappeared from the city, returning with her eyes downcast.

Brent shook Caroline from his mind and continued, "Each of you is here because you have a talent, a magic that is not like other Magii. Most Magii pull their talents from the natural elements. But as a Mist Keeper, you use the surrounding Mist—the Effluvium, as some may call it—to harness your abilities. This allows each of you to see the world of the dead...and to do things otherworldly."

Brent opened his palm. In it, the story of a dancing tree appeared. Yaz laughed while Milo and Chander shared similar smirks.

He closed his palm again. "Everyone's magic will be different. There are different ways to harness the Mist, something that Tomás will teach you about another time." Tomás clenched his hands together and nodded ever so slightly. Brent continued, "I do not want to put one rumor to rest, though: your magic is not dependent on you becoming a full Mist Keeper. Our focus right now is to prevent your magic from overwhelming you. Don't worry about being a Mist Keeper right now. The dead can wait."

Brent stepped out from behind his desk, scanning over the room. "Now everyone, gather around, a'ight?

We're gonna dive into our magic—don't be scared. We're here to help."

He motioned for each of the students, as well as Malaika and Tomás, to form a circle. His hands shook as he moved, limping toward the center of the group.

"So, to help each of you, we gotta understand your magic. Now, if you don't wanna show us here, that's a'ight. We can do a private session. But I don't think magic should exist in the shadows. We should be proud of what we can do...although, I know that it can be hard. Our hope here, whether it's today or tomorrow or next week, is that you will think differently of your magic and see its beauty."

None of the students said a word.

"Now, I've already shown you my magic. So..." he spun around, "Malaika! Would you like to show off your magic?"

"Absolutely." Malaika snapped her finger. A globe wove into existence before her, spinning on its axis. "What should I look at?"

"Hmm...any suggestions?" Brent asked his small class.

"Look at Zephyr!" Yaz chimed.

Malaika obliged, fixating on her globe. After spinning it once, Zephyr appeared on its surface, soaring through the sky.

"Wowee!" Yaz exclaimed.

Malaika snapped her fingers and took a bow.

"Now tell me," Brent said, "What would you say is the most difficult part of your magic?"

Malaika pondered, "That is a good question. My magic does not mess with my head as much as some others' magic. It's kind of independent from me. But it is unreliable. I've had to learn when the map is lying...because certain things aren't visible. I guess...if I get too reliant on it, it causes its own slew of issues."

"Thank you," Brent turned to Tomás. "Now Tomás...what am I thinking, right now?"

Tomás chuckled and closed his eyes. Brent refocused his thoughts, waiting for Tomás to recite his thoughts.

"You're visualizing a pineapple...and thinking 'vile demon fruit.'" Tomás shook his head with a laugh.

"Well, it's true," Brent grinned as he motioned to Tomás again. "So, as you can all see, Tomás reads minds."

Tomás took a slight bow.

"Now Tomás can do more, too, but for the purposes of this demonstration, we'll leave it at that."

"How do we know he actually read your mind?" Chander spoke up, arms crossed.

"I can read your mind if you are such a skeptic," Tomás replied.

"Fine."

Tomás closed his eyes again. A beat passed.

"Now, Chander, aren't you a little young to be using that kind of language?" Tomás opened his one good eye.

Chander flushed.

"Can you hear thoughts all the time?" Yaz asked.

"No—well, not anymore. I used to...which was quite difficult."

"That would be bad."

"Quite. And to answer your next question, it took many years for me to learn to control my thoughts. Many, many years. But I did it by finding something to ground me—a constant in my life. Someone who I loved and could confide in."

"You mean you fell in love?" Yaz leaned forward, eyes wide.

"Yes, you could say that." Tomás's head fell. Brent didn't need to read his mind to know how much Tomás missed Varden.

Before Yaz asked any further questions, Brent redirected the conversation. "Every Mist Keeper has faced their own challenges. So we want to help you face whatever challenges have come your way. We'll start with Chan—" Brent stopped as Chander shook his head. "I mean, Milo! Why not show us what you can do?"

The spirit pushed his glasses up the bridge of his nose and rose to his feet. From his pocket, he removed a small metallic harmonica. He brought it to his lips and, with a swift movement, produced a sad melody.

As he played, the room fell silent, and the Mist danced around him. It told a story of a child running from fire, away from his home and to the shoreline. There, the child played his own song, begging for money with each passing day. The visuals filled the room. Brent could feel the story in his grasp; there was something familiar about it, as if it connected to another story that he had tried collecting. Which story? He couldn't remember.

The music enchanted everyone, wrapping around their emotions and decorating the Mist. As it trickled to the end, it was as if they came up for air, all gasping at once as Milo placed the harmonica back in his pocket.

Yaz broke the silence, "Wowee…"

"Impressive," Chander added.

Milo took a slight bow before fumbling back to his seat. His head hung to the side, one eye gazing at the wall. With his music, it was as though he broke out of Ningursu's spell. But now, he had returned to as he was: a spirit of his former self.

"So Milo, your magic allows you to tell stories with music, yeah?" Brent asked.

Milo nodded.

"What do you hope to learn now that you're here?"

Milo sucked in his cheek, then with his finger, he tapped on his desk: ....-...--.

"You want to learn how to help?"

Milo nodded again.

"I think we can do that."

Milo then tapped one more statement. --..- ..... -.-. / ... - ---.--.

"But you also want the music to stop? Do you hear the music all the time?"

Another nod.

Like my stories. Brent stared hard at Milo, watching as he shifted in the chair. "We'll find a way for the music to stop. Don't worry."

Milo smiled, revealing a row of rotting teeth. Behind that smile, there still existed a young man eager to learn about the Mist. He must have been the same age as Brent when he first was pulled into the Mist. What was his story? How did he end up becoming Julietta's apprentice?

No wonder Julietta always confused me with him. Brent grimaced. Julietta was her own predicament now. With her mind altered after the Diabolo wiped her sense of self clean, Tomás turned her into Jewel, the new leader of the pinstripes. But it did not stop the Erasure from impacting her. Last time Brent saw her, Julietta—or Jewel—had been wearing her frustration like a badge, swinging around an empty pistol like a paintbrush.

Perhaps she would become a pupil here at the school...if he could get her to agree.

Brent thanked Milo for sharing, then turned to Yaz.

The little girl squirmed. "I don't know how I can share my magic. I just control monsters..."

Brent knelt beside her. "You don't have to share if you do not want to, Yaz."

"But I want to! I want to learn."

"A'ight, then just close your eyes. Focus. Tell me what you see."

Yaz did just that. With her eyes shut, she wrinkled her nose, focusing hard. A wisp of yellow smoke escaped her mouth, just for a second, and then a gasp.

Her eyes flew open again. "They're just...circling. The monsters, I mean."

"Circling?"

"Around the plains. Waiting or watching or something. But they're here!" Her face paled. "I saw them...and that's what's so scary. I see them, but I can't control them really and—and—" She glanced between Chander and Brent. "I dunno what to do."

Brent offered Yaz his hand. She took it, squeezing his fingers tight. He wanted to promise that it would be okay, that the Diabolo would stay away, and that they would teach her to use her magic properly. But, if the look he shared with Tomás and Malaika meant what he thought, then really, there were more pressing matters.

Ones he hadn't wanted to consider.

Not when he was trying to teach.

CHAPTER TWELVE

A New Home for a Town

Brent waited at the front of the classroom, watching as his small collection of students filed from the room. Yaz clung to Malaika's hand as they left, while Milo stayed close to Tomás. Chander followed the rest of them with his head down, leaving a heavy air of silence behind him as he walked. Yaz's discovery lingered over the rest of the lesson, where they discussed the differences in everyone's magic while sharing personal anecdotes about their own magical discoveries.

Why hadn't the Diabolo attacked? What were they waiting for, if anything?

What was Ningursu planning next?

That was it, wasn't it? No one knew his next steps.

Brent tapped his desk, then rose from his spot, heading out of the classroom and toward the street. Exhaustion crept over him. The past twenty-four hours had been relentless, but now wasn't a time to rest. There was still work to be done.

Nighttime had fallen over the Chessboard Plains. The white flowers glistened in the glow of the town while the black whistled like the currents of a deep sea. With the Mist dancing on the surface, the plains existed in their own realm, harboring stories that Brent feared. So many lives had been lost out there; wars battled for centuries, all to paint the white flowers red.

He could hear the stories calling for him. With everything occurring, he hadn't committed much time to releasing souls. Not like he had intended, at least. The job of the Mist Keeper, a true Mist Keeper, was to release the dead. He wanted more than anything to follow the stories, to help those souls cross. That was his job: to help.

But there were more pressing matters.

He wandered through Neorama toward the metallic box in the center of town. It really was nothing more than that: just a windowless box with a single door and a dusty path. It sat between two buildings, with grand columns and carvings on their walls. No signs of life came from the box.

But Brent still knocked on the door.

With a collection of clicks, the door swung open. Szyman waited for Brent, his thick beard pulled up in a smirk. Behind him, gears pulsed with smoke. A faux window reflected with an iridescent glow, creating shadows of the town just outside.

"Knew you'd be coming by," Szyman remarked.

"You... How did... You did?"

"Peaked in on your lesson. Was quite a show, really. You got a knack for it—woulda thought you were a performer."

"I did have an act in the circus for a bit."

"Of course you did," Szyman chuckled. "It showed in your lecture."

"Oh, um, thanks...I think."

"It's a good thing, don't worry. Kept me entertained for a while."

"How long were you there?"

"Long enough to hear Yaz say that the Diabolo are near."

"So you know why I'm here then?"

"You want to discuss shifting the town, right?"

Brent nodded. He had yet to witness the true talent of Neorama. With the strange control room behind him, Szyman not only created the town but allowed it to move across the world, shifting out of the Mist like a Mist Keeper.

"It's probably overdue. Usually, we don't stay in one place for too long," Szyman hopped onto his stool, looking over his array of levers and gears. "We can shift her now if you want—I imagine you've told Malaika where you wanna go?"

"Uh...no. Not yet. I—I mean, I don't want to risk it. I know Malaika doesn't have a tight connection with Ningursu, but I don't want to risk any control he might have over her." Brent leaned on his cane. "Besides, I think we can wait a few days before shifting."

"Well, I need some sort of idea where we're going."

"I can show you if you want."

"Very well." Szyman clicked a few levers, then spun off his stool. "Lead the way."

"Now?"

"The night is young...and quite frankly, until Dobroslawa comes back, I don't have much to do. She and I have a standing card game every quarter moon...and she's late."

"Oh, um, a'ight then. We can take the Tunnels."

"Lead the way."

"Right." Brent slowly exited Szyman's control box, hobbling forward into the street. Fatigue tugged at his eyelids, begging for a moment of rest in a warm bed.

Just stay awake and don't fall out. Please. Don't fall out. Brent blinked a few times. His eyes didn't listen, though.

Instead, they danced in the street before him, glistening orbs, cackling.

Once Brent willed his eyeballs back into place and pushed away any stories that dared cling to his psyche, he led Szyman to the tunnel entrance beneath a wiry tree not far from Neorama. The white and black flowers of the plains cascaded inside the Tunnels, acting as a guide one step at a time. Despite their beauty, Szyman showed no amazement over the Tunnels, instead picking at the flowers and scowling at a collection of mud on his feet. When Brent first uncovered the Tunnels, they shocked him with amazement. Now, he still found them spectacular, but not because the Mist Keepers built them. Rather, he marveled at how Bria kept them alive with a mere flick of her wrist. Every turn brought him back to her with detailed vines and branches.

Rather than leading Szyman to the Library entrance, Brent continued south, where the Tunnels guided him toward the humid, muddy swamps of Volfium. If he turned right, then he would arrive at Bria's palace.

But instead, he turned left, where the tunnel began to climb above ground, with a collection of pine needles collecting in its path. At the end of it, early morning sunlight welcomed them to an empty green pasture bordering pockets of cypress swamps.

"Volfium?" Szyman asked, his brow raised.

"It's close enough to Rosada but out of Ningursu's reach. We're past the Vermillion Swamp, not far from Stilette…so we have a hub for supplies and such. I think…I mean, it makes sense. Plus…" He glanced towards the swamp. "Bria's not far from here. It's where she built her castle."

"Castle?"

"Oh, yeah, um…I've kept it kinda quiet. Bria…she built a castle out of the cypress trees. She's…it's amazing."

"Ah, I see." Szyman eyed the area. He lowered his hand to the ground, sticking his finger into the dirt. "Yes, this seems firm enough. How far is Stilette from here?"

"About a fifteen-minute walk down the road there," Brent motioned to the road at the end of the farm. He flinched as a story of a creaking auto entered his vision, followed by the abrupt hollering of cows. "All the stories…they…they don't show many visitors. Should stay quiet."

"And your girl's castle?" Szyman asked.

"Through those trees there, down into the depths of the swamp. That's a longer walk…no more than an hour-long walk."

"I would like to see this palace of hers…since I am an architect in my own right."

"Don't tell Alojzy," Brent chided.

138

"Oh, I would love to rub what I can do in Al's smug face."

Brent had collected parts of Szyman's story. It was intertwined with Malaika's and Alojzy's past. While Malaika was open about how she recruited Szyman for an apprenticeship, and he declined, it was Alojzy's side of the story that was more interesting. From Brent's understanding, Szyman was good friends with Alojzy's wife and, convinced of an affair, Alojzy ended Szyman's life. That was before Alojzy knew he was destined to be the next Mist Keeper and build the tunnel system, as well as the Library itself.

"Al might think he's a good architect, but you can only build up so far. Sometimes, you need a bit more creativity," Szyman continued.

"Maybe that's why he lost control of the Library to Bria."

"It could be one of many reasons. But either way, clearly she's got a knack...and I'd love to see what she did with her palace."

"A'ight, yeah, it's this way. I dunno if Bri will be around..."

"It's not like she can see me right now. I just want to see this palace of hers."

Brent obliged, and with Szyman beside him, he led the way into the wall of nearby cypress trees.

The mud gathered at his feet as they waded through the swamp. In the distance, the chirping of crickets in the early evening danced through the warm air. Green glowed from the trees while the water around their ankles bled red.

But with every step, the plumes of smoke rose around Brent, sending stories flurrying over him. These swamps harbored countless stories, from the bird flittering in the sky to an alligator sinking into the mud to a child lost in its woods, and even to the Council itself, using these very trees to hide before Alojzy constructed the Library. Tales of monsters climbed within the branches, rippling through the very soul of the swamp.

One step, and he was following in the monster's footsteps, seething against chains and fighting against imprisonment.

Another step, and he was the child, screaming for his mother.

Another, he was Malaika, sitting on a stump, knitting a sweater, while a monster stared over her.

And another, he was Ningursu.

He was Ningursu...

The story wrapped around him, a deep darkness settling into his core. It wove into the countless stories he had collected, tugging from Nedo's story that he had collected almost a year earlier.

Nedo - Ningursu's brother - had spent a life imprisoned.

And now he saw Ningursu's story, unguarded, clear.

Spiraling...

Spiraling...

Spiraling...

And then, with a single blink of an eye, he was a skull positioned on a log, unable to move. In silence, he sat, willing for the black smoke to gather around him. When he closed his eyes, he knew all; he could feel his Mist Keepers crawling across the globe.

Come to me. It is time. Ningursu's voice echoed.

But it exited Brent's lips as if it belonged to him.

And he spiraled...

Down...

Down...

Down...

His knees quivered. Now, he was Ningursu, perched in Nedo's hands, staring at a collection of spirits, writhing and crying as yellow smoke gathered at their feet. They begged, speaking in half-fledged sentences and sobbing as their bodies convulsed. He looked on, unmoved, as their bodies fell to the ground.

"See this, Nedo," he said. "This is just the beginning."

Then, a deep chuckle escaped his lips as Brent collapsed against the muddy ground.

CHAPTER THIRTEEN

FINDING TRUST

Bria stood in the kitchen of the tavern, sorting through a few pieces of fruit. She popped a strawberry into her mouth. The moment it touched her tongue, a clump of roots sprouted, lacing into her teeth.

She spat the roots on the ground and cursed. Just the mere touch brought the strawberry seeds to life. It reminded her of when she first discovered her magic. At six years old, any seed that entered her mouth bloomed. Now, it wasn't lack of knowledge that caused the seeds to react, but too much.

After spitting the remaining pieces of strawberry into the sink, Bria settled on a slice of plain white bread. Even the ground wheat tickled her, but at least in its bread-like state, she would give bloom to an entire field.

With each bite, she recited a different element.

Nitrogen.

Carbon.

Helium.

It kept her grounded as she picked at the bread. She didn't glance up as Hue entered the room, taking a seat across from her at the table.

"Are you planning on leaving again?" Hue asked.

"Huh?"

"Lana ate the same way when she was planning something."

"What do you mean by that?"

"Grazing and picking at different foods. You're more similar than you know."

Bria inhaled and met Hue's stare. "I can't stay here. I have a job to do."

"Freeing people from the Pits?"

Bria nodded.

"Isn't it dangerous? Aren't you afraid that someone might turn you in?"

Bria didn't know how to explain that Brent had looked at each person's story. His magic wasn't as honest as Marisol's ability to force the truth out of any one person's mouth, but it showed their past without hindrance.

But to explain that to Hue seemed far more difficult.

Instead, she said, "They're no more dangerous than Knoll's Pit."

"Perhaps, but Lana and I spent years curating rela-
tionships with our allies in Knoll. These are strangers."

"But they're the ones suffering."

"And you are the one with a bounty on your head, Bria.
I am not trying to undermine all the wonderful work that
you did, but I am being practical. We cannot risk losing
you."

"That's what you all say..." Bria closed her eyes.

"It's the truth. And, frankly, I am worried about you.
Lana was, too."

"I'm fine."

"Do not pull that on me. I know that trick."

Bria sighed and opened her eyes. "What do you want
from me?"

Hue's eyes twinkled behind her thin-rimmed glasses.
"I want you to be honest with me. I'm doing you a cour-
tesy by asking these questions without Marisol here—I
want to give you a chance to speak."

"So you'll force me to talk if I don't?"

"No, but I would like you to be honest with me."

Bria glanced at the locked cellar door. Why didn't she
just leave? It would have been easy to avoid these questions. But she also knew she couldn't hide forever. She
needed Hue's support. Now that Lana was gone, she'd
slipped into a clear position of leadership. Hue had the
connections to keep Rosada thriving.

"I'm scared. That's the truth. I'm terrified," Bria whispered. "I have no control over what is happening in the world, so I'm doing the only thing I can...freeing people. It might come at a risk to me, but...it's not like I'm a politician or natural-born leader. I'm...I'm a gardener. I'll always be a gardener. So I've had to figure out how to use that to thrive in this world."

Hue reached across the table and patted Bria's hand. It was an awkward pat, but it came with a tenderness. "You do not have to do this alone. We've already created political connections throughout parts of Rosada. If we can reclaim the Senate, then these connections will help bring the country back to its former self...or better."

"Oh...good." Bria stared at the table. The nails on her good hand dug into the wood, leaving behind a few twisting twigs.

"But I just ask that you be careful. You don't know who you can trust."

"I know..." Bria pondered for a moment. "Maybe...Marisol can come with me...back to where everyone is. She can vet them for me."

"That is not a bad idea...but remember, even magic has its limitations. There are ways to deceive even the strongest magic."

"Are you speaking from experience or speculation?"

Hue smiled, "A little bit of both."

"From all the time in the Pit?"

"You could say that."

Bria took advantage of the conversation's redirection. "How'd you end up in the Pit? You're a doctor...I'd think there'd be value in that for the Order."

"Ah, that's a story. I suppose you could say I grew up surrounded by rebellion."

"You mean here in the tavern?"

"That's right," Hue replied. "Growing up, I used to help Aunt Nan—or Doris, as you know her—here in this tavern. It used to be filled with magic and stories, although not without its encounters with the Guard." Hue took an apple from the bowl on the table. "Aunt Nan had a run-in with the guard at one point. They took out her tongue. That's why she uses tap-code for everything. Luckily, my brother, Lester, has a good understanding of it. Better than me...but he has a mathematical brain. Mother was so upset when he decided not to go to the Academy. She was an alumnus of their law program and hoped that all her children would also attend. But...Lester loves this tavern...more than he ever loved school."

"I'm glad he stayed. This tavern is important to a lot of people." Bria recalled when she took Brent there the first time. A smile had gathered on his face in a way she had never seen. Then, when he told a story, and his magic took foot, it was like nothing else mattered.

"Yes…it means a lot to me too. Even though I left, I loved growing up here. But I wanted to pursue higher education, so I applied to the Rosadian Academy."

"That's the old campus here in the Capital, right?"

"Yes…but it used to bustle with life just like the city. It's a shame how dead it is now. So many students found love there…including myself."

"It sounds like everything was going well then."

"It was. I obtained my medical license without issue, and my spouse Rory and I moved out to the factory town of Siskin's Corner. Have you ever been there?"

"A while ago."

"It's a mountain town, prone to earthquakes and landslides. Not really the best place to live, so they send vagrants there. I'm positive that they have a larger vagrant population than Knoll, depending on how you measure it. All industrial-they make their vagrants labor twelve hours a day. Rory was contracted by the government to run one of the factories. They discovered the horrors early into their tenure. Terrible working conditions, constant illness. I wrote to my mother to ask about the legalities of it. Since all the workers were vagrants, in the eyes of our government, the endeavors were perfectly sound.

"So there wasn't anything we could do. Within a few months, a large growth appeared on Rory's neck. We removed it, but the growths had already spread to other parts of Rory's body…" Hue paused, swallowed once, then continued. "Since Rory was a civilian, it presented a new question of legality, and my mother was quick to launch an investigation. She asked me to serve as her eyes and ears while she put together her case. So during the day, I offered medical help to those sick under the guise of keeping the factory running while Rory recovered.

"But Rory never recovered. They died a few weeks later despite all my best efforts. We concluded that the materials used in the factories poisoned the workers. I can't say if the materials occurred naturally or had magic, but there were absolutely no safety protocols. When I discovered this, I wrote an article to the newspaper, exposing the working conditions in the factories."

"I can't imagine that the Order liked that," Bria interjected.

"Not at all. I hid from them for over ten years, pretending to be a vagrant while healing the sick. They didn't really pursue me, as I was an annoyance…not a threat. I thought they forgot about me. Until I learned that my own mother was sick."

"And did they find you because you returned home?"

"Yes, they were waiting for me outside the tavern. No one could stop them from arresting me. When my trial came around, my mother was far too ill to defend me in court. She introduced me to some of her other connections, but it was all for naught. I lost the case, and the Order branded me and sent me to the Pit. A year later, my mother died. Two years after that, they relocated me to Knoll, where I met Lana." Hue shrugged. "That's how I ended up there. That's why I want to make a change now."

The gears in Bria's mind turned. *Siskin's Corner.* She hadn't thought of the town as a potential location to search, but now it rose to the top of her list. She whispered, "Thank you for telling me this, Hue. This helps a lot. Really."

"Just...be careful, Bria. Whatever you are doing, please, be careful."

"I will," Bria promised. And she meant it. "I...appreciate all you've done so far, Hue. I'm glad you're continuing what Lana started."

"As are you."

"As am I..." Bria tried not to think about Lana. While her relationship with her mother had been obscure at that, without Lana's leadership in Knoll's Pit, they never would have made it this far.

But Lana hadn't done it alone.

"I can show you where I've been if you want. I...need help." Bria finally admitted, her voice cracking. "I need help."

"I know."

"I was going to head back now. I can't leave where I've been for too long."

Hue frowned, "I cannot leave abruptly. Perhaps Marisol can go with you—I'm sure she'd be willing."

"Okay," Bria picked at the table again.

"I'll go ask her—you stay here. Eat. Rest. Okay?"

"Okay."

Hue rose from the table, smiled once, and then left, leaving Bria alone with the bowl of fruit mocking her.

Marisol had no reservations about joining Bria. As nighttime fell over the farmlands, they snuck out of the tavern, walking side-by-side toward a hanging oak tree at the edge of the road. Marisol babbled, talking about her partner, Jeremy, with delight in her eyes. Bria nodded to her words, not really absorbing them, as she eyed the landscape through the foggy lenses of her gas mask.

In the center of the field, charred grass gathered with the winter's frost. She approached it, running her gloved hand over the ashes.

"Bria?" Marisol stopped and glanced over her shoulder.

"Was this where the Death's Mourn pyre was?" Bria asked.

"Yes, it was."

Bria removed one of her gloves and placed her hand into the grass. A few blades turned green, forming a small circle amid the burnt grass. Then, she reached behind her ear, willing a white camellia flower to bloom.

She winced as she plucked it, then dropped it into the center of the circle.

"I'm sorry I wasn't here..." Bria whispered.

"Lana would have understood," Marisol responded.

"I know...but...still."

Marisol placed an arm around Bria and hugged her. Bria flinched but accepted it before they departed the charred grass and continued along to the tree.

"Nix is coming, by the way. She's been following you," Marisol said.

"Oh..." Bria's stomach sank.

"I know...I'm sorry..."

"It's not your fault."

"Yeah, but I feel bad."

They continued to the tree in silence. When they arrived at its roots, Bria stuck her foot beneath it, hoisting them off the ground. Beneath them, the earth opened into a ladder made of taproots.

"Wait...what?" Marisol laughed. "What is that?"

"Just a ladder to some magic tunnels," A smile twitched on Bria's lips. Excitement and a twinkle of bewilderment filled Marisol's eyes. She never got over that glimmer of amazement. It just showed that the world still had a bit of color despite everything.

"But how?"

"Does magic need a reason?" Well, she knew it did—there was Alojzy, the very architect of these tunnels, but that was not a story she wanted to tell.

Marisol stumbled behind her, gawking as they wandered through the Tunnels. Bria led the way, avoiding the junction and instead detouring south, where the air thickened with humidity. Lush greenery dotted the path. Mud layered the ground. Bria glanced back once as she led the way, then smiled. Pawprints dotted the mud beside Marisol, the exact size of Nix's feet.

Good girl. Bria returned to the path. The distant glow from the moonlight filled the Tunnels.

And with its beams as her guide, they exited at the edge of the vermillion swamp.

"Wait...how did we get here? Bria! This is—wow!" Marisol brought her hands to her mouth.

Bria removed her mask and said, "These tunnels can take us almost anywhere in the world. I discovered them as a child...and they're mine."

"So you've been living in the swamp?" Marisol asked.

"No, I built a home not far from here. Here, it's this way."

"Through the swamp?" Marisol lifted her shoes from the mud, scowling.

"Of course," Bria motioned for Marisol to follow.

Her friend grumbled but followed Bria deeper into the swamp. Nix ran ahead, leaving footprints in the mud. Bria yearned to see her dog's face, to hug Nix tight, but at least the pawprints gave her some solace.

But then, those same pawprints darted forward, throwing mud backward as they ran.

"Nix!" Bria and Marisol shouted at the same time.

They exchanged a glance, then, without speaking, raced after the pawprints into the cypress trees.

CHAPTER FOURTEEN

MUDDIED

A wet nose against his cheek woke Brent.

He groaned, leaves sticking to his body, before rolling over. Upon opening his eyes, a boxed-headed ghostly dog greeted him.

"Nix!" He laughed. The dog wiggled her way under his arm, her tail whipping in the air.

He pressed his face into her fur and laughed, "I missed you."

Footsteps approached, causing Nix to shoot her head up, ears open. Brent leaned on his elbows, sitting up slightly to see through the trees.

To his surprise, Marisol stumbled through the swamp. She exhaled, "Nix! There you are!"

Nix barked.

"What are you doing—oh! Brent! What're you doing in the mud!?" Marisol exclaimed. Brent didn't know too much about Marisol, but they had met back in Knoll. She'd adopted Bria as a friend, and from the whiffs Brent caught of Bria's story, he knew that Marisol was a constant companion through the thickening Mist.

"It's kind of a strange story."

"Well—oh! Hold on!" Marisol spun around, waving to someone behind her before dashing back into the trees.

If Marisol can see me...then she must have an inclination to the Mist. Brent scratched behind Nix's ears as the dog chewed on his cane lying in the mud. While Marisol's footsteps echoed, the Mist hovered above the ground, dancing to the melody of the swamp. Szyman was nowhere to be seen. Had the stories scared him away? Had something happened to him?

Yet, Brent had no time to put together the pieces as Marisol rushed back through the trees. Bria stumbled behind her.

"Look, Bria! See! Brent's here!" Marisol pointed at Brent.

But Bria's head fell, and she shook her head.

"She can't see me," Brent said.

"But you're right here!" Marisol exclaimed.

"I am...but your magic is different from Bria's. So while you can see me, she can't."

Bria finally whispered, "I know he's here, but I can't see him."

"He just told me," Marisol replied. "So you've been spending time here then? With him?"

Bria nodded. Her sadness flooded the air, humidity thick. Tears filled her eyes.

Marisol opened her mouth to speak, then stopped. She approached Bria, "I'll give you two a couple minutes but...I expect you to explain everything later, okay? I'm going to go take a breather, just past those trees."

Bria didn't reply as Marisol strode back into the trees.

Once she was gone, Brent lifted his cane from the ground and hit the nearby tree in tap-code.

Bri. Sit. Please.

She approached where he tapped the message out again. By instinct, or perhaps by her own magic, she sat on the dry ground beside him.

"I can see your outline in the mud..." She choked as she removed their notebook from her coat. She placed it and a pencil on the dry ground beside her. Brent scooted over and took the pencil in his hand to scribble on the page.

You alright?

Bria didn't reply at first. Another tear fell from her eye.

Bria.

"It's not fair..." she inhaled, then continued. "And I feel ridiculous for saying it. But...it's just not fair. Why does Marisol get to see you when I can't?"

The Mist isn't fair.

"I know, but I'm...I'm so angry!" She slammed her fist down beside her. Mud bubbled at her fingertips. "And I shouldn't be. It's not like it's her fault, but I'm just–why does she get magic that lets her see *you*? Why can't I?" She closed her eyes as another tear fell. "Why do we have to deal with any of this shit? I just want to be normal."

Brent inched closer to her but didn't touch her. *You know, I was thinking the same thing recently - how we'd never have that life we talked about by the cows.*

Bria sniffled, "The cows..."

Remember, you were drunk and named a cow "Pig"?

"Right, the cows," she wiped her eyes. Nix inched closer to her, pressing her snout to Bria's calf. She didn't flinch at the dog's attention.

But we'll figure this out. We'll make it work.

Bria pressed her hand to the notebook page. Another tear fell down her cheek.

Bri, please. It's going to be alright.

"I'm just...I'm tired. I've been trying to fix everything, but nothing works. The world is still masked in a yellow...the Order is continuing its reign...and you are...like this. And I can't do anything!"

She wiped her eyes. As hard as it was to watch her cry, it gave Brent some relief. She was *feeling*. For the past few weeks, she had been so distant and aloof. But now, without a doubt, she was letting her emotions run. Perhaps it meant she had embraced her kingdom.

As she cried, the air grew heavy. A gentle drizzle broke in the air.

Brent scribbled in the notebook again, *I know you can't see me, but if it's alright...can I give you a hug?*

"Please..." she sniffled.

Brent carefully put his arms around her, pulling her close. She sobbed heavily. While Brent didn't search for her story, her tears still weighed on him. He let them hang in the air, brushing back her hair, breathing in rhythm with each sob. As they sat there, embracing, Bria's little branch found his arm and slowly wrapped around it. It gave him a temporary exoskeleton, and as he brushed one of her tears away with the new appendage, she gripped his hand tight.

This was the closest thing they had now; the shadows, the branches, and the mud.

They stayed in their little corner of the swamp for a little longer. Brent told her how the stories had overwhelmed him upon arriving in the swamp. He still couldn't put the pieces together, the glimpses spinning around him like a storm. Bria read each of his words, clinging to the outline of his arm. Her tears had dissipated to sniffles, eyes still puffy.

"Why didn't you tell me the stories had gotten so bad," she asked.

Brent wrote, *I can usually control it. This time was different though. It was worse than usual because I saw Ningursu's story.*

"What? Anything useful?"

I'm not sure. I have to write it down, see if it makes any sense. Brent licked his lip, then wrote. *It had to do with the spirits...and the Diabolo. I think he was turning them into vessels.*

"Like he wanted to do with you?"

Right. It was clear now that Brent wasn't the first attempt—nor would he be the last. *It must all be for control,* he wrote in the journal.

"That's all he wants. Remember, he can control Magii too..." Bria brought her hand to the little branch behind her ear. Ningursu had plucked one of her very flowers and utilized it for his own means of control. "Though, I haven't heard him in a while."

It's because I yanked that flower from his mouth to stop him.

"I don't think that stops the effects."

You don't know that.

"It seems too simple."

Fine. Then I can say something sappier like 'you're stronger than him' or something.

"Well, you're definitely stronger than him."

Easy to be stronger than a skull.

Bria smiled, just barely. Brent placed his hand on Bria's shoulder, letting her branch wrap around his fingers again. He forced himself from the ground, using the nearby tree for support, then with one hand on Bria's shoulder and the other on his cane, they walked out of the clearing. Nix rolled in the mud, then bounded to her feet, racing around in a circle. Just for now, they could pretend that everything was right. They could pretend they existed in the same world, pretend that there was no difference between Life and Death.

They found Marisol sitting on a log beneath an opening in the canopy. With her eyes shut, she turned her chin to the sky, basking in the light. As they neared, she smiled and opened her eyes. "I missed the warm air."

"Winter will end soon," Bria replied.

"I hope so."

As they continued walking, Marisol inquired about the forest and about Brent's current state. While Bria's gaze glossed over, Brent explained to Marisol that he had a connection to the Mist. He approached the topic delicately, explaining that he had become a Mist Keeper and that he was more part of the Mist than others. While answering, he tapped Bria's wrist with the twigs on his fingers, summarizing in brief words what he said. He could sense her frustration beneath her story, and the last thing he wanted was for her to be left out as Marisol's questions continued. Her magic tugged at his tongue for answers, and without overwhelming her, he covered the very basics while offering her a chance to sit in any classes she desired.

The trees bled as they entered the deepest crevasses of the forest. And amongst them all stood Bria's intricate palace, where Marisol's questions ceased. Brent couldn't help but smile each time he saw it. *Szyman was right; she's an architect in her own right.*

Around the palace, countless people gathered from Bria's excursions. Horton moved about them, checking on each person to ensure they were well. Yet, to Brent, their stories bled, sharing a common tale: a life in the Pit, all for the same reasons. Magic, eye color, or storytelling; some entered the Pit due to their own experiences, locked away because of a war they had fought years earlier.

He tightened his fingers around Bria's wrist. Her heartbeat grounded him; she was still there. They were both still there.

"Brent!" Szyman hurried through the crowd. "I was trying to find help, but no one noticed me. Are you alright there? You were convulsing quite a bit."

"Yeah, the stories...it was a lot at once. But I'm a'ight. Bria, Marisol, and Nix found me."

"Oh, good to hear! Was worried there, but let me say it was quite impressive, really. Never knew you could throw your voice like that."

"Honestly, I surprise myself every day."

A smile appeared under Szyman's thick beard. Then, his attention shifted to the palace, hands on his hips, admiring it in awe.

"What is this place?" Marisol asked beside Brent.

Bria responded, with her voice low, "It's where I've been taking everyone. I built it with my magic. It's not perfect...and a lot is unfinished...but it's close enough to Stilette where people can get supplies...or flee."

"You've made your own kingdom here!" Marisol exclaimed.

Bria shrugged.

"The girl is modest," Szyman added. "But it's a work of art, isn't it?"

"Oh, without a doubt," Marisol replied. "Can we go inside?"

Bria nodded once.

"Oh, good!" Marisol lunged ahead, grabbing both Brent and Bria's hands. Brent flinched once. He'd seen parts of Marisol's story before—that of a cheerful mask that hid her pain—but the mere touch absorbed him. With a single blink, he was accused of manipulation, taken from home, and imprisoned in a tower.

"No..." he tugged his hand back and shook his head. *My name is Brent Harley.* He recited the line to himself, then glanced up at the palace again. This time, it breathed with stories from its core. With the Library as its base, it was impossible to hide from hundreds of years' worth of history.

"Brent? What's wrong?" Marisol dropped Bria's hand.

"I'm gonna stay out here."

"What's going on?" Bria asked Marisol.

"He said he is going to stay outside."

"You can go on ahead then. The palace is safe. I'll be in shortly."

"Are you sure?"

"Yeah, it's fine," Bria turned in Brent's direction. Despite the invisible wall between them, Bria still had a way of reading him like a book.

Brent motioned for Szyman to go with Marisol, and as the two disappeared into the palace, he found a seat on a log outside one of the small houses Bria had constructed from cypress trees. His feet sank into the mud, and Nix plopped beside them.

Bria took a seat next to him. She didn't speak, briefly acknowledging one of the refugees walking by with two children but otherwise remaining quiet.

Brent removed the notebook again, writing on the next clean page, *The stories are still acting up. I'm sensing everything.*

"Are you taking your medication?"

Kek told me to stop.

"What!?"

It's a no-win situation. If I take it, then the Diabolo is weakened, which lets Ningursu into my head. If I do take it, the Diabolo still has some presence so Ningursu will move slower, but the stories will also grow louder. It's the sad truth of what he did to me in the Library.

"That doesn't make any sense!"

For now I just have to be careful.

"Then...this place is dangerous for you. I can't imagine what the Library or this swamp does to you."

Don't worry, I'm still going to come. I think there's a story here, looking to be uncovered. But I need time to gather more pieces before exploring it.

"You mean a story about Ningursu?"

Yes.

Bria stared at the words on the page. "I don't like how quiet he has been. What do you think he's doing?"

Not sure. Right now, the only evidence we have is what is going on in Rosada.

"Abolish magic, control stories...it's all the same..."

Look for the small things. There's something there. I would look if I could.

"I know..." Bria furrowed her brow and wrinkled her nose. Brent knew that look; it was a familiar one when a thought struck and wrangled its way into her head.

What're you thinking?

"About where I am going to go next. I have an idea."

What is it?

"I need to go to Siskin's Corner—the factory town."

Why there?

"Because if they're doing anything, it's in the factories."

It made sense. But with every plan, his stomach twisted. He couldn't help Bria as she threw herself into each risk. Her narration was her own, and rather than tell her story, he could only watch it unfold.

Just be careful.

"I will," Bria held out her hand.

And Brent took it, letting the branches wrap around his fingers, gripping each other tight.

CHAPTER FIFTEEN

INQUIRIES FROM AN ANNOYANCE

The speakeasy reeked of sweat. It kept Todd from sleeping, and when he tried to eat, the food even tasted like salt. The cramped facility was bolstered, though, with some patrons whispering stories while others played with magic in the palms of their hands. When the excitement ceased, the barkeep handed out sleeping cots, where most now slept.

Except Todd, who stared at the ceiling, checking every few minutes that Garrett rested soundly beside him.

Every one of his instincts fought the reality of being here. It wasn't safe. This would only lead to further harm. Why did he dare follow in the first place? It was something that Lex would have done. And what good did that do? If Lex had just stayed quiet, kept away from all this magic, then maybe things would have gone differently.

He sat up as a shadow moved through the speakeasy. Most continued to sleep, undisturbed by the moving figure. Todd clenched his fist. Who was up at this hour?

What hour was it even?

Did that matter?

Then, the figure moved into the glow of the candlelight.

"Oh, it's you," Todd grunted.

Nils glanced in Todd's direction, his fingers snapping the buttons on his shirt closed. "Morning."

"What're you doing up?" Todd hissed.

"Making a run to the apothecary. You need anything?"

"What? No. Why are you going? That ain't safe!"

"Listen, people need their meds, including me."

"You're on meds? For what?"

"None of your business. Sheesh, relax."

"How can I relax?! You've trapped me in a basement that smells like shite."

"Aw, it's not that bad," Nils said as he pulled on his jacket. "Besides, at least you got a roof over your head. Your kid looks content."

"He doesn't know where he is!"

"Aw, come now, give the kid some credit."

"No, it's probably for the best," Todd brushed Garrett's hair back. The child didn't flinch.

"He's blind, right?"

"Good job, you're not."

"No need to be rude, just a comment is all..." Nils watched Garrett and rubbed his scruffy chin. "You know, the kid might be more aware than you know."

"Yeah, well, he's gone through a lot of shite. Wouldn't you give up if your eyes were stolen?"

"So he hasn't always been blind."

"Why does it matter? He's been through enough! Thought you were just helping us get outta this damn city—not host a fucking inquisition." Todd snarled.

"Listen, I'm just wondering 'cause the boy doesn't look good. I can always pick him up something at the apothecary if you want."

"He's fine!"

"Not even for pain?"

"I said he's fine, you fucking annoyance!" Todd nearly shouted.

Nils furrowed his brow. They looked like caterpillars as they pressed together while his lips puckered into a scrunched frown. "I'm just trying to help."

"Yeah, well, I know what's best for my son. You don't know nothing."

"You're right, I probably don't. But I know people who know things."

"Then let them do the talking."

"They would if they weren't picked up by the Order a few weeks ago," Nils said.

Todd crossed his arms and leaned against the wall. Nils was just trying to get him to talk. He'd fallen for this trick before; the Story Collector back in Mert did the same thing. What was his name? Brent? He tugged Todd's own story from his lips, leaving him empty and vulnerable. No. Todd wouldn't give into Nils's empty statements now. Not without reason or cause.

"I get it. You don't have a reason to trust me. But I'm just saying, there's something odd with what is going on there with your boy."

"You don't know anything that happened!"

"I know that his eyes probably were bleeding, yeah?"

"Yeah, because someone carved them out of his face!" Todd cursed under his breath. Despite his own volition, the truth came out with a single stream of consciousness.

"Now that's different from what my sister saw..." Nils shrugged. "Forget it then. Can't help you."

"Wait! What? Why not? You were just hounding me nonstop, and now it doesn't matter?"

"My sister was investigating the spontaneous bleeding occurring in eyes that started a couple months ago. She attributed it to some disease," Nils turned. "Sorry, can't help you."

"Right, I'm sure it's just a coincidence," Todd grunted.

"Well, I don't believe in coincidences…" Nils paused, then asked, "When were his eyes removed?"

"I dunno. Sometime around when Senator Cordova was killed."

"And do you know how they were removed?"

"I don't know! Some prick delivered him to me… and his eyes were gone!"

Nils crouched beside Garrett, eyeing him closely. He furrowed his brow again. "It seems too convenient to be a coincidence."

Todd crossed his arms. Nils had a way of rambling that eluded no facts whatsoever. If he wouldn't provide any useful thoughts, then why speak at all?

Nils shifted, then reached for Garrett's bandage. Todd reacted at once, grabbing Nil's small hand and squeezing it. "Don't you dare."

"Listen, I didn't study medicine like my sister, but I do know it's good to let wounds breathe if they've scabbed over. Is he still bleeding regularly?"

"It's better that he keeps them covered."

"Fine," Nils rose, "but he shouldn't be ashamed of his battle scars."

Todd climbed to his feet. "He wears them for his safety…"

"I don't think the Order would care about some kid who had his eyes removed. There are more gruesome crimes they leave rotting in the street."

"But they're the ones who did it!" Todd's voice quivered. He'd been resistant to vocalizing it. He couldn't even be certain they were responsible. But who else? Who else dared remove the wide red eyes of a child?

"And so the Year Glass shatters…" Nils whispered.

Todd closed his eyes and muttered to himself. Lex would not have beaten around the bush for so long. She would have trusted Nils, opened up to him, and done everything and anything to save her child. Why couldn't he be so brave? Why did he create stone barriers that prevented others from entering?

"So the Order removed his eyes…around the same time as Senator Cordova's death—"

"The same day as his death," Todd admitted.

"Same day? Now that is definitely not a coincidence."

"What does that mean?"

"Not sure. My sister would have a better idea. As I said, she's the one with the brains."

"Then go get her!"

"Can't. The Order arrested her a few weeks ago."

"For what!?"

"For her opinion articles in the gazette. Have you seen any of those?"

"Which ones?"

"About the bleeding eyes."

Todd grimaced, then nodded.

"She thinks it's a whole conspiracy. Maybe your son here is part of it, too."

Todd scoffed. Conspiracy? No. The Order decided to torture a child. How hard was that to understand? There was no special reason.

Nils took one last glance at Garrett, "He's rather aloof, isn't he?"

Todd couldn't believe what he was hearing. "Now you're insulting my son!? Weren't you just saying he might know more than he lets on?"

"Well, I did think that, but now I'm taking a better look. He just doesn't seem very aware of his surroundings. It's like he is...a lukewarm coffee. Not quite present, but not quite lost in a daydream."

"Yeah, well, he's been through a lot. Lost his mother and everything. Wouldn't you be like this too?"

"I don't know...it's just something. I can't explain it. Just a shame my sister isn't here." Nils sighed, then returned to his peppier grin. "Anyway, I am off to the apothecary. Are you sure you don't need anything?"

"Just get away from me," Todd snarled, taking a seat on the ground beside Garrett again.

Nils didn't say anything else. He waved once to Todd, then disappeared into the dark corner of the bar, where the Witch Tunnels waited.

Todd mumbled curses under his breath. Why did he humor that man? What was the point? It just left him frustrated.

"Fucking annoying twat..." he grunted.

A voice hissed from the cot next to him, "Can you shut up? We're trying to sleep."

"Nils and I were talking for who-knows how long...and now you want me to shut up?"

"Nils has a nice voice. You sound like a discontent cow."

"What?"

"Just shut up!" The figure rolled over and muttered their own slew of curses.

Todd groaned. Beside him, Garrett shifted but did not wake. One of his bandages slipped ever so slightly from his face, catching the edge of his cheek.

Without waking him, Todd unwound half the bandage. The empty, scabbed pit that once held Garrett's right eye was shut, deep in sleep. In this light, Garrett almost looked like himself.

But he wasn't the same child anymore.

He was a little warrior with battle scars and a story that had only just begun.

CHAPTER SIXTEEN

THE FACTORIES OF SISKIN

Bria sat with Brent for hours outside of the palace, exchanging anecdotes and developing a plan. He intended to shift the ghost town near the swamp to avoid potential tracking from Ningursu or the Diabolo. She could almost hear him stammering through his plans. On paper, he wrote eloquently, as if nothing could hinder his words. But there was still an essence of Brent on the page.

Meanwhile, she detailed to him what she had learned over the past few days...and where she next planned to go. Every decision she made around the Pits resulted in a slew of questions and fear. But he never stopped her.

Just as she wouldn't stop him.

Instead, when she mentioned Siskin's Corner, Brent wracked his brain over his own experience and searched his collection of stories for factoids that might help. It may not have been much, but any little bit helped.

Ultimately, as the sun set, he left, and Bria returned to Marisol, where she marveled at the palace. Together, they returned to the Tunnels, where Marisol launched into one of her long-winded, excited babbles.

"Hue is going to love this! It's just...perfect!"

Bria affixed the gas mask on her face. "It's worked out so far."

"See, this is what we needed. I don't know why you hid it from us!"

Bria didn't know either. She just wasn't ready. But she wouldn't say that to Marisol.

Instead, she said, "So you'll talk with Hue about moving some people here? I'll make sure the Tunnels remain open for you."

"Yes...but you best not disappear again, okay?"

"I won't."

"And you'll be careful?"

"I will. I promise."

"Good. So you'll be waiting for us at your palace?"

"Yes," Bria stopped at the exit to the tunnel. "Just come back the way you came. The Tunnels will remain open."

She placed her hand on the wall, ordering the Tunnels to listen. *Guide them. Don't let them get lost.*

The vines curled around her fingers in acknowledgment.

"Alright," Marisol grabbed hold of the ladder leading to the surface. "See you soon."

Bria waved, then watched as Marisol climbed to the surface. The moonlight glistened through the opening, then turned dark as she shut the door behind her.

She would have gone with Marisol, but there were more important things in which to attend. Her own attention shifted with the change in light, and the little branch behind her ear clawed over her face in its familiar mask. Once again, she was Rho. Not the Forest Queen. Not Bria. Just Rho, venturing across the world with her determination as a guide. As Rho, she navigated the Tunnels without a thought, letting them take her from humid greenery to the chilled dead paths of northern Rosada.

Rather than taking the more familiar path towards Knoll, Bria kept to the west, pulling her coat on tighter. The vines tried to hold her back, to tug at her hair, and to pull her back to safety. But she ignored their pleas, riding on the determination of the oxygen in the air.

As she reached the tunnel exit, she double-checked her gas mask, braving herself for the suffocating onslaught.

And there she emerged from a crack between two buildings, just narrow enough for a child to crawl. Steam flooded the sky, intertwining with the streams of yellow marching across the land. She kept to the walls, commanding the stones to hide her from the clear view. But for her footsteps, all was silent. No one celebrated in their late-night endeavors. Only the shadows of guards lingered.

But with the dead trees as her subjects, Bria climbed above them in the canopy, sprinkling hints of green with each of her steps.

Siskin's Corner suffocated on smoke and death. The glow of gas lamps caught the town in a sepia tone, breathing in and out, each gasp of life more horrible than the next. Bria held back the itch to cast her hand over the street, to blanket it with green, and bring life back to all. It was one thing to give buds to the dead trees and another to bring back life where everything had died.

But the moment she brought her magic out, everyone would know she was there.

Later.

She inhaled once, then raced between the walls, listening to earth to guide her. Any semblance of magic haunted each of her steps. She could hear it pulsing through the earth. The elements shifted with magic; they behaved in ways that echoed in her ears, singing unfamiliar songs. The break in oxygen, a pause in iron, or a tremor in gold told her that magic had been brought to life. No matter how small, no matter how infrequent, it was enough.

So Bria followed magic's call, keeping to the walls. With the approach of guards through the city streets, Bria pressed herself into the stone, forming a cocoon that camouflaged her with the buildings. Once the guards passed, she hopped back on her feet, heading toward the smokestacks towering over the town.

She tightened her gas mask as she neared the factories. The smoke grew thicker, and she had never been more relieved to wear her mask. There was a heaviness hiding in the smoke, and she could feel it pressing on her. This smoke tainted the earth, stealing the worst elements and suffocating life. It wasn't like the Effluvium or the Mist Keepers; this had carbon, oxygen, and nitrogen, each one burning away and throttling the air. She could push the elements aside, but they would only come back with an equal vengeance.

Bria slipped between the crates outside the first factory. A dull light trickled from the window, and once sure no guards waited nearby, she peaked inside to get a better look.

Long benches filled the room, where children—no older than twelve—sat. With hunched backs, they worked, painting away on sheets of metal. The paint they worked with glowed, forming a nefarious hourglass shape that branded far too many people across the nation.

A guard walked past the row of children with his hands behind his back, a long smoke in his mouth, and a club on his hip.

In the back of the line, a small girl's head drooped. The paintbrush fell from her hand, hitting the floor. Bria didn't hear a thing, but the guard turned at once. He shot over to the little girl and tugged her head up by the hair. The girl's eyes widened as muffled shouts slammed into the windowpane.

How many children are working like this? Bria clenched the nearby wall. She counted at least thirty at the closest table, but more shadows waited beyond there. Did the other factories harbor similar tales? Why were they here in the first place? What about their parents? Hue hadn't mentioned anything about children. Only that people had gotten sick...

...and that they had died...

Her mind raced as she ducked back behind the crates. If she freed these children now, what would happen to the others in the factories? Would they be punished? Would she even be able to help the others escape?

But if she abandoned these children, could she live with that choice?

I wish you were here, Brent. You'd help me figure out what to do. She inhaled, forcing back the nervous tears. She had to think creatively. What did she know about Siskin's Corner? She hadn't ventured here much when she explored the Tunnels on her own. Brent must have mentioned something when they were talking.

What did Brent say about this area? Nothing much that helped. He had only been here briefly during his time in the circus, and his focus had been more on escaping than the factory town. The mountains in the distance provided no help.

But what forms mountains?

The answer came to her like a quiet breeze. First, the thought passed her by...and then she savored its angry roar.

She rose to her feet, shaking. It seemed almost impossible...but...would anyone suspect a thing?

Nerves mounting, she planted her feet on the ground. *I'm a tree. I'm taking root...let the earth collapse around me.*

Not only did her little branch flourish around her, but the ground replied with a rumble. Around her, the crates and buildings rumbled just for a second.

Then it paused.

Bria glanced back inside as the rumbling ceased. The guard froze, glancing over the children. As one child climbed under the table, the guard shouted.

"Keep working!" His voice echoed against the glass.

Bria stomped her foot. Another light rumble captured the building.

"I said keep working! A little quake isn't enough to stop anyone."

She wrinkled her nose, then pressed her heel deeper into the ground. This time, the rumbling lasted for a few more seconds, long enough for one of the pistols to fall to the ground.

That caused the guard to freeze. With a wave of his hand, he ordered the children beneath the table. The children flooded to the floor, their panicked expressions glowing in the weak light of the gas lamp. They clung to each other, looking towards the guard for guidance.

But the guard gave them none.

Instead, he crouched beneath his own steel desk on the far wall, covering his head and neck.

*If this goes wrong...*she stopped the thought. No, it couldn't go wrong.

It wouldn't.

She dug her heel deeper into the ground. The rumbling escalated, shaking the windows and gas lamps in the factory. With the earth's shouts dominating, Bria took the chance to pick a handful of pebbles from the ground and send them flying into the windows.

And then it cracked.

She raced forward, the earth now controlling its quakes. In the factory, bookshelves had already fallen over while the children all huddled, some crying, some wide-eyed, and some uncaring.

Just a few more things need to fall. Another bookshelf. Or two. Enough to block the guard.

But, rather than a bookshelf, the chain to one of the gas lamps snapped.

The fixture swung downwards, landing on its side on top of the bookshelves.

With cracking glass, fire took shape, crawling along the side of the bookshelves closest to the children.

Bria cursed. Without waiting, she pressed her hands to the outside of the window. The stone compressed, breaking the final fragments of the window.

Not caring how the broken glass scraped her, Bria toppled into the room. She glanced towards the guard. The fire masked her presence in a fit of smoke, rising higher, a beast rising from the ashes. She held her breath, pushing the oxygen in the opposite direction, away from the children.

Toward the guard.

She ducked beneath another piece of falling debris, crouching to the children's height. They all gawked at her, wide-eyed, as if trained not to speak.

"I'm going to get you out of here, okay? Just form a long chain by looping your arms together...and hold on tight. Okay?"

The first few children nodded, then linked arms.

Bria raced along the back of the table, sending the instructions along. She then hurried towards the remaining tables.

More tables than she imagined greeted her. Six tables, each with at least two dozen children, filled the small factory floor. There were at least one hundred children in this factory, if not more.

"Everyone check—do I have everyone from your table?" she asked as she recounted one last time.

The children all nodded as another rumble shook the ground.

Bria reached the first table again. The children had all gathered close, arm-in-arm. "Okay, good. Listen, it's going to get loud and shake even more...but just hold on close. It will be over in a second, and you'll be safe. Okay?"

The children nodded.

"Okay, so count with me now. Five...four...thr–"

"MISS!" a child shouted.

Bria paused.

"Emily won't hold my arm, miss!"

Bria's stomach dropped. She raced over to where an older boy waved his hand. Beside him sat the little girl she'd seen nearly pass out earlier. Her cheeks were pale, eyes heavy, each breath wheezing.

"How long has she been like this?" Bria asked.

"Dunno..." the boy responded.

"Okay, grab hold of his arm," Bria motioned to the other boy beside her.

"I don't wanna hold Maurice's ha—" The room quaked again. The glow from the fire rippled across the scene.

"Do it!" Bria shouted, lifting the small girl into her arms. The child's breathing came in labored laps as if suffocated by, well, Bria couldn't be certain. It might have been the yellow smoke, or the factory's poison, or the flames roaring behind her. It didn't matter.

Without much of a thought, Bria took a deep breath, then removed her facemask. She affixed it to the girl's face the best that she could, then returned to the front of the group.

She held up her hand to the child in the front, then slowly counted down with each of her fingers.

5...

4...

3...

2...

1...

"Your hand is wilting!" The child in front shouted.

Bria didn't have a chance to react. Another quake rocked the entire room. This time, rather than breaking around them, the ground opened.

And Bria fell into the ground with the children.

As they toppled, she used her last bit of magic to close the ground above, hiding her and the children from any further attention.

The fall was short, but Bria still summoned a bed of leaves to secure their fall. Upon landing, Bria placed the little girl in her arms on the floor and then stumbled to the side. Her head spun. Around her, the world constricted with yellow smoke.

The children cried out.

"Someone...follow this path to get help..." she choked.

Then, before Bria could say another word, her little branch withered to the floor, and she with it.

CHAPTER SEVENTEEN

LOSING HIS HEAD

Brent scanned Neorama from the steps of his schoolhouse with Nix at his side. After returning from Bria's palace, Szyman had launched into preparations. With Yaz's visions showing the Diabolo, time was of the essence. They would need to move the town to protect not only themselves but the magical haven of Mert.

He glanced back at the empty schoolhouse. The first lesson, really, was a success. Small, a bit disorganized, but it set the direction for the school. All he could hope, really, was to help those struggling with the Mist understand and to give them a choice for their future. Unlike him.

It wasn't just the fact that being a Mist Keeper was thrust upon him. All through his own schooling, he didn't have options. The black stamp marked him from a young age. He, as well as the small cohort of others stamped as children, never had any chance to grow. They learned, but they were always placed in the back of the class; the teacher never offered tutoring, and their supplies were used and decrepit. Most of the others with black stamps gave up by the time they were twelve or thirteen, but Brent stayed, trying to learn despite the stamp on his wrist.

All because he was born with silver eyes.

And all because he loved stories.

But the teachers never looked at him except to reprimand him for telling stories to the younger children.

It was the life he had accepted, but he made it work. He never had the best handwriting, nor was he ever very good at math, but he tried. The teacher once commented on his writing ability, saying offhandedly how his handwriting would work perfectly in the Pit, but his writing reminded her of scholars.

He used to wear that compliment with pride.

But now, he knew there was so much more.

Let this be a home where future Mist Keepers can seek safety and knowledge. This is the start of not just the school, but our new Library. A true Library. One that does not harbor fear. He ran his hand over the wall. *One that does not hide from the world and lock monsters away. A Library, a school, and a home for all. Because we shouldn't fear the Mist.*

He expected his Diabolo to respond, but despite not taking his medication in days, the monster had not returned.

He could see the story before him, just a glimmer of it like a gaze into the past. Yaz would sit eagerly at the front of the class while Chander sat a few rows back, his expression nonchalant but his ears open. Beside them, faceless pupils gathered, listening as they learned about their magic. Yet, while Brent couldn't see the future students, he did recognize the ones gathered in the back. The spirits watched in awe and hesitancy. They didn't speak or interact.

But they were there. Thriving.

Learning.

Free.

And from there, the story only grew, the future more pronounced. It would no longer just be a single house but an academy. A place of learning, of adventure, and of magic. It was so vivid, like any of his stories.

But then, it faded.

Just my imagination going. The future is still a blank page.

With his hand tight on his cane, Brent limped from the schoolhouse. Nix followed close behind him, wiggling ahead, her tail rampant, unaware of the stories bubbling in the air.

For the most part, Brent had grown used to Neorama's stories. They told him about how Szyman built the town and nomadic ghosts who joined his side over time. Brent could spend hours watching these stories, enamored by how the buildings crawled out of the Mist. What other talents did the Mist Keepers hide? What could they have done to make the world...better?

And what had Ningursu suffocated?

Ningursu...The stories from the swamp still haunted him. The answers lay with Ningursu's story. He'd been avoiding looking back into Nedo's story to uncover Ningursu's past. Ever since Nedo showed him the tale of the Pool, of Kek and Ningursu's tenacious past, and of how Nedo lost his autonomy to his brother's rage. But Brent never dared look beyond that glimpse, fearful of what the tale might do to him.

Yet, when else could he begin? It was quiet, all things considered. There was no sign of Ningursu, no hint of Diabolo, and he could think. His fears hemorrhaged around Bria's actions; she willingly ventured into danger to save so many people from a life of dismay.

That was the beauty of being alive; she could change so many things in the world. But here Brent stood, no more than a ghost, carrying the burden of stories on his shoulders, capturing history in a single breath. But history couldn't be changed.

Only learned from and repeated.

Brent paused at the edge of the Chessboard Plains, gazing back towards Mert, Nix slowing her pace beside him. The city waited peacefully for him to return. While behind its buildings, chaos never ended, there was an element of serenity to the city. People didn't know of the suffocating Mist or the monsters in the sky. People could live.

As they should.

No one deserved to carry the burden of the dead. Their stories lingered, no matter how old.

Including Ningursu's tales.

They were everywhere if Brent just knew where to look.

But few knew Ningursu well.

Very few.

But there was one...

"Nedo...help me..." He whispered, clutching his cane tighter. The memory of Ningursu's ghostly brother and servant filled his mind. As part of the treaty between the Palaver of Immortal Magi and the Council of Mist Keepers, Nedo agreed to serve by Ningursu's side. He took a vow of silence to protect himself and those he cared about.

As Brent closed his eyes, he could see the ghost standing amid the peonies in the Library. He told Brent the story of the war, of Merta, and the beginning of Ningursu.

Nedo's memory of the war came back to him at once. He had shown Brent a story of the Chessboard Plains, of Kek and Ningursu, of blood loss. It had been but a glimpse, but now, he saw it as he opened his eyes.

There, on the Chessboard Plains, Ningursu's story beckoned him.

And he just had to take a step...

Ningursu walked before Brent, a man of strength and pride. His hair fell to his shoulders in thick curls, resting around his clean-shaven face.

His eyes were silver.

On his hip, he carried what looked like a farmer's scythe, sharpened to a point like a sword. The Mist gathered at his feet.

And he walked without hesitation.

Behind him, his army followed like a storm cloud. Monsters rose from the Mist, pulsing with yellow, while tethered to Ningursu by streams of black. In the distance, the glistening capital of Merton waited, guarded by an army of equal force.

Brent walked with the story, inhaling Ningursu's rage and determination. From the story, he already learned that Aelia stayed back, working on her alchemy and remedies. Tomás, though... He left Ningursu with a foul taste. The mere thought of the man made his stomach churn with deep-seated anger. How dare that man betray him! How dare he run from his duty and war!

Brent shed the anger, recounting his name once as he walked in pace with Ningursu.

At the top of the hill that overlooked the capital, Ningursu paused. He raised his hands, catching the tendrils of black smoke. Like a puppeteer, he beckoned his monsters towards the army at the bottom of the hill, guarding the city.

And that army rushed forward with the same resolve.

Elements collided. The monsters roared. Mist masked everything.

Blood.

Death.

It stained the chessboard plains, a game of chess coming to its final collision point.

But any tactile plan had long been lost, replaced by a disorganized charge and a bloody bath.

Each story of the warriors twisted through the air; their deaths left a stain of their own. Brent caught a glimpse of Edith slaughtering a Diabolo, her eyes thirsty for blood. She had not changed a bit since the war. Blood, iron, death—all part of one forsaken tale.

Brent pushed aside these demanding stories to follow Ningursu into the battle. He used his scythe like a sword, slashing open the Magi as they attacked. Their magic stood no chance against death; despite their strength in air, water, fire, and earth...death always found a way. If the Seers gave them predictions, it proved nothing.

Until Ningursu came face-to-face with Kek.

"Finally," Ningursu spoke, his voice rumbling.

"Death only has so much power," Kek unfurled their own sword.

"But what sort of power does an alchemist have?"

"An alchemist is part of Life. All of us are. We wield her power now."

"But everything dies."

Their blades clashed. Equally matched, the two fought like a dance. Mist poured. Elements roared.

When it all parted, Ningursu stood there, scythe blade to Kek's neck.

"The balance is broken because of you. Magic should never counteract death." He growled, pressing into their neck.

"You helped me create this. I trained Aelia for you. Do not act like any of this comes as a surprise."

"That was back when you were nothing but a naïve royal. Now...you've raised an army to fight me."

"Do not blame me for your failures, Ningursu. You could have had an army, but you settled for monsters instead. You dared to stop anyone who showed a hint more of talent than you. All you are is Death...and no one respects you using your magic

to control them. That is not leadership, power, or being a god. A true god would not have to lift a finger to get their subordinates to obey."

"You know nothing."

"You slaughtered the Gods that existed before you; you stopped most who existed after you. You are alone."

Ningursu pressed the scythe further, "I am the God of Death. People will bow to me."

"Then prove it. Without lifting a finger, command your followers."

Ningursu snarled and raised the scythe in the air.

But before he could use it, a small figure emerged from the smoke with blazing red hair.

Edith leapt onto Ningursu back. With a swift motion, the metallic blade of his scythe disintegrated. She fought the dark tendrils as they wrapped around her, keeping her own knife close to Ningursu's neck.

Kek rose to their feet. "Prove you do not have to lift a finger to garner respect," they said as they approached. They unfurled another, sharper blade from their hilt. The edges glistened with the silver twinge of the Pool.

Black smoke continued to seep from Ningursu's mouth, "Let go of me. You will regret this!"

"Prove it," Kek said again.

Then, they sliced open Ningursu's throat.

And the world turned black and yellow.

Brent collapsed, holding his own throat. Was he bleeding? Why couldn't he see? Everything was black. Everything was yellow. The world was spinning.

"Enough!" Someone shouted in the distance.

Or was it in the past?

He couldn't tell. He couldn't see.

A dog barked.

Or was it the wind?

He couldn't know.

He only knew that everything had changed.

He had no body.

No throat.

No sense.

He withered against the chessboard plains.

He had to fight.

He had to win.

Otherwise, was he any sort of God at all?

CHAPTER EIGHTEEN

PUPPETEER

Chander lit a smoke at the edge of the foggy Chessboard Plains. Anandi's scolding wrung in his ears, but he ignored it. The first lesson from the School of Mist, as he had dubbed it in his head, haunted him. All these Mist Keepers had phenomenal magic… What good could his do? He saw through the eyes of others. What did that matter? Even Yaz had a better talent than him—she could control monsters! He didn't belong here. It'd be better to just go live alone somewhere, away from anyone who could haunt his vision.

He closed his eyes. To his relief, he saw only black. *Yaz must still be asleep.* He removed the smoke from his mouth. She'd been distraught after her vision of the monster. Even the brief reassuring touch he offered haunted his sight.

But now, as he opened them, at least he could see solely what was in front of him and nothing more.

What he saw gave him pause, though. The fog had settled, and a ghostly dog raced up to him.

"You... I recognize you." He approached the dog. He remembered seeing this ghostly dog around Knoll's Gully with Bria. "What're you doing here?"

The dog barked once, then raced back into the Chessboard Plains, trampling over the collection of black and white flowers.

Chander dropped his smoke on the ground, jamming the embers into the dirt with his heel, then followed the dog. As he moved into the plains, the fog thickened around him, capturing the air in twirling whirlwinds. With each step forward, the whirlwinds changed, taking shape like ghosts.

But this was a story.

The smoke told the story of war, of monsters, and of magic dancing across the plains. Chander couldn't make any sense of it.

But he knew, in the center of it all, waited Brent.

Nix led him straight there, where Brent seethed in the center of the stories. His eyes had rolled back into his head while foam gathered at his lips. He stumbled back as the Mist swirled around him, taking a knee and holding his throat.

"Brent?!" Chander called.

He sputtered in response as if choking.

"Brent! Are you okay?" Chander stepped forward as Nix performed an anxious loop around them.

No response.

Chander moved closer with his hand outstretched. Brent showed no signs of violence, his head drooping from one side to another like a rag doll, his lips opening and closing like a fish. Chander placed his hand on Brent's shoulder. The tip of his finger brushed Brent's skin.

And Chander closed his eyes.

But when he looked through Brent's eyes, he only saw himself staring back.

"C'mon, we gotta get you help," Chander said, eyes still shut. He took one step backward.

To his surprise, Brent followed.

Chander's throat tightened, and he opened one eye. With each step, Brent followed, his eyes glossed over, his steps shaky and uncertain. But, when Chander opened his second eye, Brent stopped and stumbled back to the ground.

At once, Chander closed one eye again, and with half his gaze through Brent's eyes, he took another step.

And again, Brent followed.

Nix circled around them in excitement, barking. Chander nearly tripped over the dog as they neared the edge of the plains. Neorama still remained dark, undisturbed by the shift of Mist, and not a single glance at the seething Mist Keeper strolling through the streets. With one eye open, Chander kept Brent close, searching for any sign that someone could help.

But the last thing he wanted was to bring Brent into the school where Yaz slept. What would she do if her *hero* was a monster?

Perhaps Szyman would be walking about, or Tomás, or Malaika.

There had to be *someone*.

And at the end of Neorama's one road, there was someone. Chander slowed as he approached.

Caroline, the Mist Keeper drenched in black, stood there. Her blue eyes twinkled beneath her melted features, her skin blotched and pruned as if thrown underwater. She sent a shiver through Chander's body, but he forced himself past that fear.

"Oh good, you are here," Caroline said as they approached. Her twisted lips immediately fell, forming a disfigured frown. "Wait...what is wrong with him?"

Chander opened his other eye. Beside him, Brent fell to the ground again, gurgling with spit and clenching his neck. Nix lay beside him.

"Well? What happened?" Caroline spat, her voice shrill and pointed.

"I found him like this in the plains...and I got him to follow me or something with my magic...but I don't know what's wrong..." Chander exhaled. As he said the words, his head started to spin. How did he get Brent to follow him? He'd never done this before; all he wanted was to see what Brent saw, but instead...this happened.

"You...controlled him?" Caroline asked.

"I...guess so," Chander diverted his attention to the ground, kicking up a few weeds. *I didn't mean to control him, though.*

Caroline's eyes widened, and for a moment, they sat there in a silence that could slice open the air. Chander didn't know what to say. He couldn't explain what happened. It merely...happened.

Finally, Caroline spoke though. "Go find Tomás. He is probably at that tavern in Mert with Juliet—I mean Jewel. Tell him Brent is having one of his incidents. He will know what to do."

"But what about Brent?"

"I shall stay with him," Caroline knelt beside Brent's writhing body. She placed a hand on his chest, stopping him from twitching. "Go—I would hate for anyone else to see him like this."

"Oh, um, alright. Of course. Yeah," Chander shook his head and then, without another thought, darted back along the road toward Mert's glimmering shadow.

Chander walked in a daze back to Mert. His mind churned. What happened? How did he control Brent? He hadn't intended on doing it, but somehow, he managed to get Brent to follow him. His magic had never done anything like this before! It had only ever been a glimpse, a vision, not...control.

He swallowed once as he entered the city. In the early morning light, the dusty air glowed like fairy dust, casting an eerie glow on the otherwise dead plants and grass.

The streets of Mert sat quiet in the early morning. Chander's pace slowed as he neared the otherwise uninteresting Pinstripe Tavern. A narrow shop front beneath a collection of murky windows, there was nothing all that interesting about the Pinstripe Tavern. It sat on an unassuming street, away from the airfields and main plaza, without the lurking attention of merchants. Really, if he, Anandi, and Yaz hadn't met Mitzi, the deputy of the Pinstripe Gang, he never would have noticed this tavern at all.

Chander stopped outside of the tavern, staring at the otherwise unassuming door. His stomach flipped. How could he even describe what happened? What would Tomás think?

Or worse, what would Anandi say to him?

He hadn't spoken with his sister in weeks. She kept busy, working alongside Mitzi, not daring to humor his "dumb magic talk," as she called it. What would he say to her now?

And what would his grandfather think? He had promised to protect Anandi...but now, he was wrapped in all of this Mist Keeper nonsense. It was almost easier back when they lived in hiding with their grandfather in Grover's Marsh, with only fleeting memories of their parents. They just had to hide their magic, keep their heads down, and stay out of harm's way.

But, one day, after he bumped into a Sister of the Order at the nearby train station, Chander found himself enthralled with visions of torture hidden deep in the crevasses of a nearby Temple of the Order. When he brought it to the local authorities, they immediately arrested him. His grandfather stepped in, claiming to have the visions himself.

And from there, they had been taken away by one of the towers, led like lambs for slaughter to Knoll.

His sister was only strung along because of her relation to Chander and his grandfather.

Now, she was here...and he had abandoned her.

Maybe this Mist Keeper thing isn't for me. Chander's hands shook as he reached for the door. He controlled a *person*. He didn't want that! It would only do more harm than good.

With a deep inhale, he opened the door to the tavern. The tavern was empty, but for a man passed out at the counter and Tomás sitting in a booth towards the back. Beside him, the blonde-headed Jewel, the aloof "leader" of the Pinstripes.

Although, since she became invisible due to the so-called "Erasure of Sight," she hadn't been much of a leader to anyone at all.

Chander gulped and approached Tomás. "Um...Tomás?"

The Mist Keeper raised his head. Jewel turned her head as well.

"Um, Caroline sent me because...well...Brent was having one of his story nightmares, I guess? I don't know how to describe it." Chander blinked a few times. As he blinked, he saw Caroline's face as she watched Brent.

Tomás stood and straightened his pants. "Very well. We knew this would happen again. Where is he?"

"Neorama."

"I'll go see him then. Thank you." Tomás stepped from the booth.

"Oi, where you goin', Tom?" Jewel snapped. "Don't leave me here all alone again—no one's noticing nothing, you know."

"I tell you every time that you are allowed to come with me. You are the one who chooses to stay here."

Jewel huffed and rose from her spot. She pulled on her tight pinstriped blazer, managing to fasten one button, before climbing out of the booth. "I'm sick of this—I'm coming. You're supposed to report to *me*."

"You are no longer queen anymore."

"Yeah, that damn Mitzi is in charge now."

The two continued to blather as they left, leaving Chander standing alone in the tavern. He collapsed in the booth, flinching as the door slammed. He could have followed them, but after everything, all he wanted was a warm meal and a comfortable bed.

But if he slept, would he control Brent again? What would become of his dreams?

That didn't matter. As soon as he lay back on the hard seat, his eyes began to droop.

And for once, only the undersides of his eyelids stared back at him.

CHAPTER NINETEEN

LIKE HER MOTHER

W hat were you thinking?" Hue asked as she finished replacing the bandage around Bria's good arm.

Bria didn't reply, wincing when the antiseptic touched her skin. She had awoken back in the speakeasy on her usual cot on the second floor. From what she gathered, one of the children had found Marisol, and they brought her and the children from Siskin's Corner back to this very location. When Bria had finally regained consciousness, she lay for hours in the bed, not moving, her mind racing over the events from the previous nights.

She didn't reply to Hue as the doctor tied off the bandage, then moved over to the deformed branch on Bria's left shoulder.

"Have you tried to reform it?" Hue asked.

Bria shrugged.

"Bria…I swear…you are so much like Lana. Never talking. Always acting. Talk to me. Please."

With a sigh, Bria inhaled and then said, "I did what I had to do."

"At what cost?"

"I weighed my options, and I have to live with that choice. I know people might have died, and that terrifies me." Bria gulped once, forcing the tears back. "It absolutely terrifies me that someone might have lost their life. I tried my best to contain it…I really did…"

"I'm not talking about that! I'm talking about you, Bria! You're going to kill yourself."

Bria glanced down at her hand and discombobulated branches. "I'm fine…"

"Bria!"

"I am! See!?" She willed her hand back into its shape. "I can do this. People are waiting for the Forest Queen to come…and as…ridiculous as it is, I can't ignore it."

Hue sighed. "It's noble. And I understand. But we can't save everyone. We don't have the space here."

"I have space back at my castle. Marisol was going to show you, but—"

"That doesn't matter right now. What happens if you're hurt…or worse? What happens then?"

"I trust all of you to carry forward."

"You really do sound like Lana."

Bria looked away from Hue. "At least Lana left behind something..."

Hue groaned. "Please...just keep me in the loop with your plans. I will support you, but we can't risk losing you."

"You keep saying that." Wincing, Bria rose from her spot. As she rose, the wooden dresser beside her sprouted with a leaf.

"Look at everything you've done, Bria. You are instrumental to our movement. You've rescued people, you've hindered the Order—"

Bria shook her head. *This is the same story. I'm just a tool. Like I was for Ningursu, for Kek, even for Lana. I'm a weapon.*

Hue grabbed Bria's arm to stop her from leaving. "And we care about you."

Bria froze.

"You're young, and it's not fair that you have to endure this. You should be getting married, having a family, and living the life you wanted. Not...leading a rebellion." Hue shook her head. "There are too many young'uns like you who are so deeply involved. My mother was the same way...so was my aunt...everyone in my family. It's not fair. I just don't want you taking unnecessary risks."

Bria glanced toward the window, overlooking the dusty field outside the tavern. Marisol sat outside with her love, Jeremy, where they watched the children from Siskin's Corner play. It was like a glimpse into the life she lost, a life where she and Brent could live here in peace. It would be like the little cabin they once talked about. Hadn't they always talked about a little home with a nice garden, a bookshelf filled with stories, and even a family?

They used to sit by the fields and name the cows. They had Pig...and once, Brent derailed the conversation and chose the names for their future children.

The children they would never have, but in the meantime, they would protect.

"The children..." she whispered to herself, then turned back to Hue. "How's Emily?"

"Who?"

"The little girl that I gave my gas mask to."

Hue's shoulders fell, and she turned her attention to the loose bandages left on the bed. Slowly, she rolled the first piece. "Not well. She's in our makeshift infirmary downstairs. It's...not good. I saw this back when I lived in Siskin. Her lungs are tarnished by the smoke and unhealthy chemicals. With our resources, I don't think she'll survive."

Bria's heart sank. The girl couldn't be older than seven years of age. How long had she worked in the factories? What sort of chemicals had she been exposed to in her time?

Where were her parents?

How many more children suffered the same fate?

"Is there anything you can do?"

"I can only guess what sort of chemicals she was exposed to in the factories. Perhaps radium or barium...or it may be a magical compound."

"Like the silver pool..." Bria murmured.

Hue didn't hear her, continuing her own ramble. "It is a complex situation. I'll make her comfortable and do my best to help but...I fear the worst."

"Then we should find her family before then—"

"You realize they are most likely dead."

"There has to be someone!"

"And how will you find that someone? Scour all of Rosada? Return to Siskin? She doesn't have time."

Bria turned away from Hue and towards the door.

"Where are you going!?"

"She shouldn't be alone."

"Bria—"

She left with steady determination and headed down the stairwell. There had to be something they could do for this little girl. It wasn't fair that such a young child rotted away at the hands of some unnamed poison. She was a child; she had no say in her fate.

She nodded once at Old Lady Doris as she left the stairs, turning into the small parlor where a collection of cots had been assembled. A few other vagrants and fugitives from the Capitol lay in bed, the scent of death, injuries, and illness hanging deep in the air. The few who rested on the makeshift cots did not move with her arrival.

The little girl rested in a cot by the window. An oxygen container leaned against her bed, a long cannula twisting around an intravenous line before looping into her nostrils. The gasmask waited beside the bed. Emily did not flinch as Bria approached the bed. Her eyes rested, not in a sort of peaceful sleep, but of the type that reminded Bria of her grandpapa before his death years ago. She remembered it vividly, and upon talking with her grandpapa's ghost months earlier, the memory was clearer now than ever. It was a final gasp, a last moment of life, hanging on by a thread.

For Emily, each breath was empty. No life flushed her cheeks.

Hollow.

Broken.

Bria took the little girl's hand. "I'm sorry, Emi—"

She paused. Beneath the surface of Emily's skin, the elements spoke to her. The oxygen in the blood, the carbon in her lungs, and the sodium in her tears. It all bubbled, like the top of a pond.

But there was something else, something deeper. It burned within, and when Bria closed her eyes, a blinding light terrorized her.

The elements interacting with Emily's body screamed.

And Bria squeezed the girl's hand tighter. Could she separate the terrible elements from the good ones? Could she bring back life to the little girl in a single grasp?

But as soon as she traced the bright elemental radiation in Emily's body, it darted away, unable to be found amongst the thousands of particles of oxygen and carbon.

"No..." Bria bemoaned, releasing the little girl's hand. "No...you're not allowed to—" she stopped herself, watching as Emily's body rose and fell with uneasy gasps. She had said the same thing to her grandpapa, and he held on...but at what cost? It wasn't her job to play Life or Death. Would it be unfair to the little girl if she forced her to stay? "Emily, try to fight this. We'll...we'll try to help...Emily, please..."

But there was no response.

No sign of recognition.

Nothing.

Bria released Emily's hand and leaned back in the chair. She wouldn't leave. Not until Hue returned.

But then, it would be back to the Tunnels.

Back to the Pits.

Back to her swamp.
And back to being the Forest Queen.

JUST A STEP OUTSIDE

The basement oozed with a pungent odor. Even after days, Todd still couldn't shake the pungent smell of the basement—not even when he ventured upstairs to use the lavatory or when he dared to sneak outside just for a quick breath of air at night. He only stepped outside once, sneaking through the back entrance of the restaurant's kitchen to take in the fresh air while Garrett slept. The restaurant itself sat along the far wall of the Capital, where a narrow river intersected with the sewage system. He checked once that no one was watching before sitting outside for a good five minutes to relieve his nostrils.

But the relief did not come.

With the stench lingering, he snuck back inside, snatching a newspaper from the restaurant's front porch before heading back into the basement, where Garrett continued to sleep on his cot. The boy had barely woken the last few days, acknowledging only the smallest amount of food and resorting to wetting the bed rather than letting Todd know he needed to relieve himself. In fact, Todd couldn't be sure if the child had spoken at all since they had arrived at the speakeasy.

As he arrived back inside, Todd searched for Nils. The man was the only one Todd had made any acquaintance with since arriving. While he didn't *like* Nils by any stretch of the imagination, sitting in silence was just as difficult. None of the other refugees or vagrants wanted anything to do with him, forming their own cliques in separate corners of the basements. Every day, a different person would arrive from the Witch Tunnels, gathering a group of five or so at a time. Then, someone else would come later with another band of refugees.

Everyone just keeps on running. Todd slinked against the wall beside Garrett. He opened the newspaper in his hands and, as every morning, skimmed the articles.

For the most part, it was all the same. Formal decrees filled each page, signed by an anonymous government agent. The single signature, a fluid line, bore no name, no identity. He stared at it for a moment, then moved on, scouring the page for anything that might show times would change.

How much longer could they live like this, in the palm of some faceless government? At least with the Senate, the representatives had names.

Todd flipped to another page. The headline caught his attention.

Massive Earthquake hits Factory Center of Siskin's Corner

Three nights ago, at a quarter after midnight, an earthquake struck the factory center of Siskin's Corner, the industrial center of Rosada. Five of the twenty factories experienced debilitating damage, halting operations until further notice. Factories on the western coast will take over production of some assets.

Fourteen individuals sustained injuries in this event. No notable deaths have been reported. One hundred and forty-eight unremarkable individuals are currently missing.

Todd grunted to himself and flipped the page. Earthquakes weren't uncommon in Siskin's Corner. When he joined the Guard as a boy, bright-eyed and eager to leave his otherwise normal life in Maedee's Outlook, he had a small tenure in Siskin's Corner. His captain at the time reiterated the importance of these factories to Rosada's safety. The towers, the airships, the weapons, and even some of the safeguards in the Pits all came from those factories. Now, with everything else happening, who knew what else was constructed behind those factory walls.

Yet, Todd doubted it would take them long to rebuild. What was a little earthquake to Siskin's Corner after all?

But perhaps nature itself decided that the Guard needed a hindrance.

Todd adjusted Garrett's blanket and leaned against the wall. He eyed the entranceway to the Witch Tunnels, hidden by the wall of fake liquor bottles. *I gotta be in a group coming soon, right? I mean, my son's sick. I've seen a lot of healthy people get priority, which is a load of bull if you ask me.*

Once Nils returned, Todd would give the little man a piece of his mind. Quite frankly, this was getting ridiculous.

His thoughts continued to wander as he waited, sending him into a conscious sleep. His eyes remained open, his ears alert, but he was no longer in the speakeasy. Rather, he fell back into his dreams, imagining a time in Mert again with his family. It felt like a fantasy, those few years of peace.

He should have known they wouldn't last.

He should have never gotten comfortable.

He shouldn't have dropped his guard.

Especially now.

A crash above brought him back to the present. Everyone in the little speakeasy paused, the silence slicing through the air. Another crash followed.

The response within the speakeasy came without a command. Todd lifted Garrett from the ground and, with a hoard of others, moved toward the door to the Witch Tunnels.

Another crash.

Followed by a scream.

And the familiar command of the Guard echoed from the floorboards above them.

Was that a gunshot? A scream?

It didn't matter.

The speakeasy immediately jumped into motion. With chaos bristling and voices shouting, the refugees crammed together. They tripped over each other, nearly trampling Todd and Garrett in the process.

"Watch the fuck where you are going!" he shouted as he forced his way through the refugees.

They didn't pay any attention to him as they clawed open the door to the Witch Tunnels. In clumps, they pushed into the tunnels. The panic connected all of them, no matter how familiar or unfamiliar they had begun. One unified goal, one shared fear, and they all arrived in the sewage-filled Witch Tunnels.

The last person slammed the door, and the others with them barred it with stacks of heavy crates.

And then, with realization as its tether, panic settled in Todd's core. He knew this was a bad idea! Where would they go now? They couldn't just stay in these Witch Tunnels, surrounded by waste and water. The crates would not protect them for long. Surely, the Guard would find the entrance. And then what?

Would they all end up in the Pit? Or worse?

"Oi!" A shout pulled Todd back out of his fears.

Nils stood on top of a crate with his hands cupped around his mouth. "What's going on here? Why you all out here?"

"Guards!" Someone shouted.

Nils's expression grew sullen. He asked, "Are Tilly and Cliff still inside?"

"I'm here!" A small middle-aged woman piped from the back. "I don't know about Cliff, though."

"A'ight, it'll be okay," Nils scanned the audience. "Listen, half of you go with Tilly. Take 'em to the train yard, a'ight? The rest, come with me."

Todd joined Nils's group. It didn't really matter who he traveled with, but he had conversations with Nils. Any trust went a long way in these times.

The groups traveled together at first, all in silence, but for the sloshing of sewage and the occasional cry of a child. Despite the commotion, Garrett still did not speak. If he had awoken, he showed no signs of understanding what occurred. Right now, it was for the best.

Let him sleep. Let him think everything is okay. Todd shifted the boy in his arms. *At least you're still tiny for your age. Any bigger, and my arms might fall off.*

Where two tunnels intersected, Tilly's group turned to the right. Nils waited for a moment, then tapped the wall with his fingers.

Within seconds, the bricks at the far end of the tunnel caved in on themselves. Like dominos, the path in which they came disappeared, turning into nothing more than a thick wall of rubble. To his surprise, the ceiling above did not cave in, though, still perfectly supported by the collection of bricks.

"Magic..." Todd grumbled.

As if Nils heard him from the front of the group, he said, "The Magii who built these tunnels are something, huh? Managed to link sound with the bricks. Still love it...and keeps those pesky guards off our tails."

A few mumbles replied, but no one waited long. Rather, they continued in haste behind Nils, weaving in and out of a collection of tunnels. No one spoke, not even the children. Rather, each turn came with further uncertainty. Todd didn't ask any questions; he knew better than to ask.

After what felt like hours, Nils slowed in front of another set of doors. This one, with its intricate golden accents, exuded a history that Todd couldn't quite place. This door had seen things. If it could speak, the stories it could tell would be endless.

Nils tapped on the door again. A few moments later, with the click of a lock, the door opened a crack.

"Password?" A man asked behind the door.

"Octopus."

The door swung open. An older man stood in the doorway, blocking a golden-accented bar glistening in an otherwise dim light.

"Hey, Lester, sorry for arriving like this...with thirty-some people," Nils said.

"Yeah. Wasn't expecting you today at all. What happened?"

"Walleye was discovered. Tilly and I got the lot out. Not sure where Cliff is."

"I'll put out a notice." Lester stepped to the side, allowing everyone to come inside the doorway.

As Todd approached, he could see the decorated interior of another speakeasy. Larger than the first, a good twenty people gathered around the tables, sharing drinks and stories.

Nils and Lester continued to chat as they all entered. Todd managed to catch their exchange as he rounded the counter with Garrett.

"Really? Walleye was discovered? Thought that place was locked down." Lester mumbled to Nils.

"Yeah, unless someone left when no one was looking. There's that watchtower that can see into the alley."

Todd froze. *Watchtower?* He hadn't seen a watchtower. Sure, he had stepped outside...but that couldn't have been enough to get the Guards' attention. He could have been anyone in the alley. No—it couldn't have been his fault.

Right?

Todd shook his shoulders and took another few steps into this new speakeasy. It didn't reek of sweat, at least. In fact, there seemed to be a lighter atmosphere here than in the other one, as if people came here not just to escape but for a good time.

No way it was my fault. Nope. I'm allowed to get fresh air if I want. He just had to relax, maybe have a drink or two. This wasn't his fault. There was no way he was the first one looking for fresh air.

No way at all.

Todd approached a table where only a single man sat. The man didn't look up as Todd took a seat across from him.

"You know," the man said as he raised his head, "you could have asked if this seat was taken instead of just assuming I was alone."

"Oh, sorry. I just assumed..." Todd's words tapered off as he locked eyes with the man.

Or lack thereof.

Because the man's empty eyes bled a deep red.

CHAPTER TWENTY-ONE

THE DIVIDE

For a while, he was the moon.

Then, he was a flower.

And finally, after the flower wilted, he was Brent Harley once again.

He woke with a jolt, nearly ripping the intravenous line from his arm. A bell rang as he rose.

"Bri—" he called out, then stopped. No—she wasn't here. This wasn't the Diabolo.

He sank back into the bed. Nix lay in the bed beside him, her silver eyes staring straight at him, tail wagging. Her smoky fur pulsed in and out of the otherwise sterile room. *Back in the Sanitorium again...shite.*

Last he remembered, he had been on the Chessboard Plains, enamored with Ningursu's story. But the story weighed heavily, and for a moment, he thought he had become the moon.

Or that Ningursu was the moon.

The story made no sense. But did that matter?

"Shite," he rubbed his head. Again, a bell rang. He flinched at the noise, only to discover a thin string attached to his wrist. He traced along it, discovering a small bell above his bed, ringing with every movement.

The door to the sterile room opened. Kek peaked in, their hair "Brent? Ring the bell once if you're awake."

Brent obliged.

"Excellent," Kek entered. They placed a notebook and a pen on the bed before taking a seat on the nearby chair. "How are you feeling?"

Brent reached for the notebook, and with a shaky hand, he wrote, *Head hurts. Vision is blurry. But I'm here.*

"Good," Kek eyed the wall, where Brent's shadow reflected from the dim light. "The intravenous line is still in?"

Yes.

"Good, Tomás inserted it, but I couldn't tell how precise he was being." Kek checked one of the bags of medicine flowing into the line. "Tomás and Caroline brought you here after you seemed to slip into the stories. You kept talking about the moon, but you sound lucid now."

I don't remember honestly.

"It took a while to get you on a dosage that wouldn't exasperate the rot on your abdomen..." Kek continued to stare at the medication bag. "It's a shame Aelia has pledged her loyalty to Ningursu. I am sure she would have answers."

So you know Aelia?

"Almost as well as I know Ningursu. Her alchemy skills come from pure study and talent. She lacks the magical touch, but she understands it better than most."

Brent adjusted in the cot, wincing once as he clutched his abdomen. The stories remained fresh in his mind, begging to take him to the moon and back. But in those stories, questions remained, and this was the perfect moment to get the answers he needed.

What do you know about Ningursu?

"Hm?"

The reason I was on the Chessboard Plains was to look for Ningursu's story. I think the only way to stop Ningursu is to understand him.

Kek shook their head and turned back to their chair. "You have Nedo's story. Is that not enough?"

He doesn't know everything.

"Then look at my story. Why should I bother telling it to you?"

Because I respect your privacy. Also the older the story, the more overwhelming it is. I highly doubt you want to inject me with another round of medication. Brent scratched his arm where the needle entered his vein. Unlike the medication Kek initially prescribed him, this one chilled his skin. But like that same medication, at least he could think clearly. It didn't completely dull the stories, though, and as he glanced around the room, Kek's past darted in front of him like a dust tornado.

Kek's shoulders fell. At first, Brent thought they would leave the room without a word. But then, they said, "What do you want to know?"

Brent pondered the question. What did he want to know? That mere question could unravel countless stories.

He would have time to collect them. For now, he needed to understand what Ningursu wanted.

What caused the One War, all those years ago? I know it had to do with the balance of magic and death...but what exactly caused it? I feel like what is happening now is part of that war in the first place.

Kek laced their hands together. After a moment, they sighed and said, "It's complicated."

I have time.

"Very well," Kek stared ahead at the wall. They waited a few moments before starting. "You need to understand that Ningursu and I used to have a good relationship. But, even when Ningursu and I respected each other, even when we were friends and equals, we never saw eye-to-eye on what our roles should be in the world. I saw my job as a defender of magic. I sought immortality so I could create that position for myself, and with In Domumus Divitiae, I did just that."

In Domumus Divitiae?

"The silver liquid I use for everything."

You mean the Pool?

"Do you honestly think I just call it the Pool?"

No one ever said the name.

"That would be like calling the Diabolo something like 'Death Monster.'"

I don't think the Diabolo would be insulted by that.

"The Diabolo do not think. Of course they would not be insulted," Kek said.

Brent didn't waste time arguing. With his Diabolo near silent in the back of his mind, he knew that there was more to each of the monsters now. They were born out of Ningursu's fear; he reconstructed them with the souls of the Dead, and even in the darkest, most complicated Diabolo, there was a child begging to be set free.

Brent continued his questions. *So did immortality cause the fallout?*

"Absolutely not," Kek replied. "No, for a long time, Ningursu saw me as his equal. But he did not like that I would connect with other Magii, as you call them. I would offer them a taste of immortality while asking for their assistance to protect magic and give life back to the earth. I created countless groups before and after the war to protect our position. My dear friend, Xiuying, helped me expand the Divitiae. Meanwhile, I provided support to the different elemental Magii across the globe, allowing them to maintain the balance. It wasn't a perfect system, and I will admit that the Seers suffered under my hand. For a long time, I saw them more as a resource to increase the strength of the Divitiae. It wasn't until Varden came along that I began to change my tune."

Brent recalled Nedo's friendship with a young woman named Merta, a story he had long pushed to the back of his mind. Many years ago, Merta had given her life to the Pool.

Or, really, her life had been taken by it.

And even now, Seers continued to die, using their final breath of magic to grant immortality to the lucky—or perhaps unlucky—few.

Kek continued, "While Ningursu did not support my interactions with Magii, he didn't stop it, as for a long time, he did not see it as a threat. A single Magii, at the time, did not harbor enough magic—not like the way your Rhodana has magic."

Brent reached for the betrothal mark on his wrist. It remained stable, a collection of roots gathered on his skin.

Kek continued, "As more Magii entered my Palaver, he did grow antsy. Many years before me, there had been powerful Magii, but they had since faded. He worried that their power might return, especially as Seers began to whisper prophies but a strong Magii who would bring balance back to the earth. It was with those prophecies that the legend you know as Rhodana the Forest Queen was born."

Brent scribbled his next question. *So the Seers were predicting Bria?* He imagined Bria's reaction. Every time the idea of a prophecy or a chosen fate entered the conversation, she derailed its feasibility. He didn't blame her. Why would anyone want a prophecy resting on their shoulders that defined their lives?

"Yes. The circumstances of Briannabella Smidt's birth made her the perfect storm. Is she the most powerful Magii? Right now, in our current environment, I believe she is." Kek rubbed their chin, lost in clear thought. "Between you demolishing the structure Ningursu had created and Bria's unfounded magic... This is why Ningursu is scared. And rightly so, in my opinion."

I didn't want to demolish anything.

"Your very survival demolished his structure. Ningursu had carefully curated every one of his Mist Keepers. Even once the prophecy gained traction, Ningursu did not find a worthy successor for another five hundred years. He went through countless apprentices, more than I can recall. Each one did not meet his stand-ards...until Aelia.

"Aelia was obedient and quiet. She didn't argue with him, and that he liked very much. I didn't put the pieces together at the time, but he had Aelia train with me—since she is an alchemist in her own right. I think he wanted her to gain insight into any plans that the Magii might have. At the beginning, we had none.

"What began to tear our friendship to pieces was not my collection of Magii...or his repugnant ways of finding apprentices. I think...now that I can recall it...that what tore us apart was when Aelia stole the Divitiae."

Brent could almost see the story brimming from Kek's skin. The anger they felt as their precious gem lost its sanctity. The disappointment when Ningursu did not come to their defense.

And deep within it, a regret.

Kek did not stop there. "Of course I do not know for certain, but based on my own research of the Diabolo...it was with my very magic they created a beast that would seek out my destruction." Kek bowed their head. "The Diabolo did not reach their full strength until the war, but that was the beginning. I saw there that Ningursu desired more power, even if it threatened the balance of Life and Death."

None of this was anything entirely new to Brent. Yet now, with the pieces in front of him, Ningursu's story no longer hid only in the Mist. Rather, it bristled with revelations.

But there was more.

So much more.

Brent asked, *You said I disturbed everything Ningursu constructed though. I'm guessing...that's it because he didn't select me.*

"Precisely. Ningursu has curated each of his Council members. Aelia was obedient and could match my talents; Tomás had been groomed since he was a young boy; Julietta forgot her past, so she was a clean slate; Jiang was distracted by his own heart; Malaika was generally uninterested in complicated affairs; Alojzy worshipped him; Caroline was self-absorbed."

Brent picked up the pen to protest but stopped. He had seen glimmers of everyone's stories. What Kek said was true, however simplistic.

"You, though... You were independent and had magic that even he couldn't control. So with Bria representing what he feared of the Magii, and you representing an alternative to the Council...Ningursu has every right to worry.”

So this was all inevitable.

“In a way, yes. Everything aligned.”

But this isn’t enough. I still don’t know what he is planning.

“I think what you are doing is right. You need to unravel his past. Only then you can destroy his future.” Kek turned away from Brent and moved to the door, “It is something I could never do.”

Brent scowled to himself.

“Now get some rest. I’ll be back in a bit.” Kek opened the door. “I’m glad someone has hope in all of this.”

Brent didn’t know how to respond as Kek left the room. He had to have hope that things could get better. It was what kept him from being thrown into the Pit at a young age.

It kept him thriving now as he sank back into the bed, running his hand through Nix’s fur. He couldn’t ignore how Ningursu’s past continued to circle through his head.

When he closed his eyes, he went back in time.

To become a man fearful of horses.

And a man obsessed with his own reign.

But even then, Brent did not accept the stories.

No, there was more to discover. More to learn.

And there were others who had answers.

The stories couldn't hide from him forever.

CHAPTER TWENTY-TWO

A BLESSING

Brent waited until the sky darkened to leave his bed. His body ached as if it had only just been reconnected to his head. With quaking knees, he exited the room. Kek had instructed him to remove the intravenous line once he was ready. Without the fluids, his head spun, and he took each step slowly, using the wall for balance and each blink as a chance to refocus.

No one waited for him except for a plate of crudites, Kek's private suite otherwise empty. Brent picked up a carrot and popped it into his mouth. The crunching echoed in his ears, and he swallowed abruptly.

Was that always so loud? He limped over to the window and peered out into the street. Mert, once lively with magic and laughter, had been layered with a broken yellow tinge. No one spent time in the streets, ruled instead by the Rosadian Guards and Pinstripe Gang. Every day marked warfare, death, and uncertainty. Brent wasn't sure if what he saw now was another conflict or just a story from a previous day, replaying in an otherwise empty street.

In just a short year, Ningursu had transformed the world into his fantasy. A world where magic hid in all corners, where the yellow smoke tinged the sky, and where his powerful Mist Keepers hid in fear.

This won't last, Ningursu. It can't. You know, I know it. So stop hiding. But what would he do once he found Ningursu? How could anyone destroy the so-called God of Death?

And even if he figured it out...would he be able to end this rule?

First, he had to move the school. Once that was safe, he could focus his efforts on Ningursu. He had to keep finding the stories, keep supporting Bria in her quest to protect Rosada, and keep focusing on his mission.

Before the stories overwhelmed him.

Before his mind became lost.

Running water pulled his thoughts back to the present. He turned away from the window, where the door to the latrine opened to a swirling black cloak.

And there stood Caroline, her face still lopsided, her lips no longer painted red.

"Caroline! What're you doing here?" Brent asked.

"Well, I was returning to Neorama when Chander found you convulsing in the plains. Tomás and I brought you here." Caroline picked at her nail, not making eye contact with Brent.

"Oh, good, yeah, um...I just didn't expect you to be here. You've...not been around lately."

"Well, someone has to complete the routes."

"The routes...you mean you've been releasing souls?"

"It is our job."

"It is..." Brent's shoulders fell. He released souls as they came to his attention, but with everything else occurring, the core function of being a Mist Keeper escaped him. He was supposed to be helping the dead reach their peace, but instead...he was fighting a skull garnished in chaos.

"Do not be ashamed, Brent. You have bigger fish to catch. Besides...this is where my skills lie. My magic is limited; I am not aware of the full history of the Council, and I am not a teacher."

"You taught me."

"You taught yourself. I only introduced you to this world."

"But you still taught me...and because of that, I am here now."

Caroline dismissed the comment. "It does not matter. I am perfectly content completing the routes while you fix this madness."

"Doesn't it exhaust you, though? Isn't that why I became your apprentice?"

"I do not know if it exhausts me or not. I think that is just one of Ningursu's rambles to control us. But even if it does," Caroline glanced up at the ceiling, "it keeps me preoccupied. I do not want to get lost in thoughts around Julietta. And it is not like I can confide in Tilda either, with this whole sight malarkey that we are dealing with right now."

"Right..." Brent hadn't spoken with Julietta, or Jewel as she went by now, for quite some time. He had learned how Tomás had rebranded her, not just once but multiple times throughout her life. With a blank mind and fragmented thoughts, it was easy for Tomás to replace Julietta's mind with that of someone best suited for the task at hand.

"I just wanted to make sure you are okay, Brent." Caroline turned back to him. "You gave me a scare back in Neorama."

"I'm a'ight. I promise."

Caroline nodded, "Very well. I must continue with my routes. Tomás is downstairs with the spirits if you wish to see him."

"Thank you."

"It is my pleasure," Caroline turned toward the door.

Brent called out, "Caroline, wait!"

She stopped.

"I hope you…I want you…you should know that I think you are invaluable. And…you have a place in my school once it's running. Because, I mean, I need someone to teach about releasing souls. That is the true job of a Mist Keeper, after all." Brent inhaled once and counted backward before saying, "I want you to be part of this. That is, if you want. A'ight?"

Caroline's lips curled into a half smile, and then she left the room, leaving the door ajar behind her.

As Caroline said, Brent found Tomás downstairs with the spirits. The spirits sat in the open living space, playing games of cards while mumbling in a language Brent couldn't understand. At the piano against the far wall, Milo played a tune, letting stories escape with each of his notes, capturing everyone in a prayer. Brent caught the story of a dove in hands, cradling it for a moment before letting it take flight again.

Tomás rose as Brent entered the room. Julietta sat on his left, watching Milo as he played. On his right, with that usual blindless stare, sat Varden. Unable to see, his eyes bloodied and lost, the Seer was nothing but a shadow of his former self, unable to see the world he'd known for thousands of years.

"I see you are up and about, Brent," Tomás remarked.

"As much as I can be." Brent gripped the couch for support. Neither Julietta nor Varden moved at his presence. Julietta remained enchanted by Milo, her hands close to her chest, the fierce demeanor she had adopted as Jewel disappearing.

"I suppose you are not aware, but Milo is Julietta's son," Tomás said.

"What?" Brent hadn't seen a single story that suggested that fact. "I thought he was just her apprentice?"

"He was." Tomás watched Julietta and Milo closely. "Julietta gave birth to him when she was still Julyana, only a few months before death claimed her. She has never managed to remember the fact they are blood—only that he was her apprentice for a short while."

"So being a Mist Keeper was in his blood?"

"It would seem," Tomás shrugged.

Brent kept his eyes locked on Milo. "Does he know?"

"Yes. He has known for a long time." Tomás took his seat beside Julietta again. She didn't flinch.

Brent watched Milo for a moment. The music visually wrapped around Julietta as if pulling her back toward her true self. But who was Julietta truly? Was she the Pinstripe Gang leader, Jewel? Or was she the Mist Keeper,

Julietta? Or perhaps Julyana, Spinozan Royalty? Or someone else? Brent couldn't find her story in the muddied smoke.

"She should come to your school with the others," Tomás said.

"What?"

"Being with Milo seemed to bring back part of her. I think, given the opportunity to learn again, she might return to us." Tomás crossed his legs on the couch and leaned forward, drawn in a trance by Milo's music. "She and the spirits will do well at your school. I have no doubt of that after your first lesson."

"It's gonna be a joint effort. You, Malaika, Caroline—"

Tomás cut him off, "Someday, yes. But for now, I must stay in Mert. There are spirits here not ready for Neorama...and Kek cannot take care of them alone."

And there is also Varden. Brent didn't judge Tomás for wanting to stay. He would do the same with Bria.

Tomás continued, "Szyman has done a fantastic job hiding Neorama for centuries. Without a doubt, it is one of the safest places for the spirits...that can tolerate the voyage. The sixteen in the room here are the ones Milo has worked with, and while they still struggle with their magic and comprehension, they are becoming more human each day. Neorama will keep them, as well as Julietta, safe, while the others here will continue to heal until they are ready." Tomás took Varden's hand. The giant did not flinch, staring straight ahead, neither conscious nor asleep. "I was skeptical of your school, reflecting on my own time under Aelia's teaching, but I know you will do well, Brent. Just...be careful."

"I know," Brent glanced once at Julietta. Would she slip back into her Pinstripe leadership once at the school? How would the kids fare?

"I do not just mean Julietta," Tomás replied. "The next Ningursu could be brewing right in your school."

"I doubt anyone is going to be like Ningursu."

"Chander," Tomás stated. "Chander very well could be."

"Chander?"

"Pay attention to his magic. Well, pay attention to everyone's magic, but his in particular."

"Why?" Brent couldn't imagine why Tomás would make such an assertion. Chander? The kid wasn't any kind of threat. If anything, his magic seemed more like a burden than anything else.

"He controlled you like a puppet. Like Ningursu does with the rest of the Mist Keepers."

"Puppet..." Brent furrowed his brow. "I don't remember..."

"It was when you were lost in the stories. He controlled your body to move it back to Neorama. While I do not sense anything malicious within him, I just want you to know that the next Ningursu could very well be in our midst."

Brent gripped the back of the couch, his attention turning toward Milo. The melody haunted him. The next Ningursu? It just didn't seem possible. But what made Ningursu—his magic or his past? To protect Chander, to protect any young Mist Keeper to follow, Brent had to find those answers.

"I'll keep an eye on him," Brent said.

"I do not doubt you, Brent."

With that, Tomás did not speak again. A final reassurance, a final blessing; Brent would be able to start his school, Neorama would shift, and together they would all uncover the truth within the Mist.

As long as the Mist didn't thicken first.

CHAPTER TWENTY-THREE

INHUMAN

Bria guided another entourage of vagrants through the Tunnels. She'd gone just north of Siskin's Corner to one of the villages bordering the Kainan border. In the brittle air, she entered their small Pit—a single building located inside a decrepit old hospital—and freed the seven vagrants they kept within its walls. Hue's concerns echoed as she guided them into the Tunnels. How did she know that none of these vagrants were guards in disguise? With the Pits being freed, they had to know Bria would arrive like a force of nature.

Brent had done well at reading the stories, but she couldn't keep asking him to open himself up to more tales like that.

The body changes when people lie. Chemicals react. Elements shift. She paused and turned to the small group. The oxygen and carbon in the air shifted in a constant rhythm, brushing her cheek. These elements... They danced, a swaying movement in a melodic breeze. "Can I trust all of you?"

"Of course," one vagrant said, and the others agreed as well.

The oxygen and carbon remained the same.

If there was a liar, they were skilled—but otherwise, Bria could only assume they told the truth.

They continued through the Tunnels in silence. Bria adjusted her gas mask, pausing only once as a stabbing pain shot through her abdomen. After a moment to catch her breath, they continued into the junction, where the doors to the Library waited, covered in vines and moss. Bria slowed by the door, placing her hand against it, letting a few more vines crawl over the surface.

Just as she redirected her attention to the next tunnel, echoing footsteps caught her attention. She froze, motioning for the vagrants beside her to crouch against the wall. With her branched hand, she readied the vines and took her stance at the corner where a tunnel met the junction.

As the footsteps neared, Bria shot out a vine.

"Bria! It's me!" Marisol's voice rang.

Relaxing, Bria recalled the vines and stepped into the Tunnels. Marisol stood there with a dozen or so refugees from the speakeasy. Beside her, Edith smirked at Bria while gripping Tilda's arm. The Seer didn't react, each step slow and steady as she pressed her hand along the wall.

"What are they doing here?" Bria asked.

"You told me to bring people as we vetted them. Remember?" Marisol replied.

"No, I mean Edith and Tilda."

Edith piped up, "What? Are you being selective about who you let into your kingdom? Isn't that just as bad as the Order?"

"Oh, don't play that game."

"Bria," Tilda spoke, her voice low, "we needed to come. Edith is our connection to Kek, and I could no longer bear being in that tavern with the other miserable Seers."

"Oh, um, right." Bria wasn't entirely sure about linking Kek in with her hideaway. While Kek was a powerful ally, trust was a term Bria used loosely around the alchemist.

"Were you heading back to the swamp?" Marisol asked.

Bria nodded, then called for the vagrants she had rescued to come out of the shadows. With the new collection of individuals, she walked beside Marisol, who launched into a blathering tirade.

"You know, this whole tunnel thing you showed me couldn't have come at a better time. There was a raid at one of our sister speakeasies, and about two dozen or so people got moved to us. We were out of room, and we didn't have another secure transport for at least a fortnight or so...but this works out! Our transports go to Volfium anyway, and now...well, this is faster. Once I get back, I'll start vetting the new people, and I think we'll be able to move more out here instead. Which is great because it'll make it easier for Hue to enact her plan."

"Wait, Hue has a plan?" Bria asked under her breath.

"She's working on one."

"Why didn't she tell me?"

"She didn't want to involve you until it was finalized. You have your thing you're doing." Marisol waved her hand in the air, motioning to the refugees behind them.

"Yeah, but shouldn't I at least be aware?"

"Maybe. Really, I don't know. I only know about part of it because Jeremy is involved. Hue wants to send him to Aeterno Village to infiltrate the Order. He has some background in the scripture and such, so...I guess she hopes they can damage them from the inside. Jeremy told me the other day about it."

Edith hissed from behind her, "Really, little queen, I wouldn't worry. Let your subjects handle this petty business with the Order. You have far more important quests."

"Be quiet," Bria snapped.

"It's true. Don't forget that Ningursu is your enemy. Not some petty Order."

"It's all the same."

Marisol didn't seem to hear the exchange, continuing with her babbling. "Trust me, Bria. Hue will pull you in when it's time. For now, just keep doing what you're doing...and don't forget to rest."

Bria kicked the ground with her heel, wincing as a familiar cramp ran rampant through her abdomen. Rest. If she rested, what would haunt her? At night, she would lie awake, trying to decide the best course of action. Because what was she doing? She was freeing people and bringing them to a swamp, but what good did that do? Horton had

As they passed through the entrance to the swamp, Bria paused, staring out at the small collection of houses she'd helped construct. Horton greeted them as they exited the hollow tree, a smile on their face. Their bright green blouse shimmered with newly embroidered, beaded trees around the buttons.

After a soft greeting and a wide smile, they led the refugees toward the intricate building at the foot of the palace.

Edith and Tilda stayed, though. But much to Bria's surprise, Edith didn't even speak, marveling instead at the small kingdom Bria had constructed. *If she behaves, maybe she can finally help me build the latrines,* Bria thought, slowly removing the gas mask from her face to take a breath of fresh air.

"I know I told you this already, but it is gorgeous here," Marisol said to Bria.

"I wish I could see it," Tilda whispered, closing her bloodied eyes.

Edith added, "I gotta say, it is something."

Bria thanked them with a whisper.

Marisol continued, "We'll bring those kids you rescued next time. Hue wanted me to observe this all a little more before we, you know, bring kids here."

"I already have a small group of children. An old schoolteacher I rescued even started up a small schoolhouse. She's hoping to ultimately coordinate with the school in Stilette once it's safe to do so," Bria replied. "With Horton's help, it really has become a little community."

"Oh Horton! That's their name! I remember them from Knoll!" Marisol remarked.

"I visited Knoll a few months ago, and Horton asked if I needed any help. They took over the logistics without much questioning, really, and I'm forever thankful. I couldn't have done this without them."

"No, you can't do this alone. That's part of being a community—we work together and thrive."

"Yes…I know." But it was so hard to ask for help. It would be easier to just run everything herself, but the picture of a thriving community required everyone's help.

It was like a loose promise. Too many unknowns sat in the way of her kingdom bolstering in this swamp. But with the help of more people, with talents that left the Order in peril, they could build this swamp into something new. Maybe a new tavern or a restaurant or café for those looking for a new escape. Hue could set up a hospital to treat the sick. And perhaps, even someday, it would be safe enough to open the Library for all.

Children wouldn't need to work in factories. Adults wouldn't need to work in mines. Here, at least, people would have a chance to be something greater.

"How are the children doing?" Bria asked Marisol.

"Good—most of them are coming out of their shells." Marisol bit her bottom lip, then lowered her voice, a somber tone on her lips, "You should know, the little girl…the one you gave your gasmask to…she passed away a few hours after you left. Hue said there was nothing she could do. I'm sorry."

"You mean...Emily?" Bria gripped her gas mask in her hands. "Are...are you sure?"

Marisol nodded.

"Did we find out anything about her? Who she is, her parents, anything?"

"No. No one knew anything about her."

"She can't have died alone..."

"I'm sorry."

Bria inhaled. Her little branch crawled around her ear, touching her cheek with a gentle caress. *Brent can learn about her. He can save her and give her peace. He has to...it's his job.*

"Thank you for letting me know," Bria whispered. "I...I need time alone."

"I'll be here if you need anything."

Bria turned away, and without a word, she trudged through the swamp toward her castle. She was sure Edith said some mocking statement as she walked away, but Bria didn't dare engage. People died, she knew that, but there was something about that little girl that rocked her core. *I tried to save them. I really did.*

She entered her palace and ascended the stairs toward her private suite. The vines and roots followed her up to the top of the stairwell, where she stopped. She glanced back at the winding paths and knotted branches and leaves. How could she create something like this and not even save a little girl? She could have—she felt it in the palm of her hands. The child's life was there, begging her for help. She could still feel it, a distant patter that she had pleaded with to stay alive.

But the idea of playing god scared her, and she let the child's life crumble in her hands.

Just like she did with her grandpapa all those years ago.

She had the ability to create and destroy. Even now, with a single flick of her wrist, she could destroy her palace, her artwork, and everything in between.

Let everything crumble.

Including herself.

She shook the idea away and entered her suite. After kicking off her boots and checking that Brent hadn't left any notes in the notebook, she collapsed on the bed, pulling her pillow close. Another cramp reached for her ribs and swallowed, staring instead at her empty hand. There, she let a single camellia bloom before letting it wither.

It didn't matter what she did. She could build a kingdom, but it didn't matter.

How long could this be sustained? Sooner or later, she would be stopped. Suffocated. Eliminated.

Sure, she was the Forest Queen.

But everything she planted would die if she dared look away.

So why close her eyes?

Why bother to sleep?

Even if it meant a moment of peace?

Her eyes drooped as she pulled the pillow tighter.

Why bother to do any of this if everything wilted?

She was a tree.

And camellias rained from her hair.

The forest she stood in basked in the sunlight, and for the first time in a long time, everything was peaceful.

Everything was quiet.

And she could breathe.

She laughed, but her laughter was the wind.

And the wind carried the leaves, the pollen, and the butterflies to freedom. She could control everything with a breath. From her spot in the forest, she could sense everything; she could taste life, curl away from death, and embrace the Mist.

And when the Mist finally came, in an incandescent exhale, she welcomed it with a whistling song.

But its colors soon dissipated, filled with a void of yellow.

And out of it emerged a shadow holding an ax.

"Hello, Briannabella," it hissed.

The wind bellowed around her, but she couldn't speak.

The figure approached, its shadow unrecognizable, but the voice carving...

Twisting...

Confusing...

"It's a shame...you are nothing but a useless, empty tree." The shadow hissed. "You cannot fight—nor will you ever win."

Another gust of wind acted as her reply.

"Give up. It's the easiest option." The shadow raised its ax.

She couldn't move.

Nor cry.

And the ax slammed into her trunk.

"NO!" she screamed as she woke. Sweat coated her body.

She sat up, pulling her knees to her chest. The orange glow of dusk painted her room.

She wiped her eyes, then glanced at her branched hand. *I'm still human...right? I'm not a tree...I'm still human...*

As she swung her legs out of bed, another sharp pain ripped through her abdomen.

And behind her, blood stained her bed sheet rather than sap.

CHAPTER TWENTY-FOUR

THE ODD COUPLE

Todd sat at the table with the blinded man. Neither spoke nor left. Sure, Todd learned there had been others blinded, but he brushed it to the side as coincidence. It had nothing to do with him—or with Garrett, for that matter.

But there was no denying that the man had a similar stare to Garrett. Unmoved. Vacant.

The only difference: the man's eyes remained, bleeding but in place.

His red eyes.

Like Lex's eyes.

The stalemate broke with a woman's voice. "Yeshua! There you are! What're you doing down here?"

The woman strode, a thing of beauty in the dim light. With her stunning heterochromatic eyes, it was hard not to admire her. She moved like fire and ice, bundled into one person, sifting across the floor of the tavern. If Todd believed in a god, he might have thought her a goddess. She was ethereal, magical, and without thinking, his mouth opened slightly in awe.

But then Lex's face filled his vision, and he turned back to his untouched mug of ale on the table. Garrett shifted slightly in his arms but still said not a word.

"I needed a change of scenery," the man mumbled to her.

"You could have waited for me, my love," the woman took the free seat beside Yeshua, "I am sure it was difficult coming down here, yes?"

"I still have my memories to guide me."

"I would have preferred you wait for me upstairs."

"I couldn't keep sitting with those other seers. They're not the most enlightening company."

"Have you tried making small talk?"

"I'd rather kiss Kek." The man reached forward, feeling along the table until his fingers wrapped around a glass of water. With a trembling hand, he raised it to his lips.

"Very well, I'll go order us another round then." the woman kissed the man's forehead, then glanced once at Todd. She raised her brow and asked, "You want anything?"

"I still got my glass," Todd mumbled.

"Yes, but it is lukewarm."

Todd glanced at his mug and scowled.

"Unless you like it like that, of course."

"I don't need another," Todd grumbled.

"Very well. What about the kid?"

Todd shifted Garrett onto his other knee. The child still did not react. "I don't know if he's hungry."

"I'll bring over some bread. He can snack on that if he wants," the woman winked with her shimmering blue eye, sending Todd's entire core somersaulting. Yes, she was stunning, and her voice reminded him of melted chocolate, but he knew better than to give in to temptation. Something so sweet always had its consequences.

Besides, whenever he blinked, he still saw Lex, with her skin glistening in the moonlight and platinum hair like the sea on a bright but cloudy day.

"You hungry, Garrett?" Todd asked his son.

To his dismay, there was no reply.

"How old is your son?" Yeshua asked, turning his chin up as if to get a better look.

"Oh, um," Todd counted on his fingers, "he turned five around Death's Mourn."

"Quiet for a kid his age."

"Yeah, well, he's not doing great. Been through a lot."

"Haven't we all?"

"You certainly have with your…well…you know."

"My eyes?"

"Uh, yeah."

Yeshua smirked, leaning back slightly in his chair. "Honestly, I have not been bothered much. It has been…freeing to not see everything all the time."

"Seems more like a burden."

"When you see as much as me, sometimes you struggle to differentiate good from evil."

Todd let the conversation end there, tracing his finger around his glass of ale. It no longer bubbled, a dull brown color mocking him. *Why do I always get stuck with these damn loons speaking in riddles?* Sure, people spoke in these riddles to hide from the Order, but in closed quarters? Why did it matter?

The woman came back over with a round of drinks and a loaf of bread. She dropped them on the table and then collapsed in the chair beside Yeshua.

The two spoke in a hushed tone, their language foreign. Todd grunted and broke off a piece of bread. Carefully, he placed it in Garrett's hands.

The child fumbled with the food, missing his mouth once, before finally resting the bread on his tongue.

"The child is blind," the woman remarked from across the table.

"You don't think I know that?" Todd spat.

"Of course, you know, but it was an observation, nonetheless." She leaned forward, grabbing one of her mugs and bringing it to her lips. "He's a seer, though, right? His eyes started to bleed randomly?"

"No, they were already cut out of his face. I've gone through this goddamn explanation already with Nils."

"His eyes were cut out?"

"Gisela, let it be," Yeshua grunted. "We agreed we would stay out of this from now on."

"We still have a duty," the woman hissed.

"No, we don't. We made our mistakes, and now we must lie in them."

"How many times have you said that before, my love?"

"All those other times I could *see*."

"But you can't see this time! This child's aura... It glows with your similar warmth. This child's a seer, just like you."

Not this again... Todd rose with Garrett in his arms.

"Wait!" Gisela rose with him.

"I'm not doing this. All you magic folk are all the same. My son's eyes were torn from his face by the Order, and he's traumatized. He's never gonna be himself again. It doesn't matter if he was a seer or something—he's nothing now."

"If the Order did something in regard to his magic, there may be a way to help him. I know someone—"

"Why would I trust you?"

Gisela didn't respond.

"C'mon, Garrett." Todd started to turn.

"Garrett?" Gisela rose as she spoke. "That means you're Lex's husband!"

Todd froze.

"We helped her escape Knoll before those vagrants attacked it. Ask her! She'll tell you about Yeshua and me."

"Well, I would…except she is dead."

"Dead…oh, I see." Gisela's face hardened. Beside her, Yeshua frowned.

Todd brushed off their woes. "Listen, I ain't putting my trust in any magic or bullshite like that. I'd rather seek out medical help. Nils mentioned a doctor—"

"Hue won't be able to help you," Yeshua said, attention latched to the wall. "There's another researcher, though…the one in the papers. She had an idea of how to help. Something to do with heightening the senses, but just as she was making a breakthrough, I lost communication with her."

Todd furrowed his brow. "You mean Nils's sister?"

"You know her?"

"Nils spoke to me about her."

"Unfortunately, I am unsure what happened, but…if anyone can help your son, it's her."

Todd huffed. From what Nils told him, his sister had been captured by the Order. But still, even if she had been researching these blind *seers*, how would that help Garrett? His eyes were cut from his head—there was no curing that form of blindness.

But perhaps she can help Garrett live again. The voice in his head sounded like Lex.

Would it be worth finding Nils's sister? If she could give Garrett a chance to *live*, then why not try? It would be difficult, frustrating, and perhaps fruitless. But...at least he would be able to fix something.

For once.

Without saying another word to the odd couple, Todd carried Garrett to the stairwell leading out of the speakeasy. He'd seen a few people already come and go from upstairs. The stairs creaked as he ascended them, and he winced as the door opened.

But unlike the previous speakeasy, this stairwell opened into a spacious tavern with shuttered windows and a bustling presence. No one flinched as he walked out of the kitchen and into the hallway, where he found Nils talking to an elderly woman in a rocking chair. The woman tapped on the arm of the chair when replying to Nils, her voice hoarse and jumbled.

"Oh, look! It's Scruffy!" Nils exclaimed as Todd entered.

"Scruffy?" Todd asked.

"Well, you never told me your name, so that's just what I've been calling you."

Todd groaned.

"What brings you out of the cellar, Scruff?"

"I ain't allowed to walk around a bit?"

"I don't know. I thought maybe you were a mole person."

"I like my fresh air," Todd replied. "Those basements wreak of sweat."

"Eh, better than blood."

"S'pose so."

Nils shrugged, then glanced at the elderly woman. "Doris here told me we got some transport arranged. We should be able to get you and your little man outta this cursed Capital soon."

"Oh…good." Todd adjusted Garrett slightly. The child showed no reaction to Nils's statement. He never showed any reactions. What sort of dream had he been locked into for this long? He knew he couldn't leave Garrett in this state permanently. But it was hard to know who to trust.

He'd trusted the wrong people more than once in his life. Could he dare risk it again?

"Have you…received any words on your sister?" Todd asked.

Nils raised an eyebrow. "Now you're interested in her?"

"You said she can help."

"You didn't seem all that interested in her."

"I've had…time to think." Todd chose each word carefully. "You said she was taken prisoner by the Order? Where to? The Capitol?"

Nils nodded.

Todd gritted his teeth. He'd spent time at the Capitol back before being reunited with Garrett. He and a handful of doubtful guards fled into the Witch Tunnels, leading out of the facility and into the depths of the city.

And these very tunnels could help anyone return to the Capitol as well.

Not that he ever thought of returning.

"I think I have an idea how we can rescue your sister," Todd said, his voice shaking.

"Really? How?"

"We use the Witch Tunnels."

"We've never found a way into the Capitol via the Witch Tunnels before."

"Just bring me a map, and I'll show you." Once again, he was a lieutenant in the Guard, demanding his subordinates to follow. In the Capitol, he had led the way into these very tunnels. He just had to remember that guise of command. He was, and always would be, a guard.

Whether he agreed with the Order or not, his life had been defined by them. He just had to find the right cause.

And as Garrett shifted again in his arms, wrapping his small fingers around Todd's collar, he knew what flag to fly.

It was the flag he should have flown back to Mert.

It was the flag he should have worn when Captain Carver demanded his obedience.

But now, he would fly it high and proud.

Everything for Garrett.

Everything for Lex.

Everything for his family.

LIKE A WORM

Chander sat cross-legged on his cot in the Pin-stripe Tavern. Yaz buzzed around the room, gathering her few belongings still in the room, her glasses nearly slipping off her nose. She babbled relentlessly about the school, the fear she had over her own vision of the Diabolo gone after just a couple of days. Since she arrived earlier that day, her excitement had been nonstop. But it did not infect Chander, staring at the wall, his hands laced together to avoid touching anyone.

He had hardly left the room since returning to the tavern. Timothée checked on him occasionally, and Anandi threw food into his doorway each morning and evening, but otherwise, he sat alone in silence. Sleep came in winks, waking whenever a new dream started, threatening to send him back into someone else's vision.

"Brent stopped by the school yesterday evening," Yaz babbled as she removed a bag from under her cot. As she spoke, she removed a variety of odd-shaped tchotchkes, wiping them with the sleeve of her shirt before returning them to her bag. "He said there's gonna be about a dozen or so more students joining you, me, and Milo. We're gonna have a real school!" Her eyes sparkled as she glanced up from the bag, a smile catching from cheek to cheek.

Chander feigned a smile. He hadn't the heart to tell her that he wouldn't be coming anymore.

Besides, it was his duty to protect Anandi. Not Yaz.

Yaz removed a flower from her bag and held it to the window. The white flower still had its perfect shape, petals wide and flourishing. She traced it with her finger, then planted it back in her bag.

"You still have that flower?" Chander asked.

"Yeah. Miss Bria said everything will be okay as long as the flower keeps blooming. So everything's gonna be okay." Yaz grinned at Chander.

He frowned. *If only it was that simple.*

Yaz buckled her bag and threw it over her shoulder. "I'm gonna go downstairs. Malaika is waiting for us. She said she'll bring us back to Neorama once you're ready."

"Yeah, okay," Chander squirmed. "I'll...um...I'll be down in a minute."

Yaz continued smiling as she hurried from the room, nearly tripping over her feet as she left.

Chander sank back onto his cot, pressing his head to the wall. He didn't dare shut his eyes. Every time he closed them, he still saw through Brent's vision. The man had woken in the Sanitorium a couple of days earlier, and between visiting with those spirits and his work in Ne-orama, the visions left Chander's head spinning. But he also worried about how much further he could carry his magic. If the wrong thought entered his mind, would it cause Brent to fall under his control again? Or, now that his mind was clear, would it be okay?

Chander didn't want to find out.

He laced his hands together and frowned. They were all waiting for him downstairs, and he couldn't hide up here forever. Through the walls, he could hear Timothée and Micca bicker as usual. Chander had given up on trying to figure out those arguments. Stress ran high through Mert. With Micca unclear about what happened to some of his friends and Timothée's fixation on a ghost child, it seemed as though the arguments would never end.

But that was a small price to pay to keep his magic quiet and Anandi safe.

He practiced different explanations for Yaz under his breath. "Sorry, Yaz, I gotta stay here. No… I'm sorry, but I won't be going to Neorama. I don't think it is the place for me. No, that's not it. I'm sorry, but…" He cursed. Yaz would pout the moment he explained this to her. Just like how Anandi pouted when he told her about Neorama.

What could he say?

"I'm sorry—"

"What are you mumbling under your breath about?"

Chander glanced toward the doorway. Anandi stood there, hands on her hips, a smudge of chocolate on her cheek. She wore her dark hair up in an intricate twist, like the Pinstripe Boss, Mitzi.

"Oh. Hi, Anandi," he mumbled as he turned back to the wall.

"Yaz is busy waiting downstairs. You going to keep her all day?"

"I'm not going to Neorama."

"Why? I thought you were excited about that." Anandi sat across from him on the other bed, kicking off her shoes so they flew across the room.

"I…I promised our grandfather I would protect you."

Anandi crossed her arms. "I don't need protecting."

"Yeah, but—"

"I don't need protecting," Anandi reiterated. "Mitzi has been teaching me all about how to shoot and everything."

"What!?"

"Don't worry, I don't have a real pistol...yet. She said I have to wait until I'm ten."

"Yeah, but Grandpa wouldn't like that!"

"Grandpa's not here! Besides, I don't have magic like you...I need to find other ways to protect myself. And Mitzi has been really awesome; she teaches me all about these Pinstripes and everything. It's where I wanna be."

"Then I'll stay here with you."

"No."

"Anandi!"

"This is mine, Chander. You have your stuff at that magic school that Yaz keeps talking about."

"But—"

"No. I don't want you here, Chander." Anandi straightened her apron. "Besides, you seem happier lately."

"What do you mean?"

"I don't know. You seem more like yourself or something...like from when we lived with Grandpa. So I think that school is probably good for you."

Chander shook his head. "No, it's not."

"Why not?"

"Because...I..." he chose his words carefully. "I'm scared."

"Why?"

"Because of what it will teach me. What if I become a monster?"

"You're already a monster."

"Wha—what?"

"I'm joking!" Anandi laughed, a high-pitched noise that used to annoy Chander but now made his chest ache. "You're my brother, so you're always a monster to me. But a real monster? Nah. You're too lame for that."

"Yeah...but you don't know what happened."

"I don't care. You're not a monster. Maybe a creature, like a worm or something, but not a monster." Her smile faded, and then she said, "Monsters live in shadows. I feel like if you hide in this room, you will become a monster. Just like that giant moth we raised in our bedroom back home, remember?"

Chander could recall it at once. He had been around Anandi's age when he brought a brightly colored caterpillar into their room. They raised it under their cot, building a home for it out of twigs and broken glass. One day, it cocooned itself between two branches, where it slept for weeks.

When it finally emerged, it was not the beautiful butterfly they had expected but a large, grotesque moth that their grandfather had to chase from their room.

"When did you get so wise?" Chander asked.

"When I turned nine," Anandi grinned again.

Chander smiled back, an easy smile that he hadn't felt in quite some time. He opened his arms and allowed Anandi to hug him. Her hair smelled like the kitchen flame rather than soot and dust. There was a change in her since they had arrived. Perhaps these Pinstripes were right for her. At least they gave her a home and a purpose, something Chander could never provide.

"So you're gonna get out of here?" Anandi asked as she released Chander.

"Yeah, but I'm gonna send you letters and visit, you hear? You're not getting rid of me that easily."

"Next time you see me, I'll be running the Pinstripes."

"I doubt that."

"You never know. Mitzi's getting me an official suit next week. I'll be the youngest Pinstripe ever!"

Chander laughed. He had never imagined his little sister as a part of some gang, but here she was, fully indoctrinated.

And safe.

That was the most important thing.

She was safe.

Chander met Yaz and Malaika by the bar, where they snacked on a small bowl of pretzels. Anandi held his hand as he approached them, like they used to do when they were little. They'd stopped by Timothée and Micca's room so Chander could say goodbye. Timothée sent him off a pat on the shoulder, all while Micca snuck a pack of smokes into his bag. Chander thanked them both, but before they had even closed the door, Anandi snatched the smokes out of the bag and tossed them into a closet.

"Those were mine!" Chander hissed as they left the stairwell and approached the counter.

"They're not good for you!"

"Yeah, but I'm your older brother!"

"But I got a pistol."

"Not yet!"

"But I will," she grinned as she released his hand. Chander reveled in her touch for a moment. His younger sister had matured beyond his imagination.

Would he be able to grow like she had?

At the counter, Anandi smiled one last time at Chander, waved once at Yaz, then headed behind the counter to complete her duties.

"What was taking so long, Chander?" Yaz asked, mouth full of pretzels.

"I was getting my bag together and saying goodbye to Anandi." Chander shifted the small paper bag in his arm. It didn't contain much — a few tunics and a pair of socks — but it belonged to him.

"That's all you have?"

"Most of our stuff was Anandi's."

"Oh," Yaz jumped from her stool. "Well, we can go now, right!?"

"Yeah, yeah, we can go," Chander glanced once into the kitchen. *Anandi's gonna be fine.* He closed his eyes for a second. His vision had been replaced with Anandi's as she gathered ingredients from the cupboard, going about her business with her head held high.

"There's no rush," Malaika added at last, knitting a map together with the Mist. "Brent just left the Sanitorium with the others."

"But then we can meet up with them!"

"You're right, we can." Malaika let the Mist dissipate, then, with a wave, led Yaz and Chander from the tavern. Chander paused at the entranceway, glancing one last time past the groups of Pinstripes and back toward the kitchen. *I'll see you soon, Anandi.*

It was a promise to himself more than anything. He would not disappear from his sister's life.

Yaz returned to her chattering, telling Malaika about how she would decorate her room at the school. Chander hadn't even thought of his room—but now, it was real. He was going to have a *home* with his own room above a schoolhouse where he might learn how to harness the Mist.

Well, assuming Brent would still be willing to teach him.

He stayed behind Malaika and Yaz as they arrived in the plaza. While yellow smoke continued to haunt Mert, the outlines of airships remained high in the sky, hovering over the yard beyond the City Hall. Malaika scanned them with a scowl.

"Still no sign of my *Mystical Cheer*," she grumbled. "I swear, Zephyr better gobble up that damn pirate when I find her."

Chander exchanged a glance with Yaz. She shrugged, her attention turning to the far end of the plaza.

"Oh! Look!" she pointed.

There, Brent led an entourage out of the alley from the Sanitorium with his dog on his heels. He took each step with care, wincing as he leaned on his cane. Tomás and Jewel walked beside him. While behind them, Milo led a group of spirits. Chander and Yaz both froze. The spirits stumbled, eyes hanging from their sockets, mouths lopsided, and their feet clunking along the pavement. With their graying skin, they looked more like mist than human.

Yaz gulped.

"Did you know that he was bringing those things?" Chander asked under his breath.

"No. I just knew he had more students." Yaz clutched her bag tighter.

Chander placed his hand above her shoulder.

But Yaz shook it off, and with her bag tight in her hands, she approached the group of spirits. Chander froze as she neared the first one, a frail thing with long, graying hair and wide green eyes.

Yaz's hand visibly shook as she held it out to the creature. "Hi, my name is Yasmin, but you can call me Yaz."

The spirit's lips curved into a misshapen smile.

Then, it took Yaz's hand and shook it.

THE SHIFT

Brent wrung his hands together, sitting at the front of his classroom with Nix at his feet. The spirits wove in and out of the chairs, marveling at their new home, while Yaz babbled with a couple of them. Chander had vanished upstairs to his room, leaving a noticeable void in the back of the classroom. But class was not in session; for now, it was a chance for everyone to adjust to their new home.

A yellow tinge crawled through the windows, coating the schoolroom with a mustard hue. *The Diabolo will be here soon.* Brent didn't need *his* Diabolo to know that much. Sooner than later, another Yellow Storm would rip through the plains, taking any trickle of magic in their palms.

He pressed his fingers along his knuckles, counting backward from ten to keep his mind at ease. Every time he blinked, the stories danced over his eyelids. He saw the history of this building or a haunting moment of Ningursu...or the conniving grin of the moon. Even the yellow glow from the Diabolo carried stories. Nonsensical tales about children singing to trees and men fighting talking pigeons. They wove together as if trying to communicate with his own Diabolo.

But instead, Brent just saw it all as clear as he saw the blackboard in front of him.

The unusual chattering between the spirits pulled him to the present. It didn't cease as Tomás entered the room, his gaze somber and his hands locked together.

"Julietta is set up in her room. I told her that this was a safe house for her to hide from Mitzi." Tomás said as he approached Brent.

"Did she believe it?"

"She believes Mitzi is out to get her, so yes...I think so." Tomás fidgeted. "I hate leaving her, but...I must stay in Mert. I'm placing my trust in you, Brent."

"Yeah, I know. I'm...I'm gonna get her back."

"At minimum, help her understand that she is dead. It has worked in the past with a less resilient version of herself."

"A'ight," Brent saw the story. Tomás had worked with Julietta on multiple occasions when her memory had vanished. But that was different; In those times, the essence of Julietta remained the same.

Jewel was someone else. Brent had to help her reconnect with her old stories.

"Good luck, Brent. I have my faith in you."

"You know, it doesn't sound good when a thousand-year-old Mist Keeper puts his faith in some twenty-three-year-old."

"You may physically be twenty-three, but you've collected stories from across centuries."

"Doesn't mean I know how to use it."

"I disagree. I've seen how your mind works."

Brent grimaced but didn't say anything else, walking with Tomás to the exit of the schoolhouse. Nix followed behind them. A few spirits cast glances in Brent's direction before returning to their indistinguishable dialogue.

He stood with Tomás at the exit of the school, staring down the single road at Neorama. A few ghosts chatted in the streets while Malaika conversed with Szyman by the odd metal box in the center of town. If Brent stared for too long, the stories began to bleed into the streets, blending with the dead and tugging him into the past.

Tomás turned to him, "I hope to join you here again soon. It is important that Varden heals first, though."

278

"I know," Brent replied.

"But I know you will do quite well."

"I hope so."

Tomás bowed his head, and then, with a gust of Mist, he vanished from beside Brent.

Part of Brent had always assumed Tomás would help with the school. With his centuries of knowledge and experience as a pupil in Ningursu and Aelia's school, it would have been a fantastic edition. Yet right now, with the war brewing and the sky boiling with yellow, his ideal school would have to wait. For now, it was about keeping the current students safe.

Far away from the Diabolo brewing on the horizon and the horrific stories threatening to repeat.

He joined Malaika and Szyman by the metallic control box. The two of them engaged in a conversation marked by laughter, and they both turned as Brent approached. Nix barked once to greet them.

"Is everyone ready?" Szyman asked.

"I think so, yeah."

"Good. It means we're ready."

"I'll see ya'll around then." Malaika placed her hands on her hips. "Gotta get out of here before you shift."

"Wait…you're not coming?" Brent asked. Did all these Mist Keepers really believe he could handle the school on his own?

"I'm just taking a different way. I hate the way this town moves. It makes me nauseous. Besides, someone's gotta fly Zephyr outta here. The dragon isn't gonna be able to handle this sort of shift like you can." Malaika motioned to the sky with her chin to where Zephyr circled.

"Oh…a'ight."

"Don't worry. I saw on the map where you're heading. I'll be there soon. Although, I may take a detour if Dee's intel pans out—she thinks she knows where my Mystical Cheer is. So I'm waiting for her message."

"I still do not understand how that works," Szyman remarked.

"My map has its ways of telling me things. Don't worry."

Brent frown.

"Oh, stop pouting. You've got a handle on this," Malaika said.

"I thought I'd have one of you helping me with this. It's…daunting, I mean…yeah, it's just kind of scary."

"Well, you got Caroline."

"No, she didn't commit."

"Then why is she here now?" Malaika nodded down the road.

Brent turned. Caroline, in her black cloak that stained the landscape, meandered in the street, staring up at the schoolhouse.

Malaika pressed her fingers to her mouth and whistled a high-pitched noise. Nix yelped, ears back as she darted behind Brent's legs.

But the noise did grab Caroline's attention, and with her usual determined stride, she approached them.

"Malaika, I have told you before…do not whistle for me like a dog," Caroline spat.

"Got your attention, though," Malaika said with a laugh.

Caroline rolled her eyes.

"Caroline!" Brent stepped forward. "I didn't…I mean…are you coming with us?"

"Someone has to teach all your students how to actually be a Mist Keeper," Caroline replied as she picked at her nails. "All this magic and other malarkey is great, but there is still a job to be done."

Brent couldn't help but smile. "Glad you finally came around."

"What are you implying? That I did not come up with this on my own?" She returned the grin. It was the first time in a while that Brent had seen Caroline smile. It brought back the churning fear he felt when he first met her, marked by a spectacular beauty. She was what he pictured when he imagined a Mist Keeper. Not Ningursu. Caroline—the loyal one, dressed in her blacks that never faltered from her duties.

"Well, there you have it, Brenty-boy—you get one of us. But now, I best be off. The dragon awaits!" Malaika saluted once, followed by a bow, before turning down the road.

Caroline shook her head as Malaika left. With their laughter and their smiles, a story flashed over Brent's eyes. It may have been fake, but in some ways, it was like looking into the future. His school, filled with life, and the Mist Keepers acting together to help the next generation. Caroline would once again garner her red lipstick while Malaika bounced between the classrooms with a new adventure on her lips.

But just as soon as the story arrived, it disappeared, a mere dream waiting in the shadows of yellow fog.

"Well, are we ready then?" Szyman asked Brent.

Brent glanced at Caroline. She shrugged.

"Uh yeah, we are," Brent turned back to Szyman. "What do you need from us?"

"I just need one of you to come with me—the other should take refuge indoors."

Caroline spoke before Brent could answer, "I volunteer to go inside. I would rather not be decapitated."

"You won't be decapitated," Szyman replied.

"I am not taking that chance."

"Suit yourself," Szyman turned to his metallic box and opened the large, hinged door.

"Nix, go with Caroline," Brent said to the dog.

"Oh, do not make me dog sit. I have never been good with animals," Caroline griped.

"You volunteered to go inside."

Caroline huffed and then waved for Nix to follow, leaving Brent with Szyman in the center of Neorama.

They waited a few moments for Caroline to venture into one of the nearby buildings, then entered the strange metallic box.

Brent had been in this box before, but it still captured him with awe. Filled with an array of odd gears and wires, mist intermingled with technology, with beeping and buzzing echoing around the box. Szyman went over to the central console and pulled a few levers, causing the gears to turn. The Mist churned with it, replicating the very movements, pulsating around Szyman and Brent.

As the gears clicked, metal shutters opened on each of the walls, peering out into Neorama.

"Listen, when I tell you, spin the dial on this compass here. I'll handle the rest," Szyman motioned to a compass on the console.

"A'ight," Brent took a seat by the console as Szyman stepped on the pedestal in the center of the room. He held out his hands, letting the Mist gather around him, trickling over his fingers.

He inhaled once, and the Mist shot out from each of his fingers through the open windows and into the streets of Neorama. Dust gathered with each gust, shooting around the foundation of each building and decorating the street in a kaleidoscope of colors.

Szyman pulled on the Mist, bringing each of the buildings closer. They towered over the box, threatening to trample over it, as the wind spun and the sky turned a coat of silver.

"Now," Szyman hissed between his teeth.

Brent fumbled with the compass, managing to turn the dial with a click.

And then, it was as though he was moving through the Mist, just as he had done in the Library. Around him, stories spun in all directions, capturing his attention with each flicker, like a moving picture on a screen. The stories intermingled with the ghosts, and the buildings themselves seemed to collapse as the Mist swayed.

Only to reconstruct themselves when the movement finally slowed.

Szyman lowered his hands, letting the Mist settle. Outside, the streets of Neorama returned to normal, their buildings in place, the road unchanged.

But instead of the Chessboard Plains, the cypress trees greeted them with a blanket of humidity.

DESTRUCTION

The nightmares kept getting worse. Every time Bria closed her eyes, the voices echoed, reciting the constant threats and calling her one formal thing: a monster. When she woke, her little branch sprouted more twigs, taking away from her humanity, while her abdomen cramped and her head seared with pain.

With sleep no longer her friend and what she could only assume was Ningursu's voice echoing in her ears, she left her private suite and ventured downstairs. Her energy kept her confined to her castle, exhaustion following her every step. As much as she wanted to travel to the next Pit, free another group of vagrants, or talk with Horton about the state of her little town, any time she dared near the exit of her palace, her entire body froze with pain.

Instead, she focused on adding accents to her palace, returning to the lavatory to create some sort of latrine. The rock still did not agree with her, breaking whenever she tried to create a curve. Brent's words repeated in her memory. She couldn't do this alone.

But she wanted to be alone.

No part of her yearned to speak with Marisol or listen to Edith's obnoxious antics. The nightmares gave her enough company, and instead, she felt herself struggling through each movement.

Is this what Brent feels like with his Diabolo? Bria couldn't help but wonder. Granted, it wasn't like the voices echoed in her head. It was more of a constant nagging, echoing the same words repeatedly.

Monster.

You are a monster.

You are not human.

Monster.

And like a monster in her palace, she lurked down into the Library, seeking out a quiet place to hide, away from anyone who might come searching. The refugees did not venture down into the Library. With stairwells blocked and an intricate atrium, any wandering attention was de-railed.

The Library was hers for the taking.

Yet, as she wandered down into the rows of muddied books, the confidence dwindled. Memories echoed through every corner. The magic she first felt upon entering the Library, with Brent's arm around her and a smile on his lips, had long disappeared. Instead, memories suffocated the magic: memories of the giant, Jiang, pushing her from the balcony, or to Alojzy forcing her to drink some strange liquid, to the battle that followed months later that left the Library as a swamp. They tainted paradise with a thick coating of secrets yet to be discovered.

She paused toward the back of the bookshelves, where red peonies puddled along the floor, stemming from a decrepit archway marred by roots.

The Pool... Bria froze, staring through the arch. She and Brent had used that very Pool to escape the Library. She couldn't destroy it at the time... but now...

She stepped through the archway. The once beautiful Pool, surrounded by red peonies, had grown murky and gray. Luminescent algae pulsated on the surface, clinging together to form what looked like small sea serpents shifting through the water.

How many lives has Ningursu destroyed with this very Pool? Bria approached the edge of the Pool, running her finger along the water. It didn't breathe with the same amorous aroma anymore, producing a cough of distaste at her touch.

Right here, this was the Pool, wasn't it? The one that impacted countless lives and destroyed countless stories?

She reached forward, searching along the surface of the liquid for any element. *Mercury, gold, tin, oxygen...* she pulled the list of elements from her memory, tugging at each one as it simmered beneath the surface.

And as the elements popped, the Pool sifted, giving birth to an explosion of peonies in its center. The magic within them trickled into the Library, blessing the walls with vines and giving green a chance to breathe.

Bria couldn't help but laugh. Finally, she had done it. The Pool was gone now! Ningursu wouldn't be able to use it any longer!

"You seem happy," a voice chided behind her.

Bria spun to face Edith, leaning against the archway, arms crossed, a smirk on her face.

"I destroyed the Pool... of course I'm happy," Bria replied.

"Yes, you destroyed a useless Pool. Congratulations."

"But isn't this *the* Pool? The one that started it all?"

"Do you honestly think Kek would give Ningursu access to the original Pool? Pfft." Edith chuckled to herself. "Now that is hilarious."

"But I thought—"

"You thought wrong. Kek keeps the Pool in a secure location. *I* don't even know where it is. They trusted only a few to defend it."

Bria scowled, staring at her bed of peonies on the Library floor. *Things are never so simple.* Of course she couldn't just waltz into the Library and destroy the Pool. That would be far too easy.

Bria changed the conversation, asking, "Why are you here, Edith?"

"I have a right to poke around this Library."

"Do you?"

"It's not like you own it. Besides...if you were me, wouldn't you want to discover some of Ningursu's secrets and whatnot?"

"Did you find anything?"

"Nah. Haven't found anything but that damn giant's wine stash." Edith crossed her arms. "It's good wine, I'll admit, but it doesn't help us in any way."

"What are you looking for exactly?"

"Oh, look at you being nosy."

"Just tell me."

Edith chuckled. "Nothing groundbreaking. Where Ningursu ran off to would be one thing. Been in contact with Kek, but apparently, there are no leads. That Mist Keeper with the maps is useless, too."

"Yes, I know. Brent already told me."

"Speaking of which…I've heard your Reaper has been having some issues."

"The stories are getting stronger for him."

"Yes. My understanding is that he thought he was Ningursu for a bit."

"Well, he saw Ningursu's story in the swamp—"

Edith cut her off, "No, there was another time in Mert. He got his head in a frenzy…thought he was both Ningursu and the moon for a bit."

Bria's heart sank. She hadn't heard anything about Mert.

"Oh, you hadn't heard? I thought you two had some telepathic connection," Edith taunted.

"Be quiet," Bria hissed.

"Guess you two are losing your touch."

"Just because we're not talking all the time doesn't mean we are losing each other. We are in a war, Edith."

"And war destroys people," Edith leaned forward so her breath hit Bria's face. It wreaked of wine.

"Go away, Edith," Bria whispered. "I want to be alone."

"Oh, did I hit a nerve?"

"You always do."

"As long as it keeps you thinking. The last thing we need is a resigned queen."

Bria glowered at Edith. The woman cackled, removing a small stone from the archway. In her palm, she formed a small knife, which she spun in her fingers once before letting it clatter to the floor. The laughter only continued as she left the doorway, disappearing back into the Library. Bria sank at the edge of the dismantled Pool, staring into the murky water, where the red petals gathered. She traced them with her fingers. *Edith is just trying to get to you. She doesn't even want you to destroy the Pool. Why would she? It benefits her plenty.* But as Bria sat there, the words etched into her mind, reciting over and over again an inconvenient truth.

She had resigned herself to one duty, one destiny, but she was no closer to solving any problems. While Bria doubted that she would ever stop the casualties happening in Rosada, at least not alone, she had yet to make any progress in finding Ningursu or helping Brent. What good was constantly saving people if the world continued to suffocate in yellow?

What kind of queen just let the earth cry?

At least now, as she sank against the vine-covered wall, the earth did not cry for her. Instead, it sang a quiet tune, reminding her where she came from and where she would always return.

This time, she stood on a mountain, staring over Newbird's Arm. It was exactly as she remembered it, with its bustling market, spired temple, and dusty Pit. Home. Excitement gathered in her chest. She was home!

But, as she took a step forward, the ground rumbled. The trees blew. And the clouds gathered.

She froze. A voice whispered in her ear.

"Now, Briannabella."

"No."

"Let it all out."

"No!" Her voice ruptured the earth. Around her, the ground cracked. Steam gathered. Heat pulsed.

And as if she was a dragon, fire escaped her lips, shooting across the mountain.

Burning…

Moving…

Down…

The trees disintegrated. The grass charred.

And Newbird's Arm was no more.

"Good girl." The voice cooed.

"No…no…I didn't mean to do this…" she sobbed. With the sob, tears followed.

"This is your destiny. The only way to stop all of this. Destroy everything that threatens you."

"No!" She spun around to confront the voice.

But she was met with only smoke.

She woke abruptly, lying face-down against the red flowers. Her branched arm extended, crawling across the floor, lacing into the walls. As she rose, the branch snapped, causing dagger-like pain to shift through the arm and into her shoulder. She cursed, curling her knees against her chest and lowering her head into them. *It wasn't real. It was just a dream.* Was it, though? If she went home right now, would she discover it ablaze?

She closed her eyes. Still, she could see the town, as vivid as her dream, surrounded by flames.

"It's just my imagination. It has to be..." she whispered aloud. She hugged her knees tighter with her good arm, letting her branched hand reform one twig at a time.

Bria didn't dare close her eyes again. It would be easy now to let the peonies surround her, to sink into the earth's core. At least then, she couldn't harm anyone.

And the earth didn't dream. Not like this, at least. Instead, the earth flourished, letting the seasons bloom with each breath.

A soft tapping on the archway caught her attention. She raised her head.

-... .-. ... .- *Bria.*

"Hi, Brent." She removed the notebook from her coat pocket and placed it on the ground next to her. The peonies curled around each of Brent's steps. They flattened beside her where he sat.

She held out her half-formed hand. As he took it, her fingers extended, tracing around his hand and up his arm. She didn't tell them to stop until they traced the outline of his jaw. It was tempting to have the branches keep going, to fully outline his body, so for once, he would be there, in full, beside her.

But it would just be an illusion.

What's wrong? Brent wrote in the notebook.

She stared at the words. A tear fell down her cheek, hitting the page.

Bria?

She shook her head, choking on her words as she spoke, "I've been having nightmares. Vivid, horrible nightmares. I was destroying Newbird's Arm in the last one."

Brent didn't write anything at first. The root along his face shifted as if he were furrowing his brow.

Then, he wrote, *Did you finish the dream?*

"What? No… I woke up. I was terrified."

You need to finish the dream.

"Brent, this isn't one of your stories!"

But it is similar. If you finish the dream, make yourself the hero, then you can rest again. You know what I mean?

"Not really."

Just close your eyes… give it a try.

"I'm not a storyteller, you know this."

Just try.

Bria grumbled but still obliged. As her eyes fell closed, once again, she saw Newbird's Arm set ablaze. *It's just a dream*, she reminded herself. But if she was there in person, what would she do to extinguish the flames? How would she save her home?

Rain. It was a simple thought, a single image crossing her mind. But with that one idea, the image in her head shifted, and the clouds moved in across the town. With an exhale, the rain fell, suffocating each plume of fire and smoke, stopping the flames before they ransacked the town.

She opened her eyes, and once again, she sat in the peonies with Brent.

Better? Brent wrote.

She nodded.

Just remember, it was a dream. You're not destroying Newbird's Arm.

"I know…but…it was just so vivid…like I was there. And there was a voice…I think…it sounded like Ningursu's voice. But a bit different, too. It's hard to describe."

Ningursu's voice? A dot of ink punctuated the statement, bleeding into the paper before Brent wrote. *Well,*

Bria almost laughed and leaned into the branch wrapped around Brent's shoulder. A single breeze caught her hair, sending a strand whipping across her face.

And with it, she once again heard Ningursu's voice, cooing in her ear, a faint whisper.

Briannabella.

CHAPTER TWENTY-EIGHT

THE STORIES OF THE LIBRARY

Brent lay in the flowers with Bria, keeping his root-covered hand laced around her. She drifted in and out of a half-sleep, waking abruptly as her dreams danced into her unconscious mind. All the work she was doing had caught up with her. Ever since he met Bria, determination and righteousness coursed through her veins. A memory floated into his mind of Bria arguing with a few children who insisted that Brent play the "evil vagrant" in their game of Guards-and-Vagrants. Despite Brent accepting the role, Bria insisted that it was "mean."

It was with that same guile that Bria had built her story.

Now, it had caught up with her, though, and she sank into the flowers under the weight of her own story.

Sleep did not come Brent's way either. Nix had followed him from Neorama to the Library and spent her time running through the flowers, chasing the petals that dared to fall from the stems. The dog seemed unphased by the sudden relocation of the town.

After arrival, Brent checked briefly on the school, swallowing his own nausea. A few of the spirits held their heads in pain, while others seemed unphased. Yaz and Chander both lay in their rooms, fighting off headaches.

The worst was Caroline, who had vomited profusely. She didn't stay around to help clean, leaving a few of the ghosts to clean her mess while she marched off into the swamp.

Once the initial wonder of Neorama's movement, positioning it well at the edge of the swamp, wore off, Brent hurried to Bria's palace, where he found her by the dried Pool. Or the Divitiae, as Kek called it.

He groaned as he rolled onto his side. The pain from the ongoing rot gnawing into his stomach had progressed, siphoning his energy and leaving his body weak. He lifted the edge of his tunic to check the wound. The black tendrils climbed from his abdomen up toward his chest like branches of a tree. With each new branch, it was as though the stories grew stronger.

Now, lying by the Pool, he couldn't help but sift through the stories to pull apart the repetitive tales of

Ninguru, Tomás, Alojzy, Aelia, and even Jiang visiting the Pool. They would gather liquid, speak into the Pool, or pick peonies. Nothing ever changed. The same story, retold, in a different light.

Well, until there was a shift. Brent could not tell how far back he looked nor how many centuries had passed. But this story was different.

This time, Alojzy approached the Pool with Ningursu in his hands. They stood beside it, speaking in hushed tones that pulled Brent up from the ground. He approached the story with care, letting it take him hostage and into the past.

"So this is it then?" Alojzy asked Ningursu.

"It is."

"It is smaller than I imagined."

"Because it is not the original. It's the portion I stole from Kek years ago. I hid it here, deep beneath the swamp. The Mist has provided a barrier so Kek cannot discover it."

"I see," Alojzy said. "So Aelia uses this very Pool to lock away those monsters?"

"Not just lock them away… but to create them. That is why the crypt you are building is key. We will be able to create an army for the inevitable day we must engage in battle with Kek once more."

Alojzy wrinkled his nose, his brow furrowed, and eyes nar-rowed. "Is Kek really that dangerous? After all these years, I am astonished they have not tried to attack you again."

Ningursu stared forward, locking eyes with the Pool. His lip twitched.

"Right now, Kek does not threaten me. But there could be someone in the future, someone who Kek takes under their wing, who may be stronger than we could imagine. That is why I need this protected, so I can stop that from ever occurring."

"And how will you do that?" Alojzy asked.

"I'll show you. Let us return to my study."

The story faded as the past versions of Ningursu and Alojzy left the room. Brent stepped forward, only for Bria to shift on the ground beside him.

"Brent?" She rubbed her eyes.

He grabbed the notebook lying beside him and scrib-bled, *There's a story. I need to follow it… I think it might help.*

"What is it?"

Something with Ningursu.

"Okay…be careful."

I'm going to Ningursu's office if you want to come with me.

Together, they left the Pool and reentered the Library. Nix ran ahead, weaving between the shelves, while Brent tapped on the shelves every few steps, letting Bria know where he walked. He checked every few moments that she stood near him, sifting past the stories to bring himself back to the present. As he reached the stairwell, he paused, taking in Bria as she stood beside him. She was still the most stunning individual he'd ever seen, with her freckled face and oak-colored eyes. Even when he was betrothed to Jemma Reds and tried his hardest to force himself to fall out of love, it wasn't possible. Bria Smidt was his constant, and even though he missed the way she used to smile, the way her laugh used to make her eyes light, she was still the woman he loved.

"Brent?" Bria asked at the foot of the stories. "You stopped. Is everything okay?"

-.—. ... / ... —- .-. .-. -.— Yes. Sorry.

He continued up the stairwell, following the story. It led him exactly where it said it would, back to Ningursu's office. Around it, other tales dared to tug at his attention. Tales of Caroline, Aelia, and Tomás visiting the office. But he kept his eyes locked ahead, fixated on Ningursu and Alojzy as they entered Ningursu's study.

The study itself had been emptied. Its once glorious fixtures, with carved bookshelves, plush sofas, and a disorganized desk, had vanished just like Ningursu. Only an empty basin remained where the Pool had evaporated, leaving behind nothing but a single wilted flower.

Brent reached his hand out to Bria. Her branched hand detected it at once, sending twigs around his fingers. He held it tight as the story returned to him, sending him back into the past once again.

Alojzy sat across the desk from Ningursu, hands on his lap, while the skull sat perched on his cushion.

"Did you lock my door?" Ningursu asked.

"It is bolted shut," Alojzy replied.

"Good," Ningursu closed his one eyelid. For a moment, he sat without speaking, lost in his own thoughts. "Tell me, Alojzy, what do you know about Effluvia?"

"Effluvia?"

"I apologize, I mean Rosada. I keep forgetting that its name changed."

"Rosada…" Alojzy recited to himself. "I do not know much about it. It was never on my radar when I was alive."

"As I expected. Rosada has never been a partner or foe beyond the Schanifeld. But that is all well and good." Ningursu opened his eye again and smiled. "Rosada has been a project of mine for centuries."

"Pardon?"

"A few centuries ago, we took a powerful Mist Keeper as an apprentice. Odo Othar was his name, and he had the ability to create Diabolo and monsters with a flick of his finger. I saw him as a tool to suffocate magic. With Aelia by his side, he obtained a powerful position in Tencauri, out in Yilk. Everything seemed to

be going well until an army slaughtered him, and he succumbed
to his own terrors."

"So he is in the crypt now?

"Yes, he has gone mad. I hope to one day transform him into
a Diabolo if he is well enough. But yes, he is in the crypt."

Alojzy scowled and asked, "What does this have to do with
Rosada?"

"Ah, that is the question I was waiting for," Ningursu replied. "You see, Odo had twin daughters from his first
marriage… Rose and Ada. After their father went mad, they fled
the country, sailing across the sea to the land of Effluvia. They
settled there with a small army, where they established their new
home in a place they called Ab Aeterno.

"Now, I'd been watching Rose and Ada for many moons as I
kept tabs on them after their father's demise. Upon their arrival,
they sent their armies to explore the land, and in turn, I sent Mist
to follow them, with a message echoing through it. I gave them
warnings about magic, told them stories that needed to be followed, and promised them paradise here in Effluvia.

"They told what they learned to Rose and Ada, and the two
sisters used that knowledge to form their new rule. They had
three simple orders: no magic, no stories, and no silver eyes like
their father. The last one was not anything I told them, but I suppose Odo Othar's silver eyes haunted them, so they carried it
with them to their new country."

Alojzy nodded once, "I see. So, I imagine you are still in communication with the leaders of Rosada?"

"I communicate to their powerful religious group, the Order of the Effluvium, using that very Pool we saw below. It is paramount to keeping everyone obeying me because why should they disagree with a holy pool?"

Alojzy nodded again, "Very well. I understand. Thank you for telling me this, sire."

"I only tell you because I trust you to assist in this duty. For this war is one that will not end anytime in the near future."

The story shifted, and Brent stumbled backward, standing again in the office. He turned toward Bria, only for an onslaught of stories to enter through the doorway. Brent's head spun as he latched onto one of Caroline storming into Ningursu's office.

The door flew open, and Caroline rushed inside the room, "Ningursu!"

The head lifted from the table, eyes narrow. "Caroline, you know that you are supposed to knock."

"Sorry, sir, I apologize, but this is of the utmost importance."

"And what is that?"

"A boy saw me today! I do not know what he is—he certainly was not a seer! He did not have the classic red eyes. I promise, sir, I did not make myself visible. He just… saw me."

"I see. And where did you meet this boy?"

"In some small town in Rosada. Newbird's Arm, I believe."

"Newbird's Arm..." Ningursu shifted to address his ghost, Nedo, sitting on the far side of the room. "Nedo! Bring me to the basin."

The ghost obliged without speaking, lifting Ningursu from his spot on the desk and carrying him across the room to the basin.

Ningursu peered inside, "Newbird's Arm... there was no one there who had caught my attention."

"What do you mean, sir?" Caroline asked.

"I keep an eye on all potential Mist Keepers, but I did not notice any developing in Newbird's Arm. Quite odd that one developed like this..." Ningursu licked his lip as the liquid churned before him. "Brenton Rob Harley. I never saw him before." Ningursu glanced back at Caroline, "Keep an eye on him. He is one to watch."

The scene shifted before Brent could look away from it.

Aelia now sat before Ningursu, a ghostly child cradled in her arms. She spoke in a low tone, punctuating each statement with a sharp tongue. "He released this child, Master. It was a powerful release... One that I had not seen before. It wiped him off his feet."

"Yes, he released a soul. That is the task of a Mist Keeper, Aelia," Ningursu said without even a smile.

"This was different. I interviewed a few ghosts in the area. There was a flood of energy that escaped him, and as he released the soul, the Mist changed around him. I worry, Master, that he might be too powerful."

"Then we must force him into submission… or failure."

"Understood, but…" Aelia bit her lip.

"Yes?"

"You must know, Master, Alojzy discovered that Brent has been interacting with a Magii in the tunnels."

"The tunnels?"

"Yes…it seems one has entered our domain."

"I see." Ningursu closed his eye. "Tell Alojzy to unlock the cellar. He'll know what I mean."

"Yes, of course, Master."

"And Aelia?"

Aelia paused as she rose, the child in her arms.

"Get rid of that girl. What's her name? Maija?"

"Yes, Master. I understand."

"Good. We do not need this young apprentice flaunting his successes."

Aelia bowed, then left the room with the ghost child in her arms.

"Maija..." Brent stepped through the doorway after the story. Maija had been his first release. He had almost forgotten about her. What became of her? Was she one with the mist? Or had something else happened?

Something worse?

He glanced down the hallway, wide-eyed and searching for the story.

But another one entered his view.

Aelia walked with Ningursu in her arms, each step slow and delicate. Ningursu coughed once, a plume of black smoke exiting his lips.

"Master, I am fearful that you are losing stability. You need to find another way to survive."

"Brenton will be ready soon."

"What if he isn't? He is much more of a fighter than we initially thought."

"Then I will use other bodies to contain me. But I do not see Brenton as being strong enough to resist. Once I eliminate that Diabolo of his, then the stories will overwhelm his psyche. He will not be able to survive."

"Are you sure?"

"If not, I have identified temporary vessels, giving us time to devise a plan. Alojzy has already prepared a haven to keep my soul secure." Ningursu turned his head toward Aelia. "Do not

fret, my child. We will survive this together. You, Alojzy, and me… we are the Council of Mist Keepers.”

“Not Jiang, sir?” Aelia asked.

“Jiang is an imbecile. His trust could be easily severed by a few inconvenient truths.”

“We’ve kept those secrets long enough. I doubt Jiang will ever learn the truth.”

“We can only hope,” Ninguru replied. “Now come, we must prepare.”

Brent stumbled back again. More stories danced across his vision. They didn’t stop, bombarding him with new facts and names. He sank to his knees, gasping for air, begging for silence.

“Brent!?” Bria joined his side. She extended her arm, letting it wrap around him until she managed to find his hand. “What’s wrong?”

He tapped on the ground with his free hand. ... —- / — .- -. -.— *So many.*

“Stories?”

-.— . ... *Yes.*

Bria squeezed his hand tighter. “Come on then. Let’s leave the Library. Get some fresh air. Okay?”

—- -.- *OK.*

Using Bria's roots for stability, Brent climbed to his feet. His entire body shook as the stories continued to cross his vision.

If he didn't leave them soon, he very well may become no different from the books remaining on the shelves. A resource of history.

And a book with secrets scribbled on its pages.

CHAPTER TWENTY-NINE

WHERE THE FOREST QUEEN MUST GO

Bria navigated Brent back into her palace, sitting him down in the large dining room. She found another notebook for him, where he scribbled his discoveries in frantic chicken scratch. His hand shook under the clinging roots as he described Ningursu's puppeteering of the Order, as well as the distaste they had at Brent's first arrival to the Council. He proceeded to detail how Ningursu was also weak and in search of a vessel to carry him into the next era. While Brent had known about Ningursu's attempt to take his body, it seemed the realization was all the worse.

I know it's important to understand the past, but each story is demolishing me. I feel like I'm turning into a collection of debris. Brent wrote on the page.

"You shouldn't absorb this many stories at once. You need time to process what you learned," Bria whispered. She was still trying to comprehend each of Brent's discoveries.

How much time do we have to process this information, though? That's what I'm wondering. Brent wrote.

"I am, too," Bria replied. If they had an eternity, they might have been able to spend years writing a story, dictating the past. But as they sat in stalemate, waiting, time ticked.

Tocked.

Ticked.

We need to understand the past to save the present. Brent punctuated the statement. He didn't elaborate, a single thought hanging in the air.

But it sank into Bria, a firm reminder of the truth.

Truth she had long ignored.

Her whole life, it had been a question: why. Why was she able to master the flowers and the trees? Why didn't anyone tell her the truth of her past? Why did she get buried in the Senator's Garden the day of her birth?

Why?

Now, the answers were within reach. She had learned about her Nanni Safiyyah and her Grandpapa Tulio last time she visited Newbird's Arm. A perfect storm of magic circled her birth, and with it, her powers grew.

But even with those circumstances, a deep-rooted history hid in her blood. One that she could not answer by staring at a tree or listening to Brent's stories.

Answers waited for her abroad.

"I have stories I need to learn too..." she finally remarked.

Which ones? Brent asked. She had already told him about her grandparents, but now the story sat there at the forefront of her mind.

"What you said made me remember the story...because you're right...the only way to understand our present is to learn our past. So... I think I need to go to São Caméliosa. Where my grandpapa was born." She picked at the twigs sprouting from her hand. "I don't know what I'll learn down there... but... I think it might help me."

I know it will help you.

Bria stared at his words. Honestly, it hadn't crossed her mind since she spoke to her grandpapa's ghost, but now, it seemed like the only answer. Especially after everything she had seen over the last couple of days. She couldn't keep hiding from her story anymore.

Her next statement came with a quiver in her voice, "But... I also need proof I'm not a monster... and... I don't know. Something is telling me... I need to go down there now."

Do what you need to do. Brent paused for a second, his pen dripping on the page, before writing. *Do you want me to come with you?*

Bria shook her head. "No. Do what you need to do with your school and Ningursu. I need to go down there alone."

I understand.

Bria didn't expect any other answer. She leaned into the branches wrapped around Brent's arms, pressing her head against where they met his shoulder. It was the closest they could touch, and Bria had no intention of releasing him. If she focused hard enough, she swore she almost heard his voice, catching the wind in a gentle whisper. "I love you," it hissed, but it may have been her imagination.

She stayed leaning against him for a time. But in the back of her mind, a voice echoed, distant and taunting. Was it her own inner demons or something else whispering to her, *How can a kind man love a monster like you?*

No. She couldn't let that voice win. Their shared feelings had never been something she questioned. Why should she start now?

Brent's branch-covered hand shifted, reaching for her face. Bria leaned in as he cupped her cheek, running a finger across her lips. She exhaled, leaning forward, her body inclined for a kiss. But none came. What would someone think about the scene? It would look preposterous.

And they both knew it.

Brent's hand fell away, and a new sentence danced on the page. *When sight is finally restored, I'm never letting you go again.*

"We do need some personal space," Bria chided.

Nope. Never.

She imagined him smiling as he wrote it.

"You'll have to let go of me sometime. You have a school to teach."

Yeah, right, I do. There was a pause before another sentence. *I should probably head back soon. They're probably looking for me.*

"I'll come with you. I know I won't be able to see anything, but…I want to make sure you get back okay."

Yaz will be happy to see you.

"Oh, I'm sure."

She picked up the notebook and, with her branched hand, wrapped her fingers around Brent's hand. If she didn't look, she could pretend he was right there with her, walking side-by-side. But the silence that came with it was obvious. Even when they used to sit together in comfortable silence, at least Brent's breathing reassured her. Now, it was nothing but wind.

They left the palace, greeting the early evening glow of the vermillion swamp. Horton sat with the children, telling stories and laughing, while other refugees gathered in the makeshift homes. A few glanced in Bria's direction, including, to her surprise, Hue, who sat on a nearby log conversing with a few others.

"Ah, Bria!" Hue stood as Bria approached. "Just the person I wanted to see."

"Hue, when did you get here?" Bria let the little branch recede from Brent's arm.

"Marisol brought me here. I wanted to see where we were sending all of our people."

"Oh! Is Marisol here?" Bria asked. *She might want to see Neorama.* The mere thought hit her with a wave of unexpected jealousy, but she swallowed it. What Marisol could see was not in her control—there was no reason to hold an umbrella of disdain over their relationship.

"No, she is saying goodbye to Jeremy. He's leaving for Aeterno Village tomorrow."

"She was telling me about that," Bria replied.

"Oh really?" Hue asked, "Did she tell you anything else?"

"Only that you had a plan."

"I see. Well, that plan is exactly what I want to talk to you about. Do you have a moment?"

Bria glanced beside her. In the dirt, Brent etched the word, *Yes.*

"I have a few minutes," Bria said.

"Good, sit." Hue motioned her to the log.

Bria obliged.

The woman flexed her fingers, then said, "I received word from our contacts in Siskin's Corner. They looked into the factory you destroyed."

"They did?"

"That specific factory was responsible for assembling panels for some sort of weapon. My source doesn't quite know what weapon, but it was definitely a weapon. They are thinking something along the lines of an explosive device. The children were responsible for painting identification numbers on the panels. Nothing that important, but by destroying that factory, you set their weapon development back at least a few weeks... if not longer."

"That's good then, right?"

"It's quite good, but we must use this window to act fast," Hue said. "While we have Jeremy and a few others infiltrate the Order, we need to hit them where it hurts."

"I'm not following," Bria's body tensed. She could almost sense what Hue would say next.

"We need to destroy every factory, every government center, as fast as possible. We have some weaponry... but

Bria, you're the one who can act the fastest. It took you all of five minutes to destroy that factory… and back in Knoll, you took the tower down without much trouble at all. You could—"

Bria rose abruptly, "Absolutely not."

"Bria!"

"I'm already branded a terrorist."

"Exactly! What do you have to lose…you might as well live to your name."

"What do I have to lose?" Bria leaned forward, the wind picking up behind her. The swamp water bubbled at her feet. "Everything. I never, ever, destroy without purpose."

"The purpose is to stop the Order."

"The purpose is to make a statement. I will not put innocent lives at risk."

"They're not innocent."

"Not all of them are guilty either." Bria began to walk away, "I will not become your weapon. Find someone else."

Hue called after her, but Bria did not respond, stepping into the swamp. She ordered the branches to thicken behind her, letting only Brent follow her into the trees.

As the palace disappeared behind the trees, Brent grabbed her shoulder. The branches attached to him at once.

"I'm fine," Bria hissed but still opened the notebook for him. "I just expected better from Hue. Lana would have never asked me to do such… horrible things."

Brent scribbled on the page. *They're desperate.*

"I don't care! It's exactly what Ningursu made me do in Newbird's Arm…or even in Knoll! I can't keep leaving behind craters because I'm angry."

I know. I agree with you.

"Besides…none of this really matters if we can't find Ningursu. It will just be destruction for destruction's sake." Bria inhaled the thick swamp air. "I need to go to São Caméliosa. I feel like… there might be some answers there. I don't know what… but… I have to see."

And I'll keep searching for Ningursu's story. We're going to figure this out.

"I hope so," Bria whispered.

But once again, the voices had returned in her head. They sang a song, one both familiar and new, constantly repeating, constantly taunting.

Rhodana, the Forest Queen,
She loves to cry, she loves to scream,
She'll turn the world into a fire ring.

Rhodana.

THE PAINTINGS ON THE WALL

Chander's head finally stopped spinning. When Neorama shifted, it left him as nauseous as when he first unlocked his magic. While the shift itself had been marvelous, changing the landscape of Neorama with a sudden gust of smoke, Chander did not dare go outside once it stopped. Rather, he crawled into his bed, holding the pillow over his ears until the pounding in his head ceased.

Sleep may have helped if he dared close his eyes, but instead, he lay awake, attempting to rest with his eyes open, aware of his surroundings.

He crawled out of his bed and squinted out the window. The orange glow of sunset peaked through the swampy treeline, shooting down the main road of

Neorama and bouncing against the stone walls of the school. Neorama positioned itself well against the trees. It was as though this very piece of land had been designed for the town.

Wonder if this place has a spot everywhere in the world. Chander thought. He closed his eyes once. Darkness stared back at him. *Anandi must be asleep.*

He opened his eyes and peered out the window again. Yaz wandered in the streets with one of the spirits, pointing to the different trees. Other ghosts wandered about, sharing in the excitement. Why did they choose a swamp? Chander wondered. Sure, it wasn't as out in the open as the Chessboard Plains, but back when he lived in Grover's Marsh, the alligators and snakes proved to be constant nuisances. Why not choose a quiet meadow, away from a city, where no one could find them?

"Brent!" Yaz shouted outside, just loud enough for Chander to hear. He squinted into the setting sun. Brent strode down the road, clutching his cane. Beside him, Chander instantly recognized the Forest Queen, a gas mask clipped to her belt, the branches crossing over her body like armor. Yaz raced over to her.

Chander could tell that Yaz babbled to Bria, a wide smile on her face, but not loud enough for him to hear. Just as Chander remembered, Bria listened intently. But when Yaz pulled her forward, Bria shook her head.

Can she even see what is going on around her? Chander wondered. He had seen how Micca and others lost their ability to see. Brent had mentioned the wall that had formed between Life and Death, but Chander didn't ever think about it happening to the Forest Queen. She seemed untouchable.

But really, wasn't she just like everybody else?

Guess I should say hello. Chander left his spot by the window and moved slowly into the hallway. A few spirits gathered, talking in a strange language he could not understand. He tensed as he strode past them. While he trusted that they would do no harm, it was hard to deny how… different they were from him. It was as though someone had taken apart their bodies and reconstructed them one limb at a time. Physically, everything was in the right place… but something just felt… wrong.

He glanced into a few of the rooms as he walked toward the stairway. For the most part, the different spirits did little to decorate the rooms. Only Milo had added a personal touch, laying out different instruments on his dresser and scribblings of musical notes across pieces of parchment he hung on the wall.

Chander turned from Milo's room. The door to the next room hung open an inch, just enough for Chander to peek inside. There, the old pinstripe leader herself, Jewel, sat on the floor, holding a paintbrush in her hand.

She worked the paintbrush through the air, capturing Mist on its bristles. As she moved it, one stroke at a time, a mural appeared on the wall. First, a layer of black, followed by silver and red, coming together to form the image of a skeletal woman drowning a little girl in a pool of silver water.

"What the fuck?" Chander whispered, blinking twice. He couldn't be so tired as to imagine nightmares like *that* painted on the wall.

Jewel turned. Her blonde hair cascaded down her face, eyes wide and marred by dark circles.

"What are you looking at, kid?" Jewel snapped.

"Sorry," Chander stepped back, "I just… I saw your painting. What is it? It's… disturbing."

"It's just what was in my head," Jewel placed her paintbrush on the ground and stepped back from the wall.

Chander now saw the rest of the mural. In one corner, a diabolical creature with a knit sweater sat cross-legged on the wall. From there, the painting transformed, showing a skull sitting upon an hourglass. The hourglass itself broke, extending into unlit crypts, which ceased on a painting of Brent himself. From Brent's body, black tendrils escaped, twisting onto the ceiling and dissipating.

"I didn't know you had a dark mind," Chander remarked.

"I don't," Jewel snapped. "I don't know where these images came from."

"But you just said that you painted them."

"No, I didn't."

"Yes, you did! I saw you!"

"I don't paint," Jewel said. But just as she said it, she lifted the paintbrush from the ground. The Mist spun around it, and she brought it to the wall, eyes locked in a trance. Chander held his breath.

The movements came over Jewel as easy as breathing. With the Mist as her palette, she decorated another blank portion of the wall. The scene was less macabre, instead showing a stout, balding man reorganizing books on a shelf. Around him, yellow smoke pulsed, rising from the floorboards.

But then the image shifted, with fallen bookshelves and a monster rising from the smoke, towering over a cowering figure between the shelves.

Each painting was its own story, with details that seamlessly blended.

And as the painting neared completion, Jewel dropped the paintbrush and shook her head. After blinking a few times, she glowered at Chander. "What're you looking at, kid?"

"Nothing... just... nothing," Chander continued to stare at the painting. It was hard to ignore the artistry.

But Jewel's attention had already returned to the wall, where she brushed her fingers against the picture of the balding man. "Alojzy…"

Chander almost asked her what she meant, but instead, took a step back out of the room, nearly trampling into Brent standing in the hallway.

"Oh! Sorry!" Chander held up his hands.

Brent didn't react, peering past Chander at the images on the wall.

Jewel spun around and glared at Brent, "What's with all of you staring at me? Can't a girl get some privacy?"

Brent gripped his cane, "I'm just… I mean… the artwork. It's intriguing."

"It's hideous," Jewel spat. "Whoever painted it has a disturbed mind."

"Oh, I doubt that. I think they just… captured a memory."

Jewel rolled her eyes.

Brent took each step forward, his gaze locked on the wall. He always chose his words with care, and despite Jewel's clear hostility, he did not abandon that gentle nature. "The paintings remind me of the work of a… of a friend. Julietta was her name. Have you heard of her?"

Jewel crossed her arms. "No. Why would I?"

"You remind me of her, that's all…" Brent trailed off, running his fingers over one of the murals.

"I ain't like no one else but me."

"Perhaps you're right…"

Chander used that moment to sneak out of the room, stealing one last glance at the mural. The paintings on the wall sent shivers up his spine. He didn't know the people in the painting, but they weren't strangers. There was something familiar about them, as if they themselves had haunted his dreams or spoken to him through the Mist.

It had to do with the Mist Keepers. But that would be a lesson for history class, wouldn't it?

He descended the stairwell, pushing against the wall as Milo walked past him. The spirit grinned, revealing his rotten teeth, before disappearing into the room with Brent and Jewel.

Chander shoved his hands in his pocket and left the schoolhouse. The orange glow peered through the trees, illuminating the main road. The strange black box in the center of town still pulsed with Mist,

The swamp tree line bled red against the setting sun. Brent's dog, Nix, chased after a lizard into the trees. Meanwhile, different ghosts gathered, talking with Szyman or getting situated in their new home. Chander even noticed as Caroline reentered the town, a black cloak swaying behind her as she entered the tavern.

At the edge of town, Yaz sat on a log with Bria, babbling. Bria listened intently. She had changed since

Chander last saw her, though; there was a clear heaviness in her gaze while her magic had expanded beyond just that branched hand. In some ways, she looked more like a tree than a human, with bark acting as armor across her body.

"Hello, Chander," she said as he approached.

Chander nodded a greeting.

"Yaz was telling me everything that has happened since I last saw you. I'm glad to see you're doing well."

"Chander!" Yaz jumped to her feet. "Guess what? Ms. Bria said that she built a palace out of the trees! Doesn't that sound neat?"

"That's hard to believe," Chander replied.

"She says it's true, and we can see it if we want."

"Tomorrow," Bria interjected. "It is getting late, and the swamp is dark at night. Brent will take you to it, alright?"

"Okay-doke," Yaz said, then frowned. "I wish I could show you around Neorama."

"I know. I wish I could see it."

Chander crossed his arms. *So she is like Micca and Anandi... she can't see it.*

"I hope Brent can fix that. You need to see it," Yaz replied.

"We'll find a way to fix it someday..." Bria's voice trailed off as she said that final sentence.

Chander glanced at his hands. Why did other people lose the ability to see while he was forced to see…everything?

He closed his palms and looked away from Yaz and Bria.

That's why you're here. To learn how to control what you can see. But could anyone really help him? Jewel painted images without recollection. Brent saw stories that he could not forget.

And even Yaz's monsters never left her.

Together, were they cursed to flounder in their own magic?

If so… what was the point of shifting to this swamp but to become creatures in the mud?

CHAPTER THIRTY-ONE

RETURNING TO THE BEAST

The uniform hung on Todd's body like a smock. Its perfect fit had been sabotaged by weeks on the street, no longer hugging his muscles to amplify his presence. Smudges covered the coat, dirt dusting its sleeves. But, despite its state, Todd knew it would have to do.

He never thought he would wear it again. While he had the foresight not to get rid of it, he had every intention of burning it once he escaped the Capital.

Now, this time, without a doubt, it would be his only way to protect his son.

This came with thought, though. Unlike when the departed Captain Carver persuaded him to rejoin the Guard, every part of Todd's decision came with weighing the alternatives. He could have just left with the next group of refugees. But... if Nils's sister could help, wasn't it worth trying to rescue her?

He adjusted the cuffs of his coat, affixed his club to his belt, then left the lavatory.; Nils waited outside in an equally ill-fitted uniform.

"We look like a load of schmucks, y'know," Nils commented.

"Yeah, that uniform is like three sizes too big for you."

"This is the smallest size we got. You don't look much better."

Todd scoffed, then glanced around the hallway. Nighttime had settled over the tavern, carrying with it their mission. They'd spent the past couple of days reviewing the maps of the Witch Tunnels. With its skeletal underside, the Capital existed above this grid of tunnels, twisting in and out of subway systems and sewage lines. It took hours working through the maze, but they had finally identified the correct tunnel network straight into the Capitol.

"You ready then?" Nils asked.

"Just gotta say goodbye to my kid," Todd glanced down the hall toward his bedroom.

"He's sleeping. Let him rest. Ms. Doris will keep an eye on him."

"Can we trust her?"

"She's one of the few I trust with my life."

Todd frowned. *Be well, Garrett. I'll be back soon.*

"I promise, kid's in good hands. So we better get a move on, yeah?"

"Isn't this my plan?" Todd grumbled.

"Yeah, but you're not the only one eager to rescue your sister."

Todd grunted but didn't argue. Nils was right; no reason to disturb Garrett. It wasn't like the kid would acknowledge him anyhow.

Todd couldn't help but wonder if Garrett even knew what was happening. Did he understand that they had been wandering the streets? Had he fully processed that his eyes were missing? Was he even aware that Todd was his father?

Was the child even alive anymore, or a mere shell... breathing?

No. Todd repeated the thought to himself. *He's alive. You're gonna save him.*

But the thought didn't fend off the intrusive ideas dancing through his brain. If this didn't work with Nils's sister, would Garrett's life even be worth living? Would he be—

Todd stopped the thought at once, focusing ahead as Nils led him back into the speakeasy. As always, the basement bustled, with a few storytellers performing on stage and refugees gathered with their drinks. In the dim light, it was almost as if they were in any other tavern.

But that immediately faded as Nils opened the liquor cabinet on the back wall. He pushed aside the rows of glasses and bottles of liquor to stare into the dark Witch Tunnel leading that would take them to the Capitol.

Todd inhaled, then, without looking back, followed Nils into the tunnel. He was sure people watched as they left, but he wouldn't humor them with acknowledgment. This was his mission; he wasn't doing anything to help anyone but his son. It had nothing to do with the greater good or saving someone wrongfully locked away. He was helping his son; nothing more, nothing less.

He walked with Nils in silence through the Witch Tunnels. The man adjusted his uniform as he walked, tightening his belt so the trousers wouldn't fall, before tapping along one of the walls to open another tunnel. Nils knew most of the Witch Tunnels by heart. Todd's expertise was needed only near the Capitol.

"So, I think I've earned your name, haven't I?" Nils asked as he tapped along one of the stones. A new tunnel fell open as he finished the last line of code.

"Huh?" Todd followed Nils through the opening.

"You never told me your name. Been referring to you and your son as Scruff and Scruff Jr. when people ask."

"You don't need to know my name."

"Aw, c'mon, we're about to break into the Capitol. The least you can do is tell me your name."

"That's all the reason not to tell you—if we get caught, then you could turn me in."

"You know my name."

Todd grunted.

"C'mon."

"It's not for you to know."

"Fine…" Nils slowed his pace. "I'll just call you Lieutenant Drayton."

Todd froze, "How did you—"

"You have your last name on your uniform. Faded, but I can see it."

Todd glanced at the front pocket of his uniform. There, etched into the fabric, sat his name: T. Drayton.

Nils continued to pry, "What's the 'T' stand for? Timothy? Theodore? Thomas?"

"Just drop it," Todd hissed, then continued to walk forward, down the tunnel, toward the west where the Capitol waited.

Nils continued his prying, reciting names like poetry, "Todrick? Tobias? Taylor? Trevor?" The list went on, repeating with each beat, a bumbling annoyance in Todd's head. "Tucker? Terry?"

Todd gripped his hand, "If I tell you, will you shut up until we arrive?"

"Maybe." Nils grinned.

"It's Toddle, a'ight? Toddle Drayton."

"Toddle?"

"Todd for short. A'ight? Now drop it."

"What kind of name is Toddle?"

"I said drop it!"

Nils snickered. "Big ol' Toddle, the ex-guard? And I thought Scruffy was an insult!"

"I fucking swear…" Todd took another step forward, trying his best to silence Nils's constant taunting. The man did not know how to shut up. He seemed so poised back in the speakeasy, but here…it was like dragging a yappy dog behind him.

Every few minutes, Todd ordered Nils to be quiet, but the silence was always short-lived. Nils would begin to click his tongue or tap along the wall before diving into another ramble about Todd's name.

"Why are you so obsessed with my name, huh? Can't we just be quiet?" Todd snapped after a few minutes.

"You were the one safeguarding it. Wasn't sure if you were ashamed of it or something," Nils said.

"No! I just don't want to share my name. Risks the Guard or someone finding me or something."

"Then why not give yourself a new name? You could've lied and said your name was Trevor or something."

"Because my name is my name."

"But you should have no shame in changing it… or altering it. I have had at least four different names over the past two years. Finally settled on Nils 'cause it felt like me."

"Well, I've never felt wrong in my name."

"But you could use the name Trevor for a disguise or something."

"Oh, just shut up. You know my name now, so leave it alone."

Of course, Nils wouldn't leave it alone. So Todd continued to drown out the rambling, tuning into his heartbeat as they entered a set of narrow tunnels. The stench from the nearby sewers dwindled, leaving behind only an occasional drip of water and a thin glimmer of light.

"We're getting close," Todd mumbled to Nils.

For once, the man didn't reply.

Every now and again, the light flickered as they walked, sending a shadow over the tunnel. Stones lay scattered along the floor, where roots and vines crisscrossed, a reminder of the Forest Queen who had visited months earlier.

Todd removed the map from his pocket and traced along it with his fingers. They had left behind the dominant, artery-like tunnels, shooting off into one of the frayed capillaries beneath the main plaza. He had escaped through tunnels similar in nature; he had never intended to return.

Now, he waded through the path of rubble, clamoring over stones and pushing apart the vines, with full intent to climb into the beast's mouth.

"How're we supposed to get through all of this?" Nils asked as they approached a towering pile of rubble.

"We climb," Todd started over the first pile of rocks, pushing a few over to the side so he could visualize the path on the other side.

"What if there is some magic blocking our path?" Nils inquired as he stumbled over one of the rocks.

"The guard doesn't use magic," Todd replied.

"Yeah, that's a lie."

"It's their core fundamentals."

"Yeah, but you've seen what has been happening. The Order likes magic for its own purposes...so I'm sure the Guard is the same."

"No. The Guard still will not use magic—these tunnels are their way of finding a safe escape."

"If you insist..." Nils stumbled behind him.

They continued through the narrow tunnel, pushing aside rubble and debris. It was not an easy path to navigate. Even when Todd escaped, the tunnels felt as though they were collapsing in on him. They provided a worthy escape and had certainly served the Senate well through the years, but daily use by the Guard would be more cumbersome than necessary.

Todd stopped at the end of the tunnel, where a narrow stone door waited for them. He turned to Nils. "Now listen, we gotta blend in well here, you got it? If anyone sees us, I'm your lieutenant, and you're a cadet, you hear? Let me do the talking. Understood?"

"Yes, sir." Nils saluted.

Todd grunted, then traced his hand along the door, searching for the lock. Rather than the magic built out of tap-code, this door consisted of a multi-faceted locking mechanism. Three dials circled the hinges, each assigned a different number.

Hopefully, this works. Todd slowly turned the locks to the numbers *3,15,18*. He waited, listening for the numbers to click.

But the lock didn't budge.

He cursed under his breath, then tried a different code. *18,15,4*

Nothing.

5,6,12

Still nothing.

"Thought you knew the code?" Nils asked.

"I'm trying," Todd hissed.

"You don't think they changed it recently?"

"They might have, but how the hell would I know what it is?"

"Well, we don't got time for your guessing game. Move aside."

"What're you gonna do?" Todd snapped.

Nils spat into his hand and placed his spit onto the lock.

"What the fuck are you doing!?"

"Hold on!" Nils hissed. As he held his hand over the locks, the spit visibly cooled, freezing over the locks.

Then, once ice formed on their surface, Nils pulled the doorknob.

The locks snapped.

"Wait...you've got magic?" Todd hissed.

"Can just freeze stuff. It's not that special," Nils pushed open the door. "Lead the way."

Todd stared at Nils for a moment, then stormed through the doorway. It opened into a dark closet stacked with old chairs.

Nils shoved the door to the tunnels shut behind him. With the only light sneaking out from the other side of the closet, Todd slowly pushed the door open and peeked into the other room.

The plush velvet chairs of the Senate Chambers waited beyond the other side of the door. Without a senate, though, the room did not bustle. No one guarded the doors, and the flickering light of the chandelier hung over the Senate's table.

Todd stepped out from the closet, then froze. Bile rose in his throat, unable to turn away from the scene at the long conference table in the center of the room.

This was worse than anything he had ever seen in the Pits or in his training as a guard.

Even Nils did not speak.

There, sitting in the chairs at the conference table, waited the bodies of every senator. Flesh rotted from their skin, with flies spiraling around their corpses. Bone poked through their otherwise decomposed flesh. Vines and roots twisted around each of the senators' corpses, with visible gunshots piercing each of their bodies.

Todd only recognized Senator Cordova, in his long ruby robes, at the head of the table. A single gunshot entered his skull, while a bustling bouquet exploded from his mouth. If the Forest Queen was responsible, as the papers said, then she had certainly left her mark.

"Why would they leave them here?" Nils choked.

"Because they can," Todd swallowed his nausea. "C'mon."

Nils didn't argue, following close behind Todd as they hurried through the Senate Chambers. Todd kept to the wall, freezing at the flickering of shadows. But no one emerged from any corners.

Just the candles, Todd exhaled. They just had to locate Nils's sister. But that was the most difficult part of the mission. Todd hadn't a clue where to start or if she was still in the Capitol. What if they moved her to the Pit? What if she was dead? Then what use would come of this?

Todd gripped the club on his waist. With Nils close, he opened the chamber doors, peering out into the long marble hallway.

He didn't dare move.

At the end of the hallway, a single guard waited, back turned.

Todd held a hand in front of Nils, motioning for him to stay. Like a shadow against the wall, Todd moved slowly, balancing on the edge of his heels to prevent his shoes from clicking. He gripped his club tighter, holding his breath and clenching his jaw.

Don't turn. Please, don't turn. He took another couple of steps.

Still, the guard did not flinch.

Good. Todd unhooked the club from his hip and raised it above his head. *Just two more steps—*

Before he could finish the movement, the guard turned.

"Oh, hello, Lieutenant Drayton. I didn't expect to see you again so soon."

CHAPTER THIRTY-TWO

A Pathetic Cadet

Todd stared at Cadet Carver, the very cadet who saved Garrett.

The cadet had changed, though. While he still maintained his strength, his burned face had grown gaunt, eyes tired, and lips worn down to thin, chapped streaks. His lush blond hair had grown frailer. Even his uniform seemed to lack luster.

"Cadet…hello. I…have returned," Todd stammered.

"I don't understand…why would you? We saved your son."

"Hardly."

The cadet fidgeted, his gaze lost and broken as he stared past Todd. "Why'd you return, Lieutenant?"

"That is not for you to know, Cadet."

"Please, Lieutenant, I swear I will not turn you over to the Order. I saved your son. Please," the cadet begged. "I'm desperate to leave this shite. I should have left with you, but… I had loyalties. Or… well… I thought I did. It hasn't been right here. They're using magic. It goes against everything I stand for. Please, Lieutenant."

"Why should I trust you?"

"I saved your son."

"Only after they cut out his eyes."

The cadet bowed his head. "My plan didn't quite work out. I am sorry."

Todd glowered at the boy. *Pathetic.* The cadet was in his mid-twenties, still assigned a rank for adolescents. Yet, despite that rank, he had inner workings with the Guard. Most cadets did everything to garner their superiors' respect. What made this cadet any different?

He saved our son. Todd could almost hear Lex whispering to him. She would trust him, wouldn't she? Without him, Todd never would have gotten close to Garrett.

"Fine, but I'm watching you. If you so much as look at me funny, I'm gonna bash your head into that wall…you hear?" Todd remarked.

"Yes, sir," the cadet saluted.

Todd glanced back at Nils and waved to him. Nils ran forward, stopping a few paces away from Cadet Carver.

"What's with the schmuck?" Nils asked.

"Cadet Carver helped me rescue my son. We can trust him," Todd said.

Nils glowered.

"Here, I'll prove it," Christof unhooked his utility belt, letting it fall to the floor. The pistol, radio, and club echoed as they hit the stone tile.

Nils snatched up the pistol and club, then slammed his boot into the radio. It crunched under his foot.

"I'm keeping an eye on you," Nils hissed. "Later, I better hear at least three good stories out of you, y'hear?"

"I ain't a storyteller."

"Well, you better try."

Todd breathed a sigh of relief. At least Nils had a new person to bother as they snuck through the halls. The cadet fielded the questions without hindrance, walking slowly beside Nils as they navigated the Capitol.

The building itself was a shell of its former self. When Todd first arrived in the Capitol a few months earlier, the building bustled with senators and their staff, civil servants, and even the Guard. Even at night, activity boomed. But now, it was silent. The artwork that once hung proudly on the wall had been destroyed, torn by vines, and shattered by gunshot.

As they climbed the marble stairs, their footsteps echoed. Charred marks skidded over each step. Soot collected around their feet.

Nils' questioning continued, and Todd interjected when they reached the top step. "Cadet, listen. Do you know where they might be keeping a prisoner? A scientist?"

The cadet furrowed his brow. "I know they have been… harboring guests in the old barracks. Guards are usually hanging out there."

Todd cursed.

"Just follow my lead, a'ight? I might still be a cadet, but I got some pull with the recruits. They're kind of a bunch of dipshits if you ask me."

"Why are you still a cadet if you're in charge?" Todd asked.

"'Cause Captain Rivers don't like me much." Cadet Carver motioned for Todd and Nils to follow him down another corridor toward the back of the Capitol building, where not even windows glimmered. Todd had spent a good amount of time back here. With rows of offices, there was nothing all that remarkable about this corridor. Old portraits of the Guard hung on the wall. He read the names to himself as they walked past. *Captain Oberland, Captain White, Captain Massey…* He didn't recognize any of the names, but that was one of many lessons he skipped during the guard. What did a bunch of dead captains know about Rosada today?

Cadet Carver opened another door, leading to a familiar stench of sweat that followed Todd into every station with the Guard. Young guards sat in a common area, playing cards while drinking and smoking. Laughter bellowed about the room, few noticing as they entered.

"Carver—who's the old man?" a young guard called as he lit another smoke.

"Lieutenant Drayton. Back from assignment. Needs to visit with someone—the guests are still upstairs, right?" Cadet Carver replied.

"Yeah, in the tower or some shite." The cadet dropped his match on the ground and put it out with his heel. "You gonna come play a round when you done? Or you fucking that sister again?"

"Depends what the prize is."

"Oh, you ain't gonna win."

"Then I ain't playing."

"Fine. Have fun *praying*."

The group of cadets cackled, eliciting a half-smirk from Christof as he led them across the room. The banter never changed in these barracks. Todd had his own memories from before he met Lex of the continuous jeers and lewd remarks. It was a lifestyle that Todd had once consumed like a narcotic.

Like any drug, it was easy to return to those antics.

But he didn't humor them as he followed Christof up another narrow stairwell into a tower precariously affixed against the Capitol. Beside him, Nils tapped along the wall.

"Relax," Todd hissed.

"I can't! I dunno know what state she'll be in."

"Well, panicking isn't gonna make it any better."

Nils continued his incessant tapping along the wall.

The staircase spiraled upwards, with steel doors collecting on each landing. For the most part, each room is vacant save for stains on the floor or old clothing draped over a chair.

Cadet Carver turned to Nils. "We don't got a lot of guests here right now. What's your sister's name? Might help me narrow down her room."

"Gratz," Nils replied. "Etta Gratz."

"Professor Gratz, you mean?"

"Yeah."

"Why didn't you tell me?"

"Cause I don't trust you…" Nils grunted.

"Well, she's right up this way—c'mon!" Cadet Carver motioned them down the hall.

This professor better help Garrett after all this. Todd followed Cadet Carver down the hall. He removed a ring of keys from his hip. They clanked as he flipped through them, settling on the correct key. He then inserted it into the door.

The door opened to a dim light. At once, Nils pushed past Cadet Carver and into the room. "Etta!"

"Nils!?" A woman's voice exclaimed.

"Yeah, it's me."

Todd peered into the room. Nils had thrown his arms around a woman with graying, curly hair and thick glasses. Something about this woman was oddly familiar. It was like a ghost passing in the hallway or a shadow that painted the walls. The memory was there but faint, with no defining characteristics beyond a feeling of déjà vu.

"What are you doing here?" The woman asked Nils.

"We're here to get you out. Scruff here," Nils motioned to Todd, "needs your help and got us in here."

"I see," Etta released her brother. "So we're getting out of here? Right now?"

"If you want!"

"Yes, yes, of course—let me just get my stuff." Professor Gratz rushed over to her small cot. She yanked a small bag out from under her bed and began to shove papers into it from around the room. She buzzed about, not taking note of anyone, mumbling just as her brother always did.

"We should hurry up," Cadet Carver hissed. "Don't need the others seeing us."

"Y'hear that, Etta? Hurry up!" Nils called.

"I am! Just want to get all these papers! Don't want the Order getting their hands on 'em, you know?"

Todd exchanged a glance with Cadet Carver.

"We don't got all day, Etta!" Nils shouted.

"I'm coming! Hold your horses, sheesh."

Finally, Professor Gratz stumbled from the room, clutching her bag tight. Todd couldn't believe that this disorganized, frazzled woman was the one that everyone said would help his son. The Order had already tugged her in another direction over the past couple of weeks. He doubted she even had time to think about the bleeding red eyes. Why would she come crawling back to another hypothesis?

But Todd didn't question her about it now.

Instead, he turned to Cadet Carver, "So, how're we gonna get out of this place?"

"There's a utility tunnel at the bottom of the tower. We used it to rig this thing in place. Should lead us into the sewer system." The cadet tapped one of the stones. "C'mon, I'll show you."

Cadet Carver motioned for the group to follow him back down the stairwell. As they walked, Etta and Nils babbled under their breaths. Todd glowered at them, which caused them to drop their conversation.

At least for a minute before they began to ramble all over again.

They're like children. Todd inhaled once, then turned the corner with Cadet Carver.

He nearly trampled over the cadet. The door to the tower had opened, with two recruits in the doorway engaged in intimate relations. They didn't turn as Cadet Carver and Todd rounded the bend.

Cadet Carver motioned Todd, Nils, and Professor Gratz down another narrow corridor. He then slipped back to the doorway.

A few moments later, a thud followed,

And Cadet Carver returned.

"Easy enough to knock 'em out," Cadet Carver muttered. He cracked his otherwise unscathed knuckle.

"Didn't we take away your weapons?" Nils asked.

"There're other ways to knock people out," Cadet Carver replied. With confidence in his stride, he continued to navigate them down the narrow corridor. As he walked, Todd swore he saw smoke at the cadet's feet. But it faded almost as soon as it appeared.

A ladder waited for them behind another door. Cadet Carver bowed, motioning for them to climb into its depths.

"You sure this is safe?" Nils asked.

"I told you, will get you to the sewers. Figured you all can lead the way from there," the cadet replied.

"Yeah, but—"

"Just go!" Professor Gratz pushed her brother toward the ladder.

Nils cursed, then, with a deep breath, climbed down the ladder. The professor followed.

"Will anyone try following us?" Todd asked Cadet Carver

"It's a maze down there… but I'll take care of the ladder. Don't worry."

Todd nodded, then descended the ladder. With its rusted bars, every wrung creaked, threatening to snap under his weight.

Once he landed on the foul ground, he stepped back from the ladder. Cadet Carver loosened it from its fasteners. As the final one snapped, the ladder fell, hitting the ground with a clatter.

"Move it out of the way!" Cadet Carver shouted from above them.

Todd obliged, pushing the ladder against the far wall.

Cadet Carver leapt through the opening at the top of the tunnel, landing on his hands and knees with ease. The cadet winced, then stood, seeming unscathed by the descent.

"That was quite a feat," Professor Gratz remarked.

"My training does come in handy." Cadet Carver brushed the dust from his pants.

"I can see that."

Nils rolled his eyes. "C'mon. Let's get out of here before someone discovers you're missing."

"Of course, lead the way," Professor Gratz took her brother's arm. Todd would let Nils shine now; the way back to the speakeasy would be paved with familiarity.

They had done what they set out to do, hadn't they?

But Todd couldn't help but feel it had all been too easy.

Not that he was complaining.

As long as Garrett recovered, it didn't matter… right? Besides, he needed an easy win.

Just once.

CHAPTER THIRTY-THREE

WHERE SHE BLOOMED

Bria left her swamp in the heart of the night. With the humidity budding on her forehead, she secured her gas mask and climbed into the tunnels. Rather than heading north toward Rosada, she detoured to the south. She knew where she had to go. Why? She wasn't sure. But, after witnessing Brent collect Ningursu's stories, hiding from her own past seemed impossible. Her grandpapa had given her the starting point. Now, with the knowledge he'd provided, she would finish the tale.

Los Gardeniros n'e Diversito. She'd placed it deep in her memory, along with her knowledge of elements learned by the *Rules of the Apothecary.* But now, it bubbled to the surface; her grandpapa's last name, Gonzo, came from this very group of gardeners. Tasked with protecting the earth, they had existed for centuries.

Yet, they had also vanished, leaving behind only a group of inexperienced Magii playing with weeds.

Why had Bria ended up so much stronger than them? She had spoken with her grandpapa, with her grandmama, with Lana, and with her father. Circumstances had collided. While there was no definitive reason that Bria's magic had grown with such regard, there were possibilities. Her father's side of the family bore potential connections to the physical earth, while her mother's breathed of life and forests. Together, it tuned Bria into all the elements.

Would São Caméliosa hold the thread that bound these facts together?

Bria didn't know.

The air grew thicker as she turned further south, rich with summer. The tunnel itself exited between two towering fitzroya trees. With night still lingering, Bria squinted through her mask. The lenses fogged up as she took a step forward.

Not a tinge of yellow invaded the sky. Greenery provided a welcoming embrace.

Bria hesitantly removed the mask and inhaled. *It's not here yet.* While she had heard that the yellow smoke had reached even the likes of Mert, São Caméliosa of

Perennes had maintained its freedom. Magic could still live unscathed.

She clipped the mask to her belt and adjusted the sleeves of her jacket, hiding her branched arm. While her grandpapa told her that São Caméliosa had been his home, she couldn't be certain that they'd be so accepting of magic now. News from these southern countries never quite made it to Rosada.

There was so much more in the world. Bria had explored parts of it when the tunnels were a blessing. She absorbed the sights, from the glass cities on the coastlines to the baobab trees of the plains to the towering cities of Yilk. Even if she wanted to abandon Rosada, it wouldn't change the oncoming plumes of smoke pouring from Ningursu's mouth.

For now, though, São Caméliosa was yet to be suffocated by Ningursu.

And she could breathe.

As she exited the forest, she inhaled the early morning air. Her shoulders loosened as she walked along the path. The earth sang to her here. It wasn't crying for her attention, demanding her assistance. Instead, it welcomed her, like a grandparent welcoming home their grandchild, cradling them in an embrace.

She kept to the edge of the forest. In the distance, the ocean thrashed against the shoreline. Lights twinkled from the city, capturing the water in its glow. All slept.

She continued through a collection of homes, with vines creeping down their sides and flowers gathering at their doorsteps. Unlike the Capital, Mert, or Newbird's Arm, the homes of São Caméliosa belonged to the forest. They had not been planted there, a foreign entity, but instead intermingled with the foliage, born of the forest. The more Bria looked, the more she noticed how the roots and vines not only climbed along the walls but formed them. Just like her palace.

But these homes flourished like ancient trees. How long had they been here? Did each Magii help their homes grow?

She reached toward one of the homes but paused just before her fingers touched the wall. One branch climbed to her, but she couldn't act on it. This wasn't her palace. She couldn't bend it at will.

Bria wrung her hands together and continued along the path. Why hadn't her grandpapa told her about São Caméliosa? As a child, she would have hung onto every word. She could have followed the tunnels here...and possibly, never would have felt alone.

She followed the path through the collection of natural-born homes. Each one bore a uniqueness to it. The roots twisted in different directions, the vines hung with different flowers, and even the shape of the buildings changed. Would her little haven in the swamp be like this someday? She often wondered what would become of it all if she walked away. But if these homes remained, the architects long gone, then surely, she could go elsewhere.

She continued along the path. The roots and vines slithered beside her like snakes, guiding her along just like in the tunnels. Trees bowed to her while the drooping moss swayed over her head.

Even more than just the forest breathed. Beneath her feet, the ground shifted. With each shift, different elements pulled at Bria's attention, from the wells of water beneath the dirt to minerals fueling life in the plant.

She stopped beneath a tree at the corner of the road and placed her hand on it. The swamp burst with similar life, but it had the benefit of hiding a fair distance away from anyone at all. This was nature interacting with humanity unscathed.

As she made her way toward the docks, the city slowly came alive, a hint of dawn peeking through the tree line. Tamarins hopped between the branches. Bright-colored birds rose with the sun. All the while, the branches shifted in the presence of gorgeous wildlife Bria had never seen in Rosada.

Along the docks, a collection of merchants had begun to set up their shops. A few boats bobbed in the harbor. No one batted an eye as Bria loitered amongst the stales, pausing at the handmade jewelry, woven ponchos, and an array of handcrafted figurines. The sizzling of fried dough dragged her to a merchant operating a makeshift stall. A portable gaslit stove sat positioned on the table, where a pan sizzled with oil.

Bria stayed back, watching as the merchant fried meat enveloped in dough. Her stomach growled.

When did I last eat? She frowned. Food hadn't been on her mind much in the last few days.

She reached into her satchel. Inside, she still had a handful of Rosadian coins, but it was doubtful they had little sway here.

"Ay!" the merchant called her way. He proceeded to say something in an unfamiliar tongue.

Bria stared at him. "Oh, um, sorry. I'm not from here."

The merchant perked up slightly, speaking again with a sharp accent but fluent tongue, "Oh! You're Rosadian?"

Bria nodded.

"We don't get many of you around these parts. Was asking if you wanted one?" He held up one of the fried meat patties.

"I only have Rosadian coins on me."

"No, take it. On me."

"I couldn't."

"I've been cooking for fifty years. This one isn't perfect, but it's still good. Here," the man handed her the food in a napkin.

"Oh...thank you," Bria whispered, staring at the food. As she took a taste, she smiled slightly. It'd been a while since she had a hot meal. At least, not one where she had to scarf down before rushing off on another mission.

When she first started showing Brent the world, she loved taking him to food vendors like this. They had tried countless delicacies, allowing Brent to try ice cream for the first time and even devour pizza. Sure, he went on a tangent about pineapple on more than one occasion, but in those moments, she saw a different future. What would his reaction be to a meal like this?

He'd probably end up with half the meat on his shirt. Bria wiped her mouth and turned back to the merchant. "Thank you again. It was delicious."

"You're quite welcome. I am glad you liked it." The merchant placed another wad of dough on the stove. "I imagine it's been quite a travel from Rosada, hasn't it? Did you come with the Commeant?"

"The Commeant?"

"Sorry—the ships."

"Oh, um, yes," Bria lied.

"Quite the voyage, but I suppose anything is better than Rosada."

"You know what is going on in Rosada?" Bria asked.

"Oh, we receive plenty of information here. Rosada sounds like a wilting flower."

"Yeah…it is."

"At least you got out. I doubt there's much that can be done."

Bria silently agreed.

"I have to say, though, their hope in the L'Corona Verde is remarkable?"

"L'Corona Verde?"

"I believe you call her… Rhodana?"

Bria's throat tightened. "You've heard of Rhodana?"

"Some travelers spoke of her a couple years ago. Said how Rhodana saved a small mountain town. It's kept growing from there."

"But surely Rhodana's feats aren't that impressive here in São Caméliosa, right? Don't you have others here with her magic?"

"Pah, if what they're saying is true, then the closest thing we have are our Gardeniros. But they're a team, not a single person."

"The Gardeniros…" Bria recalled what her grandpapa had said about their family history. *So they still exist.*

"You don't know of the Gardineros, do you?"

"Oh, um, not really," Bria replied. "I've heard of them vaguely, but back in Rosada, they don't teach us much about them."

"I wouldn't think so." The merchant shrugged as he continued frying the dough. "I am not certain how long you will be around, but if you have time, visit the Governor's Gardens. That's where the Gardeniros work and train. Foreigners love watching them. Think you'll have a good time as well."

"The Governor's Garden?"

"Just follow this path, and once you reach a split in the road, turn left. You can't miss it." The merchant motioned behind him. "If you hurry, you might get to see the morning crew arrive."

"Oh, okay. Thank you so much, I'll go take a look."

"Of course. Enjoy your time in São Caméliosa."

Bria waved to the merchant one last time, then headed up the path behind him. She glanced back at him once. The docks held a sort of serenity she hadn't seen in a long time. These were good people, just trying to get by in life. In São Caméliosa, at least they could do so without fear.

As she strolled in the morning light, the flowers crooned, forming a blossoming trim along the road. The unfamiliar foliage radiated with reds, yellows, and oranges. Multicolored butterflies fluttered between them.

She knelt before one of the flowers and let the petals brush her fingers. They moved toward her with ease.

While Bria could have spent hours just sitting at the side of the road, she did not delay, following a foliage riddled-wall along the path's border. At the corner of the wall, visitors gathered, peaking through the wired gates. Children clung to their parents' hands while an elderly couple watched on their tiptoes.

Bria slipped between the crowd without much notice, managing to find space behind a few children so she could peer through the wrought-iron fence.

On the other side of the fence, a wild garden, resembling more of a rainforest than a garden, waited. A narrow path twisted through the trees. Before the gate stood a coalition of twelve individuals dressed in overalls and armed with shovels. They did not move, staring down the path, silent.

This silence did not quell the excitement. Children babbled beside Bria, their unfamiliar language catching the wind. It seemed to mix with the garden, blending into the surroundings as though part of the earth itself.

And the garden spoke back to them.

Sang even.

Bria could hear it, like a low hum, echoing from down the winding paths.

It blended in with the marching boots approaching.

And there, twelve other gardeners appeared from the trees. They lined up to face their counterparts, their own shovels firm at their side.

With an indecipherable call, they all straightened their backs.

Then, another call and the shovels rose in the air.

And with the last call, vines crawled up the arms of the shovels before exploding like a canopy over the entrance to the garden. Looped together, dripping with green, the otherwise empty entrance merged with the forest.

And flowers reigned from their branches.

The children beside Bria cheered. Behind her, the other spectators gaped. While she had done feats like this before, it was different seeing it as an outsider. She clapped along, smiling, all while her little branch tugged behind her ear, begging to participate in the festivities. It was an instinctual pull, like something inside her knew this routine.

But she refrained from participating, merely marveling at the artistry of the Gardeniros.

They placed their shovels in the ground, letting the foliage remain in their sculptural shape.

The two closest Gardeniros then unlocked the gate and stepped back with a bow. The children rushed into the garden while other visitors pushed past, all giddy to see the magic waiting behind the wall.

Despite her own excitement, Bria paused, admiring the artistry. This is where she was meant to be; here, blooming in this garden...a place where she could be safe and call home.

La Propriedad

The garden was nothing like Bria had ever imagined. In contrast to the Senator's Garden in Newbird's Arm, which fought for every ounce of life, this garden was but an extension of the surrounding environment. Colorful birds fluttered between the trees while tamarins chattered. Bria swore she saw a large cohort of rodents scurrying past with round snouts and narrow eyes. While she'd traveled through rainforests, this was different; everything had been curated, just like São Caméliosa.

She moved slowly through the garden, admiring each tree and flower. Despite her instincts, she kept her hands at her side. What would happen if she touched one of these plants? Would it unwind the work of the Gardeniros?

She followed the path around an old stone palace. The foliage had reclaimed it, crawling from windows and doors, so thick that it was impossible to view the interior. Bria removed her hand from her pocket but once again stopped herself and hurried away from the castle before her curiosity dared to take hold of her.

This is not my place. I am just visiting. Don't destroy their work. She took a deep breath. The fullness of oxygen bubbled inside of her, and she took control of each breath, ensuring it did not cause the clouds to move in the wrong direction. But, if she paid attention to oxygen, then her ability to pay attention to other elements decayed. There was, truthfully, no way around her magic. Here, it burst at the seams.

She was relieved when she exited a section of the garden where a worn archway encapsulated the path. On the arch, the words *la Propriedad d'los Gardeniros n'e Diversito* hid, barely visible beneath the stamp of time. She followed the path beneath it, entering a quiet sculpture garden. The sculptures guarded a cage composed of rotten thorns. They pulled Bria's attention, and she approached the cage on the far side of the sculpture garden.

She kept her hands away from the rotting thorns, peaking past them at an empty pedestal sitting within the cage. Dead leaves gathered on the ground. Roots crawled at the pedestal's feet.

Bria frowned. *I wonder what was in there.* She turned back to the sculptures. Like the pedestal, leaves gathered around them, a less worn path than the rest of the garden. Grime covered the statues, hiding their faces, while caked vine and dirt masked the names.

No flowers bloomed.

She circled each statue. Through the encrusted moss, she could visualize the different features of the statues: an old king from centuries passed, a god of gold and silver, and even a famous Gardeniro. Bria didn't recognize the names, nor could she read the inscriptions, but it didn't matter. Their history lived in these statues.

"Brent would love these," she said to herself as she approached another statue. This inscription she could read, and even without knowing all the words, she understood what it meant after speaking to the merchant by the sea.

L'Corona Verde. Rhodana. Bria stared at the words, then turned to the statue.

A stone copy of herself stared back.

Bria stared back, willing the statue to change. She circled it once. But it still didn't change.

"No…" Bria whispered. It had to be a coincidence! But it was more than just her braid or the sculpture's face. The sculpture bore a branch behind its ear that extended out and formed an arm. From there, the branches crossed over the sculpture's body, like a suit of armor ready for battle. Bria removed her own jacket, taking note of her branch's twists and turns down her neck and across her body.

Everything matched.

"No…" she knelt to the ground and brought her head to her hands. "This doesn't make any sense! I'm just Bria…just me."

This was different from people singing about her actions. It was more than just the vague song of Rhodana. This was her, plain as day, a sculpture of the past.

She could feel the age in the stone. This wasn't sculpted recently. Hundreds of years had passed since the sculpture first found its home in the garden.

But how? Could there have been a queen, years ago, with the same name and same appearance? Could it all be coincidence?

But that seemed all too implausible.

She swallowed, trying to retract her emotions. But her frustration had already emerged, the pathway budding with a new collection of moss. The vines around the sculptures slithered, and the thorn cage grew. Just the slight shifts changed the entire demeanor of the sculpture garden. The earth had taken over, and soon rain would come to solidify the agreement.

Bria inhaled again, reciting the elements to herself. *Hydrogen, Oxygen, Helium, Carbon, Nitrogen…*She took another breath, then climbed to her feet, holding her hand close to her chest.

As she rose, her stomach twisted. The sculptures no longer sat in stone. Rather, leaves had blossomed upon them, creating intricate woven designs. The sculpture of Rhodana had become the most detailed of them all, blooming with camellias and laced with an arm as detailed as her own.

She stepped away from the sculptures, hands shaking. *I can control this. I have to control this.* Yet, with every step, the garden bowed to her. Vines and roots crawled from the nearby walls, slithering along the stones. A new story needed to be told, and they would react to her every movement.

Control it.

She had always been able to control the plants. Here, in the garden, it was much stronger. But what made it any different from playing in the Senator's Gardens back home?

"Enough!" she feigned confidence as she bellowed her command. "Enough."

The foliage froze.

"Go. Sleep…" she whispered.

Like a reluctant child, the foliage rescinded back to the garden. Those that had captured the sculpture garden did not leave, though, taunting her as if to say, "Look what we did!"

Her knees shook as she stepped away from the sculpture garden. With a trembling hand, she used the archway at the end of the path to support herself. Even the stone wanted to play, forming small, perfect holes where her fingers touched.

"I said stop it!" she hissed at the stone.

While the stone stopped its tomfoolery, Bria's attention remained on the column. Now that the vines and moss had fled to the statues, the artistry of the column appeared. Worn images etched their way along the pillar, circling it as if to tell a story.

She ran her finger over the worn stone. With her magic, she defined the edges of each of the images.

While Bria expected to see stories of the Gardeniros, she instead was greeted by an old carving of a man striding into a garden, with curves reminiscent of smoke on his heels. Although the image had long been reduced to etchings, she could decipher his thick beard and long weaving cloak. *That looks like a Mist Keeper.* She traced the edge of the smoke. It didn't look like any of the Mist Keepers she knew, but time had a way of changing people.

She followed the story to the next picture. There, the Mist Keeper met with two individuals who bore the expression of trees. Crowns sat on their heads. At their feet knelt the Gardeniros, all embellished with vines, roots, and flowers.

Bria circled the column, arriving at the next image. There, the Mist Keeper stood on a pedestal, with subjects bowing to him like a God. Roots and vines gathered at the foot of the pedestal as if withering in his very presence.

Another step, and she found the next piece of the story. There, like fallen logs, lay the bodies of the Royal Gardeners. At their grave sat a single flower.

In the final image, a single gardener with wilted hands lifted the flower, cradling it close to their chest.

No other images remained, leaving Bria staring at the column, flabbergasted. Who was the Mist Keeper? What led to this moment? How did he cause them to wither?

And why?

She ran her finger over the flower carved into the column. The lines blurred within the image, taking away from any defining features.

But in her heart, Bria knew the truth: this was a camellia.

She opened her branched hand, letting her flower gather in her palm. What was so significant about this little flower? She'd always accepted it as part of her, but it remained as a force within São Caméliosa. Why the camellia?

She plucked it from her palm and let it fall to the ground. The stem wrapped around a root, taking its spot as a goddess amongst weeds. Her immortal camellias used to bloom in the Senator's Garden. Now, at least, they would have a place in São Caméliosa as a reminder of her grandpapa.

And of her ancestors lost to the Mist Keepers.

She stepped away from the archway. Would Brent be able to uncover more of the story?

As she turned away from the sculpture garden, the clunking of boots gave her pause. A group of Gardeniros appeared from the path leading to the old palace. Upon seeing her, one of them shouted.

Bria didn't need to understand what they said.

She merely raised her hands above her head, revealing her branched hand and a single camellia in her palm.

CHAPTER THIRTY-FIVE

THE GRIPPING SMOKE

Brent trudged through the swamp with Caroline and Nix. Behind them, the class followed, with Yaz leading the way. The other spirits all loitered behind her, with Jewel, Milo, and Chander in the back.

Brent's head pounded, and his skin crawled. That morning, as he got dressed, he paused in the mirror, taking note of how the rot had worked its way up his chest with each onslaught of stories. It was only exasperated by the last twenty-four hours, locking him in a daze. He had tried his best to put together the stories without abandoning his own sense of self. As much as he had tried to ignore the stories, attempting to teach the introductory class to his new students, his enthusiasm still dwindled. So he welcomed Caroline's interjection, where she recommended going to the nearby city of Stilette to demonstrate how to release souls.

Everything was planned. Brent kept reciting it all in his head. From the Diabolo escaping to the integration with the Order. Everything had been part of Ningursu's plan.

Except for Brent himself.

He stumbled as they approached the road. It wove between the trees, well-traveled but unaware of the kingdom lurking just a hike away.

"Are we almost there?" Yaz asked.

"I would say another ten minutes or so," Caroline replied.

Brent glanced back at Yaz and the others. The spirits stayed close together. There was childlike amazement about them as they wandered through the swamp. But also a hint of fear. Their stories, jumbled but present, echoed in the swamp. Tales of torture, of innocence, and of fear, all battling for attention.

Before their intensity grew, Brent shook his head, sending the stories to the back of his mind. Kek's words came to haunt him with every step. When would the stories take him over completely? Today? Tomorrow? Next year?

Or would he be able to push them back for an eternity?

When would he stop being Brent Harley and instead be nothing but a Library?

"Brent? Are you present?" Caroline asked beside him.

"Yeah, I'm a'ight," he replied. "It's been a long couple of days."

"Did you get any sleep last night? You do not look well.

"Not really…I mean…I was looking at Jewel's paintings. The ones on her wall."

"Oh, yes, those horrid things."

"They're helping me, in a way. I can…it gives me a chance to deconstruct the stories."

"Yes, but they're terrifying. And to come from Julietta of all people!" Caroline huffed.

Back when Jewel had been Julietta, paintings of such horrific details never seemed present, from what Brent could tell. But Jewel was different—and at least this difference gave Brent a better understanding of what he'd seen in the Library. Jewel's magic had let her capture the stories, locking them in time like a memory. Brent used his own collection of tales to dissect each image and place their knowledge in his back pocket to store for later.

Caroline lowered her voice beside him, "Do you think that she will ever be… Julietta again?"

Brent frowned. "I don't know. There're hints, though…so maybe?"

"Perhaps."

"Milo has been helping, I think," Brent took a glimpse at the spirit, walking alongside Jewel. They didn't visibly speak.

"He is helping her remember Julyana, not Julietta," Caroline replied. "She was Julietta for centuries. Julyana was but a blip in her existence."

"I think that… even if she remembers, she won't be the Julyana he knows or the Julietta you know. She will instead be… I mean, Jewel, Julietta, and Julyana will all be part of her. And whatever name or self she chooses is her choice."

Caroline clenched her hands together and murmured, "I love her, you know. She was my best friend. Sure, I have Tilda… but she cannot even see me. I saw her in Bria's palace, and she did not even know I was there. It is… odd. I do not have any of my… constants. Except for conducting these releases."

"We'll find your constants again."

"But are they truly constants if they can be stolen?"

Brent traced the root-like tattoo on his wrist. "Constants… maybe they're more like… constellations."

"You are just selecting a word that sounds similar."

"No. Listen. Constellations, I mean, they appear at night. But sometimes, the weather or sky doesn't allow for them to be visible. But they're always there… constantly in the sky. Sometimes, we just can't see them."

Caroline chuckled. "That is a ridiculous analogy."

"But it's kind of true."

With a bit more of a smile, Caroline continued to lead the way, a wave of confidence matching each of her steps. Brent could feel the stories of the dead tugging him forward, but with the stories of the spirits close by, it was impossible to pinpoint one dead man's tale.

But Caroline's focus remained undeterred. As signs of Stilette emerged with sporadic stilted homes appearing along the road, her face began to switch. Masks layered over them, revealing those of three elderly people, their lives well lived.

"We are getting close," Caroline whispered.

Brent used that moment to turn to the students behind him. "A'ight, listen, today you are just going to watch Caroline as she releases souls. No one is doing it themselves. A'ight? Just, I mean, pay attention to Caroline's movements, her reactions, as well as to the environment around her. The release of a soul is a personal experience for both the Mist Keeper and the soul. Every release is different, and every Mist Keeper has their own way of approaching them."

Most of the class listened with intent. In the back, Jewel scoffed, seeming unconvinced by the ordeal.

Brent didn't blame her. Unlike the rest, this current version of her was thrust into the school, misplaced because no one else could watch her. But he could only hope that as she reconnected with being a Mist Keeper, her past would follow.

"Brent?" Yaz tugged at his arm.

"Yes?"

"What do you mean each release is different for the Mist Keepers?"

"Good question, Yaz." Brent raised his voice so the rest of the class could hear. "So as I said, the release is different for every Mist Keeper. This starts with how we even find souls to release. For me, I hear their stories. Caroline takes their face. Malaika finds them on her map. And Tomás hears their final thoughts. Each of you will have a different way as well." Brent glanced over the group once, then continued. "The way we find souls transcends into how we release them. While I can't speak on other's experiences, I know my own. I dive into their story, travel into their personal Hell. The first person I ever released, I interacted with her..." Brent trailed off. *Maija.* His stomach twisted. Whatever became of her? He saw in the story how Ningursu had done away with her. She wasn't in the crypts. Did he eliminate her completely?

Yaz tugged at Brent's hand again. "What do others experience?"

He pulled himself back to his lecture. "It's hard to know what the other Mist Keepers experience. Perhaps

Caroline will share her experiences after releasing these souls, a'ight?"

"Okie-doke!"

The stilted houses grew in numbers as they entered the outside of Stilette. Boardwalks wove between the trees. In the trees and beneath the wood, ornamental canisters hung, some older with caked mud and others pristine and maintained.

As they neared a set of stairs beneath the boardwalk, Caroline approached one of the canisters. She cupped it in her hands and closed her eyes.

Brent stepped to the side, allowing the class to observe as she released the soul.

And as she released the souls, the Mist thickened around them.

But rather than witnessing the dead's story, another story wrapped around him and took his mind in full.

Alojzy stood in the swamp, holding Ningursu in his hands. In the distance, workers erected columns, standing half the height of the trees. Thick white Mist clouded their feet.

"It appears I finished the Library at just the right time, sire," Alojzy *remarked.*

"Yes, well done."

Brent blinked. The thick smoke laced through the city on stilts, brushing just on the edge of the boardwalk. Like fingers, edges of the smoke reached for Caroline and the class, lacing around their feet.

"Caroline!" Brent shouted. Chander glanced beside him and immediately stepped out of the way, allowing Brent to push the others in the class away from the smoke. Nix barked alongside him, avoiding the smoke and

Caroline's face had just shifted back to normal as he yanked her away from the canisters, causing them both to fall backward into the swamp.

"Brent! What are you doing?" Caroline spat.

"Ningursu controls the smoke here," Brent clamored to his feet. "Everyone, we gotta go back. He can't find us in Neorama."

"Did you see a story?"

"Yeah, I'll tell you later, but—" As he took a step forward, another story flooded his mind, and he stumbled back into the mud.

"Why are you so enamored with Rosada, sire?" Alojzy asked as they turned away from the construction.

"Hm?"

"You are always talking about Rosada. Surely a god like yourself would not care for just one country."

"Hm," Ningursu's thin lip smirked, "Yes, you would think that."

Alojzy waited for a response.

"I do not talk much about my time as a mortal, but I trust you, Alojzy."

"Thank you for trusting me, sire."

"Yes, and that is why I will tell you. Rosada, or as I know it, Effluvia was where I was born, and hence where our Council was created."

"So it is your home?"

"It is mine, and in my eyes, also mine to rule. But it is hard for the dead to rule the living. If they saw me, a mere skull, they

would make a mockery of my existence. So instead, I must control them through their own beliefs." Ningursu's voice grew soft, almost whimsical. "Someday, I shall return, though. I will take my place above the mountains where I spent my mortality."

"Mountains? The ones in the east?"

"You are quite inquisitive today."

"I am only trying my best to serve you, sire."

Ningursu chuckled, "Yes, I believe the locals call them the Newbird Mountains now. I knew them as the Fastigicaligo."

"So, the same place where I first developed my tunnel network, then?"

"Yes, it would seem so. As I said, the Mist is powerful in Effluvia."

Brent spit out a wad of dirt from his mouth and sat up from the ground. Caroline and the class stared at him. Well, except for Jewel, who sat on the ground beside him, etching in the mud herself.

"Brent? What is it?" Caroline inquired.

He glanced at Jewel, still sitting there. As he watched her, it was clear: she drew the very story he had just witnessed of a man holding a skull in his arms.

"Brent?" Caroline pressed again.

"Take the class and Nix back to Neorama. But leave Jewel here. I have a story to collect, and I think she can help me."

"What are you talking about?"

"Please, Caroline." He rose to his feet and glanced over the class. "Take the class back. I'll...I'll be back soon."

"Where are you taking her?" Caroline's eyes locked on Jewel.

"I need to...I need to go home," Brent swallowed. "I need to go back to Newbird's Arm."

CHAPTER THIRTY-SIX

DESENSITIZED

Todd slept well into the afternoon. Upon arriving back at the speakeasy, he briefly checked on Garrett before collapsing on his bed. He had no intention of sleeping that long, but his body thrived in the dreamless abyss, away from the horrors of the Capitol and the grotesque tunnel system beneath the streets.

He woke to footsteps storming down the hallway. With a groan, he rolled over and climbed from bed. His mouth tasted like three days of rotten food. Even the fresh water by his bed did little to settle the flavor.

He pulled on his tunic and then exited his room. A handful of people queued for the lavatory, and he took his place behind them, rubbing his eyes again.

Nils turned from his spot in line with a grin. "Oh! Hello there, Scruff! Finally awake?"

Todd grunted.

"Yeah, I slept in too. Was up 'til dawn talking with Etta."

Todd didn't humor him with a reply.

"She's in good spirits, considering she was held by the Guard for so long. She's with your son now."

"Wait, what?" Todd stepped back from Nils.

"She's examining him now down in the speakeasy."

"Without me? What the fuck is wrong with her?"

"Well—"

Todd didn't wait for a reply, ignoring the pinching of his bladder and racing downstairs. He nearly trampled over the barkeep as he reached the kitchen.

"Woah there, mate. What'cha in a rush about?"

Todd pushed past him and down into the speakeasy. The room bustled. His head spun, trying to pinpoint his son in the commotion. Cadet Carver sat at the bar with Yeshua and Gisela while a storyteller performed, plucking away at a lute for effect.

After scanning the room, Todd spotted Garrett sitting on top of a table. Professor Gratz sat across from him, a bowl of food in her hand. She raised the spoon to Garrett's mouth.

"Oi! What'cha giving him?" Todd stormed over to her.

The professor didn't bother turning to him. "Food."

"Yeah, what type? It looks like shit."

"It's gelatin. Go on, open up," Professor Gratz moved the food toward Garrett's mouth.

The child opened, blankly accepting the food.

Todd snatched the bowl from the professor and sniffed it. It didn't reek of anything.

He spooned a clump of the food into his mouth.

Then cursed.

Heat scorched over his tongue, clawing down the back of his throat. He gagged. Sweat formed on his brow. Even as he clamored for water, the pain did not cease.

"Why the hell—" he coughed twice, "why the hell are you feeding my son that!?"

Etta took the gelatin back. "Tell me, is your son reacting like you are?"

"No, but that's beside the point!"

"Why do you think that is?"

"Does it matter?"

"Yes." Professor Gratz wrung her hands together. She punctuated her statement, staring hard behind her thick-rimmed glasses at Todd.

"Don't look at me like I should know what you're talking about. Just explain already," Todd crossed his arms.

"Fine," Professor Gratz grunted. "If your son isn't reacting to this gelatin, which contains one of the hottest peppers on the planet, it proves to me one thing:

removing his eyes did more than abolish his sense of sight, but all of his senses."

"He was traumatized."

"That shouldn't make it so he can't taste smokey peppers."

Todd snatched the gelatin away. "Well, don't give him anymore."

Professor Gratz straightened her shoulders. "Very well. I am done with my experiments, anyway."

"Experiments? How long have you been torturing him?"

"Oh, I wasn't torturing him. Do not be so dramatic."

Todd crossed his arms.

"I was testing his senses. He did not respond to loud noises, putrid smells, or even cold ice on his skin. It is as though he is experiencing the world wrapped in a blanket." Professor Gratz motioned for Todd to take a seat.

He begrudgingly accepted.

"Now, from what my sibling told me, you do not like the *m*-word. Can I ask you why?"

"You mean magic? What does it matter?"

"Because I'll cater my answer to your beliefs."

"Isn't that lying?"

"It is me doing right by your boy."

Todd huffed, "I just don't like it. My wife... she loved it. But nothing good ever came of it. My home was destroyed, my wife died… and now my son doesn't got eyes."

"So you do believe it was due to magic?"

"No. I think the Order thought he had magic, so they tore out his eyes to stop the magic."

"What type of magic do you think he had?"

Todd almost didn't reply. After Garrett's brother, Preston, died, Lex was adamant about how Garrett would play with his brother. "My wife used to think he could see the dead. Thought he used to play with his dead twin."

"I see."

Todd glanced back over to the bar, where Cadet Carver continued to speak with Gisela and Yeshua. The boy had perked up slightly since arriving, but there was still that strange gray tone to his skin.

Professor Gratz continued, "I am not here to tell you if your son has magic. I am a magiepidemiologist—I study diseases that cannot be explained by science, so that magic is the only explanation. Your son's condition wreaks of magic, in my opinion. Something took away his senses in a similar way that it is impacting many others as well. He's different in that his eyes were removed though… which makes me wonder…"

"Wonder what?"

She raised her brow, "When were his eyes removed?"

"Dunno. It was a couple months ago, right when I escaped the Guard."

"So the Order did this to him?"

"Yeah. Thought that was clear."

"I would rather not assume…but how interesting…" she glanced over Garrett again. "I thought he looked familiar."

"What d'ya mean?" Todd reeled.

"I've been working for the Order for a long time. Was even up in Knoll before it collapsed. They were experimenting on some kids with magic for a while. Not sure what they were doing. They just hired me to keep magical ailments at bay if needed." She continued staring at Garrett. "I just thought the little man looked familiar was all. I never interacted with him… but thought I saw him with one of the Elders."

"And you didn't do anything!?"

"Oh, you were with the Guard. You know how hard it is to go against the Order's doctrine."

Todd couldn't argue with her. He sank back into his seat, watching as Garrett played with a small wooden car on the table. The child made no noise, moving the car back and forth, uninterested.

"Can you fix him?" Todd finally asked.

Professor Gratz leaned back in her own chair. "His eyesight is unrecoverable. But I hope to create something that will spark the senses in him as well as the others. I do think they're related.

"Yeah, that sounds like bull."

"It does, doesn't it? But I'm pretty sure I'm right...just not so certain how."

"Well, you better prove it."

"I plan to, but first, I'll need a laboratory. Dr. Lieu said that she would find me one—and speak of the devil!" Professor Gratz rose from her spot with a smile.

Todd turned. The resident doctor had entered the speakeasy, with a younger woman walking in step behind her.

"Hue! Hullo!" Professor Gratz remarked as the doctor approached.

"Etta," the doctor replied.

"Have you found me a place to work?"

"I have made some connections. Once we get everyone to the next safe house, I think we can sort out a good place for you to set up."

"Safehouse?" Todd asked. "What? It ain't safe here anymore."

"We're fine now, but we received a report that one of our allies was attacked. We don't have details yet, but we're trying to move as many people as possible out of the country before they get more aggressive. Once Marisol here vets everyone, we can start moving forward." The doctor motioned to the young woman beside her.

"You're seriously moving us again?"

"Trust me, where we're going is way better than this tavern," the young woman added.

Todd scowled. Once again, his paranoia took hold. Where would they take them now? How long would they need to travel? Before he could ask, the doctor and Marisol walked away, heading to the bar where Gisela, Yeshua, and Cadet Carver chatted.

He stared ahead. His son played with a wooden car beside him, blankly jamming it onto the table. Would he ever have his son back? The boy was a ghost trapped in a sensory-deprived shell.

Could Todd even do anything to help?

He had found Professor Gratz, though. However unorthodox her methods, she was an expert. Trust was not a fruitful commodity. Todd just needed to give her a little, just enough that maybe his son would shine again.

"Promise me that you'll help him," he finally whispered.

Etta smiled at him, her eyes lighting with excitement, "I will help him live again. I promise you, Mr. Dray."

CHAPTER THIRTY-SEVEN

MEMORIES FROM THE MOUNTAINS

Brent's heart thudded in his ears as he led Jewel from the tunnels and into the forest of the Newbird Mountains. It'd been almost two years since he'd been home, since he'd come back to the familiar smoke and pine of the region. He'd spent his entire life here, having never left until discovering the tunnels. But now, it was a different place. The forest did not greet him with the same evergreen trees and bubbling squirrels. Instead, the trees waited bare, thick Mist weaving through them, like the Necrowood back in Knoll's Gully. Through the thin trees, he could make out the distant smokestacks from town.

"I thought you said we were getting the best lemon cakes you've ever tasted," Jewel griped, arms crossed as she glanced around the forest. "I'm gonna get mud on my shoes here!"

"We will—I told you, I just need to do something first... a'ight? It won't take long, and I think you can help me." Brent paused for a second to rub his abdomen. Despite his head spinning from the previous story, he needed to find out what happened next, the next chapter whispering to him and waiting to be told. He had to learn the rest of the story, and he wouldn't put down the book until it was complete.

Jewel huffed, "Fine. But I want two of these special cakes."

"I'll be sure of it." Brent grinned, then motioned for Jewel to follow him further into the woods. While home beckoned him, the stories led him away. A distant pulse, a thudding in his ears. With it came Ningursu's voice in waves, followed by the tales of an ancient past that whistled alongside it. If he found the right spot, he'd be able to focus.

Breathe.

Become.

Be.

The words made little sense, reciting over and over again in his head, guiding him further through the trees.

"I really don't understand what is goin' on, by the way," Jewel grumbled behind him. "Tommy never did a good job explaining it either. It's kind of ridiculous at this point. Ain't no child."

Brent slowed his pace. Jewel, for the most part, had been complacent. He'd never quite had a conversation with her. Even when she was Julietta, there was a wall between conversation and imagination.

"Do you have any memory of…anything?" he asked.

"Not really. My oldest memory was from Mert. Found myself wandering a city with Tommy, got a little frustrated with some prick trying to sell phony luck potions, gave a piece of my mind… and somehow ended up leading the pinstripes. Honestly, it's all a blur…" her gaze unfocused. Her voice softened, more like Julietta's voice. "It's like I am trying to remember too much…so I don't remember anything at all."

"Has Tomás told you anything… about who you were?" Brent asked.

"He always avoids the subject… and frankly, I couldn't care less. At least… not until all his weird magic began…" she picked at her nails. Visible smudges of paint coated her fingertips. "Hadn't given magic much thought of anything until suddenly no one could see me no more."

"I can tell you what I know if you want." Brent turned to her. She looked smaller, younger even. It was easy to forget that she was once a young woman, about the same age as him, tackling the Mist.

"Depends…how wild of a tale are you gonna spin?" Jewel asked.

"Well, let me tell you the story… and you can decide how preposterous it is, a'ight?"

Jewel furrowed her brow, then stomped over to a nearby log. She brushed off her pants before sitting down and crossing her arms in front of her chest. "Fine. Tell me the story."

"A'ight, so it goes something like this…"

It was the first time in months he had taken the stage, doing something that came to him as naturally as breathing. He wove Julietta's story, starting with when he first met her in the Library, aloof and with her memory already failing. She had meandered between the shelves, calling him by the name "Milo" and speaking in riddles that had no real answers.

But he did not dally on her confusion. Instead, he reframed the story, speaking of Julietta's true self. A painter who could take a memory and paint it with precision. Even as parts of her memory failed, she still acted as a support for others—especially Caroline.

But in her own innocence, Julietta had succumbed to the horrors hidden deep in the crypt. It was there that a monster had taken over her mind. Even after the monster left, Julietta vanished, leaving behind a hollow body and blank eyes.

Jewel didn't move as Brent told the story. He followed her gaze as he spoke. A replica of her story played out in the Mist, a replica of the Library, and a ghost of Julietta wandering amongst the books.

Then it changed. Julietta's ghost wandered into the crypt. Around her, yellow smoke took root.

And the story faded.

Brent finished his story. "You are a Mist Keeper, Jewel. Even if you don't remember this past life, you are still a Mist Keeper."

Jewel didn't move at first, still staring into the trees. Her scowl had fallen, her stance loosened.

Her question came as a whisper. "Julietta… she lost her memory at the end there, right? Then she became me?"

"Yeah, that's the story as I know it."

"But… Julietta… she still didn't have a memory of her past either. Does this mean that I am just some… empty body with ideas shoveled into it?"

"I think there's a core part of you that still exists in every iteration."

"But who was I initially? It sounds like I have lived countless lives… but who was I when it all began?"

Brent wrung his hands together. "That story is still coming together. But from what Tomás has told me...you were once royalty."

"Royalty?"

"He only told me a couple of months ago." Frankly, it hadn't crossed Brent's mind much at all—uncovering the details of that story would require research and time. For now, he'd punctuate his knowledge with that one word. It wasn't time to bring up her dearest apprentice, and apparent son, Milo.

"I will have to give Tommy a piece of my mind... he never mentioned that to me...that twat..." She cursed under her breath, once again lost in her thoughts.

Brent fidgeted with his cane, waiting for Jewel to speak again. But she remained lost in her own thoughts. Without her questions, the distant stories of Ningursu returned, hissing in his ear. It tugged him in every direction. It was almost impossible to look back thousands of years without losing his sense of self.

Fixate on Ningursu... nothing else.

Jewel tugged him back into the present. "So why do you want me here for you, really?

"Huh?"

"You obviously brought me here for a reason, so tell me, what's the real reason? Just don't say cake."

Brent replied earnestly, "I'm trying to find an ancient story…and I worry that it will be too much for me. So if you can record the memory as I discover it—as in, I mean, if you can paint it. Then it won't…overwhelm me…and I can make sense of what is happening."

Jewel crossed her arms. "You act like I know how to do that."

"You've already done it… and I trust you can do it again."

"I don't even have any paint."

"That doesn't matter…at least I don't think it does."

Jewel climbed from her seat and shrugged, "Well, if you lose your head cause I fail, don't go blaming me."

Once she joined him, they continued through the woods. With every step, another barrage of stories crossed Brent's vision: children running in the forest, a hunter seeking a deer, and ancient workers carrying materials to build homes. He locked sights on those workers and followed them down the mountain, back into the past.

There, the trees parted around a shallow lake. The waterbed had become overgrown, browning bushes and broken trees bordering its edge. A light sheet of snow covered the otherwise barren ground.

But the stories continued, and around him, a new world took shape. A community from the past emerged, dotting the edges of the lake as a central hub for a farming community. It extended beyond the lake into the mountains, where the smoke was the heaviest.

From that smoke, two little boys emerged from the past, running through the streets, where they came face-to-face with a horse.

CHAPTER THIRTY-EIGHT

WHERE A GOD IS BORN

The smallest child ran straight into the horse. It whinnied in shock, kicking back both of its feet and nearly hitting the children.

The older child yanked his little brother away from the horse. "Nedo! Be careful!"

"Sorry, horse," the child giggled, covering his mouth as he laughed.

"You could have died!"

"Yes, but the horse didn't mean it."

"Pfft," the older kid shook his head.

"Why do you hate horses so much, Nin?" Nedo asked.

"Because they can kill you... just like you saw."

"I think you don't like that they are bigger than you."

Nin huffed, "You do not understand..."

The boys continued through the bustling road, dodging horse manure and watching as villagers prepared for the festivities. Nin cringed at every horse they passed.

He only dropped the fear when they approached the village elders.

"Grandfather!" Nedo called to one of the elders.

"Ah, children, hello," an old man with a wiry beard grinned.

"What is all of this about, Grandfather?" Nin motioned to the decorations in the streets.

"Ah, we are welcoming our next Custocaligo and Hurtovitae. They arrive in the morning to take their spots."

"What are those?" Nedo asked.

"Our protectors of Life and Death. The last ones left before you were born, little ones."

And so Nin and Nedo waited for the next day. They pushed through the crowd, where they watched as the Custocaligo and Hurtovitae arrived. The Custocaligo arrived with plumes of smoke, a calmness in her walk, and a gentleness in her presence. Beside her, the Hurtovitae emerged like a legendary dryad, looking more like a tree than a human.

Nin shuddered at the Hurtovitae's presence. There was something inhuman about it, its body moving like branches and commanding the earth as if a god.

But just as soon as the Custocaligo and Hurtovitae arrived, they joined the Elders, leaving but a thick cloud of smoke in their wake.

And with every morning, that same smoke danced across the village. Nin and Nedo spied on them for many moons, but the excitement soon dwindled for Nedo, and the boy returned to his games. Nin kept alert, careful not to interact with the Hurtovitae, fearful of what it might do to him.

But the Custocaligo did keep his attention, and he found himself following the Custocaligo into the woods most days, marveling at her abilities. Every day, the Custocaligo strode without fear deep into the brambles.

And it was there that Nin saw her approach the body of a hunter mauled by a bear.

Nin held his breath as he watched the Custocaligo kneel beside the body. She worked her hands over the body, barely touching its skin. Then, with a single beat, Mist rose above the body, forming the ghost of the dead hunter.

Before vanishing.

"Woah," Nin whispered.

The Custocaligo turned, then smiled in Nin's direction. "So you saw?"

Nin nodded.

"Then, that means you shall be joining our ranks. Come, we shall discuss with the Elders."

And so, Nin followed the Custocaligo into the smoke.

Time passed.

When Nin finally emerged, he was no longer a boy. A tall, determined Custocaligo with haunting gray eyes, he walked through town with his own Hurtovitae on his arm. He refused to look at her, eyes focused on his job: to release the dead.

"Brother!" Nedo greeted Nin at the edge of the lake. Nin waved for the Hurtovitae to leave, and with a curtsey, she left for the trees. With each of her steps, the leaves changed, and flowers bloomed.

"Hello, Nedo," Nin remarked without a smile. "I hear you have inherited the farm."

"You were away, brother. But I am delighted to see you have returned and will happily split the land. Although, I doubt you need it…as you are truly our Custocaligo now, yes?"

"Indeed. I trained with countless others who will be stationed around the world. This is where I shall begin."

"And who is the Hurtovitae?"

"Cassia. She is my betrothed."

"Brother, congratulations!"

"It is not one of choice. It is merely a statement… that Life and Death are unified," Nin eyed after the Hurtovitae. He had spent his years gathering knowledge, learning more about his role as a Custocaligo. Keepers of the Mist, they called themselves. While their job at their core was to release the dead, it was so much more.

And Nin would make sure they didn't fade.

He continued, "She only gets in my way. My job is to balance Life and Death, to ensure that all creatures die and all who deserve it go to paradise. That Hurtovitae prevents me from doing my duty. She is trying to bring life, and that is abnormal at best."

"What you describe as your duty is the role of God," Nedo replied.

"Exactly," Nin murmured, "and there can only be one."

Nedo raised his brow. "One?"

But Nin did not humor the question, pushing past his brother to complete his duty.

And that guided him, where he served his home, a constant presence, like a watchful cloud. His life became marked by death, sitting beside the most gruesome bodies to release their souls before continuing on to the next one. It came naturally to him. The spirits were released without hindrance, never a mistake. All the while, he kept the Hurtovitae at arm's length, barely acknowledging her presence. When the elder Custocaligo came to check on his performance, he planned to show them his perfection. Then, they would let him stand in their highest ranks.

Even when his dear grandfather passed, Nin did not bat an eye, capturing the soul in his palms and crushing it to dust.

"That is for giving my brother the family farm," Nin hissed as he walked away from the body.

But no one ever knew Nin's feelings. Instead, they admired him, their local Custocaligo, with honor and praise. Even the Hurtovitae paid her respects. She was a pretty thing, in Nin's eyes, growing into her features, with hair woven behind her like vines. While they maintained their civility, some days, when all *was calm, he would take her into the forest and show her why he was as powerful as God.*

At first, it was all for play. But, over time, each time the Hurtovitae opened herself to him, it allowed Nin a chance to see her in full. Life was easy to manipulate and change. Only death was permanent. So Nin used the Mist to his advantage, invading the Hurtovitae's body.

But she never noticed.

Even though each time they returned from the forest, her magic dwindled. Less greenery followed her. The trees did not bow with the same grace.

She never did voice her concern.

The village did whisper about her, though. Nin could hear them echoing in the Mist about how the Hurtovitae's abilities had floundered, and the world around them had turned brown.

But Nin flourished. With every act, his magic grew. Not only could he release souls, but the Mist spoke to him, letting him see through the eyes of others and control their every move. He would listen in on the Elders talking or spy on his brother as he tended his farm plot with his wife. But often, he infected the Hurtovitae, stopping her from blooming another flower and using her magic to promote the dying weeds. At the end of each day, Nin sank back into the Mist, to his home where no one could follow.

Every morning, he returned to his village to complete his duty.

And that is where the Hurtovitae cornered him one spring day, where the leaves on the trees sprouted in patches, struggling in the smoky air. Her hair fell like dying grass against her face, while the flowers in her hair had long wilted.

"Ningursu, what have you done?" she asked.

"Many things, my dear. But what are you inferring to this time?" Nin asked.

"My magic has wilted…and I think it has to do with our engagements in the forest."

"That is merely a coincidence, my little flower."

"I do not think so. Every time I go to sleep, I hear you in my head. You are controlling my movements, suffocating my magic."

"You have no proof."

"Look around us! Spring isn't blooming. That is proof enough!" She stepped forward, "You have no respect for the union of Custocaligo and Hurtovitae…you never did."

Nin chuckled and shook his head. Around them, a few villagers had stopped, watching the altercation. "Have you ever thought that the union is wrong? You are the one manipulating life. I am only ensuring that the balance remains. You and the others do not understand that."

The Hurtovitae shook her head. "We're only helping the world thrive because of how thick the Effluvium is—you know this, Ningursu. The earth is not equipped to bear the weight of thousands of dead tales. My people keep it from dying… and maintain the balance."

"Or perhaps your people are using it to come into power."

"We're not."

"Then why is your magic able to destroy the world?"

"We do not destroy. We give it life. Stop with these ridiculous proclamations!"

"Perhaps you need a demonstration."

"What are you saying?"

Nin smirked, and then, with the smoke growing around him, he stepped toward the Hurtovitae. He laced his fingers into the smoke. It thickened around them, darkening like storm clouds and weaving like vines through the air. They wrapped around Hurtovitae's limbs and crawled up her body. As they entered her mouth, nose, and ears, her eyes rolled back into her head. Her knees gave out.

But as she fell, the ground began to shake.

With each quake, trees tumbled. The water in the lake rose. Storm clouds danced into view.

As did the rain.

The thunder.

And the lightning.

With each shock of lightning, the dry grass birthed fire. Horses whinnied. People shouted.

But the earth had made her statement. She was the one who could not be tamed. With the winds churning, the trees falling, and the fire growing, now everyone could see the dangers of the Hurtovitae. With a mere flick of their finger, they could destroy everything.

Nin smiled as the storm finally ceased. The fire tapered. And the trees lay in shambles. At his feet, the Hurtovitae had collapsed, vines suffocating her, and her heartbeat no more. Now that the smoke cleared, the true destruction made itself known. Not only did the forest collapse, but so did the village. The homes had crumbled, and the animals had fled.

Bodies lay strewn across the ground.

Waiting…

Begging…

Pleading…

So Ningursu might free them at last.

Their God.

No one else.

But this, of course, was only the beginning.

He stood there, seething. The trees mocked him, laughing at his own fear.

They weren't powerful.

They were only trees.

But then, they parted. Ningursu walked with his hands on a young woman's shoulders, whispering with streams of black smoke.

The girl turned, her eyes wide, mouth ajar.

"Bria!" Brent shouted. But the story faded.

He stumbled backward, his head spinning as he searched the area for a sign.

There was no Bria.

No Ningursu.

No horses.

Only Jewel, standing at the edge of the lake, still as a statue. Colorful Mist wrapped around her feet.

Still shaking, Brent joined her side.

Before them, a painting encompassed the lake, recanting the very story Brent had witnessed.

He sank to his knees, locking his attention with the lake.

"It's gonna happen again…" he whispered.

But not even the trees could hear him.

L'Corona Verde

The Gardeniros led Bria away from the sculpture garden and into the old palace, where walls of vines greeted her. The palace lacked any sort of grandeur, with narrow paths and broken statues. In low voices, the Gardeniros spoke in their foreign tongue, glancing back at Bria every now and again. They led her through the palace unrestrained, keeping her moving. There was a mutual trust between her and the Gardeniros, unspoken but known. While Bria maintained her defenses, she did not attack, instead listening to the decrepit stone and flickers of the candles.

At the end of the corridor, a door carved from vines sat. The Gardeniros pushed it open, leading Bria into a barrack. Like any barrack, it wreaked of sweat. Bria's stomach crawled. The mere scent reminded her of the barracks in Newbird's Arm, where Captain Carver had interrogated her for hours. Looking back at that interaction, it had been so mild in contrast to what she'd experienced. Still, she found herself counting - the breaths, the elements, and the lights.

Yet, these barracks still held a different energy. The Gardeniros did not sit there polishing their weapons. Instead, they potted plants at the table. One took inventory of seeds, and another adjusted the shovels on the wall. Not a single pistol occupied the room, weapons of destruction replaced with something pretty.

The Gardeniros themselves did not look like warriors. Laughing together and speaking in their native tongue. Like Bria's little branch, foliage wove through their hair and skin, although not as pronounced. One bore taproots in their eyebrows, while another wore branches like a glove. *They're just like me*, Bria smiled to herself. If her grandpapa had shared this with her, then would her life have been different? Would she not be the Forest Queen?

One of the Gardeniros who led her into the castle spoke, still in an unfamiliar language. The others turned, and they conversed for a moment. The only word Bria understood was L'Corona Verde.

Her stomach shifted as they all turned to her.

The Gardeniro with taproots in their eyebrows approached.

"Please, I'm no different from any of you," Bria whispered.

The Gardeniro seemed unimpressed, grabbing hold of Bria's arm. They rolled down her sleeve, revealing her branched arm to the others.

"It's just like you…" Bria said again.

To her surprise, the Gardeniro responded in broken Rosadian, "Remove coat."

"What?"

"Take off coat."

Bria hesitated.

"Now!"

Bria obliged, letting her coat fall to the floor, revealing her branched arm as it crossed over her shoulder and up behind her ear. The Gardeniro circled her.

"Is part of you?" The Gardeniro asked.

"Yes…it is."

"How much?"

"What do you mean?"

"How much does it go?"

Bria swallowed, then carefully pulled down the collar of her shirt, revealing the way the branches extended beyond her shoulder and neck, over her collarbones, and down her chest.

The Gardeniro glanced at the others. Murmurs followed, as did that phrase, L'Corona Verde.

One at a time, each Gardeniro took a knee before her. Bria stepped back, nearly tripping over the two Gardeniros who had led her here.

"I… I don't know what to say," Bria stammered.

"You do not have to say anything," a voice said from behind her.

Bria spun. "Yusef!?"

The short man stood before her, hands on his hips, his wiry gray hair swept to the side. She hadn't seen Yusef since Knoll's Gully. While his magic focused on tracking plants, he was the first connection that Bria ever made to someone with similar magic. It was with his help that they developed Brent's original medication that kept him present.

"It is good to see you again, Bria. I had a feeling you would make your way to São Caméliosa, eventually." Yusef said.

"You knew about this place? Why didn't you tell me?"

"Honestly, I put you on a completely different pedestal than the Gardeniros. I doubted they would be much help to you."

"You still could have told me."

"And still, you found your way here in the end." Yusef motioned her to follow him out of the barracks, "Come. Let's talk."

Bria glanced back at the Gardeniros, still locked in place, admiring her… or perhaps worshipping her. Either way, it made her skin crawl, and she turned back to follow Yusef into the hallway.

"What're you doing here?" Bria asked after the barracks disappeared behind them.

"I visit the Gardeniros every now and again. Used to train with them hundreds of years ago. Sometimes I come by to say hello." Yusef shrugged.

"And you still didn't tell me!?"

"Listen, the Gardeniros need at least three people to grow a tree. You wouldn't learn anything from them."

"There's still history to learn!"

"The only history they have is failure. They haven't had magic of your magnitude since before I joined their ranks."

"That doesn't mean they don't have lessons to teach. You learned from them, didn't you?"

"Barely—they were already weakened when I joined. They may have even been weakened before Kek. Their power was nothing more than a myth, really."

"Myths have power…" Bria murmured. She could almost hear Brent reciting the same phrase to her. Stories, no matter how old, had their purpose.

"I suppose they do…" Yusef eyed her carefully.

"I'm not referring to me."

"But aren't you the most significant myth of them all? I am sure you saw the statue in the garden."

Bria didn't reply.

"In fact, I know you did—I saw what you did out there. The Gardeniros have been waiting for L'Corona Verde to return ever since Varden predicted her."

"Varden?"

"He had a vision of you long ago, described you in detail… and now, we have your statue, watching over the most significant parts of the Garden."

"Why didn't he tell me?"

"He may have forgotten." Yusef approached a moss-covered window, peering out over the sculpture garden. "Honestly, I had put the thought to the back of my mind as well. L'Corona Verde seemed utterly preposterous until I met you—like a legend from the earlier times, before the Mist grew thick with vengeance."

Bria joined Yusef, peering toward the pillars on the edge of the sculpture garden. "I saw the glyphs on those pillars. It showed what looked like a Mist Keeper destroying the Gardeniros."

Yusef nodded. "Yes—and who do you think that was?"

"The Mist Keeper?"

"Mhm."

Bria didn't need to even think. She knew, deep in her core, exactly who was responsible. "Ningursu."

"He's always been playing puppet master. The Gardeniros do not stand a chance against him, although Kek has always used them in their game. That's why I am here now—to see if they will be ready to fight if needed."

"Then we don't really have a chance, do we? Ningursu will continue to pull the strings." Bria picked at her branched hand. A small camellia budded from her fingers.

"Now, let us not give up hope yet. After all, camellias bloom even in the winter."

Bria placed her fingers on the camellia's petals. They curved around them.

"In Varden's vision, long ago, he saw a camellia first," Yusef said, seeming to recall a distant memory.

"The vision with me in it, you mean?"

"Yes—he saw the camellia, and out of it bloomed L'Corona Verde. If my memory is correct, and I believe it is, he said that L'Corona Verde would bring life back to the world. People latched onto L'Corona Verde and spun their own stories with her... including the one you know."

"Rhodana the Forest Queen…" Bria recited.

"She'll save the world and make it evergreen," Yusef sang. "How? That's where the stories seem to differ and change."

Bria let the camellia fall to the floor. She couldn't alone make the world evergreen.

But there were others—not just the Gardeniros, but her friends back home, ready to fight against a foe they did not understand.

And, of course, Brent.

"I'm sorry, Bria. I do wish I could tell you more…but the stories have been lost for centuries. Even at my age, I have not heard them all," Yusef said.

Bria picked the camellia off the ground and placed it in her pocket. She then glanced at Yusef, "Then I need to bring Brent here."

"His insights would be valuable. But… I was hoping you would stay longer to meet with the Gardeniros."

"I'll be back soon. I promise. Just… I need to talk to him first."

"Very well."

Bria nodded. She could almost picture Brent wandering in the garden, uncovering the stories with a mere wave of his fingers. He'd then scribble feverishly in the notebook, telling her everything he uncovered. His notes would help rediscover history. The stories would no longer be the victors' choice. The Story Collector told all tales.

"I promise I'll return. I want to help the Gardeniros. But I won't be able to focus until I talk to Brent and get his opinion. But I promise, I'll be back soon."

"Go. We'll be here," Yusef insisted.

Bria thanked Yusef, and then, with her head down, she hurried from the palace and back into the garden. Part of her yearned to stay, to continue to bloom with the other Gardeniros.

But there was more to this world than flowers.

NEWCOMERS

Caroline vanished as soon as she led the class back to the school, leaving them under Szyman's watch. Chander and Yaz stood on the main road of Neorama with Milo, marveling as Caroline disappeared into the Mist, moving through it like a fish in water.

"Right then, I got some work to do to stabilize this town. You know where to find me if you need anything," Szyman said. He didn't wait for a reply, though, marching straight back to his metal box in the center of town.

They stood in silence for a moment. Chander closed his eyes for a second, catching a quick glimpse of Anandi moving about the Pinstripe Tavern, then refocused on the road. If he held his eyes closed too long, he worried he might fall asleep.

"Do you think Brent is okay?" Yaz asked, sitting on the ground with Nix.

"I'm sure he is," Chander replied. Brent had seemed at least *normal* when he left. Lucid, even. But what did Chander know about Brent's magic?

"I'm still worried," Yaz mumbled.

Behind her, Milo removed a harmonica from his vest and played an ever-so-gentle tune as if to say, "Everything will be okay."

Yaz glanced at the spirit and smiled. While Yaz had gotten more comfortable around the spirits, they still made Chander's stomach twist. *What if I become one?* he kept wondering but never dared say it out loud.

"We should go inside," Chander muttered. "It's getting late."

"It's not that late yet!"

"Yeah, but you heard Brent—it might be dangerous."

"But not at Ms. Bria's castle!" Yaz hopped between her feet. "She told me all about it. It's made out of the trees!"

"Yeah, but it's a bit of a walk, isn't it? Shouldn't we wait until Brent or Caroline gets back?"

"But then it might be late. Besides, there are no monsters here. I don't feel them nearby..." Yaz trailed off, gazing toward the sky.

Chander sighed, "Fine. But if it gets too dark, we better turn around."

Yaz piped up, "You mean it?"

"Yeah, whatever."

She beamed, then glanced at Milo behind them, "Do you wanna come too?"

Milo played a quick, happy melody on his harmonica that even Chander understood.

They walked through the swamp, early evening glow as their guide. Milo played his harmonica as they walked, catching the Mist in the air and warping it into birds, dragons, and more. They soared high through the trees, as majestic as any creature and with the same harmony as a story. Nix chased after the Mist, running a few paces ahead, barking, and then returning to Yaz's side. The girl watched in awe while Chander trailed behind her, keeping watch on the distant glow of the setting sun.

As they walked, hints of this haven that Bria had created appeared. Small homes woven from in the trees emerged, with defined paths and a few people moving about, as if this was a life they had lived for years.

Chander's pace slowed as the swampy creations grew in numbers. Thicker rows of small homes lined the path, seamlessly blending with the cypress trees. They all bowed toward the clearing. There, amongst the canopy, the water sat clear and calm, glistening in the setting sun.

Roots came together, forming a clear pathway toward an intricate wove tree that resembled a castle.

Yaz jumped in excitement. "Wowee! Look at it!" she remarked.

The castle was beyond Chander's wildest imagination. The trees wove together, forming a structure that did not belong anywhere else. It towered to the canopy, with its bark engraved with carvings and flowers and moss as accents. Inside, he could only imagine how the intricacies wove together.

"Bria made this?" Chander asked Yaz.

"Yeah! She's the Forest Queen! Of course she made this!" Yaz exclaimed. "And all the homes, too. She's been saving people, she told me."

"Yeah… that doesn't surprise me."

Yaz turned to Milo, "You're gonna love Ms. Bria! I hope she'll be back soon 'cause she's really nice, and she is really powerful."

Yaz continued to blather as Chander observed the area. He vaguely recognized a few of the refugees in the area from his time in Knoll, but he didn't know their names. Were some of them from his time in Captain Palmer's tower? He tried to avoid thinking about that prison. They had tied him up with electric wires, which sent shocks through his wrists every few moments. If it wasn't for the Forest Queen, he may have still been in the tower.

Toward the opposite edge of the swamp, he caught a glimpse of what looked like a door opening from the ground. From it emerged a collection of twenty or so individuals. They filed out, one at a time, heads bent and bodies weary. He only recognized a doctor who had treated him in Knoll and a young woman who had been imprisoned in the same tower nearly a year earlier.

He stepped back, not to draw attention to himself.

"Those must be more people Ms. Bria saved! She must be coming back soon!" Yaz exclaimed beside Chander. She turned to Milo behind them, "I can't wait for you to meet Ms. Bria."

Milo whistled once.

Chander kept watching the newcomers, asking, "Where did they come from?"

"The tunnels, of course!"

"Tunnels?"

"Oh, right, you haven't seen them. The Mist Keepers have secret tunnels beneath the earth, but Ms. Bria told me that she controls them now."

"You spoke a lot with her." Chander was almost jealous of Yaz. The girl had a way of making friends. She'd been quiet when they first met, but now, she used her inquisitive nature to her advantage.

"Yeah, you should talk to her too. She does so much!"

They continued to watch the newcomers in silence. One at a time, they filed from the tree: a woman with wiry curls, a stout man with a receding hairline, a man with tattooed arms carrying a child, and a woman with long black hair gripping the arm of a man with bleeding eyes.

Yaz stiffened beside Chander. She placed her hand on Nix's head.

"You okay?" Chander asked.

"I… um…" she blinked a few times, "I'll be right back. I…my tummy's bothering me."

Before Chander could stop her, Yaz raced into the trees. Nix woofed once, then followed after Yaz. When Chander went to follow, Milo held out his hand and shook his head.

"Fine. I'll stay." He returned his attention to the newcomers.

Not many more people exited the tunnels. Upon arriving, they all froze, marveling at the castle.

Except for a tall man with a half-burnt face, scanning the area like a watchguard.

"Everyone, this way!" The doctor called from the front of the group. "We'll get you set up with quarters!"

The group obliged, following the doctor to the smaller fortress at the base of the castle.

Except again for that man with the half-burnt face.

The man with tattooed arms glanced back, "Carver, you coming?"

Carve waved his hand. "Yeah, I'm coming. Just…taking it all in. This shite's insane."

The man shrugged, then followed behind the others.

The younger man, Carver, continued scanning the area. As he turned, wisps of smoke gathered about his mouth, pulsating from his graying skin.

But then he smiled, locking eyes straight with Chander.

"What're you doing hiding there?" Carver called.

Chander swallowed. Behind him, Milo made not a sound.

"C'mon, ain't gonna hurt ya."

Chander didn't reply.

Carver stepped closer into the light. One of his eyes turned inward as he approached, the smile on his face almost skeletal.

That can't be real. I'm tired…that's all.

But Carver kept approaching, "Ain't gonna hurt you. Do not worry."

"How can I trust you?" Chander stammered.

"Because you have no choice." Carver snapped his fingers. Black smoke appeared at his fingertips. As it washed over him, for a moment, his face changed, revealing a gaping hole in the side of his mouth and a skeletal jaw.

But then, his face returned to normal. Another smile followed.

Chander stumbled backward into Milo. The spirit caught him by the sleeve.

Carver laughed, a low, rumbling laugh that vibrated in the air. More smoke escaped his lips.

"Go on, run. Ain't gonna be much help, though." Carver leaned forward, still grinning. "Go ahead. Run."

Chander exchanged a quick glance with Milo, and then, without hesitating, the pair rushed back into the forest. Carver's cackles followed, his voice growing louder as smoke rushed into the trees. The branches creaked, the leaves shuttered, and birds took flight.

As the smoke thickened, the last bit of sunlight fell and left the swamp in darkness. Chander tripped over the roots, staying close to Milo, not daring to look back over his shoulder. Who was that *Carver* person? What was he here to do? Surely, the Forest Queen wouldn't have let someone like that into her sanctuary.

Was this why Yaz ran?

Chander stumbled, nearly falling to the ground.

"We gotta find Yaz!" he shouted over the growing wind.

Milo shook his head.

"But she'll be hurt! We gotta!"

Milo quickly whistled a sharp tune on his harmonica.

"But—"

Milo tugged on Chander's sleeve. The spirit was stronger than he looked and nearly caused Chander to trip again. Before Chander could even attempt to pull away, Milo dragged him through the trees, with black smoke racing on their heels like a monsoon.

NONSENSE

Todd refused to believe they used magic tunnels to get to this distant swamp. It must have been some ridiculous technology, or a trick, or just a plain lie. The swamp must not have been far from the Capital.

That was what made the most sense.

But the swamp itself was out of a story, sculpted out of the trees themselves, drenched in a thick wave of humidity. Upon arriving, he had to reassure himself that he wasn't dreaming as he sloshed through the water behind Etta and Nils.

He adjusted Garrett in his arms, stealing a glance back at Cadet Carver, standing still by the exit from the tree.

"Carver, you coming?" he called behind him.

Cadet Carver waved his hand, focusing instead on one of the trees.

Todd didn't bother asking what bothered the cadet, hurrying to catch up with Etta, Nils, and the others.

In his arms, Garrett didn't react to the change in scenery. Was Professor Gratz right? Had his senses been diminished beyond just his eyes? If they had…how would this swamp help him heal?

Dr. Lieu led them into a smaller fortress at the base of the castle, peering over the swamp. With its twisted exterior, artistic in nature, it was hard not to admire the structure. Even Todd couldn't help but wonder what magic created it.

They entered the smaller fortress, which held the same artistry. Todd expected to find more of the forest inside but instead found himself in an empty dance hall, similar to the one he visited in Mert with Lex years ago. A few chairs gathered at the side, and a buffet of food lined the wall.

As they entered, an individual in a sparkling vest and a woman with frizzy red hair approached.

"Hue! Are these the ones from the speakeasy?" The individual in the sparkly vest asked.

"Yes, Horton. This is most of them. A few are heading out on caravans, but otherwise… yes. I believe we have about twenty-six total here, including myself."

The woman with red hair replied, "I count twenty-five.

Hue glanced over the group, counting, before narrowing her eyes and asking, "Where's Cadet Carver?"

"Cadet?" Horton asked.

"I already vetted him," Marisol replied, pinching the bridge of her nose in pain.

"Go lie down," Hue insisted.

"It's just a migraine."

"Go."

Marisol obliged, squinting against the dim light.

Horton watched her, then turned back to Hue, "You have to understand why I am a bit skeptical of a former guard."

"Marisol's magic has never lied to us before," Hue replied.

"But where is he?"

Todd interjected, "He's just looking around. I'm sure he'll be in here soon."

Horton nodded, then motioned for Hue to follow. "Fine. We'll get you all situated over here. Get some food, then we'll get you into a nice cozy bed."

Horton led them over to the buffet table. Todd remained in the back as the group dispersed. The woman with red hair cornered Yeshua and Gisela, leading them over to another woman with similar bleeding eyes. Nils and Professor Gratz helped themselves to the buffet. But Todd couldn't feel any more trapped. He had no clue where he was or what would happen next. It was like being in the Guard all over again.

Instead of joining others by the buffet, he sat in the corner, continuing to take in the room. Countless refugees chatted. After a few minutes, Gisela stormed from the room, leaving Yeshua with the red-headed woman.

"Scruff, what'cha doing here by yourself," Nils asked as he approached, carrying a plate of food.

"Just…am."

"That's lonely," Nils waved to his sister to join them. "Isn't this all interesting, though? I mean, we're in a town made of trees!"

"Hate to break it to you, but wood comes from trees."

"You know what I mean."

Nils chuckled.

Etta joined then, munching away on a piece of roasted chicken. Pieces stuck to her teeth as she spoke, mouth full. "This is amazing!"

"We've already been through this," Todd grunted.

"I meant the roast chicken. You should try it!"

"Not hungry."

"What about Garrett?" Etta held the chicken to Garrett. But the little boy didn't move. "Didn't think so."

Todd pulled Garrett away from Etta. "How is being in the middle of this swamp gonna help?"

"Well, to start, we're away from the Order. And I am sure we can get in contact with some other researchers from other universities or something—"

"So you don't have a clue how to help Garrett?"

"Not yet, but—"

"I think I can help," the woman with frizzy red hair interjected herself into the conversation. Todd glowered at her. He hadn't even heard her approach.

"Who are you?" Etta asked.

"Name's Edith. Is this Garrett?"

Todd interjected, "How do you know my son's name?"

"Yeshua told me."

Todd grunted again.

"Listen, you might not like it, but that's your problem. But I know someone who can help out in Mert. I can get us there."

"I'm not going back to Mert," Todd hissed.

"Mert might be the best place to cure him!" Etta added.

"I have too many bad memories there. Not Mert."

"This isn't a choice. If you care about your son, you'll come with me to Mert." Edith stepped forward, her eyes piercing him like daggers. Her voice lowered as she spoke, "There is more at stake than your son's senses."

"Why does everyone assume that I don't know what is going on?" Todd snapped.

"Because I don't think you do. There is so much riding on your son's very existence—"

"Sorry, can I interject?" Etta said. "Maybe you can tell me what is going on. I've been helping with the kid's care."

"For one day!" Todd shouted, climbing to his feet. "None of you know my son!"

Edith laughed, "Your son is the reason why all the seers lost their vision and why we can no longer see through the Mist. He started this!"

"I knew it! See! I told you!" Etta exclaimed.

Todd ignored her. "What the hell are you talking about?"

"You see Yeshua over there? He went blind moments after they took out your son's eyes if the timeline is correct."

"It's not related! Damn—you all are persistent."

"Hear her out, Todd," Etta said.

"No! This was just the Order being the Order. There's no magical, malicious thing going on with my family. I wish you would just agree to that already! I told that to Lex—and now she's dead. She's dead, and there's nothing I can do but protect Garrett from this ridiculous magic talk!"

Etta squirmed in her seat.

Edith crossed her arms, glowering at Todd. Her voice sliced through the air like a knife, "Have you ever thought that your own ignorance is what is destroying your family?"

Todd didn't reply.

"I promise Dr. Kafele can help."

"Wait!" Etta jumped from her seat, "*the* Dr. Kafele? The renowned researcher of magic diseases?"

"That very one."

"Todd, we have to go! I have studied Dr. Kafele's work for years! I can provide them with my data—then we may be able to heal Garrett!"

Dr. Kafele... The name sounded familiar.

"I'll think on it," Todd grunted, brushing back Garrett's messy hair. The boy didn't flinch, sighing quietly on his father's shoulder.

"He'll come around, I'm sure. But tell me more about Dr. Kafele! Do they have any theories about the bleeding eye?" Etta continued to pressure Edith. Nils chuckled beside his sister, picking at another piece of food on his plate.

Todd's attention drifted away from the conversation, trying to find a quiet space in his mind, away from the ridiculousness of the conversation. This had been the constant tune ever since he and Lex arrived in Mert years ago. Magic this, magic that; no one bothered to just live.

They had a perfect little shop filled with an array of goods. Between regular customers and Todd's side tattooing business, they survived.

But then Lex had to befriend Madame Owiti. Magic forced its way into his life.

And now it was here, mocking him. He could see it throughout the room now. Different Magii conducted spells and magical feats. For the most part, they were innocent, manipulating elements and performing uninteresting feats. It had never threatened him until the Story Collector came to visit.

Now it wouldn't leave him alone.

He caught a glimpse of Hue as she walked across the room toward Marisol. The young woman sat in a chair, still holding her head.

As the doctor approached, Marisol lifted her head.

When she exhaled, black smoke poured from her lips.

It flooded around her, filling the room like a storm rushing across the sea.

Todd clamored to his feet with Etta and Nils.

Beside them, Edith grabbed Etta's fork. It extended as soon as she touched it, creating a sharp pitchfork with points that could maim anyone who crossed her path. "Okay, well, no time to think—we gotta get out of here now!"

"What the hell is happening?" Todd shouted. The smoke thickened with every passing moment.

"Reapers," Edith hissed.

"What!?"

"No time to talk. C'mon!

Etta pushed in front of Todd, quick to follow behind Edith. Todd stumbled behind her, hurrying to avoid the black smoke that continued to fill the room. The smoke itself did not smell of ash, but there was something heavy about it, as if too much could crush his insides and leave him for dead. As the smoke continued to fill the room, even Garrett seemed to react, hiding his face deeper in Todd's shirt.

"It's a'ight. We're gonna be a'ight," Todd held him tighter.

Garrett wheezed.

Edith led them through a narrow doorway and into a small lavatory. Once Todd entered, she gripped the doorknob, welding the lock shut behind them.

"Wait, where's your brother?" Todd asked Etta.

"Nils is staying behind. He's been helping with the speakeasy and everything for years… he won't go leaving them." Etta replied.

"But I just risked my ass to save you for him!"

"And for that, I thank you."

"Can you two shut up?" Edith snapped. She approached the tub against the wall and turned on the faucet. The water spewed from the misshapen tap. "Gotta give it to that little nymph. She might not have full control of stone and metal, but at least she made a working tub."

"What are you doing?" Etta approached Edith's side.

Edith didn't reply. As the water continued to spew, she removed a vial from her pocket. It glimmered silver in the dim light, and upon uncorking it, a few specks went flying. For a moment, Todd was back in his little store, where silver liquid coated the walls, and Lex had collapsed due to her Phantom Rot.

He backed away slightly, but with the door welded shut, there was nowhere for him to go.

"Now that is interesting," Etta gawked at the liquid. "Magic?"

Edith still didn't reply. She swished the bottle in her hand, then dumped its contents into the tub. The contents fizzled along the top. Then, she tapped the surface in a rhythmic fashion.

After a few seconds, a slight glow highlighted the surface of the water.

Edith spoke without turning back, "Hold onto your kid."

"What?" Todd gripped Garrett tighter.

The woman didn't say anything else. She grabbed both Etta's and Todd's arms. Despite her size, she managed to drag them both forward to the edge of the tub.

Then, without a word, she pushed them into the water.

Todd lost his footing the moment she tugged. He held Garrett close, bracing for impact into the porcelain tub. He didn't have any other time to react, to process emotion, or to procure his thoughts. It was preposterous! Why would this woman just shove him into a tub?

But he never hit the bottom of the tub. Instead, it was as if he floated.

And moments later, he emerged from the water, still gripping Garrett.

Only he was no longer in the lavatory but in an operating arena.

LIAR

Even before exiting the tunnels, Bria sensed the air had shifted. There was a heaviness in the air. It was different from the yellow smoke, which acted like a landslide. This instead hung, a virus pressing on her shoulders.

Something has changed. Bria slowed as she approached the exit of the tunnels. She readjusted the gas mask on her face. As an added layer, she willed her little branch to attach to the mask and expand past her collarbone and down her body like armor.

Inhaling once, she stepped through the exit, entering a cloud of black smoke. It wove through the trees like a snake. Beyond it, she could make out shadows scurrying about in a panic.

I was gone less than a day. What happened? Bria stumbled as a refugee nearly knocked her to the ground. They apologized profusely, repositioned their bag on their shoulder, and then rushed into the center of the fallen sanctuary.

Bria pushed through the smoke. With each step, it pulled on her as if trying to tug her back to the earth. Where had it come from? There were no guards... but it didn't mean there weren't Mist Keepers lurking behind their cloak of invisibility.

It had been inevitable that Ningursu would find her hideaway, but she hadn't expected it to happen so soon. She had done well to protect it, the tunnels impassable except by those she trusted and the swamp like a maze to any who dared to venture within its embrace. But her magic clearly hadn't been strong enough. Or maybe she misplaced her trust.

But if they were here, using their Mist to dismantle her trees and casting a blanket of death through the waters, how could she fight them? They had the upper hand.

How could she defeat something as visible as the wind?

Dust blew over her, coating the lenses of her gas mask. She used her sleeve to clean them, continuing to push toward the other side of her swamp. Her palace rose above the growing fog, still standing despite the chaos.

At the base of the tree, Horton ushered people out of the small companion fortress.

"Horton!" Bria called.

"Oh, good, you're back!" Horton called, "I don't know what's happening around here, hun, but we need to get everyone out before it clogs our lungs."

"Right, good idea." Bria glanced around at the smoke. Her thoughts flashed to the children from the factory…and of Emily. The factories had them working with chemicals that produced smoke. Was this the same type? Did the Mist Keepers go as far as to infiltrate not only magic but technology as well?

Bria shook her head, pulling herself to the present, "What's the plan?"

"I'm not sure yet. We're taking the weakest of the bunch to Stilette so they can get ample medical care. Hue's already heading back to Rosada with a few others. They left me to take care of everyone else. I was gonna head back into the tunnels and figure it out from there."

"Right…that should work. Get everyone down there as fast as possible." Bria drew a mental picture of the tunnels in her head. "Take the tunnel back to the junction. Once there, turn into the tunnel that is three to the left. Follow it straight. It will take you further south to Perennes. You should be safe there."

"I guess you're not coming, hun?"

"No… no." Bria glanced around the smoky swamp. "I need to make sure everything is okay…and that no one is left behind. Once it's safe, I'll join you.

"Had a feeling you would say that." Horton smiled sadly. "Be safe… we don't want to lose someone as fantastic as you."

"It's more important that you get out—I couldn't have done this without you."

"It's your kingdom. I am just your humble subject."

"You're more than that. Really, you all are." Bria glanced around the area, "I'll help you round everyone up. We'll make sure everyone is safe."

After exchanging a brief hug, Horton vanished into the Mist. She hadn't thanked Horton enough for everything they had done. They had stepped into their role with ease, allowing Bria to do what she did best: make the world pretty.

Bria turned back to the swamp. Already, the trees had started to wither. Even her palace leaned slightly, fighting against the onslaught of smoke. The trees called for her, and even the water sloshing at her feet begged for attention. The swamp, once so green, had turned over in its nightmare.

Every home she had ever created never seemed to last.

Newbird's Arm.

Mert.

The Library.

And now… her swamp.

It was not the time to fret over her lost sanctuaries. Instead, she raced from home to home, helping people return to the tunnels. She found three children hiding in the bushes and, with a gentle hand, guided them to safety. Each inhalation and exhale gave her just enough oxygen and carbon to find the remaining refugees.

She wished that she knew how many people had lived in her swamp. With some already gone, she couldn't be certain how many remained.

But as she brought the last few children to Horton, waiting by the entrance of the tunnels, the swamp seemed to stop breathing.

"I think that is everyone… I counted sixty-three people. That should be it," Horton replied.

"Then go. If I find anyone else, I'll get them to safety." Bria's attention drifted past the border of the swamp into the trees. In all the commotion, she hadn't even thought about Brent's school. But Brent would have gotten them out…so she didn't have a reason to worry, right? Besides, based on what Brent said, Ningursu had never managed to find the little ghost town.

She turned back to Horton. "Just go. I'll complete a final check. Okay?"

Horton obliged. One at a time, each of the refugees entered the tunnels, hushed whispers and fears following their footsteps. Bria waited for a minute, then hurried back into the swamp, where all was quiet but the shifting of the smoke.

No breathing.

No gasps of air.

No exchange of oxygen and carbon.

But for a shallow gasp.

She followed the sensation. It was weak, like a whisper, pulling toward her palace. She focused solely on the gasping air, pushing aside the demands from the trees and shrubs. They clawed for her as she climbed her palace steps. And as she opened the door, it nearly snapped from its hinge.

I'll fix you later. Just be patient. She walked slowly into the palace. The black smoke had yet to make a home within her fortress, but the fixtures had already been infected from the outside.

She tiptoed along the cracking floors, nearing the labored breathing.

"Hello?" She called out, voice shaking.

"Bria?" a weak voice replied.

"I'm coming! Hold on!" She moved toward the voice, stepping over the dilapidated fixtures, moving toward the voice.

It led her to the balcony overlooking the Library. There, a body leaning against the railing. As Bria approached, it turned.

"Marisol!" Bria called, then burst into a run.

Her friend didn't move, eyes wide. As Bria neared, a hint of black smoke gathered around Marisol's lips.

"Marisol?" Bria froze a few steps away from her.

"I'm sorry... I never had this happen before..." she gasped, bringing her head to her hands.

"What has never happened?"

"He lied to me..."

"Who?"

Two hands fell on Bria's shoulders. Their owner hissed in her ear, "Me."

Bria spun around. With her movement, a branch shot out of the wall, knocking her attacker to the floor.

But the attacker climbed up at once, a wide grin on his face.

"Christof? What're you doing here?" Bria wrapped her fingers around another branch, willing it to grow thorns along its side.

"Now, Briannabella, that is not a nice way to greet someone," Christof said as he climbed to his feet.

"Fuck off!" Bria sent the thorned branch toward Christof.

This time, he avoided it in one fluid motion. "And that certainly isn't ladylike. What have I ever done to you?"

"You killed my mother!" Her voice cracked as she held back her tears.

"A necessary casualty."

"None of this is necessary!"

"It is all necessary."

"Oh enough! What're you doing here?"

"I am only reclaiming what is rightfully mine, Briannabella."

"What is rightfully yours? For the last damn time, I'm not yours—wait." She froze, staring hard into Christof's dead eyes. "You never called me Briannabella..."

Christof's smile expanded. "That did not take you long at all."

"No..." Bria whispered. "No no no..."

"Oh, yes."

"No!" Bria laced her hands into the nearby wall. She yanked it forward, pulling down the stone and forming a blockade between her and Christof.

There was no way she was right. It didn't make sense! How could Christof be... Ningursu?

She didn't dare wait to find out. Instead, she raced over to Marisol, still leaning against the railing.

"Come on... we need to go now!" She tugged at Marisol's arm.

Marisol raised her head.

Black smoke wrapped around it, her pupils like pin-points, face unexpressive.

"Marisol!?"

In a swift motion, Marisol lunged forward, knocking Bria to the ground. Before Bria could react, Marisol un-latched her facemask and threw it into the debris. Dizziness flooded Bria's head at once, the smoke thick-ening just as soon as she took her first breath.

No. Her magic escaped her. The stones around her stopped speaking, and even the trees became nothing more than a distant hum, indecipherable next to her own breathing.

Christof leapt forward like a beast, pinning Bria to the ground. She squirmed. The smoke ate away at every bit of strength she had, locking her in place.

He used one hand to cup her face, reaching behind her ear where her little branch's roots took form. With his smile unyielding, he plucked a piece of bark from the branch.

Bria held back a cry.

"I am sure you know how obsessed Mr. Carver here was with you, Briannabella. I can see why...you are a pretty thing." He leaned forward so his breath hit Bria's face. "But pretty things wilt."

Bria didn't respond.

"We do not have time for any of those fantasies now. We have work to do," Ningursu brushed a finger across Bria's lips and chuckled. "You're mine now. All mine."

With that laugh, thick smoke exited his lip, masking her vision and depriving her of any sense of truth.

CHAPTER FORTY-THREE

A Moment Called Home

Brent lost track of how long he stared at the lake. He kept returning to different images on its surface, trying to make sense of the story still at the forefront of his mind. This was only part of Ningursu's story. He had been a young man guided by power and put side-by-side with a woman who represented Life; he dared not share the pedestal.

While Brent could make assumptions, there was still more to uncover. How deep had Ningursu woven his story into the fabric of the earth? What stories had he manipulated? And why did he fear horses? Brent would have to seek out more tales. But where? Would he just need to keep his mind open for any story, willing for it to come greet him at any sporadic moment?

"Can we leave already?" Jewel grunted from beside him. "I'm hungry, and the sun's gone down. You promised me lemon cakes."

"Yeah, yeah… a'ight, sorry," Brent groaned as he climbed to his feet. His side ached as if something had clawed into his ribs. He clenched his cane as he limped a few paces forward, flinching as a few hints of Ningursu's story washed over him.

He forced the stories away as he walked back through the forest with Jewel. Even if he had words to describe the story, he wouldn't know how to weave them together. He just needed time to process.

And Bria. He needed her now more than ever.

His fingers twitched with the desire to write in their shared notebook and discuss everything he had uncovered. *Hopefully, she'll be back when I return.* She had her own past to uncover, but in some ways…this was part of that very puzzle.

He paused in a clearing, catching a glance at the distant lights of Newbird's Arm. For a moment, Ningursu's story melted away, leaving him with his own story. How had the town changed? What was his mother doing? What about his father? Or his sister? Had they returned to their lives? He could only hope they had forgotten about him, moved on with their lives, and thrived.

"Brent!"

He turned, not expecting to see Caroline emerging from the Mist.

"Caroline, what are you doing here?" Brent asked.

"Once everyone returned to Neorama, I had to come make sure you did not attempt anything abhorrent," Caroline replied.

"Too late. But I'm a'ight now."

"What did you do?" Caroline asked.

"I found part of Ningursu's story. About how he... he started to destroy the different Hurtovitae. I mean, the Magii like Bria. There was one he... he was supposed to protect the world with her. But he turned her into a monster."

"Here? In these mountains?

Brent nodded.

"That is almost poetic, is it not? Everything started here...and now you have returned."

Brent glanced back towards Newbird's Arm, "Yeah."

"Can you two stop babbling? I am starving!" Jewel interjected. "And I desperately need water. My head is killing me."

"It has been quite a cumbersome day. My head aches as well," Caroline replied.

Brent eyed the two women. They exchanged a glance, almost one of recognition. Brent didn't try to interpret the look, though. There were some gazes too intimate for him to collect.

"Yeah, let's head back… I gotta talk to Szyman about moving Neorama again, anyway. I don't trust the smoke in Stilette…" Brent trailed off. Surely, more stories lurked in that smoke.

"I did mention it to Szyman for a moment. He is preparing a few more defenses but will wait for you to give him the go-ahead." Caroline rubbed her brow, wincing again. She glanced down the mountain toward Newbird's Arm. With that brief glance, her face changed.

Just for a second.

Long enough for Brent to notice.

The face of an old woman flashed over Caroline's face. A kindly woman with deep smile lines and dark, penetrating eyes. Brent recognized her; she bore the same determination as Bria.

"Madame Gonzo…" he murmured.

"Hm?" Caroline raised her brow.

"Your face… It changed."

"I saw it, too," Jewel added.

"I do not recall."

"It was Madame Gonzo's face…" Brent croaked, "Bria's grandmother."

"Oh," Caroline frowned. "I see. I will go release her at once then."

"No, I'll do it."

"Brent, is that wise?"

"Probably not...but I owe it to Bria. I mean... yeah... I have to do it."

"Do you want me to come with you?"

Brent shook his head. "I can do this. It's... it's my home. I... I gotta do this. Can you just... I mean... if you could head back to Neorama, make sure everyone is a'ight there... check with Szyman and all. That would... yeah... that would help."

"As long as you promise to not make any detours."

"Yeah, a'ight."

Caroline gave Brent a weak smile, then motioned for Jewel to follow her back into the trees.

Brent swallowed as he watched them leave. His stomach churned. He saw Caroline's face change to Madame Gonzo's face, but he couldn't feel her story amongst the amalgamation of tales in the air.

But he trusted in Caroline's abilities. And it was with that trust that he turned toward home.

It would have been easier to take the tunnels, but instead, Brent gradually walked down the mountain, twisting between the trees. Every moment that passed, the weight in his chest grew, slowing each step with worry. Home was so close now. The trees even felt familiar. While they didn't speak to him like they did to Bria, their twists held stories he could recall. There were times when he and Bria used to explore these woods. Back when their love was innocent, they would spend time kissing and laughing between the trees. He saw whiffs of the stories from a different time.

As well as one of Bria rushing through the forest with a towering cadet chasing after her.

Bria had told him of this moment.

Her first true loss of control.

Her first kill.

Brent honored its privacy and continued along the trail. This moment belonged solely in her memories.

More tales followed him as he walked. Whenever he paused, leaning on his cane while his legs trembled, the stories wrapped around him like a blanket. They didn't stay long, though, as the pulsating pain on his side dragged him out of the fantasy, locking him tight in its anger.

He inhaled again, then exited the last line of trees, where a dirt road greeted him along the rusted fence of the Pit. The stories poured from the top, whispers of death and mourning chanting his name.

Brent held his hand out to them, letting the stories dance along his skin. Death was always apparent in Pit. The age of expiration had faded. It didn't matter whether the deaths were recent. Once someone died, they were dead—and their fate was the same.

Brent closed his eyes and tugged at the edge of the stories, searching for peace in the tales of exhaustion, of soot, of mining, and of disease. Newbird's Pit was known for working its vagrants, sending them to the mines, and ignoring their pleas. There'd been attempts to help under Brother Roy Al. But those were for naught.

But with the stories dissipating at his fingertips, Brent stopped the suffering and granted them peace.

He opened his eyes and dropped his hand, letting the stories fall from his skin. A collection of ghosts rose above the Pit before vanishing into their eternity.

I'm still a Mist Keeper… I haven't lost sight of that.

It was easy to forget his true duty after all this time. But it was there, waiting for him to return.

All of this would be easier if there were more of us. In times far gone, how many Mist Keepers had lived across the world? How many had Ningursu destroyed? At what cost…and why?

Brent slowed as he rounded the bend, then stopped. His childhood home stood before him, waiting where the Pit and forest met. While it stood unscathed, burnt grass acted as its foundation. Beyond it, further homes had not been so lucky.

The scent of burnt wood still lingered in the air.

Shite! Grass crunched beneath his feet as he rushed to the window.

His mother sat in the front room, frailer and grayer than he'd ever seen her. To Brent's surprise, his father sat beside her. In contrast to his mother, there was more light in his face, a life away from the Pit seeming to inject him with color again. His parents did not speak, though, sitting stiff on the couch, only to shift when Alexandria walked into the room.

She'd grown, a tall, lanky child with her hair still in those signature pigtails. Now, she wore wire-rimmed glasses, and behind them, her eyes had darkened, almost more black than gray.

In her hands, she carried a tray of rugalach and other pastries, which she offered to each of her parents. Her smile wasn't as carefree, an emptiness haunting her very movements.

"I'm sorry…" Brent whispered, pressing his hand to the glass. His voice cracked. The gong in his head started to play. If he had come back sooner, when they could still see him, wouldn't his family be better? All they knew was that he had vanished.

That he was most likely dead.

"Ma, Dad… Ally-Cat," he croaked, "I have so much to tell you. And I will. I'll tell you when it is all over. I promise."

As if she could hear him, Alexandria turned her attention to the window. She squinted for a moment, then shook her head.

"Shite!" He ducked. *Did she see me? If she did…then that means…no. She can't be.* He refused to humor the idea. Perhaps he had tapped the window louder than he intended. Yes, that made more sense. Far more sense.

Right?

He crawled away from the window, keeping low to the ground. As he reached the road, he began to climb to his feet.

Only for a hand to lace into his hair and yank him upwards, dangling him above the ground.

He glanced over his shoulder, wide-eyed.

"Jiang!"

The giant glowered at him.

"Hi. Um…it's been a bit, hasn't it? Um…how're you?" Brent squirmed, only for the giant to dig his hands deeper into his head.

"We've been expecting you," Jiang said.

Then, as if Brent was nothing more than a sack of laundry, the giant threw Brent over his shoulder and hauled him off down the road.

CHAPTER FORTY-FOUR

A Giant's Broken Heart

Brent's mind raced with potential stories. It'd be easy to derail the giant if he found the right one. If he created a story of a giant whale in the middle of the road, blocking their path, then it might just derail them.

He captured the story on his fingertips, only to pause. *Wait.* There were far more stories to uncover. He just had to play his card right.

So instead, he asked, "How'd you know I was gonna be here?"

"Ningursu always knows."

"Does he? Then why hasn't he bothered me until now."

"He has a plan."

"Does he? Are you sure?"

"Yes. He sees all."

"Can he really?"

"Wherever there's a Mist Keeper, he can see."

"He's never been able to see where I am though." Brent glanced toward the mountains behind him.

"Even if he can't control you, he knows you," Jiang hissed.

Brent squirmed, only for Jiang to grip him tighter. His large hand squeezed Brent's ankles, sending waves of a story across Brent's psyche.

He'd seen glimpses of Jiang's story back when he first harnessed his own magic in Mert.

When he discovered it then, the story had gone that Jiang's hatred of magic stemmed from a sorcerer and his wife, who had killed hundreds to save their son. One of those people had been Jiang's fiancée.

But as Brent witnessed the story this time, it was as though someone had plucked away the weeds and removed any bit of Mist. Jiang had left his home in shame, traveling to the City of Tencauri, only to be taken under the wing of an old vintner. There, he found love in a young woman, her name stained across Jiang's story like a forgotten prayer.

Kikyo.

They wed after Jiang completed his vintner apprenticeship, and together, they prepared for a life running a successful tavern.

She was not his fiancée. They were married. What else had been wrong during the first rendition of his tale? The stories didn't lie, but was the first story something that Jiang had taken as truth?

The story continued, ringing a similar tune. A corrupt sorcerer and his soon-to-be wife rose to power. On the day of the sorcerer's wedding, he celebrated with a display of magic. He chose yellow smoke as his tool, and with it on his fingers, he slaughtered Magii across the realm.

Including Kikyo.

But none of this had been with reason. Not to save a non-existent son nor to bring peace to Tencauri.

The sorcerer may not have even known why.

Instead, the sorcerer acted with the same confusion that guided Jiang's story. Engulfed by smoke, left to his own confusion, the sorcerer met his downfall.

But not before Jiang took the fall for his Kikyo's demise, accepting imprisonment beneath the sorcerer's castle. He did not witness what became of the sorcerer, only for Death to make itself comfortable.

There, he emerged as a Mist Keeper who hated magic. He refused to touch his ability.

Especially since they couldn't save Kikyo.

"Kikyo…" Brent recited to himself.

Jiang froze. "What did you say?"

"Your wife…her name was…it was Kikyo, wasn't it?"

"That's none of your concern, boy."

"I think it is," Brent took a gamble with his next statement. No matter what, it would anger Jiang. But it planted a seed that he could nurture. "Ningursu is playing you like a puppet. He controls you with her memory."

"Her memory has nothing to do with Ningursu."

"Doesn't it? I've seen your story over the last couple of years, and it… I mean, it's not consistent. He is taking Kikyo's memory and manipulating your past. Just think about it."

"My mind is perfectly clear."

"Is it? Those who have gone mad still think their thoughts are clear."

"You don't know anything, boy."

Brent continued to pry, "I'm sure the sorcerer thought his mind was clear."

"He might have…but he was nothing more than a corrupt Mist Keeper," Jiang still hadn't moved.

"Was he? Are you sure?"

"Yes, I am sure. Ningursu and Aelia tried to control him, but they failed. Kikyo would have survived if she didn't have magic."

"Jiang. Look around…it's all…it's happening again." Brent lowered his voice, "Would Kikyo want you to be a part of this?"

"You don't know what she would have wanted."

"I think I do."

"No, you don't!" Jiang hoisted Brent off his back and threw him onto the ground. Brent landed on his hands and knees, groaning as he spun around to face the giant. Jiang's hair blew behind him with a gust of wind while the moonlight cast a partial glow over his cheeks. He glowered at Brent, then pressed a foot onto his throat.

"You don't know anything about Kikyo or my past," Jiang hissed.

Brent struggled beneath Jiang's foot, struggling to breathe. *You can't die. You're already kinda dead. Just find a story.* He held his hand out to the side, then found the tale right on his fingertips.

Beside him, the story of a woman with long black hair and a round, freckled face surfaced. She moved with grace toward Jiang, her voice like a song.

"Mĭn, do not be a fool," the story said.

Jiang spun around, blinked, and then snarled down at Brent, "Do not trick me with one of your stories!"

"Listen to her! This is your past speaking to you. Just remember!" Brent pushed Jiang's foot aside and clamored to his feet.

Kikyo's story approached Jiang and placed a hand on his cheek. "You're a good man, Mĭn. A fool at times but a good man. Do what is right."

Jiang remained locked in place. His face softened, a reflection of his younger self playing out on his cheekbones. "I can't be that person without you."

"Yes, you can. You do not need me pestering you to be a good man."

"But I do. Please…Kikyo. Stay."

"You know I cannot."

"Kikyo…"

"I love you, Mǐn." Kikyo pressed her lips to Jiang's cheek.

Then, she fizzled into the Mist.

Brent didn't speak. Jiang still hadn't moved, his hands clenched, head bowed.

They stayed like this for a few minutes, with only the distant hooting of owls and the sporadic breezes in the air interrupting the otherwise silent road. Brent picked at the charred grass. It'd be easy to sneak away, but he needed to see this out.

Finally, Jiang whispered, "Leave."

"Huh?"

"Leave. Before I change my mind."

Brent climbed to his feet, quietly thanked Jiang, then stumbled down the path. The seeds of doubt had been planted. Perhaps that was enough for Jiang to question Ningursu and cut the puppet master's strings.

And perhaps his story would finally be free to live untainted.

But Brent could not ponder the story for long. The heart of Newbird's Arm approached fast, and Brent hadn't a clue what waited for him there. Would it be Ningursu? Aelia? A horde of Diabolo?

Yet, upon crossing the bridge over the main river, a quiet night greeted him. While debris lay strewn throughout the town, with the Temple yet to be rebuilt, Newbird's Arm slept peacefully. The wall of the Pit hung ajar, with vagrants still sleeping within its border despite the freedom to flee. In the distance, towers formed sculptures in the farmland, no longer moving across the landscape, a remnant of Bria's past encounters with the Guard.

And while fire had charred the town, the Forest Queen left her mark. The Senator's Garden, though frail and brown, still bore its immortal camellias.

Despite the street's familiarity, Brent felt like a stranger. He used to walk in the town square, head bent, wincing at each taunt thrown about by the Guard and even the vendors. On the side of the buildings, he constructed makeshift stages to tell stories to the children in secret. He never quite belonged.

But Newbird's Arm was still his home.

As he approached the familiar house of Madame Gonzo at the edge of the market square, another story attacked him. This one started with a scream.

Then, a gunshot.

And silence.

That single story repeated, louder and louder, banging in his ears like a drum.

His hands shook as he grabbed the doorknob.

He didn't even need to turn it for the door to swing open.

Please, let that be another false story. Please.

He stepped inside the entrance and peered into the kitchen.

His heart sank.

Madame Gonzo lay on the blood-stained tile.

And sitting there, at her table, was none other than Jemma Reds.

CHAPTER FORTY-FIVE

FOUND

Chander stumbled behind Milo as they entered Neorama. The swamp maintained its greenery, the black smoke a distant memory. He kept calling for Yaz as he ran, but the girl never reappeared. Why hadn't he grabbed her hand? Then he would have seen through her eyes.

Milo caught Chander's attention and motioned to the box in the middle of the town with his head.

"I know we gotta tell Szyman, but can you go? I wanna make sure Yaz is okay," Chander said.

Milo frowned.

"Just um…use your magic to show him, okay? I think that's what Brent would tell you to do, right?"

Milo continued to pout but nodded once. He fiddled with his harmonica.

"I'll join you after I check the school, okay? Just... yeah, tell Szyman."

Milo whistled a single note on his harmonica, then headed to Szyman's box.

Chander waved goodbye to Milo, then sprinted toward the schoolhouse. His legs carried him without pain, and at once, he pushed. The spirits loitered inside, babbling in their obscure language. A few of them played with their magic while others scoured through the books lining the shelves. Chander slipped through them, avoiding their skin, and hurried up the stairs to the bedrooms.

"Yaz?!" He called as he reached her room at the end of the hallway. Her door hung ajar, her bag still at the foot of the bed, with her odd collection of tchotchkes lining the windowsill. But while her belongings remained, she was not in her room.

Chander cursed, then raced back down the hall, checking the open rooms as he returned to the stairwell. The spirits paid no regard to him as he checked the classroom, parlor, and entryway. By now, Yaz would have revealed herself; she wasn't like Anandi, who turned everything into a game. No—she just wasn't here!

Chander hurried back out of the schoolhouse. The night sky had grown dark with the same clouds following them from the castle. What if the black smoke had found Yaz? He didn't even know what that smoke did! Yaz had told him that there were monsters with yellow smoke, monsters that she could control. But this was different.

And who was that Carver person who released the smoke in the first place?

As he hurried down the road, he nearly toppled straight into Caroline and Jewel as they appeared from the side of a building. They both glanced in his direction at the same time.

"Oh good! Listen, something is going on with black smoke and such. And now Yaz is missing! Can you help? Milo went to talk with Szyman but...we need a Mist Keeper." Chander exhaled as he finished his sentence. "Please."

Caroline and Jewel glanced at each other, then grinned.

As they both turned back to Chander, black smoke began to pour from their lips.

Chander staggered back from the women. Their eyes didn't blink, as if someone had cast them like marionettes and controlled their movement. Whatever caused it, Chander did not want to find out.

He pivoted from Caroline and Jewel and detoured to Szyman's box. As he ran, the smoke crawled about his feet. With every step, the box seemed to get further away, as if the road was made of putty. It stretched each time he lifted his feet while the buildings around him shrunk and grew in height.

He burst into a run, attempting to beat the dizzying shifting of Neorama. Was Szyman trying to move it? Certainly, he wouldn't without warning them. Unless it was urgent.

He continued to run, finally managing to beat the disorienting town. The metal box greeted him with a thud, and Chander forced the door open without knocking.

"Szyman! Milo! We're in trouble!" he exclaimed as he toppled into the box.

Yet, upon entering, he froze. Szyman sat in his chair, smoke wrapping around his body like chains. His eyes had rolled back in his head while his mouth hung ajar, the black smoke bubbling on his lips. In the corner, Milo cowered, fixated on the opposite corner.

But before Chander could even turn, the black smoke thickened around him, and any chance of seeing what lurked fell into the shadows.

Sight returned like a parting storm. Chander had no clue how he ended up back in the schoolhouse, chained to one of the desks with the other spirits, but he sat there now. It wasn't sleep that took him here, but instead a moment of nothingness, leaving his eyes heavy with continued fatigue.

He pushed past the desire to sleep, keeping alert as the room shifted. A stout, balding man wandered amongst the rows. As he marched, the room distorted, reorganizing itself in the man's presence.

Chander shifted. The spirits did not move. Even Milo sat with his head bowed. Caroline and Jewel remained against the far wall like statues. The school had become a prison with a mere blink…masked by a thick miasma that threatened any sense of reality.

Chander's attention fell back to the stout man as he mulled about the room. Was this Ningursu? Yaz said that Ningursu was a skull, so probably not. Whoever he was, he controlled the Mist without even blinking, a natural extension of himself, to manipulate the room and doctor confusion.

The man did not speak, only turning as the door to the classroom opened. Carver entered the room with Marisol at his side. The girl walked in the same daze as Caroline and Jewel, taking a seat beside them at the desks. The smoky chains emerged from the fixture, cupping her hands and feet, and like the spirits, her head fell in defeat.

But Chander's attention remained on Carver. More specifically, on the figure he carried over his shoulder.

He got Bria. Chander gulped. If he found Bria, did that mean he also found Yaz?

As Carver moved down the aisle, Chander dropped his head, pretending to still be asleep. Carver met with the balding man a few desks away from Chander. They spoke in a foreign language. While Chander didn't understand, he did hear the name "Ningursu" mentioned once, as well as "Brenton" and "Yasmin."

Even as their footsteps neared, Chander did not lift his head. They stopped in front of him.

"Stop feigning sleep, boy," Carver snapped, "I know you're awake."

Chander peeked one eye open. Carver knelt before him, smiling. He still held Bria over his shoulder like a rag doll.

"What's your name, boy?" Carver asked.

Chander didn't respond.

"Oh, don't be shy—you're one of us, after all. I just want to help."

Chander still did not reply.

"Stubborn, aren't you?" Carver turned to the stout man, "Did you happen to get his name, Alojzy?"

"Yes, sire. His name is Chander Bhatta, according to Caroline," the stout man replied.

"Chander Bhatta," Carver recited. "I do not believe he is of significance."

"Sire, I would hesitate before saying that. Caroline told me that he shows signs of… puppeteering." Alojzy replied.

"Really now?" Carver eyed Chander again. In a flicker of light, the skeletal nature of his face emerged before reconfiguring itself again.

Chander still didn't respond. He wouldn't let this Carver—if that was his real name—know the truth about his magic. Or about anything.

Carver shifted Bria off his shoulder and into his arms. Her arm fell to the side, just barely brushing Chander's skin.

Chander flinched ever-so-slightly but still did not speak.

Carver passed Bria's body to Alojzy. "Prepare the girl, Alojzy. This body needs some time to rest… and I would like to spend time with Mr. Bhatta here."

"Yes, sire. Shall I involve Aelia in the preparations?"

"Not at this time. She has other tasks to complete."

"Yes, sire. I understand." Alojzy bowed his head once, then left with Bria in his arms.

As soon as Alojzy left the room, Carver's demeanor shifted. He collapsed on the chair in front of Chander. He wrung his hands together. Blue and violet bruises covered his pale hands. His shoulders curved inward. Without the guise of confidence, Carver's body had abandoned all youth. The skeletal face that Chander had seen returned.

He's like a corpse now. In some ways, Carver's body was worse than that of the spirits.

"This vessel is a short-term solution," Carver said as he flexed his fingers. "But my problem should be resolved soon."

Chander did not let his curiosity hijack his tongue, remaining quiet.

"You are a stubborn one, aren't you? No matter. I will break that habit."

Still, Chander did not speak.

"You and I, we're quite similar if what Caroline told Alojzy about your magic is true. But I am sure it is true... I know Caroline's mind well."

Chander blinked once, but no vision filled his mind's eye.

"Of course, you probably don't have a clue what I am saying. So, let me tell you a secret, Mr. Bhatta," Carver leaned forward, his voice low. "You have my magic. If you follow my lead, perhaps you will be a god someday."

Carver sounds like a stupid name for a god. Chander thought. Anandi's voice interjected his thoughts, berating him for using the word 'stupid.'

As if to answer his thought, Carver said, "Of course, you don't even know my name. How can you trust that I'll help you become a god? Well, let me tell you." Carver leaned forward, one eye inverting, revealing only his white sclera. "My name is Ningursu, and I am the God of Death. And you, my dear boy, shall be my apprentice."

CLEANSED

Brent rushed to Madame Gonzo's side.

"She's not dead yet," Jemma said, still staring at the pistol in her hand.

Brent lifted Madame Gonzo from the ground. Blood pooled from the woman's hip, raspy breaths catching the air. Using his well of stories as knowledge, Brent removed his coat and wrapped it around the old woman's waist, compressing the wound. He focused on tying it tight, pushing away the story of the attack as it echoed about the room. Jemma had arrived with poise and grace, only to enter an argument with the old woman and shoot her without a second thought.

Why?

There was more to this story lurking in the shadows.

What happened to Jemma?

And why could she see him?

He turned back to her, eyes wide. She had changed, aged almost in the short time since he last saw her. With pale, paper skin and graying red hair, she did not look like the woman to whom he'd been betrothed. There was something inhuman about her, captured by the yellow tinge in her eyes.

"What happened to you, Jemma?" Brent asked.

"I saw the Effluvium," Jemma recited, "I became Sister Jey Ma."

"No… something's wrong… this isn't you," Brent applied further pressure to Madame Gonzo's leg. The woman groaned.

"How would you know? You never knew me."

"We were betrothed for nearly three years… of course I knew you."

"How could you know me? We never kissed, never shared a bed."

"Because we didn't want to—we…we never loved each other."

"Oh, Brenton, is that what you have gotten in your head?" Jemma rose from her seat and approached him. "Think about it, Brent. We could have avoided all of this. If that corrupt Magii hadn't cast her spell on you, we would have had a bright future in this little town. You, a rehabilitated storyteller, and me, a pious sister. We would have raised a family and proven that even demons can thrive." Jemma knelt before Brent and placed a finger on his chin. "All of this that is happening in the world, we would have avoided it. We would have peace."

"Jem, don't you remember? We called off our betrothal together. You were as opposed to it as I was." Brent flinched at her touch. There was confusion in her story, masked by yellow.

Just like the yellow that used to dance in his head.

"No. The Magii corrupted us. Look what she has done now—Newbird's Arm burned! Knoll fell! The Senate has collapsed! It is not outside her realm of magic to manipulate us to play her game."

"No, that's not what is happening."

"It is. She made it so we fell out of love."

"Jemma, I know that's what you think...but it's not what...I mean...let me tell you what would have happened if we got married...because I've seen it. The story... well, it's not entirely clear, but it's there." Brent recalled the stories he had seen months earlier, tales that played out like nightmares in the back of his mind. "It would have been a loveless marriage. We would have resented each other... and... I probably would have returned to my ways... ended up in the Pit... maybe even ended up right here all over again. It would have been for nothing."

"You don't know that," she whispered. More yellow smoke poured from her lips as she spoke.

"I know who I am. Do you know who you are, Jemma?"

"I am Sister Jey Ma."

"And who is Sister Jey Ma?"

"The one who has done everything to protect Rosada."

"The Jemma I knew used to hold her morals close. She never would have done this." Brent motioned to Madame Gonzo. The woman's breaths continued to labor. "With everything going on, your own beliefs have been corrupted."

"My beliefs are as pure as they've ever been."

There was no arguing with her. Every bit of yellow smoke clouded her judgment. How long had her mind been flooded with it? What fears did it plant in her thoughts? What became of the real Jemma?

Rationality wouldn't work. But, if he could find her story, then perhaps Brent might be able to break through to her.

"Are they the same beliefs you had when you ran away from Newbird's Arm with Micca?" Brent asked, recalling what his friend had told him about their adventure across the country.

"Beliefs change as we learn the truth," Jemma said. "My beliefs back then led me away from this town and into the arms of the Effluvium.

Brent continued to pry as the yellow smoke rose around Jemma. "And did these same beliefs bring you back here?"

"Yes, they did,"

"Which led you to assault Madame Gonzo?"

"Only because she wouldn't listen… and because I had to."

"Why?" If he could get her to question her own rationality, then it may just open the door to her mind.

"Because I did—she refused to listen! I warned her if Newbird's Arm didn't start cooperating… more fires would be in their future! They would burn… all of them."

"Even your family?"

Jemma blinked. Her face softened for a moment, but it vanished within seconds, her eye darkening again. "Yes, even them."

"That doesn't sound moral to me."

"A necessary casualty."

There were those words again. Just like Jiang said in the forest. A necessary casualty. This was all just a necessary casualty—for one person and one thing.

"How many necessary casualties must be committed for your morals?" Brent asked.

"You don't understand, Brent." Jemma placed a hand on his cheek. "You don't understand. You're just a ridiculous boy who plays with stories. Sometimes, death is needed to bless the Effluvium. So the Effluvium can thrive… and so we can thrive too. Think about it, Brent. You and me together, overseeing the Effluvium. I would be its guardian, and you would be its gatekeeper. Doesn't that sound far more enticing than your current life?"

"Jemma, you're not making any sense," Brent placed his hand on top of her hand. "I… I can help you though."

"My mind is lucid. I know what I believe." But as she said those words, her eyes darted, her face quivering. Behind the guise of persuasion and smoke, there was a girl struggling to find her own mind.

"Let me help," Brent reiterated.

Jemma didn't fight as he took her hand in his hands, holding them tight. He knew she was in there, fighting. He could feel it in the story dancing across her skin.

Brent opened himself up to the tale and its befogging song.

Jemma drank the poison.

But she was told it was to save the world.

Fog muddled her vision, but through it, she watched as magic destroyed the tower she loved.

Ab Aeterno fell.

Knoll burned.

And she left with the Order through the dying forest to safety.

She followed behind an Elder and a Senator, yearning to please and maintaining all focus.

More poison arrived in chalices.

And smoke became a companion on her lips.

With the smoke came Effluvium's voice, whispering in her ear.

Sing your song, little bird.

Let it consume you and lift the curse of magic.

The voice whispered to her every night. It didn't matter where she lay, whether in the arms of a towering Guard or alone with only the scripture in her hand.

She had to stop the magic from destroying the Effluvium.

Purity would follow.

And the Effluvium would thrive.

This was her duty.

After everything, it would bring peace.

So she sang her song, the scripture as her guide.

She sang it for the Capital.

Then she sang it for the Senate.

Gunshots performed like the beat of a drum, leaving behind trails of blood.

So much blood.

Senators fell.

But it's magic's fault. When the Forest Queen comes, she'll take the blame.

The voice continued to mock Jemma every step of the way.

Controlling...

Controlling...

Even when the Forest Queen came to play.

And with the senators dead, the Forest Queen fled.

Jemma echoed the words of blame, placing them on the queen and issuing a decree. Martial law would rule across the land. All magic, stories, and vagrants would be cleansed and branded.

She was the invisible strings, pulling the laws, commanding the Guard.

Or was she?

The voice kept growing louder. Her own thoughts became nothing but dreams.

Restless.

Uneasy.

Inside, she was nothing more than a little girl begging for help.

When news came of a fire in her home, Jemma saw a chance to reunite with her past. She packed her pistol in her robe and strode from her chambers. With only her loyal Captain Rivers, the towering giant, she fled in the dead of night.

By morning, she arrived in Newbird's Arm.

She strode through town like an empress, her guards at her side. Despite the longing to see her parents and home, the voice told her to go to the Temple, where she would stay tucked away for days. Praying. Alone.

Letting the voice pull the strings.

Her knees would not budge. She could not rise like the sun. Instead, she waited.

And waited.

Until her fast ended, and the voice pulled her into the streets.

Citizens waited for her, confused and fearful. But Madame Gonzo, as headstrong as ever, approached Jemma without hesitation.

"What are you doing here?" the old woman asked.

"This is my home. I have come with a warning, but only with one request: where is the Forest Queen?" The words came from her lips, but they belonged to the voice.

"Why would we tell you that?" Madame Gonzo asked.

"Because we can squash this rebellious town with our arsenal."

"You have already tried, and you have failed."

"But we shall not fail again. So tell me, where is the Forest Queen?"

"No one knows."

"You lie."

"I speak only the truth. Now go home, Miss Reds. No one wants you here." Madame Gonzo turned and walked back through the crowd.

The crowd remained, neither praising nor demeaning, only watching in shock.

They'll make a mockery of you, *the voice hissed.* Show them what you can do.

Jemma readied a song and, with a gentle hum, she cast her blanket of yellow over Newbird's Arm. It thickened around her, painting the town with nightmares. Coughs and cries joined her hymn, leaving her to walk forward undeterred.

With her determined pride, she strode straight to Madame Gonzo's front door.

She knocked once.

The door opened.

"What now?" Madame Gonzo asked.

"I request access so we can discuss your granddaughter," Jemma said.

"There is nothing to discuss."

"But there is," Jemma removed her pistol from her robe. "Now talk."

"I told you, I do not know where she is."

"If that is the truth, then you serve no purpose. Are you sure that is your answer?"

"It is the only answer I have."

"Very well." Jemma raised the pistol, her hands shaking. It was an easy shot, straight through the heart, but then her hands lowered, just slightly, as the pistol recoiled.

Leaving Madame Gonzo collapsed on the floor of her home. Blood splattered across the hallway.

The old woman curled her body in pain, sobbing.

Jemma did not pass words of comfort. Instead, she dragged the body to the kitchen and took a seat.

No words.

No comfort.

Her mind spun.

Spinning…

> *Spinning…*

Voices chanted.

Chanting…

> *Chanting…*

Yellow smoke rose.

Falling…

> *Breathing…*

Clogging her vision, leaving nothing but yellow.

Brent continued to grip Jemma's hands, her eyes wide, mouth ajar. The yellow smoke exited her body in a flood. Brent inhaled, letting the smoke's story fill his mind and body. It chanted Jemma's story like a song in a deep rumble that reminded Brent of Ningursu.

He let the story fill him before pushing it to the back of his mind. It was hard to ignore this one, with its taunting voice and controlling hands. But he was stronger than the stories.

And now that Jemma was cleansed, he hoped she was too.

I have to stay together for Bria. We need to get Madame Gonzo help.

Jemma sank to the floor, her entire body shaking. The yellow tone left her eyes, leaving her frail and weak. She stared at Madame Gonzo.

"Jem?" Brent asked.

"I shot Madame Gonzo..." Jemma whispered. Tears filled her eyes. "I killed...so many...I killed..."

"Jemma, it wasn't you," Brent said.

She showed no signs of hearing him.

"Jemma?"

"Help..." sobs filled her throat. With each inhale, they grew louder, growing with her obvious confusion. "Help...help me! Please...help!"

Brent still wasn't sure if she even had sight anymore. With her mind free of the monster, whatever magic it had bestowed upon her might just fade.

He climbed from the ground and limped into the foyer. The front door hung open a crack, but he proceeded to push it fully ajar, revealing the clear nighttime air. The yellow smoke had dissipated. Few occupied the streets. All sat quiet.

Until Jemma's wail deafened the silence and haunted the market square.

CHAPTER FORTY-SEVEN

WHERE QUESTIONS GO TO HEAL

The last place Todd thought he would return was the Sanitorium in the heart of Mert. This was the very facility that diagnosed Lex's phantom rot and the very facility in which his life had changed for the worse.

The strange silver liquid fell from his body as he climbed from the tub. For once, Garrett reacted, shaking his head so the liquid escaped his hair. But that was it. While most children would have reacted with excitement or fear, Garrett settled back into Todd's arms without a sound.

Todd adjusted Garrett on his hip. Etta circled the pool, rambling to herself about its magical properties. Only her excited scream derailed her rambles as Edith popped from the tub.

Edith climbed from it without a word, letting the liquid fall from her body. She walked across the operating theater, undeterred by the sudden movement, as if this itself was a normal occurrence.

Despite Etta's questions, Edith didn't provide any further explanation, guiding them out of the theater and into the Sanitorium. Todd held Garrett close as they walked. The boy perked up ever-so-slightly as they walked, moving his head to the sound of carts rolling past.

Edith led them through the narrow halls of the Sanitorium, away from the main treatment area, opening unassuming doors and navigating them to a narrow flight of stairs. Pipes lined the walls, creaking and bursting with steam. A puff blew in Todd's face.

"Where you taking us?" Todd finally asked as they continued to climb.

Edith ignored him.

"We're going upstairs," Etta said matter-of-factly.

"No, really? I never would have guessed."

Etta chuckled.

Todd groaned. "What are you so giddy about?"

"I've been dreaming of visiting Mert since I learned Nils had magic. Never seemed possible… but now I'm here! I didn't have to do anything but jump into a tub!"

"Yeah, I don't get it."

"Magic!" Etta wiggled her fingers in the air.

Todd grunted.

The stairs seemed endless, only exasperated by the few lights lining the railing. But, after moments of gnawing silence, they finally stopped before a narrow door.

Edith removed a key from her trousers and inserted it in the door. She kicked it open.

Behind it, a well-kept suite with pristine upholstery and a large kitchen welcomed them. Edith strode inside, kicking off her shoes and calling out, "Kek!? Are you here?" She opened another door. "Tarek? Kafele?"

No one responded, so Edith instead collapsed on one of the sofas. "Take a seat. I'm sure they'll be around soon enough."

Etta obliged, taking a seat across from Edith. But Todd remained standing, still holding Garrett close.

"Why are we here?" Todd demanded again.

Edith rolled her eyes. "So we can help your boy. Dr. Kafele is a world-renowned doctor."

"Dr. Kafele…" There was that name again. He wracked his brain, the name's familiarity mocking him.

"I think they were the one who diagnosed my wife with Phantom Rot."

Etta perked slightly from her spot but didn't speak.

"Yeah, Phantom Rot is easy," Edith picked at her nails. "Your son might be a more difficult situation, though."

Todd had no qualms with the doctor. They seemed good at their job, but with all this magic, could they really help?

"Why are we in this suite, though? Shouldn't we be down where the action is?" Etta asked.

"This is where the doctor lived. I used to live here too when I was a nurse at this place."

"You worked with Dr. Kafele?"

"For quite a while."

"That's amazing! Dr. Kafele is spectacular! I've read all their papers! Their dissertation about the impact of dragon blood on wounds is fascinating. Let me tell you, I wanted to go out to Spinoza to research it, but the Academy wouldn't give me the grant money. Quite a shame, really, because—"

Etta continued her rambles as Todd paced the room. He paused by the window and peered outside.

A yellow glow encapsulated the city, casting a haze over the few twinkling lights. The Chessboard Plains captured the glow in its white flowers. In the distance, in the light of the half-moon, the clouds towered, streaks of lightning dancing across them.

He moved to the other side of the room, looking down at the alleyway below the Sanitorium. At night, no one mulled about, except for the trace number of Rosadian Guards lingering. They still hadn't left, maintaining their rule over Mert, a constant presence.

But without the strength of the Order behind them.

I wonder what became of my shop. Todd had sold what remained of it before they fled Mert to some fellows in pinstripe suits. It felt like a lifetime ago.

Really, all of it was strange, staring down at Mert from this window. In a way, he supposed he had missed this annoying city. Those years he spent here with Lex hadn't been all that bad.

At least they were happy.

"Oi, you want something to drink?" Etta called, standing in the kitchen.

Todd shook his head.

"Suit yourself," Etta removed a bottle of wine from the shelf and popped it open.

As Todd turned back to the window, the door to the suite opened. A towering man with red hair stumbled in, his eyes bloodshot and staring with no destination.

"Kek?" he called as he stumbled into the room.

"They're not here," Edith grunted. "Surprised you could even navigate up these stairs."

"Edith? What are you doing here?" he asked, turning toward her voice.

"This is my home too, you know."

"Yes, but you have always despised it here. What's going on?"

"I found a solution to our problem."

"Our problem?"

"Well, more your problem."

"You know what my problem is?"

"I can see what your problem is."

"Oh...you mean my eyes," Varden shook his head. "That's not important right now. Something is happening to Tom—I could feel a shift in him and the spirits. Like there was smoke blowing. I managed to get out and lock the door... but I doubt it will remain."

"Oh, that? Yes, the reapers are being non-compliant. As per usual."

Todd didn't understand a word of the conversation, glancing back and forth between Edith and the giant. The man caused Edith to look remarkably small, but there was little threatening about him.

"Well, we can't do much about your Reaper until we can see him. But if Ms. Gratz here is as smart as she lets on, I think we got an answer." Edith pointed at Todd and Garrett. "We found who started this all."

"What?" Todd spat.

"Explain," the giant pressured.

Etta spoke up, "Hello, um, Mr.—"

"Varden. My name is Varden."

"Yes, Varden, hello. I'm Professor Etta Gratz, magiepidemiologist." Etta bowed slightly. "I think that the boy here, Garrett Dray, was used somehow to infect people like you with otherworldly sight. I was hoping that someone here could help me research it... because we might be able to create a cure."

"Garrett Dray..." Varden turned his attention in Todd's direction. "Preston Dray's brother?"

"How do you know about Preston?" Todd asked. Garrett moved his head at the mention of his brother's name.

"I've met him."

"He's dead! How could you have met him?"

"I have my ways." Varden turned again toward Edith and Etta, "You know where the Pinstripes hide out, yes?"

"Of course I do," Edith replied.

"Take Mr. Dray and his son there. Find Timothée. I'll wait here for Kek," Varden felt along the edge of the couch.

"Very well," Edith headed toward the small narrow door, "C'mon then. You heard the man. Let's get going."

"Seriously?" Todd stared at her. "You know the Pinstripes are a gang."

"Oh, yes. Of course I do. I created them." Edith winked, then opened the door.

Todd gawked at her, frozen in place. But Etta tugged on his arm, and despite his entire body screaming to run, he followed them back down the stairwell and into the streets of Mert.

ALL THE SAME

Carver, or well *Ningursu*, moved Chander to a space beside Brent's desk at the front of the room. Still chained, Chander remained silent. How was this young man Ningursu? Yaz said he was a skull. But as he loitered about the room, it was obvious he was more than just some guard. He approached each of the spirits, lifting their attention to face him, then tugging at their lips with smoke. The spirits whimpered in his presence, sinking back as the smoke wrapped around them.

Ningursu continued about the room, stopping in front of each spirit to perform the same routine. Something about the way the spirits retreated, their eyes falling, and bodies stiffening. It was almost as if Ningursu robbed them of a sense of self.

As Ningursu completed his rounds, he kept stealing glances at Chander, a smirk on his face. In certain lights, the skeletal structure of his jaw reappeared. The very sight caused Chander's skin to crawl.

Just my imagination.

Ningursu approached him as he finished his last loop around the room. The black smoke trailed behind him.

"You have to admit, it is interesting, yes?" Ningursu said. "Imagine being able to control anyone, just through a single connection."

Chander still did not respond. He'd been around enough horrible people to know not to speak.

"Come now, I can see how it sparks your interest. Surely, you've wondered what purpose your talents serve. You can see through anyone's eyes...I am sure it has perplexed you since you were small."

It is not a talent that I am proud of.

Ningursu continued, "And you've had a quick taste of control, have you not? With our dear Brenton Harley?"

Chander frowned.

"Let me tell you, when I was a young man...in a far different body and a far different life...it scared me too. There were things I never wanted to experience, visions I never yearned to see. I watched as a farmer got trampled by a horse...through his own eyes. Have you ever felt life leave someone's body?" Ningursu leaned forward. "It is terrifying. That moment made me realize that I would do anything to maintain control of my destiny. Should we not be the ones to choose how we die?"

Chander had never witnessed death like that; while he'd been in the minds of the most corrupt people and the most innocent, he'd yet to feel life escape his body.

"You and I, Mr. Bhatta, have been blessed with a gift. We can write our own stories, play our own game of chess, and control our pieces without fear of repercussions. Think about it—I am sure there are times when you yearn to change your fate. With a mere thought, it is possible. Like... oh... when your sister decided not to come with you?"

How does he know about Anandi? Chander swallowed, still keeping his voice in check.

"You could have lured her to come with you. And that is only the beginning—think about it, Chander, you could have controlled the Guard. I know it all seems impossible, especially when you can barely control one mind right now. But, if you follow my lead, I can teach you how to lead an army with a mere thought while watching the world through someone else's eyes."

Chander fidgeted. *Does this mean I could push the visions away, too? Let them operate in the back of my head while collecting others?* The last question finally escaped his lips. "Wouldn't that overwhelm me?"

"Ah, so you can speak. Very good," Ningursu smiled. There was something uncanny about the way the man's face moved, like he had hijacked it and let it rot while he continued forward with his choices.

Chander kept his words close this time, waiting for Ningursu's reply.

"You must curate your sight accordingly. One thought at a time. While I am sure Brenton has been telling you to focus on your *constants* or something abstract of similar regards, the way to harness your sight is to embrace it."

Why can't I do both?

"I can help you harness it, Chander. The visions won't haunt you anymore." Ninguru said.

Chander could not recall a day when the visions did not plague him. Was it possible to stop them, to finally see clearly again?

"Let me help you, Mr. Bhatta. Be not afraid," there was that smile again. It didn't even belong on this body's face.

Chander whispered, just barely audible, "I want it to stop."

"Then, let's try our first lesson," Ningursu placed his hands on the chains by Chander's hands. Their grip loosened ever-so-slightly. "Tell me, who was the last person you touched?"

Chander frowned, pondering for a moment. "My sister."

"I want you to take a peek through your sister's eyes. Do not fret; I won't ask you to do anything invasive."

Chander paused. Should he cave to Ningursu's request and put Anandi at risk?

But he would ultimately see through her eyes when he slept. Just a peak wouldn't hurt. It was not like Ningursu would learn anything but how to serve coffee from Anandi.

"Go on," Ningursu insisted.

Chander closed his eyes. Darkness stared back at him.

"What is your sister doing?" Ningursu asked.

"She's asleep," Chander replied.

"Ah yes, I see. As your magic grows, you may be able to see her dreams. But for now… tell her to wake up."

"Wake up?"

"Yes. Just think the words. Project the thought out from your body, just as you do with your sight. It may take a few tries, but I know you can do it."

Chander frowned but obliged. His thoughts started as a soft whisper. *Wake up.*

The darkness didn't shift.

He tried again, louder. *Wake up.*

Nothing.

Wake up!

Still darkness.

Dammit, wake up already!

Finally, a slither of light entered his vision. Chander couldn't resist the smile twitching on his lips.

"You woke her?"

"I did." Chander kept his eyes closed. The light solidified, pulling him not into Anandi's room in the tavern but instead into a dark cavern with gas lamps flickering on the ground.

Wait… where is she?

He pushed his vision, attempting to see more of the room. A strange cylinder chugging with smoke sat on the ground, with wires buzzing about the room.

"I will leave you with your sister," Ningursu patted Chander's sleeve. "We will continue our training once we have shifted."

Chander didn't reply, still locked in the vision. Ningursu's footsteps echoed as he left.

In the cave, a shadow moved about the room. He pressed forward with his sight, attempting to see past the smoke building around them.

What's happening to you, Anandi?

At last, the smoke solidified, taking shape as the balding Mist Keeper, Alojzy.

Wait… Chander forced his puppet's eyes to lower. Fingers, composed of branches, waited at the body's side. *This is Bria.*

Then he remembered. Bria's unconscious hand had brushed his skin. Just barely. Enough to take his magic and hold it.

He kept watching as Alojzy moved across the room. Bria didn't have sight—did she know this Mist Keeper was there?

Would she be able to fight an invisible foe?

Chander wanted to scream, to tell her to watch out. But he was trapped in the schoolhouse. He didn't have any way to help.

All he had was sight.

He closed his eyes tighter. A single word echoed across his mind, *See.*

With the single word echoing across his mind, he opened his own eyes, letting the classroom come back into view. Bria floated to the back of his mind, like a constant weight, like the knowledge of his sister in Mert.

Otherwise, the classroom stayed quiet, the spirits sleeping, undeterred by otherworldly visions.

Nor disturbed by the shadows moving outside the schoolhouse windows, enshrouded in yellow.

CHAPTER FORTY-NINE

CYCLICAL

Bria's breathing labored. As she opened her eyes, the thick yellow smoke surrounded her, pouring in through the mouth of the cave. Water sloshed at her feet while chains kept her stable against the wall. Carved shelves lined the cave, mingling with the stalagmites.

On the ground in front of her, a strange metal cylinder laced with wires and chugging with smoke produced a metallic odor with each putter. Wires extended out of it, which kept adjusting as an invisible hand guided them.

She wracked her brain over what had happened. The swamp had been in chaos, and upon arriving in her palace, she found Marisol. But something had changed, and before she had time to process it, Christof, controlled by Ningursu himself, grabbed her.

She had lost consciousness as the yellow smoke filled her lungs, and now she was here, in the cave, unable to sense her magic. At her side, her branched hand threatened to wither.

One of the wires from the mechanical cylinder rose in the air and approached her, carried by an invisible Mist Keeper. She flinched as the wire met her collarbone. There, the Mist Keeper secured it with a needle into her skin.

I wish I could see. With her magic suffering against the yellow smoke, she couldn't even use the elements to help her resist.

Again, the Mist Keeper placed another wire, this time on her chest. Each placement came with a gasp of cold air as if fingers danced on her skin.

She once again eyed the cylinder. With each wire and a small motor on its side, it kept puttering along. *Why would Ningursu use something electric like this?* It reminded her of the tower that transported her to Knoll all those moons ago. When Captain Palmer captured her, the Guard embellished her with wires, only to use their magic to fuel the tower itself.

Do they want to use my magic for something?

But what? And why?

She strained her neck to get a better look. Even then, she couldn't determine *what* this thing was or its purpose.

If only she could *see*, then she would be able to thrive.

See. Was it too much to ask to just see her captor? Instead, they acted behind a blanket, pulling the strings but never taking the fall.

But she just wanted to *see* and to face them.

She wouldn't be able to fight, but if they were to end her life, then at least it would be with dignity.

Just *see.*

See!

The word reverberated in her mind. But this time it felt different, as if owned by another person.

With that single command, a blurry haze filled her vision. Now, a shadow carried the wires. As it moved, the Mist continued to solidify around it.

First, it outlined the body.

Then, it worked its way, etching across the figure's skin and into his clothes.

Colors brightened, and with the Mist finally parting, there stood Alojzy, working with the electric wires and cylinders, unconcerned about Bria.

She didn't dare speak, keeping her head low as Alojzy placed one last wire to her temples. Then, he patted her cheek without a word.

Bria flinched.

As Alojzy returned to the cylinder, she tried to summon any element. Nothing reacted, though, fizzling before she could even inhale, the magic sitting in her chest like a rock.

Alojzy switched the lever attached to the cylinder. The machine began to shake, buzzing about the room. On her skin, the wires tingles, scratching into her skin.

Then came the shock.

It coursed through her body, sharp and abrupt, clawing into her bones and twisting around her veins. The rock in the center of her chest broke, and with that mere gasp, her little branch extended, wrapping around the cavern and sending her back into darkness.

The cycle continued for what felt like hours. She would wake to Alojzy gone, but her magic unable to flourish. He returned with a new cylinder every time, reattaching it to the wires and performing the same ritual.

As he prepared his sixth or seventh cylinder, Bria could do little to even raise her head, sweat dripping from her nose. *What can I do?* If she dared try to summon her magic, it only sparked the machine or failed against the yellow smoke. How hard was it to operate through the yellow? It was just the Mist, composed of sulfur, oxygen, nitrogen, and carbon. Any other Mist, she'd be able to disassemble.

What made the Mist Keepers different?

Ningursu had destroyed the Gardeniros years ago, but he'd never stopped the camellias from blooming. She had their immortal blessing thriving through her veins.

She shifted as Alojzy readied the next cylinder. *Whenever the shocks begin, it opens my magic for a few seconds. Can I use that?* Electricity was just a reaction, possible to manipulate with the right focus and the right willpower. Her body ached, her mind spun, but she couldn't keep going through his buzzing ritual. Any more, and she might wither entirely.

Alojzy flicked the switch again. She anticipated the shocks this time, holding her breath as they began to rip through her body. The magic in her chest disseminated. Instead of letting it leave, she focused on how it gathered on her fingertips, using what little she could muster to trace along the elements in the air. Sulfur crawled, oxygen echoed, nitrogen chilled; with just a single breath, she tore them apart. The yellow smoke rescinded toward the mouth of the cave.

Upon noticing, Alojzy did not switch off the electric box, approaching Bria. The shocks continued to pulse, reaching through her body.

She recited the elements to herself.

Hydrogen.

Oxygen.

Carbon.

Alojzy gripped her face. She stared ahead, pretending not to see him.

Nitrogen

Helium.

Sulfur.

He squeezed her neck, scowling.

The elements on his skin tingled.

Sulfur.

Iron.

Calcium.

Like in the air or in the water, it was easy to deconstruct the elements. One at a time, they would break, standing on their own, a single entity.

Phosphorus.

Potassium.

Magnesium.

With the electric shocks growing, she kept her focus on each element, tugging at each one, pulling at their mere existence. It was the only way she could keep herself conscious, as her breaths grew thicker and more compromised.

Then, as Alojzy pressed his hand tighter, he gasped. With a wave of her magic, the elements exploded around her.

And Alojzy's hand vanished.

Then, his arms.

Followed by his torso.

Legs.

And finally, his face, with eyes wide, turned into smoke right before Bria.

Bria cried out. The chains holding her to the wall broke. Instinctively, she yanked the wires from her body, shaking. Tears filled her eyes as she leaned against the wall.

Did I just kill him? She stared at her hands. No, it couldn't be... right? She had seen it happen, though. He had vanished into the smoke, nothing more than the elements of the earth.

She sat there, frozen, as the machine continued to buzz. The wires flew about in the air, tangling around stalagmites and fixtures in the wall.

I bet he's still here. Watching. Waiting for my powers to weaken again. He's not gone. He can't be gone. If it was that easy to deconstruct a Mist Keeper, who was to say that she couldn't deconstruct... everything?

She swallowed her tears. *He can't be gone. It can't be that easy.*

The machine fell over on its side, continuing its ongoing disarray. Bria crawled over to it. As her hand fell on it, another electric shock climbed through her body, then sparked on her fingers.

There, the silence sat.

Before the box exploded with a wave of roots, vines…
and peonies.

CHAPTER FIFTY

CAPTAIN OF THE DEAD

Brent sat on the front steps of Madame Gonzo's home, watching as Captain Randall walked Jemma from the house. The local doctor had also arrived to tend to Madame Gonzo's wounds. The town itself remained quiet, unscathed by the incident, resting peacefully in the late veil of night.

Jemma's cries still haunted him. This was Ningursu's power. He could manipulate in the shadows, compromising beliefs and unweaving any sense of self. While Brent and Jemma had never been close, he knew her well enough to know that she had been a moral person wishing to bring peace.

But Ninguru's peace, even during eras without blood, was not Jemma's peace.

Brent used the railing to climb to his feet, wincing as his side burned again. *I need to get back to Neorama before anything else happens.* He turned down the road toward the familiar path to the Senator's Garden. He paused as he met the watchful eye of the Order's Year Glass, mocking him. If it could talk, he was sure it said, "You will never be free of me."

He headed down the familiar path away from the market square. His fingers twitched, reveling in the distant story of him and Bria, walking hand-in-hand as they approached the immortal camellia bushes. Now, while everything else in the garden withered, those flowers remained bright and strong.

He stopped by one of the flowers and stroked its petals. How was he going to tell Bria what happened? Madame Gonzo was alive, but her injuries would still take time to heal. Bria would be eager to visit her grandmother.

Would it be better not to say anything at all?

The idea of lying made him queasy. He made a promise to her, back when he discovered she was Rho.

No lies.

And it was a promise he intended to keep.

Bria's childhood home sat within the depths of the garden, quiet and undisturbed. During the day, the bolstered, with workers maintaining the greenery. The garden had always been a welcoming place. As a child, he played games like Come-Find-Me and Guards-and-Vagrants with the other children. When he outgrew the games, he spent time smoking along the fence line with Micca or getting lost in the hedge maze with Bria instead.

Now, those were but stories, loitering in an otherwise dead garden.

Colorless.

Even without the color, he recognized the old oak tree with gnarled roots, where he had watched Caroline enter the tunnels for the first time.

If he hadn't followed her, his life may have been different.

In fact, he knew it would have been.

He could see the stories. Instead of following, he would have turned around, back into a loveless betrothal. Caroline would have found another apprentice. The Council's cycle would have continued.

And more people would have continued to suffer.

He reached for the gnarled root. The door opened without a fight, the old ladder still there, waiting for him.

Brent descended without looking back, stopping midway down to catch his breath. The pain in his side continued its obtrusive clawing, working up his neck and even knocking on his face. Upon reaching the ground, he paused to lift his shirt, checking the black rot expanding over his side. It crawled over his veins, almost seeming to pulse with each beat of his heart.

He poked one of the rotting veins. At his touch, it steamed.

Well, this is great. Brent let his shirt drop and refocused on the tunnels. Stories of his own past returned in waves—him toppling into the tunnels, Caroline attacking him, the vines Bria used to save him.

Brent followed that story, where a lattice of dead vines greeted him. He peaked through, where Bria's little hideaway remained untouched. A few old newspapers lay on the floor, and in the center of the hideaway, a small tree grew amongst them. A small yellow fruit grew on its branches.

Brent slipped through the lattice and approached the tree. He smiled. *It's a lemon.*

As he removed it from the branch, twisting it to not damage the branch itself, a thud caught his attention. He pivoted, where the tall, looming shadow of Jiang had arrived from the ladder.

Brent froze as the giant faced him.

"Good. You're here." Jiang said. "We need to hurry."

"Why? What's going on?" Brent asked, placing the lemon in his pocket.

"Ningursu's plans are in motion. Your... wife is in danger."

Brent stared hard at Jiang. His story remained calm, without malice, attention seeming to focus on the past. "How do you know?" he asked.

"Because Ningursu knew you were coming here. You are just a pawn in his game." Jiang walked a few paces forward, his hand against the wall. "We all are."

"So he wanted to distract me while he went after Bria."

"That is my understanding of it."

"Bria wasn't home though… but…" Brent never finished his sentence. Even if Bria wasn't there, she had gathered refugees from across Rosada. Worse yet, he had moved Neorama.

Surely, Szyman moved the town before Ningursu crept down the streets.

But Brent still didn't delay, following in step with Jiang as they hurried through the tunnels. It was odd pacing Jiang. The giant had never been welcoming to Brent, often mocking him or grumbling about the Library. Bringing back Jiang's lost love, just for a moment, seemed to awaken something within him.

Jiang spoke, his voice low, "Thank you…for helping me find my truth again."

Brent paused, taken back slightly by Jiang's gratitude. "Yeah, of course."

They didn't exchange any other words, walking in silence as they continued through the tunnels.

As they approached the junction, voices echoed. Brent slowed as he approached and peaked into the opening.

Cohorts of refugees from Bria's swamp moved through the junction, heading in a line toward the tunnel leading further south. *They escaped.*

Jiang scowled but said nothing.

Brent took a moment to catch his breath as another wave of pain rocked through his body, then continued down the tunnel toward Bria's swamp.

The humidity thickened as they reached the end of the tunnel, enshrouding the collections of moss and roots. Yet rather than the richness that had defined Bria's swamp, upon exiting, they were greeted with streams of yellow and black intermingling with the mud.

"He's here..." Brent said aloud. The smoke masked Bria's palace, derailing stories and sending Brent's own head spinning. Stories of Chander and Milo running into the swamp, of Yaz and Nix cowering between two stumps, and of... Christof carrying Bria?

Brent followed after the story. The smoke wrapped around Christof as he walked, seeming to obey his movements. As he turned toward the east, the side of his face transformed, revealing the skeletal outline of Ningursu.

He followed a few more paces after the story. Yet, as he rounded a broken cypress tree, another, more recent, story intersected it. This one showed Alojzy dragging

Bria's body through the swamp. It was stronger, more recent.

Brent froze. Christof's story headed to Neorama, while Alojzy's headed the opposite direction, deep into the swamp. *Should I check Neorama first? Or go after Alojzy?*

"What's wrong?" Jiang asked.

"The stories... One heads to Neorama, and the other heads after Alojzy with Bria. If Ningursu finds Neorama, then he'll gain access to more power. But I'm almost positive that Bria is with Alojzy..." Brent scratched at his wrist.

"Go to your Bria," Jiang said. "I'll protect Neorama."

"Are you sure?"

"Yes, I can fight this on my own." Jiang turned his back to Brent, facing Neorama's direction. He opened and closed his hands. Mist gathered around him.

"Wait...are you using your magic?"

Jiang did not reply. The ground beneath their feet shifted. Brent stepped away, letting Jiang embrace the Mist.

Every time that Brent spoke with Jiang, it was under the guise that Jiang did not have any magic. While Brent knew that to be a lie, the stories showing hints of Jiang's own abilities, he had never quite uncovered their true nature.

But now, with the Mist growing and the ground rumbling, it was clear that the giant's power was more than just his height.

The Mist swirled about Jiang's feet. Then, he raised his hands up ever-so-slightly.

With this movement, a frail, skeletal hand emerged. Then another.

And another.

More hands crawled from the ground, pulling up decomposing bodies behind them. These weren't Diabolo, but something different. Reanimated corpses, responding to each of Jiang's movements. They rose around him, an army of the dead, eyes blank and soulless but ready to join his side.

"Go," Jiang ordered.

"Thank you," Brent said again, then stepped backward as the army of the dead marched with their captain into battle.

CHAPTER FIFTY-ONE

A Delicate Bomb

Bria climbed out of the cave. Flowers, vines, roots, rocks, and more clung to her body like armor—everything attracted her very being. As she shifted, the vines curled around her skin, and bark thickened like an exoskeleton across her body. Behind her, the cave continued to flood with foliage. Red and white flowers poured from the mouth of the cave and into the swamp.

But behind this very beauty was a delicate fear. The power behind these plants could suffocate even the strongest person.

And this was only a fraction of her magic.

She stared back at the cave. Smoke drizzled at its edge, steaming from the dismantled contraption.

It's like they siphoned my magic into a bomb. She clenched her hands. Taproots hung from her branched hand, reaching for the ground. Despite the yellow smoke still hanging in the air, her magic thrived, too strong to be diminished.

But at what cost?

The trees swayed as she stumbled away from the cave. The air tasted like rotting eggs, and through the canopy, the yellow clouds encapsulated the moon. Each gust of wind caught nightmares as if the Diabolo themselves had been sewn into the fabric of the world. There was no escaping their anger. Instead, they would always be there to tell the truth.

The world was not pretty.

She whimpered with each step, the roots pulling at her skin and lacing to the ground. As she raised her feet, the roots pulled back before snapping. Blood congealed at the edge of each root.

Every step carried her with no destination. Where could she go now, though? Would it make sense to go to São Caméliosa? Or Mert? Or should she just stay here and face Ningursu and try to end this all before it was too late?

And then return to the forest whence she came?

The cypress trees reached for her as she approached one of their knobby roots. Their leaves glued themselves to her hair. *Monster…* The word rang in her head. She was more of a monster than a human. The trees claimed her as their own.

Monster…

It would never end.

You'll never make it pretty.

The world is worse than petty.

She wrapped her hand around the root, then paused.

But I can make it pretty.

Bria turned, ripping her fingers from the bark and returning her attention to the swamp. Even if she didn't recognize the cave, she knew the swamp. It told her stories of life beating within its grasp. From the heartbeats of alligators to the flapping of wood storks and the croaking of the frogs. Each movement, each step, manipulated the swamp to its whims. If she just listened closely enough, she could find the anomalies.

The footsteps of a deer.

The whistles of an ibis.

Then, there was that heavy heartbeat, forced to thrive in uneven beats.

The heartbeat of a dead man walking.

She followed it, letting the exoskeleton of foliage thicken. It formed a layer of armor, coating her from head to toe. Last, her little branch passed over her face like a mask. This was the uniform of Rhodana the Forest

Queen. She was the woman who would always find a reason to laugh despite the screams.

And she would fulfill her promise to grant the world's reveries.

I am not scared of Ningursu. I defeated Alojzy—I can defeat him too.

She marched forward, cradling her confidence with every step. The song played in her head, each stanza changing, never the same.

Rhodana,
The forest queen,
She will fight for rights,
She will fight for everything.
The trees will bow,
They'll secure her now.
Rhodana.

She would fight. What would running do but prolong the battle? Now was her only chance. Otherwise, Ningursu might vanish again, continuing his reign from the Mist.

Her fingers shook as she rounded another set of trees. The explosion from within the cave had ignited something in her. Yet, adrenaline had a short life. Sooner or later, it would cease, leaving her wreathing in her own pit of anxiety.

She passed through another gathering of trees. Swamp water sloshed at her feet, gathering in her boots. She kicked them off, letting algae and moss form a layer of protection around her toes. There was no reason to fear the swamp.

It was her domain.

As she reached the edge of the water, dripping with sludge, she spotted a figure standing between the trees. It turned to face her.

"Ningursu!" she shouted, the confidence in her voice a surprise.

Ningursu smiled. Christof's body had rotted further since she last saw it, half of his face dismantled, while the flesh of his arms and legs sagged from his bones. Ningursu had taken his place, permanently scarring the cadet beyond repair. "Ah, Briannabella, I knew you'd be coming."

"I'm done playing your games," Bria stated.

"Oh, I'm sure you think that. I bet after dismantling Alojzy, you're feeling particularly confident."

Her stomach flipped. "How did you know?"

"I bet you think you defeated a Mist Keeper, didn't you? Oh, my sweet queen, you are mistaken. Do you not understand that only *I* can destroy the Mist Keepers? Some petty dryad could never do such a thing."

"Alojzy is gone. I saw it happen," Bria replied. Her voice quivered.

"It was only a minor setback—he is back, and frankly, he is quite bitter."

Bria shook her head, "I deconstructed his elements..."

"Yes, but you may have forgotten...smoke always rises."

Bria took another step toward Ningursu. She refused to humor this conversation. He was trying to upset her, overturn all of her confidence, and lead her into the palm of his hand. So she ignored his jabs, lifting one hand from her side and summoning the surrounding trees to rise.

Their branches raced toward Ningursu with the command. He didn't budge, letting them wrap around him and pull him from the ground.

Bria commanded them to tighten, squeezing him so that his body may not move.

"Now come on, Briannabella. What good will this do? Are you truly that afraid of what your magic can do?" Ningursu taunted.

"I could deconstruct every element in your body if I wanted," Bria replied.

"Then do it. You hate me, do you not?"

She stared hard at Ningursu. But all she saw was Christof's body, hanging limp in the trees. She had every right to destroy him. He had harassed her for years, destroyed her life, and killed her mother. But… perhaps being Ningursu's vessel was bad enough.

But it would be so easy to seek revenge…

She swallowed. Ningursu clicked his teeth together once, grinding something in his mouth.

Do it. Her vision blurred. *You're just as sensitive as that bomb. Do it.*

The ground at her feet rumbled. Deep beneath the surface, beyond the limestone and bedrock, the core of the earth warmed her feet. Everywhere, everything; it all beckoned her to let her magic loose.

To let it capture the world.

To ignite.

To blaze.

To destroy.

No. Stop! She trembled as Ningursu continued to chew on something in his mouth. It mocked her, a consistent clicking rhythm echoing of his decaying teeth.

Up and down…

    Side to side…

Up…

    Down…

"Go on, Briannabella. Destroy me," he mocked again.

She flared her nostrils, then instructed the branches to throw Christof's body across the clearing. He toppled through the air, landing on the ground with a thud.

A laugh escaped his lips as he pulled himself from the ground. Before he could stand, Bria allowed the branches to lift her over to him. As she landed, the limestone beneath Ningursu rose, shackling his feet to the ground and securing him in place. From there, with each step, she listened to the slow thud in his heart, the flow of blood from organ to organ. Iron and oxygen banged against his veins.

Small.

Sharp.

Prickling.

And iron could be forged into blades.

And as the iron shifted in his blood, cuts struck his skin, opening it like scissors in paper. Ningursu's laughs didn't cease.

"That's right, little flower. Accept your thorns."

The cuts appeared on his face, carving beneath his eyes.

One of those eyes stared at Bria, wide and fearful.

It didn't belong to Ningursu.

She lowered her hands. *No.*

The cuts ceased appearing on Christof's skin, leaving behind only the collection of bloodied wounds.

"I won't do it..." she murmured. If it had just been Ningursu, maybe, but despite everything that Christof had done, he was just a scared boy. The single gaze remaining on his face, a relic of a time before Ningursu, said all of that. Christof had been a horrible man. He loitered in her nightmares nearly every day. But if she carved him from the inside out, was she any better than Ningursu?

The ground stopped shaking. The shackles around Ningursu's ankles disintegrated.

His body fell for a second, breathing heavily. Bria stared at it, unable to move, her gaze locked.

"Thank you for sparing me," the body whispered. It's raspy voice nearly sounded like Christof's voice.

But she knew better than to trust it.

Ningursu raised his head, "How can I repay you?"

Bria stepped backward, nearly tripping over a cypress root.

He climbed to his feet and approached Bria. With the Mist on his heels, he raced forward and, in a single motion, laced his hand around Bria's neck.

"Don't forget, little queen. You are mine, and you always will be."

Black smoke bubbled around his lips as he spoke. As he leaned forward and pulled Bria's face to his lips.

With the horrid kiss, black smoke wrapped around Bria's head.

And she was every element, in every moment, across the swamp.

CHAPTER FIFTY-TWO

THE MONSTER IN THE SWAMP

The earth roared. Brent gripped a tree, taking a moment to catch his breath and refocus on the story. Alojzy's story had become jumbled with ancient tales mingling within the trees. He caught more glimpses of Ningursu—from before and after his decapitation — but he didn't have time to deconstruct them.

As he gripped the tree, the bark peeled, rot setting into its trunk. He lifted his hand. As soon as he lifted his weight, the tree swayed once, then snapped, missing Brent by only a few inches as it toppled to the ground.

He stumbled backward into another tree.

As soon as he hit it, that one collapsed as well.

They fell around him like dominoes. Above, the sky thickened with clouds. They teetered there for a moment, then with a burst of lightning and thunder, rain cast itself over the swamp.

"Bria!" he shouted. Despite the pain digging into his body, he burst into a run, swallowing the bile in his throat. As he ran, the earth shifted as if turned inside-out by an invisible hand. Trees continued their fall, their roots withering. Bushes crumbled. Moss peeled away from the ground, slipping into the murky water.

With the swamp's collapse, the stories grew as muddy as the ground. Tales of archers, of alligator tamers, and of travelers mingled with Ningursu's and Alojzy's stories. He tried to stay focused, but it was difficult to ignore the commotion gathering about him.

Bria. Focus on Bria.

He slid through the mud, jumping over the cracks in the earth and avoiding the ever-deepening pits of water. The mud continued to chase him as he ascended to higher ground, along a bed of pine needles, where a wall of thin trees had formed.

He clawed through them, tumbling down a small hill into another clearing where the swamp water met the shore. He nearly walked straight into a mother alligator, minding her younglings, and found himself instead face-down in the muck. He brushed it off, then pushed through the crumbling trees.

At the next clearing, he halted.

There stood a figure pulsing with Mist.

Ningursu.

Even though he commandeered Christof's body as his vessel, his identity was obvious. At his feet, Bria had curled onto the ground, black smoke weaving in and out of her body as it convulsed.

Panic formed a lump in Brent's chest. Rather than breaking it open, he instead reached for the story of the archers, readying them in position beside him. He took over the role of their leader, counting down until it was time to bellow the order, "Fire."

The arrows flew straight into the invisible target on Ningursu's back.

Ningursu spun as the arrows hit him. The black smoke loosened around Bria, where the earth's quaking slowed.

"Brenton! That was quite rude of you—it would have been better to say hello," Ningursu remarked.

"This ends now, Ningursu," Brent shouted.

"Your little nymph said the same thing. Do the two of you share one mind?"

Brent slowly marched into the clearing, collecting the Mist on his fingers. With his left hand, he gathered the story, while in his right, he pulled the black smoke away from Bria, letting it cling instead to the wound on his side. As it assaulted him, clawing at whatever remained of his Diabolo, the stories escalated. Was there really a talking alligator? Or was that just a myth, spoken in the trees?

"I won't let you repeat what you did to Cassia," Brent said.

"Cassia?"

"You don't even remember your Hurtovitae's name?"

"Oh! Cassia! That's right. You heard about that then, did you? Do not worry... I shall not be doing that. Your nymph is far more powerful than that Hurtovitae ever was. Watch." Ningursu snapped his fingers. The black smoke puddled around Bria again. She screamed out as it tightened.

"Bri—" But before he could do anything, every particle in his body tingled. One by one, he destabilized into nothing more than Mist, starting with his fingers, then progressing down his torso and around his legs.

Floating.

Deconstructing.

Collapsing.

Falling...

Falling...

Falling...

And then taking another breath.

He had landed on his hands and knees, the body solidified.

"What... what happened?" He glanced around. Ningursu stood in the same spot while Bria sobbed on the ground.

"Your little nymph happened," Ningursu said.

"What?"

"*She* did that to you."

"No, she didn't. You made her do it."

"Oh, you have no proof of that, Brenton."

"Let go of her," Brent hissed through his teeth.

Ningursu held up his hands, "I'm not holding her."

"You know what I mean!"

"I am merely just giving her the spark to reach her full potential. Isn't that what you want? For the Forest Queen to reach the stars?"

Brent gritted his teeth while searching the area for another tale. Wisps of Bria marching through the forest, readying for an attack, caught his attention. She had momentarily restrained Ningursu.

Before he could claim the story as his own, his body disintegrated back into the Mist again.

Around and around...

With every breath, his body continued to shift, in and out of the Mist. If he could just summon the right story, he'd be able to stop this madness.

But which one could he harness while shifting?

He fell to the ground again, heaving. His fingers twitched, smoke pooling from beneath his fingernails.

"Just abandon your determination, Brenton," Ningursu said. "You cannot keep this up forever. I can hear it in your voice. You are tired. Just let go."

"Yeah, no thanks," Brent focused on his heart, beating in his chest. His ribs ached as he inhaled once.

Then his body slipped away from stability again.

Rather than focusing on Bria's story, he concentrated on himself, with the way his body pulsed in and out of the Mist to the disintegration of his fingertips in the air. It wasn't just the Mist that weighed on him and pulled at his very fabric, but that of the past, the present, and the future. He had heard people say that Kek's Pool, the Divitiae, was the lifeblood of the earth. But really, it was stories mounting around him, growing by the moment.

And he was a story himself, living in that very moment.

As his body began to solidify again, he ordered his own story to follow. Rather than just himself, standing alone, facing Ningursu, he commandeered his tale, creating duplicates of himself standing in the forest. Their hearts beat in unison, their footsteps moving as one. As he inhaled, so did the duplicate stories of himself.

I look horrid. He shared a glance with one of the stories. His curls fell against his face, plastered to his skin by sweat. The black veins crawled from his neck up toward his face, while dark circles danced with his bloodshot eyes.

"Oh, you think fifty copies of you is terrifying? I'd say it is far more annoying." As Ningursu spoke, it was like a slither of Christof returned.

Brent shared a smirk with his duplicates and took a step toward Ningursu. Despite Ningursu's chuckles, he did not feel the same prickling sensation on his skin. He tried to steal a glance back at Bria, but his duplicates blocked the path, all turning with his gaze.

While he remained secure, the earth's persistent reaction to Bria's magic continued. The trees continued to collapse, and the swamp water bled vermillion.

Ningursu stepped forward, black smoke swirling around him. Yet, his body swayed beneath the plumes, just like the weakening trees.

Brent let the smoke gather at his and his duplicate's feet. He expected it to swirl, to react, and to attack his very fiber like Ningursu had in the Library.

But none of that happened.

It just hung there, circulating the duplicates, unable to fortify its attack.

"You're only as strong as what you can control, Ninguru," Brent said as he neared. "Your vessel is weak…and you used your energy on Bria…and now…now you have nothing."

"This body does not belong to a Mist Keeper. It was only a temporary solution. But now I have everything I need. Thanks to you, I now have access to more Mist Keepers than ever before…as well as your little nymph." Ningursu leaned forward, blowing a puff of smoke in a duplicate's face. "And soon you will rot away in your own stories, Brenton."

Brent didn't respond, watching closely as Ningursu clenched his jaw as if chewing on tobacco or a hard piece of candy. A distant memory returned of Ningursu chewing on a flower.

He uses the black smoke to connect and strengthen Bria, but he cannot control her without a piece of her. The first few times Ningursu laced his control over Bria, it had not been with the same power. But that was before the black smoke.

I need to remove whatever he is chewing from his mouth. Brent took note of his duplicates. Without moving, he ordered half the duplicates to step forward, circling around Ningursu. The smoke rallied at their feet, dismantling each of the duplicates, forcing Ningursu to spin in every direction to stop them.

With Ningursu distracted, Brent found a story of a whinnying horse. It rose from past the trees, racing into the swamp, straight for Ningursu.

As another whinny broke the air, Ningursu turned.

But not fast enough.

The story slammed into his body, sending the body flying.

He landed in the mud with a thud, coughing. There, a small, chewed twig fell from his mouth and into the swamp water. As it sank, the rain slowed to a drizzle, and the earth's rumbling ceased.

Letting his duplicates subside, Brent raced over to the body. It heaved, in and out, frail and broken. Brent could feel its story beneath his fingertips, begging for a release.

It was a story of a young man seeking approval from his father.

The story of a young man desperate to impress the woman of his dreams.

The story of a young man falling in step behind an enthralling leader.

And the story of a young man who gave himself over for a cause he did not understand.

Since turning himself over, Christof lost everything. His body had given up long ago, stuck between its last two heartbeats. His mind only knew nightmares, while any movement belonged to an entity playing puppet master with his broken body.

There was no escape.

No sense of self.

Nothing.

Brent pulled at Christof's story, unraveling the threads that tied it to Ningursu's control. Each stitch snapped, and as Christof's story grew clearer, Ningursu faded into the background.

In the final breath, Christof lifted his head and locked eyes with Brent.

"Thank you, Harley," he grunted.

And his body collapsed, allowing his soul to reach freedom.

With the last breath gone, the black smoke spiraled from Christof's body. It wrapped around Brent with laughter, Ningursu's voice echoing.

This is but the beginning, Brenton.

Then, the smoke fell away, leaving Brent swaying in the center of the swamp. The stories dissipated around him.

"Bri…" He turned, hoping to catch one final glimpse of her.

Only for his footing to give out and for his body to fall into a smoky hand of nihility.

CHAPTER FIFTY-THREE

The Architect and the Necromancer

Chander sat with the weight of Bria's vision in the back of his mind. He didn't dare look through her eyes but let it hang there, a constant entity. To ignore it, he spent time observing the room. The spirits remained in their permanent exhaustion while Caroline and Jewel sat like guards, watching over them. Did Ningursu control them now? And if so, why hadn't he taken control of Chander?

All remained silent until the door to the classroom flew open. Alojzy exploded into the room, steam rising from his skin. His dark eyes locked on Chander, and seething, he stormed over to him. The smoke raced with him, and with one movement, he lifted Chander from the ground. The chains around Chander's hands and wrists snapped.

Chander squirmed, Alojzy's cold fingers digging into his skin. For a second, Alojzy's vision flashed over his gaze.

But Chander retreated into the back of his mind, where Bria's sight continued to weigh. Rather than stealing her gaze, he let his thoughts sit there, pulling away from Alojzy's glower.

"What did you do?" Alojzy demanded.

Chander stared at him.

"The only way she could have *seen* me is if you interfered. What. Did. You. Do?" Alojzy's composure shattered with every word. But frankly, Chander had no clue how to respond. He could see through Bria's eyes… but did he do more than that? Did he help her… see?

If so, he hadn't any idea of *how*.

Alojzy cursed and tossed Chander to the floor. As he seethed, the smoke grew thicker. Chains rose from the floor, wrapping again around Chander's wrists and ankles. Around him, the room twisted, the ceiling lowering, and the walls closing in around them.

Before Alojzy did anything more, Caroline's voice rang. Her voice sounded deeper, as if being controlled by someone else from far away.

"Alojzy! Not now!"

"But sire—"

"We will deal with him once we leave this swamp. Understood?"

"Very well," Alojzy stepped back from Chander. The room stopped turning.

"Prepare Szyman. We must shift soon."

"Yes, sire. If you insist."

Alojzy left in the same storm cloud, slamming the door behind him.

Caroline turned her attention to Chander, "You are much stronger than I anticipated, Mr. Bhatta."

That's Ningursu. Chander shifted beneath the weight of the new chains on his wrists.

Next, Jewel spoke, taking over Ningursu's sentence. "You and I will need to talk, Mr. Bhatta. Your potential is quite impressive."

Marisol, still chained to a nearby desk, took the next words. "But we shall discuss this when we meet soon, Mr. Bhatta. It shan't be long now."

Chander scanned over each of them, waiting for more. But they did not speak again, their heads falling like rag dolls perched on their seats. The spirits beside them did not move. The class fell silent but for the wind bellowing against the building.

Chander turned back into his thoughts, locking onto Bria's vision. In it, she ran through the forest. Tears masked her vision.

Chander backed out of her vision at once. It felt awkward to witness her distress; whatever had happened wasn't for him to experience.

But as his thoughts climbed back to the forefront of his mind, he grazed Alojzy's sight. The man stormed through the street, phasing in and out of the Mist as if he couldn't stabilize his body. Around him, the sky glowed yellow, with clouds marching through the sky like monsters. Yet none of these derailed him.

Except for a looming figure standing at the end of the road. Behind the figure, an army of discombobulated creatures followed.

Alojzy's body shook with a laugh.

"Well, well, well," Alojzy's voice was muffled as he spoke. Chander focused, trying his best to hear. "You look particularly pathetic today, Jiang."

The figure—a giant with long black hair and a stone cold gaze—stepped forward, his army following in step. Their movements teetered to the side, similar to the spirits. But unlike the spirits, they moved as one, obeying the giant's commands without question. When the giant raised his hand, they all stopped. In the foggy moonlight, their bony bodies and rotting exteriors quaked.

"What are you doing with those corpses, Jiang? You know as well as I that your magic does not have the strength of the Gods."

Jiang replied, but Chander couldn't hear it, like a whisper caught by the wind.

Alojzy laughed again, "Your army doesn't scare me. You've used your magic all of four times if I am not mistaken."

The giant spoke again, hands clenched, eyes narrowed.

Laughter rocked through Alojzy's body again, causing Chander's own body to shake. He did not flinch as the giant took another step forward with his army. There was a hesitancy in the way the giant moved, fearful of each step. Chander could tell that the man was out of practice. His army, although following him, had not much else to their movements. With their skeletal bodies and vacant stares, they were no more powerful than rotting trees.

But then, Jiang's expression darkened. He raised his arms into the air like a bird. With a swift movement, he scooped the Mist into his arms, then pushed it forward in a wave. His army traveled with it, rushing straight at Alojzy.

Chander opened his own eyes as the army threw Alojzy's body in the air. He caught his breath and took a quick glance toward the window. Shadows speckled the road, but he could not witness the fight from his current seat.

So he closed his eyes again, swallowing his fear to take another look.

Alojzy climbed from his spot and snarled. Around him, Neorama began to distort. Structures changed. Their bricks melted. Around them, buildings collapsed. But as they fell, it came with a purpose, each one dropping mere inches from Jiang as he marched through the street.

If Chander hadn't known any better, he would have thought Alojzy's magic was like Bria's magic. He manipulated the buildings like he was part of them, a true architect of nature.

As a small tavern fell, Alojzy reconfigured its stones with the Mist as his mortar. Each stone traveled down the road, coming together to form an architectural feat. Even in his fear, Chander marveled at it.

With the broken buildings of Neorama, Alojzy constructed what appeared to be a giant hand.

Alojzy held out his own hand, letting his new structure mimic his movements. The stone fingers reacted with hefty ease, opening wide, then wrapping around the giant. Alojzy raised his hand, and the stone structure did the same with Jiang. There, with one swift movement, it flicked Jiang into the trees, far away from the border of the town.

Once Jiang disappeared, the bodies dropped. Each corpse made a new home on the ground, a lifeless pile of bones. Alojzy kicked one of the bodies, relaxing his body so that his magic might finally rest. The buildings ceased quaking, and in their stead, rubble remained.

Except for Szyman's little box and the schoolhouse.

Alojzy approached the box and thrust open the door. After all the destruction, everything inside the box remained the same. Only one thing had changed: a collection of half a dozen strange cylinders sat on the floor, with thin copper wires buzzing along their surface. Alojzy moved one to the side and then approached Szyman, who was still sitting in his chair, eyes vacant and body slouched.

Alojzy stood over the console and fidgeted with a few of the gadgets. If Chander was stronger through all of this, he might have been able to stop Alojzy. But all he could do was see.

Nothing more.

At least not with this Mist Keeper.

Alojzy adjusted a few of the dials and levers, then turned to Szyman. "We're ready, sire."

Szyman raised his head and extended his fingers. As the Mist swirled around him, the shuttered windows of the box slid open, allowing each tendril to expand out and into Neorama.

Then, Szyman clenched his body and tugged on the Mist.

Chander opened his eyes just as the room started to spin. The walls folded in on themselves. Just like before, Neorama was shifting.

This time, it groaned with its movements, compressing with smoke.

If the Mist could sing, this would be a chant.

A scream.

A gasp.

And then, a sigh as everything froze.

Chander blinked, his head spinning as the classroom stabilized. None of the spirits, nor Caroline, Jewel, or Marisol, reacted. He extended his neck, trying his best to get a glance out of the window. The early morning sky glimmered, a hint of purple painting the edge of the window frame.

Despite the nerves prickling his skin, Chander closed his eyes again.

Alojzy had exited the box. Although dawn arrived with a hint of sunlight, the thick fog that highlighted the landscape provided no distinguishing factors. In the sky, the feint outline of an airship hovered.

But otherwise, everything maintained its purple hue.

Alojzy strolled down the one road of Neorama, away from the schoolhouse, into the thickening fog. At first, only white filled the vision.

But as Alojzy moved forward, the image began to shift. The smoke parted, and in its place stood an old fortress, staring out across a sea of black flowers. Alojzy approached the fortress without hesitation, letting the building itself bend to his every whim. While he had controlled Neorama, this was different, as though the fortress itself was an extension of himself.

While the fortress loomed, the inside was simple. Little furniture filled the room, the signature piece a stairwell hidden behind a case of books. Alojzy followed it up, gliding along each step. Even ascending the stairs brought out Alojzy's powers, and before him, the stairwell itself twisted, only to lead him to an abyssal room where a basin of gold sat. A woman with perfectly pinned hair sat over the basin. She guided her fingers over the liquid, using the Mist as her tool.

"Aelia," Alojzy spoke, his voice firm.

"Ah, Alojzy. Ningursu told me of your conquest. Neorama is here then?"

"It is outside."

"With the Prayers?"

"Prayers?"

"That is what I am calling your little experiment," Aelia smirked.

"Ah, yes. The Prayers." Alojzy replied. "I managed to create six of them."

"That is all we'll need," Aelia lowered her hand into the basin. "And what of the vessels?"

"Not counting Caroline and Jewel, we have approximately two dozen fresh faces."

"That will be plenty."

Alojzy neared the basin. "You must know, Aelia, that we have lost control of Jiang. He remembered his past."

Aelia appeared unphased by the comment. "It was only a matter of time before the Story Collector unraveled our work. So be it. Jiang is not needed."

"But without him or Tomás, will it be enough?"

"Ningursu seems to think so."

Alojzy reached the edge of the basin and gripped its rim. He peered into it, where a putrid liquid, glimmering with a hint of silver, yellow, and black, spun. As he stared into it, an object bobbed to the surface.

"You will rise soon, sire," Alojzy reached into the basin and turned the object over.

In the center of the basin, a skull stared up at Alojzy. With pieces of flesh rotting on its bone and a crooked smile, its single white eye peered straight ahead.

Through Alojzy.

And right at Chander.

"Fuck!" Chander cursed as his eyes flew open. Once again, he sat in the classroom. *Ningursu saw me. He saw me. Fuck!*

His heart raced in his chest. There was no way to flee. Nowhere to go.

He just remained stuck in the classroom, only his breathing as a friend.

And nothing more.

CHAPTER FIFTY-FOUR

SYMBIOSIS

Every instinct told Bria to run. As the smoke cleared, as the air grew stale, and as the color escaped the trees, it seemed like the only option. Her magic was a bomb waiting to explode. She had to find someplace where she could control it, where no one would be harmed. Perhaps, even if it meant turning into the forest itself.

She was already transforming. Taproots hung from her body like webs, while her little branch extended beyond her body, like the arms of a willow tree. She was more tree than a human. Perhaps the soil was where she belonged.

But as the last of the smoke cleared, all that desire fled. Brent stood there, swaying on his feet. Black smoke pummeled his body, tearing at his skin and entering his eyes, nose, and mouth. He stumbled back and collapsed in the mud.

"Brent!" She raced over to him. Carefully, she rolled his body over. A bright yellow lemon fell from his pocket. His hand dropped beside it, where Mist gathered on his fingertips. Black veins scared his face. With each breath, his body twitched, creating stories out of the air around his ear. Incomprehensible stories about waddling ducks and glowing fish. But as a tale of a majestic eagle flew past his brow, he convulsed again, sending the tales back into the Mist.

Each breath labored. Black smoke gathered at his lips. *No.* Bria touched the veins on his face. *No!*

If Ningursu was finally laying his claim, then it was over. The Mist Keepers would fly into this war like an owl, plucking every last hope from the field.

She cupped his face, pressing her fingers against the veins. There was something about elements beneath his skin. They pulsed, deconstructing his very fabric with each passing moment. Her fingers trembled as she tried to differentiate each element. What if she pulled at the wrong one? What if he vanished again and couldn't return to her?

How many times did she already make him vanish? One more, and could it be the last time?

Bria almost removed her fingers, tempted again to flee.

But stopped.

If she didn't try to save him...then what?

Brent would want me to try. She pressed her fingers tighter. *Pull apart the heavy Mist. Focus on what makes him...Brent.* It was like unraveling branches of a woven lattice, each piece more ingrained with the next. Who was Brent Harley? A kind storyteller. A teacher. A Mist Keeper. And the Story Collector.

But he was so much more.

He was the man who smiled in the face of uncertainty. The man who hated pineapple but loved lemons. His kindness belonged to everyone, but his heart settled on morals that he never questioned.

"You can fight this, Brent," she whispered. One at a time, she let the elements unwind. She recited them to herself.

Hydrogen.

Oxygen.

Carbon.

With each element, the scarring on his face hardened like the skin of trees.

And as each tendril rescinded, the black smoke around his mouth lightened before vanishing entirely.

But Bria still didn't know if that meant anything of significance.

She removed her fingers, letting the last bit of unusual Mist fade from Brent's skin. *Why didn't you tell me it got this bad?* Brent had told her of his injuries and the way the stories assaulted him, but he never complained.

But did he ever? Even when he was branded, when he was forced into a loveless betrothal, he never complained.

He just…thrived.

And he would thrive now…right?

Bria continued to hold him, letting his head rest on her shoulder. She picked at his knotted curls. A thought continued to gnaw at her, begging her to leave before she did any further harm.

I made him vanish multiple times. For all I know…I caused this.

But she willed herself to remain in place, keeping Brent's close to him. She couldn't move him herself, nor would he leave his side. Not this time. Not again.

So she stayed there, letting the roots and ground take hold, healing her own body while protecting Brent.

There was still something odd about seeing him. While her vision was clear, it felt unstable, like a single piece of thread that could easily snap, or that she gazed through a pair of foggy goggles. His breathing was labored, but she could hardly hear him.

In and out.

In and out.

Bria's own exhaustion threatened her. Every part of her yearned for sleep. But if she dared to sleep, what if Brent vanished? What if she ended up back in that cavern, layered with experiments?

Only to become a bomb again.

As Brent's breathing relaxed, stories drifted in the air. Nonsensical tales of fairies riding on snowflakes and dragons darting through the clouds. Above his head, a miniature palace grew, where the fairies and dragons inhabited.

She watched the story. *He's a storyteller even in his sleep.*

Bria raised her hand to one of the imaginary dragons. It fluttered into her skin and vanished.

The remaining story disintegrated in trickling waves.

And as the last dragon vanished, Brent's eyes flickered.

"Brent?" She whispered.

But he didn't wake.

She lowered her head in defeat. The longer she sat there with her thoughts, the more the events from the last few hours taunted her. Ningursu had laid claim to her. While the trance was broken, she knew he would return. He always did.

Taunting.

Remember your constants. Brent always said that when fighting his own stories. Perhaps if she clung to her own constants, she could fight Ningursu.

Remember your grandmama.

Your father.

Brent.

And…your camellias.

She removed a camellia from her trembling branched fingers, letting it drift onto Brent's cheek.

But nothing changed.

She scanned the swamp, looking for any sign of change. Her heart sank. A few feet away lay Christof's corpse. Mud covered half the body, his rotting flesh drawing the attention of vultures and other scavenging animals. *How long has he been like this?* While Christof had done horrible things…did he deserve this fate?

Did anyone?

She commanded the ground to take hold of his body. It opened enough to swallow him, letting him return to the earth for his final resting place.

"Have the sleep you deserve, Christof Carver," she said softly, then returned her attention to Brent.

Bria remained there, holding him close, listening as the night moved through the swamp. The earth changed with every hour. Owls woke, birds slept, mice scurried, and alligators croaked. If she closed her eyes, she could label every hour just by the sound of the swamp.

Her attention drew to the trees, an unfamiliar shift to the surroundings drawing her attention. Footsteps sloshing through the swamp water sent ripples up her spine. These belonged to a person. But...who approached? Did she have the energy to fight them?

Or was it just her imagination?

That much was false as a tall figure stumbled from the tree line. *Jiang!*

She didn't move as he scanned the area. He looked as though he'd been thrown through the canopy, with sticks and leaves latching to his body. His long black hair fell against his face, dripping with sweat. Scratches covered his face.

She used her last bit of strength to command the roots. They approached Jiang's ankles.

He turned as they grabbed hold of him, then growled, "I'm here to help."

Bria didn't respond. *Maintain your focus.*

Jiang kicked away the roots, taking another step toward Bria and Brent.

"Stay away!" she shouted. But she didn't have the strength to fight.

"I told you, I'm here to help."

"And why should I trust you?"

"You don't need to, but that won't stop me," he snatched the lemon from the ground beside Brent's hand. He slowly peeled it open, revealing the stringy insides of the fruit. He pulled it in half, dropping the other part of the lemon to the ground.

Bria acted at once. She listened to the sour notes, finding the seeds inside the core of the lemon. As Jiang stepped over it, she ordered the tree to grow.

And in one motion, a tree sprouted from the ground, tripping Jiang.

The giant kept his footing, stealing a glare at Bria. "Listen, do you want to make sure your husband is okay or not?"

"Just tell me what you're going to do."

"You could have asked."

"Tell me!"

Jiang huffed. "I am going to unlock his senses with this lemon."

"How?"

"Flavors have memories. I am sure he has a memory associated with this fruit," Jiang held out the lemon.

Bria stared at the fruit. Nothing strange moved about its translucent yellow body.

"Fine, but if you so much as blink the wrong way, I'm sending you back into the canopy."

Jiang knelt beside Brent. With his index finger, he opened Brent's mouth slightly and squirted the lemon juice onto his tongue.

Brent's lips twitched, forming a half-smile in his sleep.

"Is that a normal reaction for him?" Jiang asked.

"Yes," Bria's voice cracked. "He loves lemons."

Jiang threw the lemon behind him, then shook Brent's shoulder. "C'mon. Get up. Can't stay lying around here—Ningursu won't be idle for long."

Brent groaned and rolled onto his side.

"That's also normal. He's a heavy sleeper," Bria whispered.

"Well, we don't have time for this." Using a single arm, Jiang hoisted Brent off the ground and over his shoulder. Then, without looking back, he marched toward the tree line.

"Wait! Where are you taking him!?" Bria chased after Jiang, tearing her taproots out of the ground in the process.

"Away from here. Do you really want Ningursu to find him?" Jiang called over his shoulder.

"But we can use the tunnels!"

"That seems like a worse idea than staying here."

"I control—"

"No. You don't."

"But—"

"You only thought you controlled them. This world belongs to Ningursu. We're but puppets on his strings."

Bria had no other rebuttal. With silence settling, Jiang continued his stomping through the trees, with Brent hanging off his back like a pendulum. Each step brought him further into the swamp.

"Wait!" Bria chased after him, away from the scene of her destruction and leaving behind an explosion of green.

CHAPTER FIFTY-FIVE

SONS

Commotion filled the Pinstripe Tavern as Todd arrived with Edith, Etta and Garrett. Upon entering, they discovered half the chairs missing. Before they could inquire about the situation, a squirrelly man raced down the stairs, and without even acknowledging them, grabbed another set of chairs and raced back up the stairs.

Shouts echoed from the stairwell. Of the few pinstripes sitting in the booths, none seemed all that disturbed, more focused on their cups of coffee, bottles of liquor, and barrels of their pistols. A little girl carried a tray of drinks to one of the booths, pausing as the squirrelly man snatched another chair from a nearby table.

"What the hell are we doing here?" Todd hissed.

Edith ignored him, marching straight to the stairwell. As the squirrelly man toppled down the stairs again, she grabbed hold of him, pressing him into the wall with all her force.

"Oi! I needa get those chairs!"

"Why?" Edith asked.

"Wouldn't you like to know?"

"Listen, I could break every bone in your body by blinking. So speak up… cause it's a disaster here. And I know I didn't leave it like this when I was last here."

"Yeah, well, I don't think you'll care about my man having some bizarre fit!"

"So you're stealing chairs?"

"Only 'cause he's being violent! Never knew him to be violent, but now he's like a madman."

Edith's scowl fell, both of her brows raised as she asked, "Is this mad man named Timothée?"

"How'd you know?"

Edith dropped the man and motioned to Etta and Todd, "C'mon. Up here."

Todd grumbled, "You want us to visit a madman?"

"He has what we need," Edith said as she climbed the stairs.

Etta followed without question. Todd exchanged a glance with the man on the floor, then hurried into the stairwell.

The scent of cigars filled the stairwell while the walls breathed of liquor. Todd had lived in Mert knowing of the Pinstripes, but he had always imagined them living in a vault, where gold was plentiful, with their shoes polished and suits pressed. Not in an old, run down, unassuming tavern just a few streets away from the central square.

A makeshift barricade filled the upstairs hallway, with chairs upon chairs stacked against the nearby door. Banging continued from beyond the door, with obscene shouts echoing against the wood.

I'd be shouting, too, if I was locked in here. Todd shifted Garrett again. The boy did not sleep, though his attention perked ever-so-slightly at the noise.

Edith climbed over the chairs, then with her hands cupped over her mouth, she called into the wood, "Listen, Reaper—got a question for you if your thick skull can process it."

An inaudible scream responded.

"No, that's not my question. I wanted to know—where's the boy?"

A slew of curses shrieked from behind the door.

"Now, that isn't very nice."

Another scream followed.

The squirrelly man joined them in the stairwell, carrying another chair. "He don't understand a word we say. Just keeps on screaming." The man squeezed another chair into his barricade. "Never realized Tim was all that strong until he almost broke down that door."

Edith shot a glare back at the squirrelly man, "If you know him so well, then tell us… where's the kid?"

"Shite, are you all about that Preston kid? I kept telling Tim it was in his head, but then Yaz and Chander said he was there. Thought they were kinda messing with me. Then some doctor came asking about him too, and now I dunno what to think."

"Finally!" Todd exclaimed. "Someone speaking sense around here! There's no way Preston was there—he's dead!"

Garrett winced and mumbled to himself. Todd swore that the boy whispered, "No."

Edith ignored Todd and asked the squirrelly man, "Which doctor?"

"I dunno! They came storming in here a few hours ago, right around the time Tim went a little mad. They had a mask, though. Makes 'em look like a bird." The man repositioned one of the chairs, balancing it precariously against the door. "Didn't seem to give a flying shite what was going on with Tim."

"Where are they?"

"The doctor?"

"Yes."

"One of the rooms. I dunno. It didn't matter. Doesn't anyone care about Tim? He's gonna kill half the pinstripes if we don't get him under control soon!"

"We'll deal with him in a bit. Just keep doing what you're doing."

"Making a barricade? You know there's only so many chairs…and I think the Pinstripes might have my neck if I don't stop soon." The squirrelly man continued his ranting, but it did little to grab Edith's attention as she climbed back over the chairs.

She didn't say a word as she marched down the hallway. At each door, she paused, kicking open each one. The doors banged against the wall, receiving a barrage of curses from the occupants inside. Not that Todd could blame them—he would do the same.

Edith did not care, continuing down the hall like she owned the place. As she pushed open another door, a gunshot rang from the room. Edith reacted at once, holding out her hand in a swift movement. The bullet froze midair. Then, it fell, disintegrating as it hit the floor.

"We'll talk later, Mitzi," Edith growled, then slammed the door closed. She stormed to the next few doors.

Despite her size, Edith was stronger than most Guards. Even in the short time since meeting her, that truth became obvious. Todd made a mental note not to be on the opposite side of her. Something told him that one wrong move might just result in his last breath.

"Finally!" Edith shouted after she opened the next door. She stormed into the room.

Todd followed in step with Etta. She had been quiet through all of this rather than her usual babbling self. As they approached the door, she flexed her fingers, muttered something under her breath, and then entered the room behind Edith.

Once again, that itch to run haunted Todd. Every move, every statement, it all seemed preposterous. How hard would it be to return to the streets of Mert—or even head back to his own home? Here, he could start anew. Like he did with Lex.

But instead, he followed Etta into the room.

The room itself was no different from a room in any other tavern. With a single cot and a window overlooking the street, Todd could have been in any tavern in any country. Yet, the occupant did not belong to any country. Only in Mert would he find a doctor sitting on the bed, holding a beaked mask. At their feet, pillows lay scattered, built into the shape of a small fort. Across the floor, crayons had been scattered about, with a few colorful lines climbing up the walls.

"You really make it inconvenient to find you, y'know," Edith grumbled. "Varden still thinks you're at the Sanitorium. He's waiting for you."

The doctor shushed Edith.

"Don't shush me!"

"Just be quiet, Edith. You'll startle him," the doctor said.

"What? The kid?" Edith glanced at the empty spot on the floor. "How do you know he's there?"

"I came by to do my usual check-in on Preston. That's when Timothée started to smoke. I convinced him to hand me the boy before he lost his mind."

"But how d'you know he wasn't lying?"

"The crayons. See," the doctor motioned to the walls. "Gave him free rein."

"Mitzi won't be happy."

"She is never happy."

Todd rolled his eyes. *Now they're trying to convince us that Preston drew these pictures. Pah.*

Etta pushed past Todd and approached the doctor, still fidgeting with her hands. She spoke low, in a way that made her seem like a child compared to the doctor. "Excuse me… Dr. Kafele?"

The doctor turned. Now that the light hit their face, Todd recognized them. Their face remained burned into his mind, describing to him Phantom Rot in the Sanitorium. He knew that name sounded familiar.

"Yes?" Dr. Kafele asked.

"My name is Etta Gratz… I'm a huge fan of your work. But you're much younger than I thought—no offense! I just thought you were older."

The doctor smirked ever-so-slightly.

Etta continued, "I swear, I read your thesis on Magical Encumberment at least twenty times. It's phenomenal! I actually wrote my thesis on it and expanded the idea, researching how Rot—"

"We don't have all day. Just make your point already," Edith interjected.

"Right, right, well, what I was going to say is that I've been researching what is going on with the bleeding eyes and this kid," Etta motioned to Garrett. "I think, with your expertise, of course, I can help."

Dr. Kafele's lips twitched as they rose to speak with Etta. "Professor Gratz… yes, I believe I read your work a few years ago."

"You did? Really? I'm sorry…but you are such an inspiration, and I never thought I would have a chance to meet you. I always thought that you were dead—"

Etta continued to ramble, but Todd's attention fell to Garrett. The boy squirmed, nearly toppling out of Todd's arms and to the floor.

"Where you going?" Todd asked as he lowered Garrett.

The boy climbed along the pillows. He wobbled on his feet, nearly tripping multiple times, before finding his way to the open floor in the center of the pillows.

"Hold on," Dr. Kafele said, placing their hand up to stop Etta's rambles. They kept watching as Garrett plopped down in the center of the pillows.

No one spoke.

Garrett leaned his head forward and opened his palms. It was the most movement he'd had in months. He hadn't reacted like this to any threat they encountered, any spicy food, or even the shifting of environments. But here, in the middle of this room, something captured Garrett, reigniting his lost senses.

"Garr?" Todd whispered.

The little boy just barely smiled as he reached his hands out in front of him.

It took one breath. Just one.

Then, a mirage shifted in front of him. It created a mirrored image of Garrett, flickering and holding tight to Garrett's hands.

But this mirror image did not have missing eyes... only dried bloody tears.

The mirage flashed in and out, whisking through the air like smoke.

Todd's mouth dried, and his head spun. A tear fell down the side of his face. *Preston?*

"What's happening?" Etta asked Dr. Kafele.

"The building blocks for our cure," Dr. Kafele's lip twitched, forming a smile.

"So that's what he was disconnected from, right? I had a theory that the reason why he was desensitized was because a connection was severed. I didn't know it was…this." Etta laughed nervously. "Wow."

"Yes… but you and I have much work cut out for us, Professor Gratz. If you will help, that is."

"Of course I'll help!"

"As I knew you would," Dr. Kafele said, still smiling. Etta took a seat against the wall, marveling at the two boys. Edith hopped onto the bed, kicking off her shoes in the process. She smirked in Todd's direction.

But Todd didn't care about her snide remarks or mocking grin. Instead, he took a knee beside his son.

No.

His sons.

Garrett and Preston.

A Fallen Kingdom

Brent's mouth tasted like lemon. He licked his lips, savoring the sour taste. If his mouth tasted like lemon, then he was human. It meant that he hadn't forgotten who he was or how to find something pretty on a battlefield.

He smiled and opened his eyes slightly. Once again, Jiang carried him like a common potato sack, the swamp passing in waves behind him. *What happened?* He remembered how the black smoke wrapped around him after freeing Christof's body from Ningursu's grasp, but not much else. Had Ningursu taken hold of him? Was this all a figment of his imagination as Ningursu pulled his puppet strings? And what became of—

"Bria!?" he flailed, toppling out of Jiang's arms and onto the muddied ground. He stumbled to his feet, wiping the mud from his shirt, to meet Jiang's disapproving glower.

"Hi, Jiang. Um…sorry."

"Hmph." Jiang turned his attention to the treeline, and with a single motion with his chin, pointed behind them.

Brent spun. There, Bria stood, camouflaged with the trees. She wore armor composed of foliage. Her eyes hung heavy with the events of the past few hours.

He stumbled toward her. While his side no longer pulsed with pain, a weakness continued to hang onto each of his steps. As he reached the tree line, he grabbed hold of a branch to catch his breath.

Bria reached for the same branch. With a snap, it fell, and in its place, she reformed it into a new cane. Its intricate weavings melded perfectly so Brent's hand could fit solidly over the top.

She lifted it and held it out to Brent, hand shaking.

He took it, staring hard at Bria. "You can…see me?"

She nodded.

"You can see me," he repeated, then his lips curved up into a smile. "You can see!"

"I can see," she replied, her voice quivering at the confession.

Brent dropped his cane and then, in one motion, pulled Bria into a tight embrace. She stiffened for a moment, then relaxed in his arms, pressing her face against his chest. Her body shook as she stifled her sobs.

"Hey…it's a'ight. I got you. It's a'ight," Brent whispered.

"You're okay."

"Yeah, yeah, I'm a'ight."

"I thought your rot had taken over. I stopped it, but…I thought…"

Brent raised one hand against his own cheek. Rather than raised skin where the black veins used to rip through his skin, the sensation of bark greeted him. He then lifted the side of his shirt. The black veins, while still there, had softened, intermingling with the same tree-like coating that he felt on his face.

He glanced at Bria again. "What did you do?"

"I cured you," Bria whispered without looking at him.

"But…wait. How?"

"I made it pretty…by revising the elements. Just like I did when I made you vanish."

"Bri—"

"I thought I couldn't control it," she choked out. "I tried so hard, but until you came…Ningursu's grip on me was too strong. I couldn't fight it, and I thought…" She shook her head.

Brent cupped her face, brushing the dirt away from her cheeks. "But you're controlling it now. You're a'ight."

She didn't respond.

"You're a'ight. A'ight? You're a'ight."

"I guess."

"Say it."

"I'm alright."

"A'ight?"

"Alright," she laughed as a tear fell down her cheek. "And you're alright?"

"I'm a'ight."

"Good…because I missed your hideous face so much."

"Oh, now we're going there?" Brent grinned.

"You're covered in mud! Of course you're hideous!"

"Oi, you're not much better!"

"But I'm allowed to be covered in mud. I'm the Forest Queen." Her smile fell. "I'm the Forest Queen…"

Brent didn't need his stories to see the gears in her head turning. It was not just a statement but a declaration.

"You're the Forest Queen," Brent agreed.

"I'm the Forest Queen," she said again, this time with a strength in her voice. Then, she raised her eyes. A glint of pride shone in her oak-colored eyes. It belonged to a queen.

In that fleeting moment of confidence, she pulled Brent closer.

And with the power of a queen, she kissed him.

It took Brent aback for a moment, but he smiled as she pulled back from the kiss.

"That's all you're getting until we both bathe," Bria said.

"Fair," Brent laughed.

"And until you cut your hair."

"Okay, that's just mean. What if I like my luscious locks?"

"You look more like a swamp monster than me."

"I am but your loyal subject—maybe I should be a swamp monster."

"I'll cut it myself if I have to."

"Oi!"

Before Bria replied, Jiang's looming shadow towered over them. "Ahem."

Brent could feel his ears turn red as he turned toward the giant.

"As lovely as this is, we do not have time for this childish flirting," Jiang said.

"Sorry." Brent clamored to his feet. Bria handed him his cane, which he instinctively positioned on his side. "Where are we heading?"

"To safety," Jiang said as he led them back through the trees.

"Where is that?"

"Away from here."

"Wait…what about Neorama?" The questions started pouring, his head ringing like a gong. Beside him, Bria grabbed his hand, pressing her fingers into his palm.

"That is where we are heading."

"So it's safe?"

"You'll see."

That doesn't sound good. Brent squeezed Bria's hand. She strode in step with him, her pace slowing. The moment of confidence had long passed, and she sank into her own thoughts, gazing far ahead of the trees. This was Bria Smidt at her core; even when they were young, he always noticed the true gaze in her eyes. Everyone used to say that she was a happy girl, bubbling with flowers and kindness. And she was kind, and she was as lovely as a flower, but she was also so much more.

Brent knew that he would speak her mind when ready. He knew better than to pressure her. While he could easily unwrap her story as it danced on her skin in whiffs of smoke, he ignored it instead, letting the comfortable silence fall between them. It was her story to tell.

Instead, Brent focused on the commotion loitering in the stories and the trees. Remnants of Bria's magic weighed the trees down while stories of the feat itself sang through the wind. Like any destructive storm, Bria's magic would be remembered. The trauma would remain in the songs of birds, in the gasps of the Mist, and in the heartbeat of the earth.

This story won't be forgotten. Ningursu won't take it away this time.

Brent continued to take in the story of the swamp as they followed Jiang. No one spoke as they finally reached the edge of the tree line, where Neorama waited.

Well, it had waited.

In its place, decrepit corpses painted the field. Bria gripped tighter to Brent's arm as they walked amongst them.

"What happened?" Bria asked.

"Jiang tried to defend Neorama using his magic…" Brent replied.

He would tell Bria more later, adding it to the pile of stories he needed to tell her.

As they passed each of the corpses, Bria's magic took hold, using the roots to bring the corpses back into the ground before covering each grave with flowers. Along with the corpses, the story of the events haunted the field. Alojzy had found the town and, one by one, imprisoned the spirits. No one was safe from Ningursu's grip, and each one fell into Ningursu's embrace. Not just the spirits but Caroline, Jewel, and Marisol as well.

Jiang arrived with a vengeance. His army stood ready to fight. But he was a novice, and Alojzy bested him, using his grip on the Mist's architecture to win the battle.

Once he ejected Jiang from the town, Alojzy used Szyman to move Neorama far away, where not even Brent's stories could follow.

"It's gone…" Brent murmured. "They're all gone."

Bria squeezed Brent's hand tighter.

"Thought it might be. Tried to stop him, but that damn architect is too strong," Jiang grumbled beside them. "I'm out of practice."

"Thank you for trying. I should have done more…" Brent replied.

"No, you needed your Kikyo—erm, Bria." Jiang watched as one of the corpses returned to the earth.

They didn't speak as they loitered through the field. Brent paused in the location where the schoolhouse once stood. The story of his classroom returned, but this time, the tale spoke of the spirits, Caroline, Jewel, Marisol, and Chander tied to the desks. Imprisoned in the very place that had promised them freedom. He clenched his jaw. Had he led all of them to Ningursu? What if he had gathered more students? How many more would have been at risk?

"None of this is your fault," Bria said beside him.

"How'd you know I was thinking that?"

"Because I know you."

Brent grimaced. *It's not my fault.* He had done everything with good intentions.

Ningursu was the one who acted in malice.

They circled the field, pausing by the road. A pair of headlights puttered up the road, flickering as they bounced on each indent in the ground. Brent held up his hand. Beside him, Bria readied her little branch, her armor tightening around her body.

A chugging caravan approached them. It slowed to a halt alongside the field.

As it stopped, a dog jumped out of the back.

"Nix!" Brent shouted.

The dog ran towards him and Bria, leaping up and down, barking excitedly. Bria's face lit up as Nix knocked her over.

"Brent! Ms. Bria!"

Yaz leapt from the back of the caravan and raced towards them. A smile crossed her face, unscathed by the events that had passed.

"Yaz!" Brent hurried over to the little girl.

She ran into his arms, hugging him tight. From the quick whiff of her story, one thing was certain: Ningursu did not control her.

"You're a'ight then?" he asked.

"I'm okay. Ms. Kai and Mr. Nasr rescued me before Ningursu could take me." Yaz waved behind her at Gisela Kai, climbing from the front seat of the caravan.

Bria joined Brent and Yaz's side. "What's Gisela doing here?"

"Ms. Bria!" Yaz released Brent and beamed. "Ms. Kai saved me from Ningursu."

Brent and Bria exchanged a brief frown but broke the shared expression as Gisela approached. Bria had told Brent what Gisela and Yeshua had done.

But was now different?

"Ah, Bria, it is nice to see our little Forest Queen thriving," Gisela said. She did not pay any attention to Brent.

"What are you doing here, Gisela?" Bria asked.

"Protecting our assets."

"What does that mean?"

"That you should come with us. To safety. And Brent, if you are here—which I assume you are—you should come, too."

"Wait, you can't see me?" Brent asked.

Bria repeated the same question. "You can't see him?"

"Of course not. Sight is still gone. Why...can you?"

"Yes, I can..." Bria stared at Brent again. He reached for her, assuring her with a mere touch that he was not in her imagination.

"Huh. Peculiar. Yeshua will be jealous." Gisela shrugged. "Yasmin, come. You'll sit up front with us. Let the lovebirds have time to themselves."

"But Ms. Kai!"

"Now!"

Huffing, Yaz followed Gisela back to the caravan. Brent watched, searching through Gisela's story. No signs of treachery or misguided behavior haunted her steps. Right now, her story held one goal: travel away from here to safety.

"Can we trust her?" Bria asked.

"I… I think so. We don't have a choice, really. We gotta get out of here," Brent said.

"And what about Jiang?"

Brent glanced over the field. Jiang had vanished.

"I think he has a mission of his own."

"And we have ours?"

"We will…after we rest." Brent held his hand out to Bria. Carefully, she took it and squeezed it tight.

Together, they walked toward the caravan, leaving behind their fallen kingdom of Mist, swamp water, and corpses.

Don't miss the conclusion to the Life & Death Cycle

Learn how it ends in...

THE STORY COLLECTOR'S ALMANAC

Also by E.S. Barrison...

Tales from the Effluvium

Speak Easy

These Sanguine Tides

The Unsought Fairytale Collection

Author's Note

Thank you so much for taking the time to read *Children of Cypress*.

If you enjoyed this book, I would appreciate it if you could:

Review this book. Reviews are a great help to an author. If you enjoyed this book, please consider leaving a review.

Tell Others. When you share this book with others on social media, you're allowing others to discover this story. Word-of-mouth is one of the best sources of marketing for an author.

Connect with me. If you want to find out about my upcoming releases, stop by my website at www.esbarrison-author.com or connect with me on social media.

Thank you!

E.S. Barrison

ACKNOWLEDGMENTS

To all the following, my thanks, for your support, friendship, and kindness throughout this process:

To Moira, my cover artist – I know the cover was difficult for this project, but you brought it to life in more ways than I could ever imagine.

To Charlie, my editor, for always being honest, and giving me confidence in my writing.

To Matthew, for putting down your video games and reading this story. I know, how dare I force you to read this behemoth.

And finally, to my readers, Thank you for your continued support as we follow Brent, Bria, and the others through their story.

Without all of your support, this story would not have been possible.

ABOUT THE AUTHOR

E.S. Barrison has been writing and creating stories for as long as she can remember. After graduating from the University of Florida, she has spent the past few years wrangling her experiences to compose unique worlds with diverse characters. Currently, E.S. lives in Orlando, Florida with her family.

www.ingramcontent.com/pod-product-compliance
Lightning Source LLC
Chambersburg PA
CBHW070259310726
48976CB00005B/1486